OLIVER EVER AFTER

8 MILLION HEARTS - BOOK 3

SPENCER SPEARS

West, introducing his students (and many other Westerners) to the traditions and practice of the Bauls of Bengal, India, a love-drunk sect of wandering beggars, singers, dancers and devotees of God. He recognized in this Path the purest reflection of his own revelation, and a means of communicating ages-old teachings in a way that was fresh, moving and deeply grounded. He was a guru, friend, poet and lyricist, as well as a beloved father, a rock & roll singer and a lover of sacred art. First and foremost, he always considered himself the long-time devotee and "Heart Son" of Yogi Ramsuratkumar (1918–2001), the revered beggar-saint of Tiruvannamalai, south India.

How spiritual slavery and a radical reliance on God could be lived functionally in the world was evident in Lee's life and work. While directing the sadhana of his students, managing businesses, keeping a grueling schedule of travel and teaching, attending to the personal needs of his large extended family, Lee deepened and intensified a fiery love directed to God through the tangent point of his own master, Yogi Ramsuratkumar. To rely upon God for all the details of one's life, for all the places and things that will absorb one's attention, and perhaps even to the degree of reliance for food, clothing, shelter . . . that's what the astute observer saw in Lee.

Lee presented his teachings in several dozen books, hundreds of talks and seminars in the U.S., Mexico, India and throughout Europe, and encoded his heart's devotion in volumes of poetry to his master, in scores of song lyrics for his several rock and blues' bands, and in the reverencing of sacred art from diverse spiritual traditions. At the root of it all, Lee Lozowick inspired many with both non-dual and theistic teachings applied within daily life. He was a dedicated champion of conscious relationship (*The Alchemy of Love and Sex* remains one of his most widely read books) and conscious parenting (his book by the same name is acknowledged as a classic), envisioned within a return to the simplicity and sanity of sacred culture.

Lee founded Hohm Press in the summer of 1975 as a means of sharing his teaching with spiritual seekers of the time. Since then, the Press has continued to publish Lee's work, along with books in many different fields, including religious studies, parenting, yoga, transpersonal psychology, and children's books on health and nutrition (through its affiliate Kalindi Press). Foreign-language editions of Lee's books have also been published in German, French, Portuguese, Spanish, Hungarian and Romanian.

Lee Lozowick was a ruthless warrior when it came to unmasking ego in its many guises. He supported no easy, "white-bread" solutions to the pain of human suffering. Rather, he demanded practice—working with mind and emotions, self-observation, meditation, study, diet and exercise, right livelihood, the intention of conscious relationship—as the only sane alternative to a life of comfort-driven solipsism. And, he begged his students and friends to turn unceasingly to the source of All, within one's own heart, and through the agency of that One, as clearly manifest in the person of the true guru.

A distinguishing element of the Baul tradition is that one draws from many authentic paths, many traditions, in seeking food for sadhana. In this regard, Lee introduced his students to many profound spiritual dignitaries of our age. In the 1990s, he encouraged the creation of a conference on "Crazy Wisdom and Divine Madness" in Boulder, Colorado, a gathering of Buddhist teachers and masters, Christian contemplatives, and Hindu ascetics. He took his students to Zen monasteries where they received the teachings of roshis; to France, where he introduced them to the French teacher Arnaud Desjardins, and the work of Swami Prajnanpad, Arnaud's master; to the coast of California to meet with Sufi teacher Llewellyn Vaughan-Lee, and to the outskirts of Sacramento to meet E. J. Gold, the radical 4th Way teacher and visionary who had supported Lee's early teaching career and maintained friendship throughout his life.

An uncompromising stand for truth, "kindness, generosity and compassion" and a call to "pay attention and remember" were the hallmarks of Lee Lozowick's life and his teaching. These remain his legacy to his students, followers of all spiritual and transformational paths, his readers, colleagues and friends.

Lee attained Mahasamadhi on November 16, 2010.

Contact Information

HOHM PRESS is committed to publishing books that provide readers with alternatives to the materialistic values of the current culture and promote self-awareness, the recognition of interdependence, and compassion. Our subject areas include the teachings of Lee Lozowick and other eminent authors in the field of religious studies, as well as books on parenting, women's studies, the arts and poetry. Our affiliate **KALINDI PRESS** presents titles in the fields of natural health and nutrition, and the acclaimed Family and World Health Series for children and parents.

To learn more about our press, and/or about the teachings of Lee Lozowick, please **contact us at**:

HOHM PRESS, PO Box 4331, Chino Valley, AZ, 86323, USA
928-636-3331 or 800-381-2700 (U.S. only)
publisher@hohmpress.com

Visit our websites at:
www.hohmpress.com
and
www.kalindipress.com

INTRODUCTION

Free Bonus Epilogue

Join my mailing list and instantly get access to *After Midnight*, a free, explicit epilogue for *Oliver Ever After*. You can't get *After Midnight* anywhere else! You'll also be notified of my new releases and when I have more free stuff, you'll be the first to know.

Sign up at: http://eepurl.com/diQHrb

Thanks for downloading this book. I appreciate your support. Visit my website or my Author Central page on Amazon to see the rest of my catalog and keep up with my new releases.

www.spencerspears.com

For J

with love

and a Mama Celeste pizza

To love at all is to be vulnerable. Love anything and your heart will be wrung and possibly broken. If you want to make sure of keeping it intact you must give it to no one, not even an animal. Wrap it carefully round with hobbies and little luxuries; avoid all entanglements. Lock it up safe in the casket or coffin of your selfishness. But in that casket, safe, dark, motionless, airless, it will change. It will not be broken; it will become unbreakable, impenetrable, irredeemable. To love is to be vulnerable.

— C.S. LEWIS, THE FOUR LOVES

1

LUKE

I should have known it was going to be a bad day when my juicer broke.

That probably sounds pretty dramatic but listen—when it's dark and cold and seven o'clock on a February morning, and you've just gone for a six-mile run down the West Side Highway with the wind doing its best to push you into the Hudson River, and you're finally back in your apartment, but it's still chilly because you try to keep your utilities down, and you have to be at work in half an hour because your boss is loading you up with extra assignments in preparation for the promotion he's been promising you for five months, well, sometimes, looking forward to your daily eight-ounces of liquified kale is the only thing keeping you going.

So when that kale refuses to liquify, when your juicer just makes weird grunting noises that sound like it's laughing at you and then spits a little bit of last night's beet juice up into your face like it's giving you the middle finger... suffice it to say that when I looked back on it, I could see that that spray of beet juice across my face was an omen. I was just too naive to see it that early in the morning.

Don't worry—by 9 a.m. I had it figured out.

I spent ten minutes trying to fix the juicer and failing, which meant I barely had time for a shower and was shit out of luck when I realized all my shirts were still at the cleaners. I was late to the office but, thank God, I was also the only one who ever got there that early, so no one saw me roll into Mortimer Bancroft LP in dress pants and my college rowing sweatshirt. I kept a backup suit in the office for exactly this kind of day—though I hadn't ever actually had to use it, and apparently all the lifting I'd been doing in the past year had paid off because I could barely get my arms through it.

I know, I know—poor me, too jacked to fit into my clothes. But when I finally got to my desk and checked my email, I discovered that Harvey, my boss, had set two client meetings for me before lunch—in other words, before I'd have time to run to the cleaners *or* pop out to grab something from the juice bar around the corner. Plus, he'd asked me to "check in" with my coworker, MacFarlane, about the status of some reports he was working on, and I'd rather have gone to ten back-to-back client meetings completely naked than deal with that.

MacFarlane Boyd was Harvey's nephew by marriage, and even though he'd only joined Mortimer Bancroft six months ago, he already had the same position as me. Which wouldn't have been an issue—if he had any idea how to do his job. But, um, he didn't. Nor did he have any inclination to learn.

On top of that, three months ago, MacFarlane happened to

pass me on the street outside a club when I was making out with a guy I'd met—and never saw again. While I wasn't exactly hiding my sexuality, I wasn't going around advertising it at work, either. Harvey was part of an older generation, and while I was sure he liked to think of himself as open-minded, he'd made some comments in passing that had me thinking he might not be thrilled to find out I was gay.

I know—gross. It's the 21st century, and no one should be discriminated against, and we all need to fight the good fight for equality. Totally true—but that wasn't a fight I was up for right now, not with this promotion on the line. Unfortunately, that basically meant that me "checking in" with MacFarlane ended up with me just flat-out doing his work, while he dangled his bullshit blackmail over me. I couldn't wait for the day that I outranked him.

I mean, Harvey had basically promised it to me. When he'd announced he was creating the position to help Mortimer Bancroft expand into new sectors, he'd pulled me aside and told me he had me in mind for the job. But on a work trip a month ago, after a few rounds of tequila shots that our investors had ordered, he'd told me the job was mine to lose.

To be honest, I'd actually been thinking about looking for another job, when Harvey had first told me about the VP position. I'd ended up in finance because I was good at it and it paid well—not because I was particularly passionate about it. I didn't like to think too deeply about what it said about me, that I was willing to put up with a whole hell of a lot of extra assignments in a job I didn't even really like, just for the prospect of becoming a VP by age 26. But I certainly didn't need those extra assignments to include doing MacFarlane's job for him.

So yeah, the day wasn't off to a great start. But it was the text message at 8:55 that clinched it.

I shouldn't have checked it. I *knew* better than to do that. It was my personal phone, not my work one, and no one I knew would have been texting me this early. My mom was a teacher so she was already in the middle of her workday. And my little brother, Tyler, and all my friends had creative jobs, which was code for *"probably not even awake yet."* But like an idiot, I swiped my phone on anyway.

MATT BAR: hey so um... at the risk of sounding totally crazy, i really feel like we kinda had something? like there was something between us? i know you said you weren't looking for anything but didn't you feel it too?

Fuck.

Matt again. Matt—whose last name wasn't Bar, whose last name I didn't even know, but who I'd *met* in a bar—was a guy I'd hooked up with almost a month ago.

Once.

And he was right—I *had* told him I wasn't looking for anything. I told that to every guy I slept with because it was true. I didn't do relationships.

It wasn't that I had anything against them—for other people. Take my brother Tyler, for instance. His co-star for his final film was Gray Evans—an ex-porn star who happened to be one of the nicest guys I'd ever met. The two of them had fallen in love during filming and were over the moon for each other. Or my friends Ben and Adam, who I'd gone to college with. They'd gone from best friends to boyfriends last summer, and I couldn't be happier for them.

But me? I wasn't a relationship person. And I was up front about that. I'd made it clear to Matt that if he came home with me, it was a strictly one-night-only deal. And he'd said he was cool with that. We'd had a good time—he was cute, fun to dance with at the bar (and okay, fine, make out with at the bar, too), and I'd made sure he came—twice—back at my place. When we'd said goodbye the next morning, I'd figured that was the end of it.

It hadn't been.

It had started with a text that afternoon. And then another one two days later. And another a few days after that. Matt *"just wanting me to know he'd had a great time!"* Or *"just wanting to say hi!"* Or, worse, *"just saw this and it made me think of you!"*

It was the kind of thing that would be sweet and great if I had any interest in dating the guy, but I didn't and he *knew* that and goddammit, we'd only spent nine hours in each other's company. How could a romper covered in pineapples remind him of me?

I'd responded politely—but minimally. I wasn't trying to be mean, but I didn't want to encourage the guy. Only, apparently, I should have just ghosted him because pictures of pineapple rompers led to pictures of red velvet lattes led to suggestions that we *get* red velvet lattes together, or a drink, or a bite, or any number of things he'd asked if I wanted to do in the past three weeks.

I told him I wasn't interested—and reminded him I'd told him that from the beginning. He said yeah, yeah, of course, he got it… and then three days later he'd text again. It was getting ridiculous.

I sighed and looked at the clock. 8:59 a.m. I had to text him back and put an end to this.

LUKE: Matt, I'm sorry, but I'm really not interested. I don't want to date you but I guarantee you if you put half as much effort into finding someone who does instead of texting me, you'd have guys beating down your door. I don't want to be rude but please stop texting me. Good luck out there.

I hated how much of an asshole I felt like. I hated knowing that I was hurting Matt's feelings, probably ruining the poor guy's day. But I wasn't having the greatest day myself, and I'd already spent too much time thinking about a guy I was never going to see again.

Besides, if I wanted to do that—wanted to dwell and angst and internally castigate myself for being an utter and complete asshole to a guy I wasn't going to see again, I already had someone for that role. And had, for seven years. A guy I'd royally screwed over, a guy who—if I were being honest—was probably the reason I didn't date, because what I'd done to him had shown me what a shitty person I was.

And before I knew what I was doing, my fingers had swiped their way over to Facebook, to the event page for my high school reunion, to the guest list, to check for his name.

Oliver Luna—no response.

The same as it had been yesterday, and the week before that, and all the months since Grace Tighe, our class president and my ex-girlfriend from junior year, had announced we'd be having a seven-year reunion instead of a ten-year one, due to a capital campaign and upcoming construction at Astor Hills Preparatory Academy.

I didn't know why I cared. It wasn't like I was going to the reunion anyway. And it was even more unlikely Oliver would be. He'd hated high school. I couldn't imagine he was eager to revisit the place and people who'd ostracized him for years. And even if he did show up, what, was I supposed to apologize, beg his forgiveness after seven years of silence? Tell him I knew now how big an asshole I'd been, how sorry I was for all my mistakes?

Hardly.

I hadn't needed seven years of reflection to realize I'd treated Oliver poorly. I'd known it since senior year, since the night of the dance when I'd—

No—I didn't need to relive that memory. It was already the memory that plagued me at four in the morning when I couldn't sleep, Oliver's dark eyes, messy hair, and serious expression haunting me. I didn't need to start giving it space at nine in the morning too. Oliver didn't need an apology from me and probably didn't want one. He'd moved to California and become this crazy successful computer genius, from what my *if-I-can't-sleep-anyway-I-might-as-well-google-him* late-night searches showed me. He'd moved on.

I clearly needed to do the same thing. And I had, really. It was just this stupid reunion that had me thinking about the past. And work stress. And a million other things that had conspired to get me thinking about a boy I'd known so many years ago. He wasn't the same person anymore. And neither was I.

With a sigh, I put my phone back in my pocket, adjusted my too-tight shirt, and walked out to the lobby.

***

"Jesus, Dad, just leave him alone, will you?" I said, turning angrily to block my father from reaching Tyler as my little brother slid into the waiting cab. "He doesn't want to talk to you—and *your own lawyer* doesn't want you to talk to him."

"Luke, this is between me and your brother," my dad responded. "Get out of the way."

"No." I planted my feet firmly. "I won't. We're leaving. The meeting's over, there's nothing more you can do, and it'd frankly be best for you if you just dropped this."

"Oh it'd be *best* for me?" my dad sneered. "Listen, you might think you're so high and mighty, but no one invited you or your holier-than-thou attitude into this—"

"Actually, Dad, *I* did."

Tyler's voice took us both by surprise, and I spun to see Tyler leaning out of the back seat of the cab.

"I asked Luke to be a part of this," Tyler continued. "Because I knew that you'd be like this."

"Tyler, I'm just trying to—"

"No, Dad." Tyler shook his head sadly. "I don't wanna hear it. Please, just go."

"But you have to—"

I took advantage of my dad's spluttered reply to slide into the cab next to Tyler and shut the door. I gave the driver the address, and as the car pulled away from the curb, my dad still yelling angrily outside, Tyler let his head fall back against the seat.

"I hate this so much," he said, letting his eyes close. He sounded exhausted.

"I know." I squeezed his shoulder. "But you did great, with the lawyers. I promise it's going to be fine."

When Tyler was six, my dad had brought him to an audition for a children's TV show and he'd actually gotten the part. Within a few years, my dad had moved Tyler to LA while my mom and I stayed in New York. It would have been great, if Tyler hadn't ended up hating the attention and isolation that came with being the most famous child actor in the country—and if my dad hadn't systematically cut him off from his friends and family.

By the time my parents got divorced, we barely saw Tyler anymore, and my dad made it sound like Tyler wanted it that way. It wasn't Tyler got arrested and ended up in rehab that we found out my dad was the one trying to keep us apart—which would have been bad enough. But then we realized my dad had been stealing from Tyler for years—millions of dollars—and lying about it, telling Tyler he was so irresponsible that my dad had to be in charge of his money.

Things were better now—Tyler was back in my mom's life, and mine. He'd taken a break from acting, gotten into producing, and had fallen in love. And when he'd decided to sue my dad for embezzlement, I'd supported him—I was the one who'd figured it out, after all, when Tyler had asked me to try to teach him about finance. I was going to have to give testimony anyway, and when Tyler asked if I'd come to all the meetings with lawyers for support, I'd said yes. Gray, his boyfriend, came to as many as he could, but he was shooting a movie right now and couldn't always get away from the set.

"I just wish it were over," Tyler said. "Sometimes I wish I'd never decided to sue him. I hate having my life raked through the mud like this."

As much as we'd tried to keep it quiet, more than a few tabloids were running stories about Tyler's suit. He might not be acting anymore, but he was still a famous, recognizable face. And since he'd come out during the process of shooting his final film, he was also a face that moved copies and sold magazines, so they'd take any excuse to put him on their covers.

Not me, thank God. I was the brother no one knew Tyler had. We had different last names (my dad had changed Tyler's to make him sound more approachable), different childhoods (my mom and I had scraped along the bottom of the middle class in Long Island after the divorce), and different lives. Sometimes it felt like the only thing we had in common was that we were both gay.

It wasn't that I wanted the attention Tyler got—quite the opposite, actually. But Tyler was my little brother, and things had gotten so fucked up for him, and I hadn't been there to protect him. Wasn't that what big brothers were supposed to do?

"It will be soon," I said, trying to make my voice encouraging. "Dad's an asshole, but all the evidence is on our side. He's just fighting this because it's in his nature to be a dick. But we're going to win, and then this will all just fade away."

Tyler opened his eyes and smiled at me. "Thanks. For saying that. But also just for being here. I really appreciate it."

"Hey, that's what I'm here for," I said as the cab pulled up outside of Maggie's, the bar that Gray owned.

Well, used to own. He'd recently sold a majority stake in it to Micah, one of our friends, who'd turned out to be amazing at running a bar—much better than Gray ever had been. The bar was always packed now, but Micah saved space for us when he knew we were coming, so Tyler and I threaded our way through the thick crowd to a big, round booth in the back, just as Gray himself came back from the bar carrying a pint.

"You're here!" Tyler said, a huge, surprised smile on his face. "I thought you guys were shooting late tonight."

"Power went out," Gray said with a grin. "We got cut early." He set the pint down on the table and pulled Tyler in for a kiss. "How'd the meeting with the lawyers go?"

"It went," Tyler said darkly.

"Do you wanna talk about it or forget about it?" Gray asked, wrapping his arm around Tyler as they sat down in the booth.

"Forget about it, please," Tyler said. "Let's talk about literally anything else."

I slid in after them and smiled at Ben and Adam across the table, who were being disgustingly cute, as usual. They were both musicians, and Ben was probably as famous as Tyler— his old label had turned him into a crazy successful popstar before he'd gone independent and started working with Adam instead. They kept a lower profile now, but they'd gotten lots of critical acclaim for the music they were making together.

It was funny to remember meeting them, freshman year of college. Even back then, it'd been obvious how devoted to each other they were—but they somehow hadn't figured out they were in love until just this past year. I was happy for all of them, that they'd found each other—as long as it wasn't contagious.

"What are we forgetting about?" Adam asked pertly.

"Our terrible father," Tyler said with a sigh, gesturing between me and him.

"Oof." Adam winced, and then raised his glass of seltzer. "Cheers to terrible dads—and forgetting they exist."

"Lawyer stuff?" Ben asked with a sympathetic smile. I nodded, and Ben made a face. "Gross."

"What's gross?"

We all turned at the sound of Micah's voice and saw him approaching the booth with a tray full of... I actually had no idea what they were. Tall glasses filled with bright green liquid, each one topped with a maraschino cherry and a little umbrella.

"You'd better not be talking about my Tiki Tumblers," Micah continued. "Because they are *delicious,* and you're all about to try them and tell me so yourselves."

"What's even *in* that?" Gray asked, raising an eyebrow.

"Oh, a mix of stuff," Micah said. "This and that. I'm thinking of using it for the cocktail of the week next week. Go on, try them."

Micah set three glasses down in front of Ben, Gray, and me. Tyler and Adam didn't really drink. I actually wasn't a big drinker myself, though that had more to do with my vanity than anything else. It's a lot easier to maintain a six-pack when you're not drinking your weight in beer every night. I couldn't help giving the cocktail a dubious look.

"Are you sure this isn't toxic?" I asked Micah.

He snorted. "Just try it, please, before you remind me that your body is a temple and you don't like to defile it with alcohol or whatever."

Rolling my eyes, I took a tentative sip—and amazingly, it tasted good. Not like alcohol at all, and actually a little bit like, well, plants.

"This is really good, Micah."

"I'll try not to take offense at your shock," Micah said wryly. "Does that mean you're actually going to finish it?"

"Well…"

"Figures."

"I swear, it has nothing to do with the drink," I protested. "It's good, honestly. But every drink I don't drink means fewer squats at the gym."

"Oh God, not the gym again," Tyler said with a laugh. "Don't get him started or he'll describe his Crossfit workout to you in minute detail."

"Hey, I'll have you know I don't *do* Crossfit. I actually—"

"Noooo, God, that wasn't an invitation," Tyler groaned. "I

was trying to *avoid* hearing about your—oh, hey, Nick's here!"

I followed Tyler's gaze to see it land on our friend Nick, weaving his way through the crush of people in the bar to reach us. His messenger bag was bulging open with books, and he had another stack of them in his hand.

"Sorry I'm late," he said when he reached us. "I was working on a paper and lost track of time."

Nick was in divinity school, studying to become a minister, and he seemed to have about ten different jobs on top of that. I was pretty sure he was even busier than I was—but he seemed a lot happier about it.

"Did you make any important theological discoveries?" Gray asked.

Adam smirked. "Prove the existence of God?"

"Please," Micah said. "My drinks prove the existence of God. We already knew that."

"God's a lush then," Ben retorted.

"Yup," Micah grinned. "Obviously."

"Actually," Nick said as he sat down next to Ben, "this paper's more of a deep dive into John Calvin's earlier writings. Some of the stuff he wrote is pretty controversial, but when you get into it, it's actually really interesting to see that he—" Nick trailed off, seeming to realize that he'd lost all of us. "On second thought, maybe it's not that interesting."

"Oh, don't feel bad," Tyler said. "Your job is at least doing some good in the world. And it could never be as boring as Luke's."

"True," Ben chimed in."Your job just evokes unsettling existential dread in me. Luke's actually puts me to sleep."

"Hey," I protested. "What is this, high school? What's with all the bullying?"

"Are you seriously trying to pretend you weren't cool in high school?" Gray asked.

Micah gave me a long look. "Yeah, I doubt that somehow. You look like the kind of kid who would have teased me mercilessly."

"Oh, come on guys," Adam said with a grin. "Let's be fair. I'm sure Luke was a very sensitive, kind fuckboy."

"Do we really not have anything better to do than make fun of me?" I said plaintively. I knew they were joking, but still... They were hitting a little too close to home for comfort. I knew I had a reputation for being a player—a deserved one. But I really did try not to hurt people.

"No," Ben said with a laugh. "At least, I don't."

Micah sighed. "I, unfortunately, do. I guess I should go, you know, actually do my job."

"God, selling the bar to you was the best decision I ever made," Gray said, smiling broadly. "Have fun working."

"Thanks," Micah said, making a face at Gray as he walked away.

Nick gave me a sympathetic smile. "Sorry, I didn't mean for them to go from teasing me to teasing you."

That was Nick for you—always looking out for other people's feelings. I didn't actually know him all that well, but from what I could tell, he was too nice to be real. That, or he was totally normal, and I was just such an asshole that my barometer was off.

"Oh, Luke's fine," Tyler said. "High school's just a sensitive subject for him right now."

"Ooh, really?" Adam asked, leaning forward. "Do tell."

Tyler grinned. "He's avoiding his high school reunion next week because he's too afraid to run into his ex-boyfriend."

"What?" Adam looked at me in surprise. "No way. You were out in high school?"

"I wasn't—he's not—it's not like that," I stammered, as Tyler snickered next to me. "I wasn't out. And Oliver wasn't my boyfriend. And for your information," I said, turning to Tyler, "I'm not avoiding him, because he's not even going—"

"Which you only know because you're stalking him online—"

"But it's not even relevant because I'm not going either," I continued. "It's silly. I'm not still friends with anyone from high school, and I haven't seen anyone from Astor Hills in years. There's no point in going."

Whatever Tyler thought, that was the real reason I wasn't going. I'd lost touch with all my high school friends once I got to college. To be honest, I hadn't even really been that close to my friends senior year of high school—it had just taken me longer than it should have to accept that. I hadn't really been close with anyone.

Well, except Oliver. But that wasn't the point.

Nick took pity on me at that point and guided the conversation to a different topic, so smoothly that I don't think anyone else realized what he was doing. I gave him a grateful smile. Then my work phone buzzed and the grateful feeling disappeared.

Harvey had sent a last-minute email asking me to get him a sector analysis by tomorrow morning—and then three more emails, when I hadn't responded to the first one immediately. I should have known better than to expect a day that started out so shittily to end well. I should have known that I'd have to pay for leaving early to help Tyler and then going to a bar.

I sighed. "I gotta go, guys, I'm sorry."

"What?" Ben frowned. "But you just got here!"

"I know," I groaned. "But I think my boss is gonna have an aneurysm if I don't tell him I'm back in the office working on this analysis in the next five minutes."

"No offense, man, but your job—"

"Kinda sucks. I know." I shook my head. "Trust me, I know."

I did know that. It wasn't lost on me that all my friends had jobs they were passionate about, jobs that let them be creative and express who they were, while I had a job that wouldn't even let me pick up my dry cleaning during the day—a job I needed to dry-clean my clothes for.

I hadn't gone into finance because it was my passion, I'd gone into it to pay off my student loans, and to be able to help my mom with her debts. And yeah, if money didn't matter, it'd be great to go follow my passion—if I knew what my passion was. But I didn't.

The worst part of it all? I sort of suspected I might be the kind of person who didn't *have* a passion. I was just boring Luke with his boring job. Or, asshole Luke with his asshole job. Any way you sliced it, it wasn't the kind of life you dreamed of having when you grew up.

Sure, I was successful. And I supposed it was an armor, of sorts. Respectable, unimpeachable. Get a job in finance, work out every day, waterboard yourself with green juices. Maybe if I kept it all up, I could forget about that nagging sense of emptiness—the other reason I woke up at 4 a.m., unable to sleep.

But there was nothing I could do about it now. I was probably just stressed anyway, and I'd feel better once I'd gotten the promotion and things had eased up a bit. But since I wasn't going to *get* the promotion if I buckled under the pressure, I replied to Harvey as soon as I got back to the office and let him know he'd have the analysis on his desk first thing in the morning. Then I got to work.

That was at 7 p.m. At midnight, I was still there and fighting to keep my eyelids open. This amount of work was ridiculous—but there was nothing I could do but keep pushing through. I was so tired that when my personal phone buzzed, I opened my messages without stopping to check who was contacting me.

I should have. Not because it was Matt—thank God—but because it was my dad.

DAD: Why don't you stop meddling in Tyler's life and let this lawsuit drop? You're not doing him any favors.

I wanted to scream. My dad was a manipulative bastard, but he was very good at it. He knew exactly what Tyler's weakness was—that he hated the lawsuit—and what mine was too—that I just wanted to protect Tyler.

I wanted to text back and tell him to shove it, that the suit was as good as won. But I also knew that Tyler's lawyer would advise against that. My dad was just trying to get a rise out of me so I'd slip and say something I shouldn't, anything that he could use.

So instead I threw my phone across the room—and even that wasn't that satisfying because I did it carefully, gently, making sure it would land on the soft carpet where no lasting damage would be done.

I was sick of everything. Sick of being at the office after midnight. Sick of dealing with Harvey's bullshit, MacFarlane's bullshit, and my dad's. Sick of trying to be careful and cautious and perfect and please everyone, sick of not seeing any other options, because I'd been doing this for so long that I didn't know how to stop.

That was the real reason I couldn't go to the reunion. On paper, I might look like I had it all together, but in reality, my life felt borderline pointless. I bet Oliver never felt this way. He'd always said he was going to move to California after high school and work in Silicon Valley and that's exactly what he'd done. He'd founded and sold two start-ups and won awards for Christ's sake—at least, that was what the internet told me. He was following his passion. He actually had one.

And why the hell couldn't I stop thinking about Oliver anyway? Maybe I should just apologize. Get it out of my system. Only, I didn't have Oliver's contact information anymore and what, was I just supposed to Facebook friend him out of the blue? The thought made me cringe.

I just needed to forget about it. Oliver surely had. As soon as the reunion had come and gone, I'd stop caring, wouldn't I? I only had to get through one more week. And it wasn't like apologizing to Oliver after seven years of silence was going to magically fix my life.

So why couldn't I stop myself from pulling up the reunion's event page again, from scrolling down the list of attendees, from searching for Oliver's name until I—

Oh.

That was different.

His name was still there—but he'd finally RSVP'ed.

Oliver Luna was coming to the reunion.

2

OLIVER

I think it was the drool that woke me up.

I could be wrong—it might have been the midday sunlight stabbing my eyes as it slanted through the window, or the incredible crick in my neck that came from falling asleep at my desk, or the sound of hammering that filled the air. But I think it was the drool.

Regardless, it was definitely the first thing I *noticed* when I woke up—the slick, slidey feeling of my cheek in a puddle. Pretty gross. I wish I could tell you that was the first time I'd woken up like that, but the whole idea of telling this story is to try to be honest, so...

It was, however, definitely the first time I'd woken up in *this* location with drool on my cheek and my head on the desk—at least, the first time in seven years. In fact, it was so disorienting that it took me a second to figure out where I was. This wasn't my apartment. This wasn't even San Francisco. This was—

Oh.

This was home.

Home home. Like home-for-the-holidays home or there's-no-place-like home or, in my case, home-because-your-dad-had-a-heart-attack-and-refuses-to-see-reason-so-you-flew-back-to-convince-him-to-listen-to-his-doctors-and-oh-God-there-really-is-no-place-like-it-and-you-remember-all-the-reasons-you-left home.

You know—the kind that just rolls right off the tongue.

God, had I really fallen asleep at my desk in my childhood bedroom? Apparently. It's not that falling asleep while working was so unheard of for me—to be honest, I did that at least once a week. But if you think sleeping with your cheek on a mousepad and your forehead jammed up against your keyboard sounds terrible, try doing it in a child-sized desk.

God, I needed some Advil.

As I straightened up and stretched, already wincing at the knots I could feel in my back, the past 24 hours came filtering back to me.

It had started with a phone call from my mom, of all people, telling me that my dad had had a heart attack—a week ago. She and my dad had divorced when I was a kid, and I hadn't seen her in ten years. But apparently my father had never updated his "in case of emergency" contact information and so instead of contacting me, his doctors had told my mom.

And of course, when I called him to find out what had happened, he'd played the whole thing off. No big deal, he said. Just a little heart attack, just a little hospital stay, just a little *total overhaul of his diet and exercise habits and recommendation for surgery from his doctors*. Nothing to worry about, apparently, because he wasn't planning on doing anything they said. The doctors had only called my mom in the first place because my dad hadn't showed up for his follow-up appointment.

It was so typical of my dad. He hated going to the doctor, thought they were all quacks. Hell, as a kid, I'd had repeated cases of strep throat and ear infections that I'd just had to suffer through because of his *"tough it out"* philosophy. I got that he wanted to be strong, got that he didn't want to depend on anybody—but the man also smoked, ate mostly fast food, and drank like a fish. Those habits didn't exactly mix well with a *"distrust anyone with a medical degree"* attitude. Honestly, the man was 58, and it was a wonder he hadn't had a heart attack *sooner*.

The most infuriating part was that he'd never even planned on telling me. If my mom hadn't called me, I'd never have found out. I'd booked the first flight back to New York after I got the news, completely ignoring my dad's insistence that everything was fine. I worked for myself as a software developer, so it wasn't like I needed to ask for time off. Besides, I could work from anywhere—case in point, my childhood bedroom.

My dad was pissed I'd come home. Didn't meet me at the airport, wasn't even at home when I got in. He'd been at the bar with some of his work friends. At a bar, the week after having a heart attack. If I weren't so worried about his health, I could have killed him.

We'd fought when he got home. Because that was what we did, my dad and me. He didn't understand me, I didn't understand him, and yet we were stuck with each other, the only family the other had. I told him he was being ridiculous, refusing to go back to the doctor, refusing to take his health seriously, even after I'd flown across the country to help. He told me it was none of my damned business and he hadn't asked me to come home in the first place. I'd told him fine, I'd get a hotel, but he was stuck with me around until he got his head out of his ass. He'd scoffed and told me it was a good thing I was a millionaire now because it would be a long fucking wait.

So. That had gone well.

Only, by the time I stomped back upstairs to repack my suitcase—while my dad opened another beer downstairs—it was midnight and slamming the door with my baggage in hand sounded satisfying, sure, but also impractical. I'd decided to wait until morning and booked a room at the most expensive hotel I could find, in some kind of futile *"fuck you"* gesture to my dad. By then, though, I was too keyed up to sleep.

So I'd opened my laptop and started working on one of my back-burner projects, programming an open-source interface for municipalities across the country to share statistical data. Extremely un-sexy, which is why I'd never tried to spin the idea into a start-up, and extremely finicky code, which made it perfect for a night when I just wanted to forget everything and bury myself in ones and zeros.

I wasn't exactly sure when I'd fallen asleep. Had light been creeping in through the windows already? It was hard to say.

I was used to this, though. Working from midnight to 8 a.m. was pretty normal for me, even in times like this, when I'd sold my last company and was mostly puttering around, looking for work that inspired me.

In fact, the only thing that was different about waking up at my desk back in Garden City, Long Island and waking up at my desk in San Francisco was that my room in Garden City was still filled with evidence of my teenage nerdery, with its geeky TV posters and *Star Wars* bedspread. I'd made a conscious effort to purge my life in California of the worst of that. I was already a programmer—I didn't need to make things worse for myself. Not that it had helped much, in the romance department.

But we don't need to dwell on that.

In all fairness, there was another difference between the room I was currently sitting in and my apartment, 3,000 miles away, and that was the distinct lack of old take-out containers, empty energy drink cans, beer cans—cans of any and all types really; I was an equal opportunity can employer—and clothes strewn all over the place. Though that was probably just because I hadn't been home long enough for my usual habits to take over.

Look, I worked with computers all day, from home most of the time, and my love life was virtually non-existent. There wasn't much reason for me to pay attention to my surroundings, let alone keep them neat and clean. And we can just skip over the part where I ended up with a diet that was no better than my dad's.

Ugh.

Speaking of surroundings, the insistent hammering that I'd

heard since I surfaced out of dreamland hadn't abated and, if anything, had gotten louder. Standing up and scrubbing a hand over my face, I crossed the room and opened the door, steeling myself for whatever lay on the other side.

Or, well, I tried. But nothing had prepared me for what I found, which was my dad, on a stepladder, hammering... what the fuck was he hammering? The trim around the pull-down stairs to the attic, set into our ceiling?

"Dad... what... what are you doing?" I asked, confused and sleepy and probably not in the right frame of mind to be having this conversation, but oh well, too late.

"Oh. You're up. What does it look like I'm doing?"

"Trying to hammer holes in the ceiling?" I said, rubbing my eyes again. "Of course I'm up, you're fucking hammering outside my bedroom door."

"Well I'm sorry I don't keep your California hours, Oliver, but some of us have work to do, and for some of us, it's the middle of the goddamn day."

Alright. I'd walked into that one. Time to try a different tack.

"Dad, please, can't you—" I stopped, trying to get my brain to actually turn on and form words. "I'm *sure* this isn't a good idea for you to be doing, in your condition. Can't this wait?"

"In my condition?" My dad's voice took on an annoyed tone.

"Uh, yeah, your condition. You know, the one where you had a heart attack and the doctors say you need to get your life together or you're going to have another one?" I shook my head. If he could be annoyed, so could I. "What'd you have for breakfast this morning? One egg? Five eggs? Did you fry them in butter, or did you use bacon grease this time?"

"Actually, I skipped the eggs and just went straight for the grease. Figured it was more efficient. You have any more smart remarks you wanted to make?"

"Dad."

"Oliver."

He looked down at me, craning his head over his shoulder, and I sighed. He looked healthy—and maybe that was the problem. He didn't look like someone who was sick, who was likely to have another heart attack, a bigger one, if he didn't get himself in shape. He looked... well, he looked like my dad. The same rock-solid, stubborn, guy who'd raised me single-handedly and thought that meant he never had to rely on anyone's help.

I sighed.

"I booked a room at a hotel," I said finally. "In the city. I'm not going anywhere until we sort things out, but at least you won't have to deal with my smart remarks at seven in the morning."

"Seven in the morning? What time do you think it is, Oliver? It's noon."

I let that pass. "I'm just gonna go downstairs and get some coffee. I'll be out of your hair soon."

"Suit yourself," my dad said, as though me getting a hotel, as though my entire trip home, were some capricious whim I was doing for the hell of it and not the result of a serious medical emergency. "There's some mail for you down on the counter, by the way."

God. Of course there was. I'd moved out seven years ago, and my dad still kept every piece of mail I got and sent it all to me in a bundle each month. It was always junk mail and always completely pointless. I never bothered looking at it when it came.

I expected to see a stack of credit card offers waiting for me when I got down to the kitchen and was ready to toss them all in the trash—because don't get my dad started on how recycling's a sham and a conspiracy of the government—but it was only one envelope, and way nicer looking than any piece of junk mail.

I picked it up as I walked over to the coffee maker and turned it over in my hands. It was addressed to *"Mr. Oliver Luna"* in that fake calligraphy font that you see on wedding invitations. Only, I didn't know anyone who was getting married. Certainly not anyone who'd have *this* address for me. I poured myself a cup of coffee and then tore the envelope open, flipping the heavy card-stock contents over to read what it—

Oh.

Oh, no.

No, no, no.

Gross.

I should have tossed it in the trash without ever opening it. My lip curled. Ugh. Definitely no.

It was an invitation to my high school reunion. My seventh high school reunion, which was a weird number to have a reunion at, but—no, I wasn't even going to waste time thinking about that. I was throwing this out. I was. Right now.

I walked over to the trash can, opened the lid—and stopped.

This was stupid. There was no way I was going to this reunion. It was pure luck I was even home for it. It was scheduled for next week, apparently, and yeah, I'd probably still be around—knowing my dad, it was very unlikely he'd have caved and gone to the doctor by then—but there was no way in hell I was going.

I'd hated high school. Hated middle school, too, if you wanna get technical about it. My dad had sent me to this fancy private school where he got a deal because he knew the headmaster from way back, and every year had been torture. I'd never fit in, and they'd never let me forget it. I would have gladly traded the supposedly incomparable education I got from Astor Hills Preparatory Academy for the anonymity of a public school, but my dad had been determined to do the best he could for me, even if it meant I'd hated it.

I wasn't in touch with anyone from school. I'd moved to California as soon as I could—doing a pre-freshman summer program so that I could leave even earlier—and I'd never looked back. I hadn't actually bothered finishing college—it had seemed kind of pointless after I'd sold my first company at age 21—but I'd never once considered coming back to the east coast.

I wasn't going to this reunion. There was no one I wanted to see. No one.

My hand hovered above the trash can.

This was dumb. So dumb. I wasn't going, I wasn't interested in going, and that was all there was to it.

So why was there a little voice inside my head insisting that I was wrong?

I *didn't* care about anyone from high school. I never had. I'd come close. Once. Or maybe more than close—maybe I had actually cared. But that was ages ago, I'd been a totally different person back then—tiny, innocent, baby Oliver, fresh-faced and 18 years old and ready to get his heart stomped all over.

It had gotten stomped.

That wasn't me anymore. I wasn't that guy. I was smarter. I wasn't as naive. Now, I knew fairy tales weren't real. Now, I knew how dumb it was to hope for some white knight to come and save me.

Right. That's why your love life's so unstoppable, and you're beating men and women off with a stick. That's why you definitely never spend most-to-all Friday nights alone in your apartment working or falling asleep with an egg roll on your chest as you watch old episodes of Criminal Minds. Because you're definitely not waiting for something special.

It didn't matter though. What would I say if I went? *"Hey, you guys were all assholes to me in high school so I thought I'd show up and... give you a chance to be assholes to me again?"*

I mean, I knew that was ridiculous. We were all in our mid-twenties. No one was going to make fun of me to my face—or behind my back. No one was going to care enough.

Correction. No one *would* care enough. If I were going. Which I wasn't.

You could, though. And show them who you are now. How much you've changed. You could go and rub their faces in the fact that you're more successful than anyone else from your graduating class. You could go and show them that you're not the same nearsighted, mouth-breathing, buck-toothed, lisping kid that you were seven years ago. The kid with the nerdy glasses and the shitty haircut who everyone made fun of for having the audacity to not conform, to refuse to pretend to be someone he wasn't.

Except that was fucking stupid—the fact was, as soon as I'd finished high school, I'd done my best to put that person behind me. I'd gotten Lasik, braces, taken speech classes until I'd finally kicked my lisp for good. Learned how to breathe through my freaking nose, once I got my adenoids removed and wasn't stuffy all the time. Decided it was worth it, getting a better haircut and nicer clothes, so that people stopped looking at me like I was a freak.

So much for having the audacity not to conform. But still...

You could show them how much you don't need them. Show them how much you'd moved past them.

Show him.

Fuck. That was what it came down to, didn't it? That was what it had always come down to, from the minute I'd picked up the invitation. *He* was the only reason, the real reason, why I hadn't thrown it out yet.

Luke Wolitzky. The guy who—oh God, this was maudlin—

had broken my heart seven years ago. Frankly, the only person who'd ever broken it. The only person I'd ever let close enough to do it.

No. No, I wasn't letting Luke back into my brain after all this time. I'd done *so well* in forgetting about him. I hadn't talked to him since senior year and more importantly, I only google-stalked him like, once a quarter. That was serious! That was maturity! That was growth.

I wasn't throwing that away just for the chance to show him how over him I was. Because if I did that, I wasn't really over him, now was I? And what kind of person doesn't get over their ex... whatever Luke had been, after seven years?

A pathetic one, that's who. And I wasn't pathetic.

Not anymore, anyway.

I was still standing over the trash can, invitation in hand, when my phone buzzed. I pulled it out of my pocket with some relief. It gave me an excuse to walk away from the trash without feeling like I was totally capitulating, for one thing.

MICAH: Hey, how was your flight? I didn't hear from you after you landed but I also didn't hear about any horrific plane crashes, so I'm assuming you're still alive?

I smiled in spite of myself. If there were one person who could get me out of any mood I was in, it was Micah. We'd been best friends when we were kids—our moms had met at prenatal yoga—but we'd never gone to the same school, and we fell out of touch by seventh grade.

But then a few years ago, Micah had looked me up out of the blue when he was visiting San Francisco and it turned out, we had even more in common now than we had as kids. And somehow, ridiculous, irrepressible, couldn't-be-serious-if-his-life-depended-on-it Micah who lived across the country from me had ended up becoming my best friend. My best friend who I'd neglected to text back last night, apparently.

OLIVER: Sorry! My dad and I had a fight and I just kinda...

OLIVER: It's not important. Anyway, I'm alive, and currently drinking shitty, lukewarm coffee before heading into Manhattan

OLIVER: I got a hotel there because of Dad stuff—honestly, shoulda predicted that

OLIVER: What are you up to tonight?

That was about par for the course for me. Get a two sentence text from someone and write a novel's worth of words in response.

Honestly, no wonder I was single.

MICAH: Omg that sounds awful. And typical. I'm working tonight and some friends are coming to the bar, but I'm off tomorrow. Wanna hang out or you busy?

I snorted.

OLIVER: Um, if by busy, you mean am I staring at a fucking embossed invitation to my seven-year high school reunion and trying to get myself to throw it in the trash where it belongs, then yes, I'm very busy and can't be interrupted

OLIVER: Sorry, not trash. *Recycling. God I've been home for less than a day and my brain is already warping. I need to get out

MICAH: Wait seriously??? You have a reunion and you didn't even tell me???

OLIVER: I didn't know about it till like, fifteen minutes ago.

MICAH: You're going though, right? Like you're not seriously skipping it

OLIVER: Um, what? No, I'm definitely skipping it

MICAH: But... Forgive me if I'm wrong but wouldn't this be a chance to see that mystery guy who you've never even told me the name of because you're fucking insane and like, show him how hot and rich you've become?

Well, that was way more accurate than I was particularly comfortable with.

I'd told Micah the outlines of what had happened with Luke in high school. But even though I knew I didn't owe Luke anything, even though New York was a giant city and Micah would never run into him, I still couldn't quite bring myself to tell Micah Luke's name. God, after all this time, I was still worried about outing him, about keeping Luke's secrets.

OLIVER: I'm sorry, is this an 80s teen drama? Did I miss the part where I became the kind of person who cared what people from high school thought of me?

MICAH: Oh no, I think I'm the one who should apologize, I must have hallucinated the part where you said you were trying to throw the invitation out and failing

Touché.

OLIVER: Okay, fair, but... I'm still not going. Anyway, I'm free. I'll text you tomorrow, okay?

MICAH: Ugh, fine. I guess I don't get to live vicariously through you and get my drama fix. You're really cruel, you know that?

OLIVER: So I've been told

I slipped my phone back in my pocket and glared at the invitation, now sitting on the counter. It was practically mocking me with its curlicue lettering and the handwritten message from Grace Tighe tacked onto the bottom.

Hey Oliver, Haven't gotten an RSVP from you yet! We're trying to get at least 80% class participation. It would be really great if you could make it!

Well, Grace would just have to get over it. I wasn't going to be one of that 80%, and that was all there was to it. I walked back to the trashcan and flipped the lid up again.

"You're throwin' that out, are ya?" I jumped and turned to see my dad standing in the kitchen doorway, hammer in hand. "I was thinking you could go to that."

"Why would I want to—" I stopped and shook my head. "Wait, how do you even know what this is? This is the first time I'm hearing about it."

My dad shrugged. "Eh, Christopher told me about it a few months ago, back when you started getting those letters in the mail." He frowned. "I've been sending them to you for months now. You mean you haven't been opening them?"

Oops. Christopher was the headmaster of Astor Hills. I hadn't realized he and my dad still talked to each other. Maybe now was not the best time to mention to my dad that I *never* opened any of the mail he forwarded to me.

"It doesn't matter." I shook my head. "I'm not going."

"Why not?"

I stared at him. "Um, because I'm just... not?"

"And what, that's supposed to be an answer?" My dad folded his arms across his chest.

"It's—since when do you care?" I asked, confused. Aside from insisting that I *go* to Astor Hills, my dad had never really indicated any interest in my school life, not even when I was *in* school.

"I care because these kinds of things matter." My dad gave me a hard look. "I know you might not think that you need anyone, now that you've got your whole life out in California, but the people you know from home, the people who've been there for you—those are the people who'll stick with you, through thick and thin."

"Dad, literally no one from high school qualifies as someone who's been there for me. There's not—"

"You think I'm not taking care of myself now, but you know how I was out with Bill and Johnny last night? It was Bill who picked me up from the hospital. Johnny who stayed over that first night to make sure I was okay. Those guys and I go all the way back to high school—but you think we'd still be friends if I'd taken your kind of attitude to this? You gotta put in some effort, Oliver."

"But that's a completely different—" I stopped and took a breath. It was too easy to get wound up around my dad, to get frustrated with him changing the topic of conversation, bending things around until they fit his point of view. "Look, Dad, I'm happy you've got Bill and Johnny. I really am. I'm not saying they substitute for, you know, licensed medical professionals, but really, it's great that you've still got friends from high school. But I never *did*. I never had anyone—"

"Well, you had that—"

"I never had *anyone*," I continued, shooting the hard look he was giving me right back at him. I did *not* want to talk about that. As far as I was concerned, my dad and I could go to our graves pretending that he never knew anything had happened between Luke and me, that he'd never had to watch me try to put myself back together after Luke broke my heart.

"Alright." My dad shook his head as if to say, *"if you insist on being this pig-headed, there's nothing I can do,"* as though *I* were the pig-headed one in the family. "I'm just sayin', I think you're missing out. Johnny and Bill and me, we—"

"Yeah, yeah, I know." I threw up my hands. "They're the brothers you never had, I get it. Johnny's had triple bypass surgery, and Bill's in remission for lung cancer, but hey, they knew you *"back when,"* so why wouldn't you rely on them for medical advice? No need to go to the doctor when you've got old Johnny and Bill watching your back."

"That's not what I'm—"

"That *is* what you're saying," I cut in. "Unless you've had a change of heart while you were doing all that extra-curricular housework that I'm sure your doctors would be thrilled to hear about? Have you decided to actually reschedule that follow-up after all, and get your surgery consult?"

"Oliver, we're not talking about that. That's not happening. What we're talking about is—"

"You're damn right we're not talking about that," I said, fully aware that I was being rude now, but I was so on edge with frustration, with exhaustion, with the pulsing fear I'd felt in my chest since I'd heard my mom say the words *"heart attack"* on the phone yesterday, that I couldn't stop. "Because God forbid you try to take care of yourself so that your son, your only child, doesn't become an orphan at age 26. God forbid you actually admit you need some help for once."

My words echoed in the stillness of the kitchen as we stared at each other—me with my chest heaving in anger and my dad's eyes going from shock to sadness to that resigned, stubborn look I knew so well.

"Oliver—"

"Forget it." I sighed. "I'm too tired to do this right now. I'm going to the hotel. I'll text you once I get there."

I set my coffee mug in the sink and pushed past my dad, walking out into the living room. I left the reunion invitation on the counter. Not in the trash where it belonged, so not a complete victory, but at least it was out of my hands now.

"If I go back to the doctor, would you go to the reunion?"

My dad's voice stopped me in my tracks, and I spun slowly, sure I couldn't be hearing that right. But my dad was standing in the kitchen doorway, the invitation in his hands, and his face had lost that stubborn look. Instead, it looked... that couldn't be concern, could it? That didn't compute.

"What?"

"Will you go to the reunion, if I call the doctor back and reschedule that appointment?" my dad asked. He held the invitation out to me.

I frowned. "Seriously?"

"What, you think I'm lying?"

"No, I just think that's a pretty weird bargain to make. Why the hell do you care so much about this reunion, Dad?"

"I don't care about the reunion. I care about you." My dad took a step forward. "Look, kid. I know we don't always see eye to eye—"

I snorted. That was the understatement of the millennium.

"—but I do care, okay? I want you to be okay."

"Well I want *you* to be okay," I said, exasperated. "That's literally all I'm here for, Dad. Me? I'm fine. I'm more than fine, I'm great."

"I know, I know. You've got your whole life. I get it, I'm not tryin' to cramp your style. I'm just sayin'—"

"That if I go to this completely pointless reunion and feel unimaginably awkward trying to make small talk with people who made my life hell seven years ago, you'll go to the freaking doctor? Because if that's what it takes—"

"I'll go." My dad nodded. "If you do."

He held the invitation out to me again, and I stared at it, considering.

I didn't want to go. For a million reasons, really. But okay, fine, if I were being completely and totally honest, nine hundred ninety-nine thousand, nine hundred and ninety-nine of those reasons were tiny, almost meaningless, compared to the final one—the only one that really mattered.

If I went to the reunion, I might run into Luke.

And so what if you do? You'll show him how over him you are. Show him how little you care.

Show him everything he's missed out on.

Ugh. Whatever voice was making those suggestions in the back of my mind clearly could not be trusted. I didn't *want* to show Luke what he'd *"missed out on"* because he'd never had a chance to begin with. I wasn't interested in him and I never would be. I didn't care what he thought about me now.

So then why hadn't I been able to stop picturing his face, that perfect blond hair, those ocean blue eyes, since the moment I'd picked up the invitation? Why was his face still as clear to me today as it had been seven years ago? Why the hell did I still care?

This was a bad idea. It just was—there was no other way of looking at it. At *best*, I was in for an extremely uncomfortable evening of making small talk with people while we all pretended that they hadn't bullied me in school. At worst—at worst, I didn't even want to think about what *"worst"* might look like.

I gave my dad a level look. "You mean it? If I go to this reunion, you won't just make a new appointment, you'll actually go to it? And you'll let me come along, to make sure that you do?"

My dad sighed. "Good to know you have such a high opinion of your father."

"Listen, it was your idea to—"

"Yeah, yeah, fine. You can come to the appointment." My dad wiggled the invitation up and down. "We got a deal?"

Closing my eyes and scrunching my face up, one hundred percent convinced that this was a terrible decision, I nodded.

"Yeah. We've got a deal."

3

LUKE

 $\mathcal{M}$ aybe it was the way he chewed on his pencil.

Luke frowned slightly to himself as he studied Oliver Luna while trying to appear to be doing nothing of the sort. Oliver, who was sitting in front of Luke, diagonally to the left, leaned forward in his chair and propped himself up with an elbow on his desk. He twirled the end of the pencil around, caught between his teeth, as he gazed down at his paper. His floppy, dark brown hair fell into his face, and from Luke's vantage point, it was impossible to tell if Oliver was deeply engrossed in the problem in the book before them, or if he was lost in thought about something else entirely.

And what did Oliver Luna think about, when he was lost in thought?

Luke shook himself and tried to turn his attention back to the class out of habit before he remembered that he was deliberately trying to *not* pay attention in calculus anymore.

Only, if he wasn't supposed to be thinking about Oliver and he wasn't supposed to be thinking about class, Luke wasn't sure what he *was* supposed to be thinking about.

The only options he could come up with were depressing: his family, and the way his parents' divorce was tearing his mom apart? How all his friends seemed to be forgetting him, now that he wasn't playing soccer this fall—thanks to an ACL injury that was supposed to have healed over the summer and didn't? Or maybe the fact that he was barely sleeping anymore, how his stomach twisted in knots over all the changes he couldn't control in life that were hurtling towards him at impossible speed? He was only 18 and everything already felt like it was falling apart.

No. None of that—Luke got enough of that every night when he tried—and failed—to fall asleep, those thoughts playing on a loop in his head.

And before he knew it, his attention had drifted back to Oliver.

It was the pencil twirl, Luke decided. It was distracting. Just noticeable enough to catch his attention, irregular enough to be unpredictable, and therefore impossible to reduce to background noise. It gave Oliver, who already had a bookish air about him, the look of an old-fashioned philosopher, contemplating things Luke would probably never be smart enough to understand. Oliver's thin, wiry glasses and the slight crookedness of his teeth only added to the effect.

Luke wished, suddenly, that he could ask Oliver what he was thinking about. He was somehow certain that it would be profound in a way that would make his own problems seem small and insignificant. But not in a bad way, Luke thought. For as much of a social misfit as Oliver was, Luke had never seen Oliver be cruel or dismissive of anyone.

It was more that Luke had the sense that whatever went on in Oliver's head, whatever thoughts played behind those dark, intense eyes of his, was light years more important than Luke's own worries. And for a brief, intense second, Luke was seized by the desire to have his anxieties put in perspective.

But what would he—could he—say to Oliver to even broach the subject? Though they'd been in the same grade at Astor Hills Preparatory Academy for six years, Luke could count on one hand the times he and Oliver had actually spoken more than two words to each other.

It wasn't just that they didn't run in the same social circle. It was that Luke's circle was at the very top of the social hier-archy and that Oliver didn't even *have* a circle. And while Luke didn't feel great about the way popularity dictated who he could talk to and what he could say, he didn't feel secure enough to do something his friends might think was strange.

As far back as Luke could remember, he realized, he'd never seen Oliver talking, laughing, or doing any of those normal *"friend"* things with anyone in school. He could call to mind years' worth of images of Oliver, but they were either of other people teasing Oliver—a thought that made Luke feel ashamed, knowing he'd never done anything to stop that— or they were memories of Oliver by himself.

He could see the sunlight catching Oliver's hair and burnishing it gold as he sat in the cafeteria, reading. Oliver's lips parted slightly in thought as he gazed out the window in their German class. Oliver's long, delicate fingers, his lean frame, all elbows and knees, doubled up on itself in the bleachers in the gym as they waited for an assembly to start. He was always alone.

And suddenly it hit Luke that he'd apparently been cataloging images of Oliver for the past six years, filing them away in some part of his brain for... what?

He shook his head, trying to clear the hot, swirling feeling he suddenly felt in his chest, and tried to move on, mentally. He wasn't going to talk to Oliver, and he certainly wasn't going to keep hoarding mental snapshots of him. It'd be better to think about calculus than that.

"Exactly, Jared, exactly." Ms. Bowman's voice cut through the fog in Luke's brain, and he realized with a start they'd moved on to a new problem in the textbook. "And so if we know that, then who can tell me how we find the limit for problem three?" Ms. Bowman paused. "Luke?"

Fuck. Of course she would call on him when he wasn't even on the right page. Luke scrambled to figure out where they were in the book, trying to glance at the books on the desks around him without actually making eye contact with anyone. He *definitely* didn't look diagonally left.

"Um, it's—you have to..." Luke began, buying time. He glanced down at the problem when he finally located it. Oh. That was simple. You just had to... Actually, it was kind of an interesting problem, Luke thought, looking at it again, because it forced you to reckon with... "Yeah," Luke said, getting interested in spite of himself. "You just need to—"

Wait.

No.

He snapped his lips shut. He wasn't trying in calc anymore. He sighed and tried again.

"Well, I mean—" he shook his head. "I'm not actually sure."

"Really?" Ms. Bowman arched an eyebrow. "Because it certainly seemed like you were sure five seconds ago."

"I'm um—" Luke could feel his cheeks flushing and ground his molars together, willing his body not to acknowledge the embarrassment. He forced himself to look up and feign indifference. "I thought I knew. But I—I don't. Sorry."

But when he looked back down at his desk, he couldn't stop his eyes from sliding just a bit to the left and— shit. He yanked them away abruptly. Was Oliver looking at *him*? Oh God, he probably thought Luke was a moron. Everyone in class probably did, which was an unfortunate but unavoidable side-effect of Luke's decision to become dumb in math when the school year began. But he could handle everyone else. It was Oliver who—

No. No, Luke *wasn't* thinking about him.

Luke looked down at his desk and didn't look up for the rest of the period. It wasn't exactly hard—they'd moved onto problem sets, and Ms. Bowman let them work in pairs if they wanted. Luke chose to work alone. None of his friends were in this class, and it wasn't like he needed to inflict his purposeful incompetence on anyone else.

The bell rang at 1:50, and Luke gathered his notebook, calculator, and textbook, shoving them into his backpack hurriedly. The quicker he got out of the room, the better, since he apparently couldn't avoid embarrassing himself.

He almost made it.

"Luke." Ms. Bowman's voice stopped him just short of the door.

He turned and looked over his shoulder, nerves suddenly jangling around in his stomach. He wasn't sure why, but he had a feeling this wasn't going to be good.

"Stay a moment," Ms. Bowman said, beckoning him to her desk at the front of the room.

"I have Euro," Luke said, which was true—he did have European History next, his final class of the day—but it was also a piss-poor excuse because Mr. Grinstead, who taught Euro, really didn't care when you showed up, as long as you kept your grades up.

"This will only take a minute," Ms. Bowman replied, giving Luke a level look that said she'd seen right through his protests. She lifted her gaze back to the door and called out, "You too, Oliver. Just a moment."

Luke's eyes widened in spite of himself, and he had to school them to stillness. She was holding Oliver back, too? Why?

When he was sure his face was set back into neutral, he turned and watched Oliver approach from the door. The only student Luke knew who carried a messenger bag instead of a backpack, Oliver slung it over his shoulder and ran a hand through his hair as it flopped down into his eyes again.

On anyone else, that haircut would have looked ridiculous —on Oliver, it looked not just natural, but... *good*, Luke admitted to himself. It made him look sort of mysterious, sort of timeless—like some French student in the 1960s who was too busy with cinema and the revolution to give much thought to his appearance, which only made it look even better. Luke spent more time than he cared to admit working out, keeping his skin clear, and styling his hair to the perfect point of artful messiness. Oliver's hair probably just looked like that naturally, which only annoyed Luke more.

"I'm almost done with the application," Oliver said as he reached Ms. Bowman's desk. "I'm sorry, I know I said I'd get it done last Friday, but then my dad made us—well, it doesn't matter—but I looked at it, and it's totally doable, so I can get it to you by tomorrow so that you can—"

"What?" Ms. Bowman blinked. "Oh, no, that's fine, Oliver. Tomorrow's fine. Really, end of the week is okay."

"Oh." Oliver bit his lip. "So what did you—"

Ms. Bowman looked from Oliver to Luke—who was doing his best to not appear nervous or even mildly interested in what was going on, despite his racing heart.

"It's not about the application," Ms. Bowman said, looking back at Oliver. "Or perhaps, in a way it is." She gave Luke a hard look. "Where are you on your college apps?"

Luke squinted in confusion. Ms. Bowman had held them back to talk about college apps? Why would she care? Sure, she was his teacher, but it wasn't like he was going to ask for a recommendation letter from her—or anyone else, for that matter. Luke wasn't going to college, but he knew every adult in his life would look at him like he'd said he tortured puppies for fun if he told them that.

"I'm um—" he paused, trying to figure out a suitably vague answer that would cut off this line of questioning. "I'm working on them."

"Are you?" Ms. Bowman asked. "I find that hard to believe. You haven't asked for any recommendations yet. From anyone. And your guidance counselor says you haven't even scheduled an appointment with her."

"Yeah, no," Luke said, unsure of his footing. Whatever he'd been expecting when Ms. Bowman had called him back, it wasn't *this*. "I will. I just—it's—I've been a little busy."

"Busy." Ms. Bowman's tone left no doubt as to how she felt about that excuse. "Well. Be that as it may, we have a problem. We need to discuss your grades."

"My grades?" Luke looked at her in surprise. He wasn't doing well in calc, he knew—but that was intentional. But the first marking period wasn't even over—why was Ms. Bowman worried now? And why the hell was she bringing the subject up in front of Oliver? "I'm not—I mean, I know I haven't done that great on the last few tests but—"

"Luke, you're failing," Ms. Bowman said bluntly. "And it would be one thing if I believed that the class really was that challenging for you. But I don't." She gave him a hard look and waited, as though she expected him to protest again.

Luke didn't. He just shifted his feet, more uncomfortable than ever. Just because he was failing on purpose didn't mean he liked having it brought to his attention. Especially not in front of someone else. Especially not in front of Oliver.

"Luke, I know you can do better than this," Ms. Bowman continued. "I've checked your grades in math for the past three years. Stellar. So why the sudden nose dive?"

"I don't know," Luke said, looking down. "I just—I don't know, it's just hard, I guess. What, I'm in trouble for not being a genius or something?"

"You're not in trouble, Luke," Ms. Bowman said firmly. "Not with me, at least. But you will be with colleges if you don't get your grades up."

"It's not that big a—"

"Which is *why*," Ms. Bowman interrupted, "I'm assigning you to tutoring. Twice a week. With Oliver."

"What?"

Luke and Oliver spoke at the same time, Luke in outrage, Oliver in what looked like surprise, before looking at each other and then glancing away again quickly.

"I'm not—I don't need tutoring," Luke said hurriedly. "I'm *fine*. I'll just study harder."

He'd do nothing of the sort. But he'd say whatever he needed to say to avoid this. Tutoring? Twice a week? With Oliver, of all people? That was—

That did something to his stomach that he couldn't even begin to understand. Luke just knew that it didn't feel good. He couldn't do this. Not with Oliver. No.

Just no.

"I'm not sure—" Oliver began, looking at Luke nervously

and then at Ms. Bowman. "I'm not sure I have time, actually. I mean, like you said, with college applications and everything. I'm taking two sciences this year and—"

"And so is Luke," Ms. Bowman said. "I've checked. You're taking the same academic load. There's no reason you can't both get into any college of your choosing. But at the rate things are going," she said, cutting her eyes towards Luke, "that's only going to be true for one of you."

"I'm sorry," Luke said. "Really, I'll do better. But I don't need—"

"Yes, you do," Ms. Bowman said. "This isn't an argument, Luke. I'm not going to let your grades remain at this level. And you're getting tutoring until you've pulled them up."

"But why *me*?" Oliver interrupted. "I don't know anything about tutoring. There've got to be other people who would do a better job than me. Why can't *you* do it?"

Ms. Bowman raised an eyebrow.

"Sorry," Oliver said quickly. "I just meant like—I'm not sure I'll do a very good job."

"There might be other people who could do it," Ms. Bowman said patiently. "But none of them have applications that are as thin on extracurriculars as yours. You need to demonstrate commitment to your community, things outside of your own academics. Besides," she added as an afterthought. "You've got the highest grades in my class, and I'm pretty sure you're not even trying."

Luke couldn't help staring at Oliver in fascination. As he watched, a blush crept up Oliver's neck and cheeks, turning his otherwise pale skin a rosy pink. It was—well, Luke couldn't exactly describe what it looked like, but it was doing something weird to his stomach—again. In fact, it seemed like Oliver in general just did weird things to his stomach, Luke was beginning to realize. He didn't like it.

But what Ms. Bowman had said did confirm one thing, at least—Oliver definitely wasn't paying attention in class when he twirled that pencil around in his mouth.

"You two can figure out when and where to meet," Ms. Bowman went on. "But I'll be giving you problem sets, and you'll return them to me, completed. In *your* handwriting," she added, glancing at Luke. "You may not like it, but I'm not going to stand by and let you jeopardize your own prospects —or let *you*," she said, looking at Oliver, "not have the best chance of getting into the schools you want when I can do something to help you both. So. Are we agreed?"

It was a rhetorical question. Luke knew that he didn't really have a choice here, no more than Oliver did. He nodded shortly and watched Oliver do the same.

"Good." Ms. Bowman smiled. "Excellent. I know you might not like it now, but one day you're going to be happy I insisted on this."

Happy? Luke thought as he walked out of Ms. Bowman's classroom. He doubted that. He had enough problems without having to figure out how to add twice-weekly tutoring that he didn't want—didn't need, in fact, though of course, it was useless to argue that point now—into his life.

And it wasn't just tutoring. It was tutoring with *Oliver*. The weirdest kid in their grade, who everyone agreed was exceptionally strange, probably gay, and possibly from another planet entirely.

The kid Luke couldn't stop thinking about.

Sure.

Right.

Happy.

4

LUKE

*D*odgeball.

As I walked into the gymnasium at Astor Hills for the first time in seven years, that's what I thought of. The scent of wax on the floor, the feel of the red rubber ball in my hands, the squeak of sneakers pivoting on the floorboards—it all hit me at once. Gym had been a requirement in high school, but one that no one took too seriously, so our gym teacher, Coach Chambers, had just let us play dodgeball, day in, day out.

Or maybe it wasn't dodgeball, exactly, that I remembered. Maybe that was just the background track to the actual memories playing on repeat in my mind—the way Oliver had looked in gym class, which we'd had together senior year. Cheeks flushed, dark hair flopping into his face, eyes constantly surprised whenever he managed to catch a ball or get someone out. I used to get distracted, my throws going wild and erratic because I was staring at Oliver instead of the person I was trying to hit.

I shook my head as I took another step inside, trying to shake clear of the memories. I didn't even know if Oliver was going to be at the cocktail party the school was hosting tonight. The reunion had events tomorrow, too, and since I didn't know which of them Oliver was planning on going to, I had to go to all of them if I wanted to find him.

God, you are such a stalker.

This was a terrible idea. I shouldn't have come. I still wasn't entirely sure why I had. But ever since he'd replied and said he'd come to the reunion, I hadn't been able to stop thinking about seeing Oliver again.

I was just going to apologize and leave. That was all. I didn't expect anything from him, and I didn't *want* anything from him—except to be able to stop thinking about him, to get him out of my head. So I'd say my piece and go and finally put this to rest.

I collected my complimentary drink tickets from someone I didn't recognize at the registration table and made my way into the gym proper. Apparently, Astor Hills was cramming the reunions of multiple high school classes together to get them in before construction began, so the gym was packed, and mostly with faces I didn't know. God, this was going to be awkward.

I walked through the room slowly, feeling a little bit like a ghost. Everyone else seemed to be talking and laughing, hugging and catching up—having a great time, basically, while I just moved through them, disconnected. I could remember who I'd been the last time I'd stood in this room, on graduation day, and I wasn't that boy anymore. The problem was that I didn't really know who I was now, instead.

Hi, I'm Luke, and I'm exactly as boring now as I was back in high school.

"Luke? Is that you?"

I stopped at the sound of my name and turned to see Kyle Richardson smiling like he couldn't be happier to see me. Kyle had been one of my best friends back in high school, but we'd lost touch as soon as I got to college. Truth be told, we hadn't even been that close in high school, which said something rather depressing about the state of my life back then that I didn't like to dwell on.

"Hey," I said, reminding myself to smile. *Just because you feel weird doesn't mean you have to be weird to others.* "Good to see you, man."

"You too!" Kyle took a step forward, and before I quite knew what he was doing, he was going in for a hug. "Dude, how long's it been?"

I blinked. I was still trying to process the fact that Kyle had just hugged me and somehow hadn't felt the need to attach a *"no homo"* to the action—something he wouldn't have been capable of the last time I saw him. It took a second for my brain to catch up with my ears.

"Uh, a while, I guess." I shook my head. "How've you been?"

"I've been great!" Kyle grinned broadly. "Grace and I got married this fall, and we're expecting a baby in June."

"Holy shit, congratulations." Kyle Richardson was having a

baby? Jesus that seemed like a— "Wait, did you say Grace? Like Grace Tighe?"

"Yeah!" Kyle's face lit up. "She and I got together after college, when she moved back from Philly. We've been together about three years now." He laughed. "She'd probably kill me for not knowing the exact date, but yeah, it's been... it's been amazing."

"That's really great." Damn. Grace Tighe and Kyle Richardson was... not a combination I ever would have pictured, but... "Seriously, congrats."

Grace had always been a total type-A who had somehow managed to perfectly balance her million commitments. Women's field hockey captain, yearbook editor, class president—she'd been our valedictorian, too. She was whip-smart, but you got the impression she'd have managed to be valedictorian even if she weren't, cowing her grades into submission by sheer force of personality.

Kyle, on the other hand... Kyle was everything Grace wasn't. Relaxed, laid-back, and completely without direction, at least the last time I'd seen him. And, to be honest, he'd kind of been a dick, whereas Grace would have found a way to be polite and friendly to someone who was trying to murder her—hell, she'd probably be able to charm them out of it, too.

But she must have seen something in Kyle, and his face had lit up with a goofy smile when he'd started talking about her, so I guessed whatever they had was working for them.

"Thanks, man." Kyle shook his head and laughed. "God, this is totally wild, I didn't think you were going to come to this. Wait till I tell Grace, she'll be—" he stopped, and his face fell. "Oh shit, dude, I just remembered. Didn't you guys date in high school? Fuck, I'm sorry, man, I didn't mean to—"

"Oh God, no. No, no, no," I said quickly. "Kyle, really, it's fine. That was ages ago—"

"Yeah, but I should have been more—"

"Kyle, really." I barked a laugh. "I'm honestly happy for you two, and I couldn't care less. I'm actually gay, so..."

There. I'd said it. Something I'd known back in high school but had never been brave enough to say out loud. It was funny how, even now, my heart was beating a little faster, waiting to see what Kyle's reaction would be.

You never really stopped coming out—that was something it had taken me a while to learn. It wasn't something where you could just flip a switch and tell the world all at once. Each person you met, you had to tell, because most people you met assumed you were straight. And while I wasn't scared of how Kyle would take it, I couldn't help being a little on edge. It was the kind of thing that definitely would have kept us from being friends if he'd known back in high school.

"Wait, what?" Kyle's eyes widened, and I braced myself for— "That's awesome. Good for you, dude."

Good for me? I had to hold back a laugh. That was... I knew he meant it nicely, but his words had come out a little condescending, like Kyle Richardson, of all people, was benevolently proud of me and how I'd grown up.

"Uh, thanks? Anyway, that's really awesome about you and Grace. Tell her congrats for me, if I don't see her."

"I will, I definitely will." Kyle paused for a second, his eyes narrowing. "Wait a second. If you're gay, does that mean that—"

"Oh, shit, Kyle, I'm so sorry, but I've gotta—" I cut him off and pretended to spot someone across the gym. "I need to go—I'll catch you later, okay? Good seeing you, man."

I waved at Kyle as I stepped away, then weaved between two clumps of people and lost myself in the crowd. That had been more painless than I'd expected, but I definitely didn't want to linger to hear the end of Kyle's question. I grimaced as I wandered through the sea of people around me. I was pretty sure I knew what Kyle was going to say, and I definitely didn't want to talk to him about it.

Maybe I should just go, I thought. The gym was so crowded, it was going to be impossible to find Oliver, even if he were here. And I didn't really need to apologize to him, did I? I just needed to make up my mind to stop thinking about him, and then I would. I could leave Astor Hills and the ghost of my high school life behind, and everything would go back to normal.

Yeah. I nodded to myself. This *had* been a dumb idea. It was time to go. I turned towards the doors to the parking lot— and stopped dead.

Oliver was walking in the entrance.

I'm pretty sure I forgot how to breathe for a few seconds.

Oliver looked... perfect. It wasn't that I was completely blindsided by what he looked like these days. Despite the fact that I was too chicken-shit to friend him on any social media platform, I'd still seen pictures of him in articles and interviews—the kind of stuff I read when I couldn't sleep and couldn't stop myself.

But still, none of that had prepared me for seeing Oliver again in person, and even at a distance of fifty yards, I was breathless. That same dark hair, those same quick, bright eyes. Those same perfect red lips always curled up on one side like he was laughing at a joke none of the rest of us would understand.

But Oliver was different, too. Taller, broader-shouldered. He'd changed his haircut—it was sleek and trim now instead of the shaggy mop he used to have. And he must have gotten contacts because he wasn't wearing the cute wire-framed glasses that I remembered.

He looked way more self-possessed now. Confident. As I watched, someone approached Oliver by the doorway and he smiled in greeting. His straight white teeth gleamed—no more of the slightly crooked grin I'd always loved.

And then Oliver shifted slightly, looking over his shoulder and out at the crowd. His gaze swept right across me as he scanned the room. I froze.

Had Oliver seen me? Would he look back at me, recognize me? Or pretend he didn't?

I couldn't bring myself to find out. I turned and slipped away through the crowd, my heart pounding. By the time I realized where I was walking, I was standing in front of one of the bar stations set up along the edges of the room and ordering a vodka soda. I felt unsteady, and vodka sodas tasted terrible, but they had as few calories as possible, and they got the job done. I tilted my head back and took a long swallow.

"Someone's enjoying himself," said an amused voice. I turned to see Grace Tighe—or was it Richardson now?—standing behind me, grinning.

"Hey," I said, trying to turn my grimace at the taste of the drink into a smile. "Sorry, I just—"

"No, honestly, no need to justify drinking to me," Grace said. "Trust me, if I weren't pregnant—and trying to run this thing—I'd be hammered."

I laughed. "Thanks. And hey, congratulations, I just saw Kyle and he told me the good news."

"Yeah, he's pretty excited. We'll see how excited he still is when it's his turn to get up for 3 a.m. feedings, but still." Grace flashed me a mischievous grin. "I'm so happy you came to this—I didn't think you were going to, you replied so late."

"Yeah, I know." I winced. "Sorry about that."

"Oh, no worries. We have to over-order on the booze no matter what, so it's not a big deal." Grace waved my apology away and leaned forward with a conspiratorial look. "The extra drink tickets—and bottles of booze—are in Palicki's old classroom in D Hall, if you're looking for any more."

"I'll keep that in mind," I said, snorting.

"Honestly, I don't know how anyone gets through these things sober," Grace said, glancing around the room. "Anyway, what changed your mind about coming? Just a spur of the moment thing?"

Actually, I've checked the guest list twice a day for the past three months and was waiting to see a yes next to Oliver Luna's name. You know. Like you do.

"I uh—yeah, something like that."

"Well, whatever the reason, I'm glad you—" Grace cut off, her eyes looking at something over my shoulder, and she cursed under her breath. "Goddammit. We've been here for less than an hour and Kyle's already shotgunning a beer."

I followed her gaze to where Kyle and Andy—another one of my *"friends"* from high school—had cans of Genny Cream Ale pressed to their lips.

"Yikes."

Grace made a face. "You mind if I go—"

"No, no, not at all."

"God, I can't wait till I pop this kid out and can start drinking again. He's gonna owe me big time." Grace smiled at me. "Good seeing you Luke—let's catch up sometime soon."

"Definitely," I called out as she walked away.

Not like that would ever happen. It didn't hurt to say it, and I had nothing against Grace, but I'd gone seven years without talking to anyone from Astor Hills. I seriously doubted that was going to change anytime soon.

The only person I wanted to talk to at all was Oliver, and even that was just to apologize so I could finally forget about this all—put it behind me. Only...

Only you're too scared to even talk to him.

God, what was wrong with me? I was an adult. It was time to

act like one and stop hiding from him. Time to man up, say what I needed to say, and put this to rest. Finishing my drink in a long gulp, I set it down on a little table next to the bar and set off to find him.

Only, of course, now that I *wanted* to see Oliver, he was nowhere to be found. I circled the gym twice before accepting that Oliver wasn't here. Had he already left? That would be just my luck.

My eyes swept across the room again and landed on the doors leading out to the rest of the school. Was there any chance Oliver was somewhere else in the building? Probably not—it was weird enough Oliver had even RSVP'ed, weird enough that he'd shown up to a place he'd always said he couldn't stand. I couldn't imagine him wandering around the school just taking in the sights or whatever.

And yet, I found myself crossing the gym and slipping through the doors out into B Hall anyway.

The hallway was dim—the lights were on near the closest set of bathrooms, but otherwise turned off. The warm wooden floors, the long rows of old lockers, the thick oak classroom doors were all dark and quiet as I passed them. That ghost feeling came back again, even stronger, and for a second, it was easy to imagine that maybe my life had really ended senior year of high school, that I'd been rattling around these halls, unable to move on, ever since.

I didn't know where I was going as my feet carried me down to the end of B hall, past the cafeteria, and then halfway down C Hall until I was standing in front of the library. Huh.

It was probably stupid. But I reached out to tug on the door handle anyway.

It wasn't locked, which surprised me, and scared me a little, too. Not like danger-scared, just... now that I was here, I wasn't entirely sure I was ready for the memories I knew were waiting for me in there. But the door opened, soundlessly, and before I knew what I was doing I was stepping inside.

I slowly crossed the main room and entered the smaller, second room with the fiction shelves and finally the third room with all the old books no one read—it looked exactly the same, just the way it had senior year. The royal blue carpet muffled my footsteps as I passed through the stacks.

Not that I could see what color it was—the only light in the room was coming through the windows from the courtyard —but I remembered it perfectly, the plush weave, the way it had felt under my fingertips as I'd sat on the floor and braced myself on one arm, leaning forward to kiss—

"Oliver?"

My jaw fell open in surprise. Oliver was perched on a windowsill in the corner, peering out into the courtyard, only a foot from where he and I had—

No. No, better not to think about that. Especially now that Oliver had turned to stare at me and I was—fuck, why was I suddenly having trouble breathing? Oliver didn't say anything—he barely moved—and I tried three times to get my mouth to work before words finally came out of it.

"Um, hi."

Great opener, really smooth.

When had my heart started pounding—and why wouldn't it stop?

"How uh—how are you?" I tried again, choking the words out and trying not to sound as panicked as I suddenly felt.

Oliver frowned, his brow furrowing, just like it had when he was studying, or working on some particularly complicated problem set in our calc class. God, I'd missed that—and how the hell could I miss something I hadn't even thought about in years? It felt like something was stabbing me in the chest.

"I'm fine," Oliver said finally. His tone wasn't cold, exactly, but it wasn't warm either. He didn't say anything else, and the set of his jaw looked... determined.

Great, me too. I'm totally cool, definitely not dying, definitely not remembering the last time I ran my fingertips along that jaw, the last time I tasted—

"Um. Good. Cool, yeah," I stammered. Fuck. If I was going to say something, this would be the time to say it. Oliver was right here in front of me. This was what I'd wanted, wasn't it? To apologize and to—

"What are you doing here?" Oliver's voice cut into my whirring thoughts. It sounded almost accusatory.

Stalking you.

"I was uh—I was looking for you?" My voice came out unsure, soft even. I hated it, wished I sounded more confident. It was just a damn apology. It didn't have to be such a big deal, did it?

"Why?"

Deep breath. God, why was this so hard? Why did Oliver

have to be so... so—so exactly what he had every right to be? So pissed. So angry.

"To apologize. I know—I know it's too late. Seven years too late. But I—I wanted—I just wanted to tell you how sorry I am."

Oliver didn't say anything, just looked at me, totally inscrutable, like how you'd watch a nature documentary on inexplicable animal behavior in the wild. Curious about what might happen next, but completely dispassionate.

God, he really wasn't making this easy for me. Not that I had any right to expect that.

"I uh—I just, I wanted you to know that I've never—I never stopped thinking about it," I went on. "I never forgot what happened. What I did, I mean. And I know it was shitty, and I know I never gave you an explanation, and I just—well, there's no excuse for it, but I wanted to let you know at least that I'm sorry, and if I could do it differently, if I could—ugh, I'm sure you don't care about that. I just wanted you to know that I'm—"

"Not really a bad person?" Oliver said finally, finishing my sentence for me.

"Incredibly sorry, is what I was going to say." I winced. "I mean, I like to think I'm not a terrible person, but I completely understand if you think otherwise. And I just wanted to say, I'm willing—I mean, if you'd give me a chance, I'd like to—"

"Jesus, Luke, calm down." Oliver shook his head as though I baffled him. "It's sweet, I guess, that you want to apologize, but honestly, I haven't thought about that night in—" he stopped and laughed. "God, I honestly can't remember. So please, don't worry about it."

"You don't—you don't—" *You don't hate me?* But I couldn't say that. I tried again. "What I mean is, you're not—"

"Still mad about something that happened when we were 18 years old?" Oliver arched an eyebrow, and his lip curled up in a wry smile. "Honestly, Luke, I have better things to think about."

"Oh." I stopped, not sure what to say next. I could feel my cheeks heating up. Thank God it was dark—I was sure they were bright red. I must have looked like such an idiot. How self-centered could I be? Oliver hadn't been mad at me for seven years—Oliver probably hadn't even thought about me since we graduated. "Oh."

"Listen," Oliver said, standing up from the windowsill. He started walking towards me, and my eyes widened in confusion until I realized he wasn't trying to come closer to me at all, just walk around me and out of the library. "It was good to see you, but I actually have to—"

"Wait." I reached out and snagged Oliver's arm. "Wait, you have to..."

This wasn't going at all how I expected. I thought Oliver would be mad at me, upset maybe. I wasn't at all prepared for complete indifference.

Which was ridiculous, when I thought about it. I should have been overjoyed. I'd wanted to apologize, to put everything behind me, and Oliver had just told me I didn't even need to bother. This was good news.

"I have to what?" Oliver said, and his eyebrow quirked up again.

He could speak volumes with that expression, and right now it was saying that he was amused at my insistence, barely tolerating my presence, and rapidly running out of patience.

"Why are you here?" If the question took Oliver by surprise, that was nothing to what it did to me. Why had I asked *that?*

"Not like, here at the reunion," I continued, for some reason doubling down on my idiocy instead of changing the subject. "But like, *here* here. The library. Why would you come back here if not to—"

"Trying to get cell service," Oliver said like it was the most obvious thing in the world. He held up a phone that I'd only just noticed had been in his hand the whole time. "This building's a black hole for service apparently, but until they do something about that in the renovation, I'm stuck looking for bars like it's 2003. And since it's cold outside, I thought I'd try this first."

"Oh." God, I was such a moron. "Oh."

A monosyllabic moron, too.

"See you around, Luke," Oliver said, and then he was gone before I had a chance to say anything.

Not that I knew what to say. *I'm sorry? Even if you don't care anymore, please just let me say it, so I can get you out of my mind?*

Yeah, because that wouldn't make me look any more pathetic.

It was better to just let it go. I'd tried—I'd done my best, and it hadn't even been necessary. Coming here at all had been pointless. It was time for me to go home.

I walked back to the gym slowly, my footsteps echoing down the silent halls. The gym seemed way too loud and bright when I stepped back inside, and I blinked against the onslaught of voices and lights. I wondered where Oliver was —talking to someone else now? Or had he gone, too?

He probably has important things to do. Unlike you, his job matters. Unlike you, his life isn't completely pathetic.

God, being here was too depressing. I needed to—

Fuck.

I didn't have to wonder where Oliver was anymore, because I could see him across the gym, talking to Grace and Kyle. And as I watched, all three of them turned in my direction, and Kyle pointed right at me. Oliver and I made eye contact. And then he turned, said something that made both Kyle and Grace laugh, and waved to them before walking towards the doors to the parking lot.

Double fuck.

What had Kyle said to Oliver? Had he asked Oliver the same question he'd tried to ask me? Oh God, what if Oliver thought I'd told Kyle about the two of us. What if he thought—

Shit, I had to fix this. I hurried across the gym floor, trying not to bump into anyone or spill any drinks as I chased after him.

"Oliver, wait!" I called as I saw him walk out into the night.

Oliver turned and looked at me, his expression changing

from surprise to annoyance when he realized it was me. I darted around a group of people and jogged to catch up with him. The sky was dark, and the air was bracingly cold. I pushed my hands deep into my coat pockets when I reached him.

"What do you want, Luke?" Oliver's voice was withering, and exhausted.

"I just—I wanted to tell you—I mean, I'm—"

"Sorry. You're sorry. You wish you hadn't done it, you really regret it, etcetera, etcetera." Oliver shook his head. "I know. You told me that already."

"No, I mean, what I meant was," I groaned, trying to make my mouth and my brain actually work together. "I just saw you talking to Grace and Kyle, and I wanted to explain—I mean, I don't know what he said, but I just wanted to make it clear that—"

"Luke." Oliver's voice was as cool as the night itself, as distant as the moon.

"Wh-what?"

"They were just telling me where the extra drink tickets were. Grace was trying to get me to stick around, and Kyle offered to get me a bottle of vodka if I stayed." He snorted. "I know it might be a little hard to fathom, but the world doesn't actually revolve around you. You were just standing in front of the doors when he pointed."

"Oh."

My word of the night, it seemed.

"Yeah," Oliver said, a note of wry amusement in his voice.

"Oh." He laughed lightly. "Was there something else you wanted to over-explain or...?"

I can't stop thinking about you and I don't know why.

Except Jesus Christ, that would be an exceptionally bad idea.

"Um." I swallowed. "No. No, I guess—not really."

I waited for Oliver to say something dry and sarcastic. Or just to leave. To make me feel like an idiot—again.

But he didn't. Instead, he just stood there, watching me.

Why *had* he been in the library? Oliver's coat looked warm, and if he was leaving anyway, why would he walk all the way to the library just to try to find service?

"Are you—are you leaving?" I said finally, not really sure what I was saying or why I was talking but suddenly desperate for the moment not to end.

"Shockingly, a free handle of plastic-bottle vodka wasn't quite tempting enough to get me to stay and relive all my warm and fuzzy high school memories." Oliver snorted. "Apparently the stuff's all in Mr. Palicki's room, though, if you're in the market."

"I know," I said, finding myself smiling, however improbably. "Grace told me, too. At the rate she's going, there won't actually be any left for people who go to look for them."

"Shit, you'd better get some while you still can. Then you and Kyle and those guys can all get drunk and throw up on the softball field like you did the day before graduation."

"Oh God, don't remind me." I grimaced. "That was such a nightmare."

"I still don't think I've ever seen anyone that hungover," Oliver said. "In seven years."

"Great, I'm glad that's the memory of me that's stuck with you all this time." As soon as the words were out of my mouth, I regretted them. That was treading too close to a topic that Oliver had already shut down, multiple times. I looked down, scuffing my shoe against the ground. "Anyway."

Oliver didn't say anything, and when I looked up, his eyes were watching me warily, like obsidian, dark and smooth. They glinted under the light on the side of the building. I couldn't move, and for a long moment, we just looked at each other.

Then Oliver cleared his throat and glanced at his phone. "My uh—my cab's gonna be here soon. So I should probably—"

"Cab?" I blinked. "Why are you—did your dad move or something?"

"No, he didn't, I just—"

"I was just going to walk," I continued, talking like a maniac because the thought of Oliver leaving was filling me with an unreasoning panic. Which made no sense. "I figured I'd spend the night at my mom's, rather than go all the way back to the city. I mean, you don't have to walk with me, of course, but I was about to leave anyway, and I just—"

"I'm not staying at home," Oliver said. "I got a hotel, back in Manhattan."

"Why?" I blurted out, before realizing just how much that was none of my business. Oh God, Oliver probably had someone waiting for him. It was ridiculous for me to assume he was single. I mean, *look* at him—he was fucking beautiful, he always had been. I shouldn't have—

"It's... it's complicated," Oliver said.

Fuck. Yup. If that wasn't code for, *"I've got somebody back at the hotel, and it's only sheer politeness that keeps me from telling you to mind your damn business,"* I didn't know what was.

"Sorry, I didn't mean to—"

"But I appreciate the off—"

We both stopped, and Oliver laughed. A car turned down from the long drive in front of the school into the parking lot and made its way towards us. Oliver glanced at it and then back down at his phone.

"That's me," he said, looking back over his shoulder.

This is where you say goodbye. This is where this ends. You don't need to say anything else. He fucking gave you permission to shut the fuck up and have a guilt-free conscience. Just let it go.

So of course, I did nothing of the sort.

"Look, Oliver. This is the last time I'll apologize, I promise. I just—I know it doesn't matter to you anymore, I'm sure you haven't thought about me in years and probably couldn't care less about what some dumbass guy you knew in high school is thinking because you're too busy making a billion dollars writing apps or whatever, I just wanted to let you know that I've never forgiven myself for what I did, that I know it wasn't okay, and that—well, well, I still think about — about it. And I'm sorry."

Oh God. It was all true. All of that. And no matter how much I tried to tell myself I was over it, I wasn't. God, that was pathetic. Oliver had *told* me to get over it, and I still couldn't.

The car pulled closer, and Oliver took a step towards the curb.

"So if there's anything I can do to make it up to you, just uh —just let me know," I said as the car slowed to a stop and Oliver took another step towards it.

Oliver stopped. He looked over his shoulder at me, then back at the car, then back at me again. That unreadable expression was back. God, he was probably going to tell me to leave him alone, which would be totally warranted because I was basically harassing him at this point and I—

The corner of Oliver's lip quirked up into a smile. "Really?" he said. "Anything?"

5

OLIVER

*O*h God.

Oh God, why did I say that? What the fuck was wrong with me?

Luke was staring at me in total confusion, and all I wanted to do was just disappear—which, hell, wasn't actually all that different from what I'd been wanting to do all night so, hey, points for consistency, at least.

Luke blinked. "What?"

God, Luke's eyes were *so* fucking blue, and it really ought to be illegal to have a gaze that arresting. A completely unfair advantage. He should have had to go around wearing sunglasses all the time—except let's be honest, while that would look ridiculous on anyone else and help level the playing field, Luke could probably find a way to make them look cool and make me weak in the knees anyway.

Because yeah, in case you were wondering, the past seven

years hadn't made him any less hot. And they hadn't given me any more chill when it came to Luke, either.

Fuck. And now I had to answer him because he was still just standing there, looking at me, like he had been all night, and I kept losing my words and just gaping at him like an idiot.

Tell him you were kidding. Play it off. God, at the very least tell him you want him to get up on stage back in the gymnasium and sing Like a Prayer *while flapping his arms like a chicken as some kind of penance. Whatever you do, don't—*

"Come back to my hotel with me."

Okay, who the fuck had taken control of my mouth?

Because it sure as hell wasn't *me* who had just said that. *I* was sensible. *I* was cautious. *I* had better sense than to invite my high school... well, my high school whatever-the-fuck-Luke-had-been... back to my hotel room for I didn't even know what, exactly.

It wasn't that I was against a casual hookup—in theory, at least. The extremely strange hours I kept back in San Francisco, plus the fact that my apartment was a disaster zone, did have a sort of dampening effect on my sex life, and I really didn't want to stop and do the math on how long it had actually been since I'd even *had* a casual hookup—but even so, I'd certainly never intended to propose one to Luke.

So why the hell was that *exactly* what I was doing?

"Come back to your—" Luke stopped and stared at me again. "Are you serious?"

I shrugged.

Or rather, the alien that had taken control of my body shrugged, and I watched in fascination from a cage inside my brain. Had I somehow used those complimentary drink tickets and gotten wasted and then completely forgotten about it?

"If you want. I'm not sure how long I'll be in town—" okay, that was technically true, if a little misleading "—so if you want to make it up to me..."

I let it hang there and took a step towards the car, idling at the edge of the curb.

"If you're—I mean, if you—if you mean it," Luke stumbled over his words.

And okay, so a tiny, very evil part of me couldn't deny taking some pleasure in seeing Luke so discombobulated. Or maybe a not so tiny part. Maybe a very large part, who was hoping that something exactly like this would happen, and who was shocked that it actually was.

Not-Oliver, or whoever the fuck was piloting my body, opened the door to the backseat of the car and slid inside. I peered up at Luke and hoped to God I didn't look like an idiot.

"It's up to you. But if you want to come..."

Apparently, Not-Oliver also knew what he was doing because suddenly Luke was climbing into the backseat of the car and closing the door behind him.

Jesus, whatever happened tonight, I definitely needed a moment alone with my subconscious to ask it when the hell it had gotten so confident. And successful. Come to think of it, I might need several moments.

"Do you—do you need to—"

I started to talk, but Not-Oliver seemed to have deserted me, and I bumbled to a stop as Luke finished buckling his seat-belt and looked over at me. Fuck me, those eyes were going to kill me.

Hopefully not before he actually does *fuck you, though.*

"Your mom, I tried again. "You said you were staying there. Do you need to—"

"I'll text her," Luke said with a shrug. "Don't worry about it."

God, how did he do that? By all rights, I was the one who was supposed to be in control here. I was the one who'd invited him back to my goddamn hotel room. And yet here Luke was, reassuring me.

"Alright then," I said, doing my best Not-Oliver impression. "I won't."

We were silent for a moment, and then another, and then another, the car sliding through the night, lights from office buildings flaring in the dark as we sped through the streets and then merged onto the Long Island Expressway, and I started to wonder at what point this was going to get awkward. I really hadn't been thinking, inviting Luke back with me. The trip back to Manhattan was a long fucking ride, and I, at least, was completely sober.

"You're in California now, right?" Luke said after a while, and I wanted to heave a sigh of relief, absurdly grateful to him.

It was a simple question. So why the hell hadn't I been able to think of something to say, to think of anything except how goddamn awkward I felt? Why did Luke still have the power to make me feel like a shy, virginal 18-year-old instead of— well, a shy but no-longer virginal 26-year-old?

"Yeah."

I nodded, then wondered if I should have said something more. Jesus, why couldn't my brain work? What had happened to Not-Oliver?

Talk. Say something else. Talk.

"Silicon Valley?" Luke asked.

"Yeah." I nodded vigorously. "Well, I mean, actually, Silicon Valley is a region at the southern end of the San Francisco Bay, and I'm in the city of San Francisco itself. But close enough."

I paused. I waited for Luke to say something. And then, when he didn't, I started babbling. Because of course I did.

"I have an office there, technically. In Silicon Valley. Well, office space—I rent it. But I do most of my work from home —it's just easier with traffic and stuff, and I can keep distractions out, and honestly I work well in isolation, so the main benefits to a co-working space aren't really that helpful for me. But I have it, in case I need to take meetings with investors or do something where I don't want to invite people to my apartment." I shuddered. "My apartment is kind of a mess most of the time. Well, all of the time. But I'm thinking about getting a cleaning service, because—well, you don't care about that. But yeah. Silicon Valley. More or less."

Jesus. Stop. Talking. What the fuck is wrong with you?

Not talking was awkward, but it was light-years better than the verbal diarrhea that had just erupted from my mouth. I risked a look over at Luke. Fuck. He was laughing at me.

"I'd forgotten," he said with a smile when he saw me looking.

"Forgotten what?"

"How much you talk when you're nervous."

His laugh was deep and throaty. Fuck, I wanted to wrap myself up in that laugh, let it pour over my skin like milk chocolate. Though I could have done without being the subject causing him so much mirth.

"I'm not nervous," I said, painfully aware of how immature and, well, nervous that probably made me sound. "It's just a general term, and I didn't know how much you knew about California geography."

"A lot less when I asked the question than I do now." Luke's eyes flashed in amusement.

I looked out the window before he could see me blush. It didn't matter that it was dark inside the car. There were enough headlights from the oncoming traffic that I didn't trust the night to hide the pink stain on my cheeks.

It seemed safer to look away, anyway—making eye contact with Luke was having a rather unfortunate effect on my heart rate.

"I'm um—I'm a little nervous too, by the way," Luke said after minutes of silence. "If that helps, at all."

"What?" I looked back at him, sharply.

"I'm nervous too," he repeated. "I mean, we haven't seen each other in seven years and now—" He shrugged. "Well, you know."

"There's nothing to be nervous about," I said, looking back out the window. I said it firmly, as much to convince myself as him. "I don't know what you think is going on, Luke, but this isn't gonna be some kind of magical reconciliation with angels and trumpets."

"No, that's not what I—"

"It's sex," I said, surprising myself—and possibly our driver, though at this point he had to realize *something* odd was going on between me and Luke. "That's all."

"That's all?"

I nodded, not trusting myself to speak.

That's all. Really. It doesn't mean anything, so don't go thinking it does. You know Luke just can't stand the idea of anyone thinking badly of him. He probably just wants to fuck you so he feels like you've forgiven him.

Well, I was fine with that. I didn't need anything more from him, didn't want anything more. I definitely didn't need him back in my life.

I wasn't going to grant him absolution. Despite what I'd said back in the library, I wasn't anywhere near forgiving him. But I sure as hell wasn't going to tell him that.

I still couldn't believe this was happening. Sure, I'd had the idle thought about just this kind of scenario during the past week, leading up to the reunion. And by idle thought, I mean roughly one thought out of every five—a full 20% of my brain space—had been devoted to what I would say, how I would act, to show Luke just how over him I was. Even if I kind of, technically, maybe, wasn't. But I'd never thought it would actually happen.

I'd only gone to the reunion to get my dad to make that damn follow-up appointment with his doctors—something he'd refused to do until I'd sent him pictures of myself actually *at* the reunion to prove I was there, which was ridiculous, but maybe also smart on his part because I probably *would* have lied and just said I'd gone, otherwise.

Ugh—I pushed all thoughts about my dad down and out of the way. There was nothing I could do for him tonight, nothing I could really do until we'd talked to his doctors. I still felt guilty, not being home, not helping out more, but he'd told me he didn't want me there, so what was I supposed to do?

Fuck my high school ex, apparently.

And I wasn't going to feel bad about it. Whatever Luke thought was happening, I wasn't misleading him. It wasn't like I'd promised him a wipe-the-slate-clean fuck—just a regular one. If he thought there was going to be some other kind of outcome—well, that was on him.

"Why'd you decide to come to the reunion?" Luke asked after another long spell of silence.

"Why wouldn't I?" I said. It was a shitty answer, but I was in a shitty mood all of a sudden.

"I just—I didn't think it was really your kind of thing."

"It's been seven years, Luke," I said, throwing his own words back at him. "Maybe it is my kind of thing, and maybe you don't actually know anything about me."

"Right," Luke said. "Right, okay. Fair." He paused. "Well, I'm glad you did, anyway."

Dammit. There was nothing in that for me to get mad at. Why couldn't Luke do me the favor of being a jerk so that I could get offended like I wanted to?

"What about you?" I asked after a minute. "Why'd you decide to come?"

Luke laughed and shook his head.

"What?" I asked.

He gave me a long look. "It's complicated. Isn't that what you told me earlier?"

"Okay." I didn't know what else to say.

"I'm kind of wishing I hadn't, now," Luke said quietly.

"Oh." I processed that. "I mean, if you don't want to—"

"No, no, not that," Luke said quickly. "This is fine, what we're doing. That's not what I mean."

This was *fine*? Jeez, try to contain your excitement, Luke.

"I just meant like..." Luke tilted his head to the side in thought. "It's weird, seeing people from your past when you don't feel like—I don't know, when you don't feel like you have anything to show for yourself. I'm not married, I don't have kids. Yeah, I have a job, fine, but it's not one I really..." he trailed off.

"You don't... like it?" I said, trying to feel my way through the conversation.

I hadn't been expecting this at all. I'd expected confident asshole Luke, not thoughtful and introspective Luke. Why the hell was he telling me this? It wasn't like we knew each other anymore. It wasn't like we were going to see each other again, after tonight. So why—

"I don't know." Luke shrugged. "I guess I just—I see all my friends, everyone I know, with these passions. And I'm not sure I have one."

"Oh."

"Like Tyler, for instance," Luke went on. I got the feeling he was talking to himself now as much as he was talking to me. "You'd think he would have been super happy acting, but he wasn't. But when he *realized* he wasn't, he actually decided to go for what he wanted to do instead. He's been working with all these different writers, and he's gonna be directing his first film this year, and I just—I don't know. Sorry. I didn't mean to make you listen to all of this."

He flashed me a smile, and I just about died. It was like seeing the sun after a storm, and goddammit, I was *not* supposed to care about that or *feel* things.

"Right," I said, trying to focus on Luke's words and not the way my heart was trying to beat its way out of my chest because—just—no. Tyler, Luke's brother, seemed like a safe topic. "Right, I thought I'd heard something about that. Wasn't he in some kind of..."

I paused, trying to figure out how to word it.

"Porn?" Luke snorted. "Yeah. That was him."

"I didn't realize he was—I mean, he came out, didn't he? I didn't realize he liked guys."

"Neither did I," Luke said with a laugh. "Yeah, we had a lot of catching up to do when he moved back to New York."

I'd never met Tyler, but I remembered how much Luke had missed him after his dad had moved Tyler to LA. His parents' divorce and losing Tyler had been... rough.

Don't think about that. Don't think about how sweet Luke was, or how sad. Don't think about what it was like to—

"Tyler lives here now?" I said quickly, trying to preempt my own train of thought.

"Yeah, he and his boyfriend, Gray, live in Chelsea. Not far from here, actually," Luke said, glancing out the window.

I blinked and realized for the first time that we were back in Manhattan. Shit, when had that happened? Suddenly I wanted nothing more but for this awkward, stilted, uncomfortable car ride to go on forever. Better that than having to deal with what came next.

Not that I didn't *want* what came next. Not that I didn't trust Luke—well, trust him for *this*, if nothing else. I just wasn't sure I trusted myself.

It's just a fuck. It's just a hookup. Something to do so that you don't sit around all night worrying about Dad and looking up heart attack statistics until you fall asleep on your keyboard. Again.

The car pulled to a stop in front of my hotel. Luke glanced back at me, his hand on the door.

He cocked his head to the side. "It's fine if you changed your mind, you know. I can just—"

"Let's go." I opened the door on my side of the car.

"I guess that answers that question," I heard Luke say under his breath.

I thanked the driver and closed my door. By the time I'd walked around to the curb, Luke was standing on the sidewalk waiting for me, his hands back in his pockets and his breath coming out in little puffs in the cold night.

We didn't talk on the walk through the lobby or on the ride up the elevator. I didn't know why Luke was quiet, but for my part, I was too busy trying not to hyperventilate to manage anything as complicated as *thoughts* or *words*. I hoped to God that Luke interpreted my silence as cool disinterest instead of the nervousness-edging-on-panic that it really was.

Luke Wolitzky was coming back to my hotel room. Luke fucking Wolitzky, who I hadn't seen in seven years, who apparently *had* been thinking about me in the interim— though surely nowhere approaching the pathetic amount that I'd thought about him and then tried to convince myself I hadn't—was coming back to my hotel room to fuck me. Because I'd asked him to.

Was I absolutely positive I wasn't dreaming?

If I'd woken up suddenly and found myself sitting at my desk back home in San Francisco, drool gluing my cheek to a packet of soy sauce, I actually would have been less surprised. I pinched myself surreptitiously and grimaced at the pain. Nope. Definitely awake.

"It's this way," I said as we walked out of the elevator. I could feel that nervous need to talk bubbling up in my chest again. "It's 1597. Which is really easy to remember, actually, because it's a number in the Fibonacci sequence. So that's kinda cool."

Jesus, that was the *opposite* of cool, and so was I.

We reached the door, and I swiped us in with my keycard. I flicked the light on as Luke closed the door behind us. When I turned, he was looking at me with a concerned expression.

I bit my lip, then unbit it. Dammit, that was a bad habit of mine, but I refused to be nervous. Or if I couldn't quite swing that, I at least refused to let Luke *know* I was nervous. Luke, who apparently remembered what I was like when I was anxious, which I couldn't decide if I found sweet or irritating.

"Oliver, I just—"

"Luke, really, it's—"

"No, no, just listen," Luke interrupted.

He took a step forward and even though there were still feet of space separating the two of us, suddenly the air felt electric. I was pretty sure I could feel every atom in the air in between us, feel the curve of the earth and all its magnetism, all its energy, concentrated into just these two feet separating me from Luke. How was the air not crackling?

"Are you—are you sure you want to—" Luke paused, swallowed, and then looked up.

I was shocked by the vulnerability I saw in his eyes. God,

when was the last time I'd seen Luke look like that? I had to yank my mind out of the past, as it tried to flash back to high school. Those memories were dangerous.

"It's just that it's been so long since we—well, talked," Luke continued, which was one way of putting it, I supposed. "And I just—if you want to clear the air or you know, talk a little before we—"

"What is there to talk about?" I heard myself say, and, suddenly, Not-Oliver was back, driving the train with his air of unstudied I-don't-give-a-fuck-ness. I was grateful. "Luke, this really isn't that big a deal."

"I know but—I mean, you said that I could make it up to you by coming here, and it's not that I didn't want to—don't want—because trust me, I do, but I just, I mean, if you want to—"

"Luke." My voice was quiet, calm, and I was amazed at how self-possessed I sounded. "There's nothing to make up. That was just my way of asking if you wanted to come back here, but now I'm realizing I should have been clearer."

"What do you—"

"Luke, do you want to fuck me? Because that's all I'm after. No deeper meaning. No feelings you've hurt, nothing you have to apologize for. Whatever happened between us happened so long ago, it would actually be really sad if I still cared about that."

Again, that was technically true. It would be really sad —it *was*.

But goddammit, I was sick of caring about it all. I was twenty fucking six for God's sake—what other 26-year-old still cared about his high school heartaches? And Luke didn't have any fucking right to the contents of the inside of my head, anyway. As far as he was concerned, I didn't give a shit.

Maybe if I acted like that enough, it would start being true.

"So that's all you—that's all you want?"

"That's all I want." I smiled. "If you want it too, that is. So the only question is: do you?"

"Do I—"

"Do you want to fuck me?" I let my smile grow. "Because while it's a liiiiiiittle hard to remember back that far, I'm pretty sure that's one thing we never—"

I didn't get to finish my sentence—Luke's mouth was on mine. He closed the space between us, and all the energy that had been waiting there was now rushing at me, sparking as we grabbed, pulled, and clung, our mouths seeking each other hungrily.

Oh God, his lips tasted the same. How could I remember that? How was it possible that I still knew exactly what Luke tasted like, that underneath the faint tingle of vodka on Luke's tongue there was that sweet, golden taste that had always reminded me of a field of ripe strawberries in the sunshine.

And a more important question. Now that I'd discovered that my brain had catalogued that flavor and held onto it all these years, what did it mean that I'd missed it?

A sudden buzzing made me pull back in confusion until I saw Luke's rueful smile as he pulled his phone out of his pocket.

"You need to take that?" I asked.

"Fuck no," Luke said. "It's just work. It can wait."

He tossed it down onto the couch where it fell next to a decorative cushion, and then his mouth was on mine again. We stumbled through the room, banging into the coffee table, bumping into the couch as we made our way to the bedroom, and suddenly I was irrationally angry that I'd reserved a suite with so much freaking space to cross before we reached the bed. Then again, maybe nothing could have been soon enough, because even once we were in the bedroom, ripping each other's clothes off, I still wanted more, faster, *now*.

Everything about you. Right now. That's all I want, Luke. Just everything about you.

There was no use in denying it, not to myself, at least. Not when it was impossible to ignore, not when Luke's hand was venturing down to stroke my already hard cock through the fabric of my boxers. I moaned at the warmth, that firm touch, and Luke's lips sought my neck, kissing and sucking on the sensitive skin there as he stroked me again.

Fuck it. I couldn't handle trying to be cool at the same time as all of this was happening. I couldn't keep up that air of don't-give-a-shit-ness, not when I just wanted to let everything go.

Enjoy this now, deal with the consequences later.

I still couldn't believe this was happening, that Luke—a mostly naked Luke—was running his hands all over my body as I did the same to him. And what a fucking body it was.

Luke had been hot in high school. Like, stupidly hot. Unfairly hot. The kind of hot that, if there were any justice in the world, would have been balanced out by him being an idiot, or an asshole, or at least having terrible body odor —something to compensate. But Luke wasn't an idiot, and he smelled amazing, of course, and as for being an asshole —well, he hadn't seemed that way, not at first. I'd learned better, later.

I'd been so starstruck, so dazed and disbelieving at the idea that Luke could possibly be interested in someone like me, that Luke even wanted to *talk* to me, that I'd abdicated all my better judgment. I'd paid for it later. But tonight, feeling Luke's hard muscles under my fingers, seeing the gorgeous man he'd become in those intervening years—I couldn't blame my past self for the decisions I'd made.

But I was going to be smarter this time. This time, I wasn't going to—

I couldn't even finish the thought, because Luke's hand dipped down underneath my boxers, and I lost control of all my senses at the feeling of skin on skin. I moaned again, desperate and needy, but I didn't fucking care. Luke drew a finger across my slit and used the precum dripping there to slick his hand and my shaft as he stroked me.

"Fuck, Luke," I whimpered. My knees felt weak.

"I've learned a few things since senior year," Luke said.

He caressed my ear with his tongue and then sucked the lobe into his mouth. My knees actually did buckle that time and only Luke's arms around me, holding us together, chest to chest, kept me from falling.

Luke laughed lightly. He looked so fucking pleased with himself, and I wanted to wipe that smirk off his face but also somehow see Luke smile like that forever if it meant he kept making me feel this good.

I kissed him greedily one last time before sliding my hands down Luke's sides. I knelt slowly. My knees seemed to want to hit the floor anyway—might as well indulge them.

"What? No, what—you don't have to—oh, fuck..."

Luke's protests turned to moans in a very satisfying way as I trailed kisses down his chest, his abs, his hip bones, until I brought myself face-to-face with the erection pressing insistently against the fabric of Luke's boxer briefs.

I inhaled deeply, pressed my nose and mouth to Luke's groin, and then rubbed my cheek against Luke's cock through the fabric. Luke moaned louder that time, and I smiled at the growing damp patch where the tip of Luke's cock lay. God, he smelled good, warm and masculine, and I let my lips drift across the outline of Luke's cock, let my tongue lap against the head through the fabric like I was so turned on I couldn't help myself. Honestly, it wasn't really an act.

"Fuck, Oliver," Luke groaned. "Jesus, that's—you're—fuck."

I laughed, letting the corner of my lip quirk up, and lifted my eyes to meet Luke's. Once his gaze was locked on mine, I licked along the length of his cock innocently.

Luke's cock twitched. "Fucking hell."

"I've learned a few things, too," I said, grinning shamelessly.

But enough with the slowness, enough with drawing this

out. I wanted Luke, and I wanted him without any clothing between us. I hooked my fingers into the waistband of his underwear and slowly pulled it down, revealing Luke's cock inch by inch.

There were a lot of inches.

God, I hadn't forgotten this part of Luke either, I realized as Luke stepped out of his boxer-briefs and kicked them to the side. I let my hands slide up Luke's thighs, brought my lips to the base of his cock where it had bounced free, and pressed a kiss to the taut skin of his groin. God, no, I hadn't forgotten this at all.

Luke's cock was a fucking treasure. His brother might be the pornstar, but as far as I was concerned, Luke was more than qualified for that profession. He'd look perfect on screen.

But he wasn't on screen. He was here. With me.

I knew Luke must have gotten more than his share of guys since high school. Looking the way he did, how could you not? I stifled a tiny flicker of jealousy at that thought. He didn't owe me anything, just like I didn't owe anything to him. This was just sex, and all that mattered was that Luke was here right now.

I didn't care who else Luke had fucked. I didn't care if he fucked someone five minutes after he left my hotel room. I didn't—really. That was all this was—one night of no-strings, no-emotions sex. I'd made that clear.

Now it was just on me to remember that.

I brought my hand to the base of Luke's cock and was rewarded with another moan. God, I'd missed this. Not just Luke really, but being with anyone. It had been longer than

I could quite remember since I'd been with anyone, man or woman, but never in a million years had I thought I'd be with Luke again.

Something flickered around the edges of that thought, and I pushed it away. Enough thinking. I brought my lips to the tip of Luke's cock and licked the precum languorously before swirling my tongue all the way around his head. I looked up, caught his eyes again, and held them as I pressed forward, taking as much of Luke's cock into my mouth as I could in one long, smooth motion.

"Jesus," Luke whispered. "Oh God, Oliver."

I moaned a little as Luke's cock filled my mouth—partly to put on a show, partly because I knew it'd feel good around Luke's cock, and partly because, dammit, I'd just wanted to. Luke's cock was big, and I had to fight the impulse to take him further down, past the limits of what was actually comfortable, just to see how Luke would react if I gagged on his cock. Knowing what I knew about him, I had a feeling he might lose his mind.

But you don't know him. Not at all, not anymore. And you're not going to.

I couldn't get caught up in all that. Instead, I pulled off and began sucking Luke in and out, building up a rhythm until he was groaning, at which point I stopped and moved my mouth to his balls before licking up and down his shaft in long stripes. I wanted to drive Luke crazy, but I didn't want him to come, not yet. Not until I had. It wasn't long before his knees were shaking as badly as mine had been, and his hand darted out to my head, stroking through my hair once before landing on my shoulder.

You can leave it there. If you like that. Put your hand on the back of my head. Pull me towards you. Use me a little.

The thought fluttered through my mind out of nowhere, and my eyes widened. I didn't really mean that, did I? It didn't matter, though. Luke's hand stayed on my shoulder like the boyscout he was.

That, I decided, wasn't something I wanted. I didn't want careful Luke, I didn't want apologetic Luke who was still trying to look out for me, to make up for past wrongs. Frankly, I didn't want Luke to remember that old version of me, the sad, pathetic Oliver who let himself get hurt. I wanted Luke out of his mind with pleasure, so swept up in who I was now and how bad he wanted me that he didn't have any room in his brain for who I'd been. And then I wanted to leave him, wanting more.

I pulled off his cock abruptly and stood up. Luke looked at me slowly, dazed with pleasure.

"What—do you want me to—" Luke shook his head as if to clear it.

Good. Be confused. Be desperate. Want me.

"What do you want?" Luke asked, a little more firmly this time. "Tell me what I can do."

"You can fuck me," I said, and I took his hand, pulling him towards the bed.

Luke's eyes widened, and I had to stifle a laugh. Had he forgotten the reason I'd asked him back here? Or had my blow job just been that good? The latter, I decided—I wanted the self-esteem boost. I grinned as my hands went to my boxers.

"No," Luke reached out, put his hands on my wrists, and stilled them. "No. Let—" he cleared his throat. "Let me."

He looked at me, his eyes soft and pleading, like he wasn't sure I would grant his request. It took my breath away.

Fuck you, Luke. Stop fucking doing this to me.

I nodded, afraid, if I spoke, that I'd say something I would regret. Something too revealing. Something I didn't even want to know myself.

Luke smiled, brought his hand to my chin, and then leaned in. His kiss was tender, and I closed my eyes as his tongue slid along my lower lip, just trying to concentrate on breathing. For a second there, it was like I'd forgotten how.

Luke was so gentle, the kiss like feathers brushing across my lips. It was so soft I could have cried.

Stop it. Don't think that way.

Luke's other hand reached for mine, and then he turned, sitting on the edge of the bed, pulling me down next to him. Slowly, he leaned in and kissed me again, a little more urgently this time, a little more pressing, and as we tilted, he brought me to lay down on my back, catching my head with his hand as it hit the pillow.

God, I wanted him on top of me, wanted to feel friction against my cock, wanted to feel the warmth of Luke's body on mine. When Luke's hand traced its way from my cheek to my neck, then down onto my chest, his fingertips like fire on my skin, I couldn't help hipping up off the bed, desperate for more contact.

Luke smiled down at me and that smile, God, that smile

flayed me open. It was so sweet and so—so focused, on me. Like I was the only thing that mattered to Luke in the entire world.

Dammit, Luke needed to stop doing that. I reached out and pulled him down for a hard kiss so I could shut my eyes, so he wouldn't see the tears building up in them.

There was no reason for me to be crying. This didn't mean anything—it never had.

They were probably just tears of relief, I reasoned. After being practically celibate for so long. Or tears of frustration, anxiety over my dad and his health and how fucking stubborn he was being.

This had nothing to do with Luke. It couldn't. Any sense of tenderness, any sense that Luke cared—that just meant that Luke was as good at pretending now as he had been back in high school. As good at putting on an act.

The only thing that had changed was that I was smarter now.

Luke shifted so he was straddling me, not breaking the kiss. I ground against him, and Luke pushed back. Finally, finally, he wasn't holding back, and it felt *good*, our bodies moving in tandem. Luke kissed his way down my neck, his fingers sliding along my chest and hooking into my boxers. His mouth followed his hands, and he pressed a kiss just below my belly button. I sucked in a sharp breath of air.

Then Luke began sliding my boxers off. It should have been awkward, really, the way I had to shimmy and wriggle my way out of them because I couldn't use my hands with Luke's in the way, like I was a doll being undressed or something, but the way Luke smiled at me once I was naked, the way he brought his hand to the base of my cock—it made my fucking heart flutter in a way that felt *very* good and *very* disturbing.

And then Luke turned his gaze back down and began to stroke me, brushing his lips across the tip of my cock back and forth, parting them a teeny bit more with each pass like he was savoring me. Fuck, that felt good, even though this wasn't what I'd expected, wasn't the pushy, aggressive Luke that I'd imagined.

Not that he'd been like that before. Not at all. God, we'd both been so nervous, so scared back then. But the Luke in front of me right now didn't compute with the Luke I'd pictured in my head for the past seven years, the Luke who'd hurt me.

I hadn't expected this Luke to be so interested in my pleasure.

It was disconcerting, and I could feel myself starting to teeter on the edge of something—something tall and jagged, like a cliff, and on the other side of it lay forgiveness. But I didn't want that. I wanted to not care about Luke anymore, yes. I wanted to be over everything that had happened, yes. But I wasn't ready for forgiveness—and I shouldn't have had to be. This was just a hookup, for fuck's sake.

Abruptly, I pushed up and over, flipping us around so Luke was on his back and I was on top this time. Luke gasped, breathless, and he smiled this thrilling little smile, the kind you'd give a friend at the top of a roller coaster right before it plunged over, as if to say, *"this is fucking crazy, but it's really happening.*" In spite of myself, I smiled back.

That had always been my problem with Luke. Even when I knew better—I smiled back.

"Stay right there," I said before hopping off and rummaging through my suitcase in the corner of the room.

It was pure luck that I still had condoms and lube in this suitcase from the last time I'd traveled for work. I climbed back on the bed quickly, back on top of Luke, but before I could do anything, Luke pulled me down for a kiss, which turned into the two of us rutting against each other, Luke's hands in my hair.

And before I could stop it, my mind was back in the library at Astor Hills, not just tonight, but seven years ago, to the night Luke and I had gone there after school, to the first time I'd ever been in this position, straddling him, breathless, my hands on his chest, my lips on his.

"Fuck, Oliver, you feel so good." Luke's voice in my ear snapped me back to the present, and I started backwards like I'd been scalded.

Luke grabbed my wrists, steadying me, and then smiled. "I have a question."

I bit my lip, not sure I wanted to hear what it was. "Yeah?"

"Were you really just trying to get service in the library tonight?"

"I—what?" I blinked. That wasn't what I'd expected at all. "I was just—I mean, I told you, I was—it wasn't—it's not like—"

Luke started to laugh. "I knew it."

I rolled my eyes. "You don't know anything, because there's nothing to know."

"Yeah, sure. Keep telling yourself that." Luke smiled. "You, of all people, probably have a phone from the future that could get signal from the center of the earth."

"You wanna keep this cute little act up?" I said, smiling in spite of myself. I grabbed a pillow from the other side of the bed. "Because I could totally smother you."

I brandished the pillow as menacingly as I could, but Luke grabbed it out of my hands with barely a struggle. He tossed it to the side and pulled me down, and I thought it was for a kiss until he swerved at the last instant and brought his lips to my ear.

"Looking for a signal, my ass."

"Shut up," I grumbled.

"Ooh, great comeback," Luke smirked. "Aren't you supposed to be a genius or something? I remember you being smart."

"I was only salutatorian," I snorted. "You want good comebacks with your sex, you gotta talk to Grace."

Luke made a face. "Please don't ruin this moment by making me reflect on the horrors of heterosexual sex."

"Then don't start what you can't finish, Wolitzky."

Luke's eyes flashed for a second, and I waited for him to say something snarky in return. But then he just... didn't. He just stared at me like he'd never seen me before, and when he opened his mouth, I realized I wasn't at all ready for what might come out. So I bent down to kiss him again, and when I pulled away, I held up the bottle of lube with a grin.

Luke watched as I pushed up, balancing on my knees, and squeezed lube onto my fingers.

"Wha—"

"Hold this," I said, pressing the bottle into his hands.

With one hand balanced on Luke's chest, I brought the other one behind me until I found my hole. In spite of myself, I gasped at the cool dab of lube at my entrance. Then I bit my lip and pushed my finger inside.

Fuck, that felt good.

I liked bottoming, always had, and fuck anyone who said that made you less masculine or whatever. But when I was on my own, I was usually too lazy to do anything other than a desultory jerk-off. It counted as a big deal if I actually bothered to move from my desk to my bed to do it. So yeah, I hadn't felt this in a while, and it was a little bit tight, but God, did it feel good.

And what made it even better was the look on Luke's face, like he was in awe of me. I loved that—loved how turned on Luke looked, how captivated. Like I was the only thing on earth right now.

I let myself moan a little as I slid my finger in and out. I was hamming it up a bit, maybe, but fuck, it *did* feel good, and besides, it was clearly reducing Luke to a drooling mess, and that was an outcome I could definitely get behind. Or on top of, in this case.

I wanted him drooling. I wanted him regretting everything,

regretting the past seven years and never saying sorry. I wanted him dying right now, thinking about how he'd left things, how he'd fucked up. I wanted him to carry *that* feeling with him for the *next* seven years.

I added more lube to my fingers, slipping a second one inside myself. I was pushing the pace a bit, and it was a stretch at first, but it was definitely worth it for the way it seemed to paralyze Luke, the way the precum beading from the tip of his cock was now dripping in a long string down onto his stomach.

Besides, I wanted to feel that cock inside me, and sooner rather than later.

"Oliver, fuck, you're—I—you're" Luke babbled, and I don't know if it was the adoring look in his eyes or his complete incoherence, but I decided I'd prepped enough.

If Luke was like this now, I couldn't wait to see what he was like once his cock was buried in my ass.

"Condom," I said, almost gruffly, and Luke blinked.

"Are you sure you—"

"Luke?"

"Yeah?"

"You're not allowed to ask me that anymore. Now give me the condom."

Luke let out a shaky laugh and nodded, grabbing the condom from where I'd tossed it on the bed and tearing the package open. I watched with pleasure as he unrolled it onto his cock, and when he was done, added more lube to my hands and began stroking him.

"How do you—do you want me to—" Luke stumbled through his words.

I could get used to that, I realized. How unsure, how off-his-game, Luke sounded.

Except you're not going to. You're not going to see him again. Just focus, for fuck's sake.

"Stay just like this," I said, a little more roughly than I'd intended.

I pushed further up onto my knees and brought myself directly over Luke's cock, rocking back just a bit until I felt his tip nestled against my hole.

"Are you sure—"

I didn't wait for Luke to finish. I sank down and whatever Luke was going to say turned into a groan of pleasure. One, I realized belatedly, that I was echoing.

"Fuck," I moaned. I could feel every inch of him inside me, pushing all the way in until my ass was resting against Luke's hips. *"Fuck."*

My voice was high-pitched, almost whiney, and Luke's hands rubbed my thighs in concern.

"Are you okay?" Luke gasped. "Are you—"

"Fuck, yes," I choked out. "Fuck. You're just so—fuck. Yes."

Luke laughed again, and it was so relieved, so happy-sounding, that when I looked down and saw how wrecked Luke was, I couldn't help laughing too.

"Good," Luke said, breathing heavily. "Because I don't think I could bear it if we stopped now."

"Good," I echoed. "Yeah. *Very* good."

"Come here," Luke said, beckoning me closer with his fingers.

I leaned down and let him pull me into a kiss. It shifted the angle of Luke's cock inside me, making me moan. Luke bit my lip, pulled it out between his teeth before releasing it, and his eyes were impossibly, impossibly blue.

"Oliver, I—"

"Shh," I said. "Don't."

My heart thumped in my chest, beating in time with... what? Luke's? The universe? All I knew is that I could hear blood rushing through my ears, feel the heat of this moment, feel an overwhelming desire, and I didn't want that to get ruined by whatever Luke wanted to say.

Luke's eyes focused on my face, his brow furrowing, and I couldn't bear that look, like somehow *I* was the one making things hard for *him*. Did he really not know the effect he had on me?

I kissed him deeply, trying to wipe that worried expression away.

"Don't," I whispered again, right next to his ear.

I kissed his jaw, his neck, everything I could reach.

"Don't."

I rocked my hips, pulling up slightly before sinking back down onto Luke's cock.

"Don't."

Rocked up, sank down.

"Don't."

It became a rhythm, and soon Luke was thrusting up into me and it felt so good, so, *so* good, like this was what I'd been missing, something I hadn't even realized I'd lost, and now I had it back, and I couldn't stand the thought of losing this again, of this moment ending, and *"don't, don't"* became *"don't stop, don't stop, fuck, fuck, fuck, don't stop."*

Our breath mingled, our heartbeats beating counterpoint to the song our bodies were making. The heat between us, the sweat slick on our chests, the motion and the sweet release were the melody. My cock was grinding down against Luke's stomach, pressed between us and fuck, it felt so good, I started to lose myself.

Luke's cock drove into me, filling me so perfectly, giving me exactly what I needed. He brought his arms around me, cradling me, stroking me. His lips were everywhere, and in between kisses, he whispered how good I was, how perfect, and fuck, no, fuck, it was all too much. I could feel myself starting to drown, and I pulled back, pushing up onto my knees to get a breath of air.

I rested my hands on Luke's chest, closing my eyes, and let myself rock back and forth, feeling his cock move inside me. This was good. I could handle this. I just needed to be careful. Needed to keep a hold of myself. I could do this.

I opened my eyes, looking down at Luke for a moment.

That was a mistake.

A terrible mistake, because Luke was looking up at me like I was every saint that had ever existed, coming down and giving him some kind of benediction. And those eyes, God, his eyes. So blue, the kind that made you feel like you were drowning in the middle of the ocean and made you happy about it.

I'm drowning in you, I thought, and something twisted in my heart. That was dangerous. I knew it, but God, this felt so good, and some part of me thought maybe this was meant to be because we'd never gotten the chance before, never gotten what we deserved.

And then Luke started talking again.

"Oliver, fuck. You're so—I need—I just—" Luke stammered.

Fear shot through me. I needed him to stop talking, to just stop talking, because I couldn't risk him saying words I wasn't strong enough to hear.

We'd never gotten our chance last time because of Luke— because I'd been dumb enough to trust him. And if there was anything tonight had shown me, it was that I wasn't any stronger now than I'd been seven years ago. And if I let myself relax, even for a moment, I wasn't sure I could keep Luke from hurting me again.

This was supposed to just be sex, but I'd been an idiot to think that was all it was—for me, at least—and even if Luke just wanted to say he was sorry, even if all he wanted to do was explain himself and then say goodbye, my defenses were down and there was no way he could do that now without cutting me to the core.

"Oliver, I'm so—"

"Stop," I said, shaking my head, angry and exhausted. "Just —just—stop."

And before I knew what I was doing, I was pulling off of Luke, climbing over to one side of him.

"What—what's wrong?" Luke asked, his eyes panicked. "What did I—"

"Nothing."

God, I was so embarrassed. What was wrong with me? Luke had already apologized like, 50 times tonight. Why the hell was I suddenly unable to hear it?

But why the hell can't he leave it alone?

"Nothing," I repeated, more forcefully this time.

I moved down the bed and leaned down, bringing my face close to his cock. Luke might be confused, but he was still hard. And I might have just made things incredibly weird, but I could still at least make sure he got off. I pulled the condom off him and wrapped my hand around his cock.

"Oliver, wait, no—"

"Nothing," I said, stroking Luke's cock, "is wrong." I knew my tone was at odds with my words, but I couldn't help that. "I'm telling you, okay? Are you really going to try to stop a guy who's trying to suck your cock right now?"

"I just—"

I didn't bother listening, I bent down and brought Luke's cock to my lips, let it slide into my mouth and caressed the underside with my tongue. Luke was looking at me like I was crazy, and honestly, that was probably warranted, because seriously, what the fuck had I been thinking?

Great job convincing Luke you're over everything that happened between you. Freaking the fuck out while his cock was buried in your ass definitely proved your point.

Why the fuck did I have to make such a big deal out of everything? And why did I still feel like I was on the edge of a nervous breakdown?

I growled, trying to push all those thoughts to the side. Maybe, if I could just concentrate on the task at hand, get Luke off, I could salvage some of the night, get Luke to leave in a post-orgasm haze and forget what a fucking *weirdo* I was. Maybe.

"Oliver—"

I picked up the pace, sucking Luke in and out, swirling my tongue around his tip. I just wanted to get this over with now, just wanted him to come. Luke's hand settled on my shoulder, and hope flared in my chest for a moment. Maybe he'd push me down further, guide me around his length. But then he spoke again.

"Oliver. Oliver, stop. Please. Stop."

Jesus Christ, you can't even get a blow job right, without ruining it and making the guy beg you to stop.

I pulled off of Luke, and the concern in his eyes only made me angrier. Why the fuck couldn't he just—

"Oliver, I can't do this. Not if we can't talk about—I mean, what the hell is going on? You have to tell me if something's—"

"I need to take a shower."

I pushed up, sliding around Luke as gracefully as I could—which was *not very*—as I got off the bed. I stalked, naked, around the end of the bed and over to the bathroom, closing the door behind me. I just barely managed not to slam it.

I threw the hot water tap in the shower on high and stepped in immediately. The water was frigid, but I didn't care. I just needed to—I just wanted a minute to—

Fuck.

I balled my fists up in front of my eyes, then gripped my head in my hands, and then slowly, slowly, found the wall of the shower and slid down to the ground. As the water heated up, I began to cry.

What the fuck was I doing? What was wrong with me? Why did I have to be so emotional and why was I letting everything get to me *now*, of all times? This was stupid—it was so fucking stupid, which suggested that *I* was stupid, and I set a lot of stock in *not being stupid*.

God, Luke probably thought I was nuts. Who invited someone back to their place to have sex—after seven years of not talking—and then lost it in the middle of him fucking me? Definitely *not* someone who'd moved on.

And now I was in the goddamn bathroom, crying while Luke was out there wondering what the hell was happening, and he was only going to have more questions when I got out of the shower, questions I had no idea how to answer.

What's wrong with me? Oh, nothing, just having that standard "didn't talk to you for seven years ago and now I can't handle it because you're being nice to me" nervous breakdown. You know. The usual.

But it wasn't going to get any easier talking to him if I put it off. Oh God, and what if he came in to check on me or something?

I bolted to my feet, ran my face under the scalding hot water for a second, and turned the tap off. The room was completely fogged up, and I had to feel for the towel rack, wrapping the thick, white towel around my waist. I paused with my hand on the doorknob, then took a deep breath and opened it.

The bedroom was empty.

And not just empty of Luke himself—all his clothes were gone, too. Mine were still there—neatly folded and stacked on the bed, of all things, which only made me feel worse. God, I hadn't been looking forward to talking to Luke, but I'd expected... fuck. I was so stupid, but given how nice Luke had been to me all evening, I'd expected him to stay. To want to talk to me.

Why the fuck would he want to stay and talk to you after the shit you just pulled?

I felt a little unsteady and walked out of the bedroom to get one of the bottles of water waiting in the main room of the suite—and stopped.

Luke was perched on the edge of the armchair in the main room, fully dressed, looking down at his hands.

"You're still here?"

The words were out of my mouth before I could think, and worse, my voice sounded accusatory. Luke's head snapped up, and his eyes went from surprised to hurt to a bruised kind of anger that I didn't like at all.

"I guess I'll leave, then," Luke said, standing up.

No. No, don't. I didn't mean it. I'm the one who's sorry, Luke, I shouldn't have said, shouldn't have done... any of this.

Except I didn't say any of that. Because that would mean I'd have to explain, and now that I was standing in front of Luke, dripping in my towel in this too-clean hotel room, I felt more awkward than I had at any other time tonight. I couldn't explain myself to Luke. I couldn't even explain myself to myself.

"Do you need cab money?" I asked, cursing myself for how dumb that sounded.

Like you're paying him off after hooking up with you—except we didn't even do that, really.

Luke's eyes were cold. "I think I'll manage."

"Okay." That wasn't a good enough response, but I couldn't think of anything else to say. "Have a good night, then."

Luke stared at me for a long moment, then shook his head. He walked to the door, opened it, then turned and looked at me like he was going to say something more. But in the end, he didn't. He just stepped through and closed the door behind him.

6

OLIVER

7 YEARS AGO

*L*uke was coming over.

Luke was coming over to Oliver's house. In approximately five minutes—unless he was late. Which Oliver was sort-of-kind-of convinced he would be. If he showed up at all.

Oliver wouldn't have been surprised if Luke just skipped it entirely and found some way to convince Oliver to lie to Ms. Bowman and get Oliver to do the tutoring work for him. Not because Oliver thought Luke was a bad person or anything —of all the jocks at school, he actually seemed like the least asshole-y one, the one who didn't go out of his way to make fun of Oliver and remind him of how much he didn't fit in. But still—why would someone like Luke spend any time with someone like Oliver if he didn't have to?

And yet, Oliver still found himself hoping, hoping so hard it almost disturbed him, that Luke would show up.

Why? He's not your friend—and he's not going to be. He's just coming over because he has to, and he's gonna leave as soon as he can, and he's probably going to hate every minute of the time he has to spend here.

But still—Oliver was excited, and he'd had a low-grade case of nerves bubbling in his stomach since that morning when Luke had pulled him aside in German and asked if he was free after school that day.

'Of course I'm free,' Oliver had wanted to say. What did he do in his free time other than read and code and read about code and generally spend all his time in his room, only furthering his dad's suspicions that there was something wrong with him? What could he possibly have to do that couldn't be moved if Luke wanted him to move it?

But instead, he'd said, "Uh, yeah, I guess?" and wondered if Luke would find him after school to walk home with him. But of course, he hadn't, even after Oliver had lingered for a few minutes in the lobby, because why would he? Luke surely didn't want to be seen with Oliver—he might be coming over, but it clearly wasn't out of choice.

Instead he'd texted Oliver just after Oliver arrived at home and said he'd be over in half an hour and now it was twenty-five minutes later—no, make that twenty-nine minutes later —and Luke was—

The doorbell rang.

Fuck. Luke was here.

The flash of panic Oliver felt in his chest made it clear that as much as he'd been hoping Luke really would come, had been weirdly, masochistically looking forward to this all day, he was absolutely terrified now that Luke was here.

What would Luke think about him, and his house? He'd

spent the past half hour trying to clean up the downstairs, doing the dishes his dad hadn't gotten to, picking up the beer bottles left next to the reclining chair, hanging his dad's uniform up in the closet where Luke couldn't see it—but there was no hiding the fact that the plaster on the ceiling was peeling or that the carpets had decades-old stains that even the most determined cleaning couldn't get out. And that wasn't even mentioning the pervasive smell of cigarettes that somehow clogged the air even though Oliver's dad claimed he only smoked outside.

There was no hiding the fact that Oliver and his dad lived in the shittiest house on the shittiest block in all of Garden City. That didn't make it a sinkhole, but the shabby, sad old house was clearly no paradise either.

Would Luke be completely disgusted once he stepped inside? Would he even want to stay? What if he took one look at Oliver's house and just walked away?

Go answer the door, dumbass. Stop procrastinating.

Oliver hurried down the stairs, took one last, nervous look around the living room, and opened the door.

Luke was standing on the front porch, one hand on his backpack strap, the other in his pocket, looking down at his feet. He looked, in a word, gorgeous. Though that was nothing new—when did he not? Oliver didn't think it was something Luke could help.

Just like some people were tall, and some people were redheads, and some people were brown-eyed, Luke was... gorgeous. It was more than a fact—it seemed to be some kind of inalienable property, something Oliver was sure couldn't be changed even if Luke had tried.

His flaxen blond hair was a little tussled, but in a way that looked cool and casual rather than sloppy. The Astor Hills lacrosse sweatshirt he was wearing did nothing to hide the muscled chest and shoulders beneath it. And his face, oh God, his face.

Oliver could have stared at it for hours. He *had* stared at it for hours, probably, if you added up all the minutes he'd wasted studying Luke's face when Luke wasn't looking, catching a glimpse of him in the hallways or parking lot or cafeteria and being unable to look away until he passed out of sight.

Luke had these blue eyes that were so piercing that it always took Oliver a second to remember that Luke wasn't angry whenever their gazes happened to cross. The color, and the focus with which Luke studied the world around him, took Oliver's breath away every time. High cheekbones, a firm, straight nose, the kind of square jaw you'd see in a Burberry ad—and lips that were way too pink and tempting to wonder what they'd feel like pressed to Oliver's.

In his eighteen years on the planet, Oliver didn't think he'd ever met someone as purely physically attractive as Luke. There was a reason Oliver tried to only look at him when Luke wasn't looking, and it was entirely selfish—Oliver wasn't sure he trusted himself, trusted his face not to give everything away if Luke caught him staring.

Luke already had enough reasons not to want to spend time around Oliver. There was no need to add, *"Hey, I've had a weird crush on you for the past six years,"* to that list. Luke might not be an asshole to Oliver now, but letting him know how Oliver felt about him would definitely push Oliver's luck.

"Hey," Oliver said, butterflies doing their best to flap their way out of his stomach and up into his throat as he spoke. He bit his lip and shoved them down, bouncing on his toes with nerves.

"Hey," Luke said, finally looking up.

He gave Oliver a look that Oliver couldn't parse—something that somehow managed to mix cool detachment with... was that *worry*? Was *Luke* nervous to see *Oliver*? There was no way that could—

"Can, I, uh, come in?" Luke asked after casting a glance over his shoulder back towards the street.

Oh. That was it. Oliver felt a flush of embarrassment as he understood. Luke wasn't nervous to see Oliver, he was nervous to *be seen* with Oliver.

"Yeah, of course, totally," Oliver said, shaking himself and stepping back to let Luke inside.

You're such a fucking idiot.

Oliver closed the door behind Luke and then walked a few steps into the living room before stopping and turning around. Luke looked at him with uncertainty, and Oliver wondered what Luke wanted him to do. Should he offer Luke something to drink? Give him a tour of the house? Make small talk? Luke seemed to be waiting for some kind of guidance, but everything Oliver could think of felt ridiculously fake and out of context.

"You wanna um—" Oliver stopped, wishing he didn't sound like such an idiot. Of course Luke didn't *want* to do anything. "I was thinking we could work at the table," he said, gesturing towards the kitchen."

"Okay," Luke said.

He shrugged like he couldn't care less, but then he met Oliver's eyes, and the next thing Oliver knew, he'd been standing there for ten seconds, silent, just paralyzed by Luke's gaze.

God, could you stop being so weird *for once in your life?*

"Okay," Oliver repeated. He blinked, then forced himself to look away, glancing over at the table instead. "Okay. Right. I'll just—fuck." He looked back at Luke quickly. "I left my notebook and calculator upstairs. Just, uh, wait here, and I can go get them."

"Why don't we just work upstairs, then?" Luke asked.

Oliver stared at him in confusion. *"Why don't we just work upstairs?"* Was Luke serious? Work in Oliver's bedroom?

I don't know, Luke, maybe because I'd never dream in a million years of inviting you into my bedroom *like some kind of creep and then you go and suggest it like it's the most normal thing in the world.*

Like, honestly, what the fuck? Did Luke really not think that was strange? Hell, maybe he didn't. Maybe it had never occurred to *him* in a million years that Oliver could be interested in him, because that's how disinterested *he* was in Oliver. Or maybe he was just afraid of someone they went to school with, what, walking up onto Oliver's front porch, peering in the windows, and seeing Luke there?

"Uh, sure," Oliver said. "It's…"

He didn't finish the sentence, just pointed to the stairs and then turned to walk up them. He could hear Luke's footsteps on the carpet behind him, quick and athletic.

"Oh, watch out for the—that," Oliver said, extending his hand towards the banister at the top of the stairs just a second too late. Luke had already grabbed it and, sure enough, it had threatened to come off, wiggling dangerously. "Sorry, it's loose. My dad keeps meaning to fix it but—"

Oliver cut off himself off abruptly when his hand accidentally grazed Luke's as he reached out to steady the banister. Luke jerked his hand away like Oliver had burned him.

So much for Luke not thinking you might like him.

Luke had never explicitly said anything about Oliver's sexuality—never made fun of him or called him names like the other guys in their grade—and he'd certainly never asked Oliver about it. No one did. They all just made assumptions.

Apparently Luke had, too.

Oliver stopped talking after that, and they walked the rest of the way to his room in silence.

"It's um—sorry it's so..." Oliver trailed off as they entered the room. He wasn't even sure what he was apologizing for. The mess or the overwhelming nerdiness of it. "I wasn't expecting anyone to um—lemme just—"

He hurriedly tried to clean up the worst of it, shoving piles of clothes under his bed, straightening the covers, then dumping stacks of books, his laptop, and a computer he was in the process of building inside an old lego set, onto the bed itself. He glanced around the room, wincing at the *Battlestar Galactica* posters on the wall, the bookcase full of science fiction and fantasy novels, the old plush *TARDIS* he'd begged for when he was a kid that still, embarrassingly, sat in the corner next to another pile of clothes. Oh God, his bedspread was *Star Wars* for Christ's sake. This was excruciating.

Oliver picked up his calc notebook, the sheet of problems Ms. Bowman had given them, and a pencil from the smaller pile of things now left on his desk.

"Do you wanna sit here?" he asked, gesturing towards the chair.

"No, no, don't worry about it," Luke said. Luke was concerned about Oliver being worried? That made... no sense. It must have just been a habit, him using that phrase. "I'm fine here."

He pushed some of the crap on Oliver's bed back a little and perched on the edge, finally dropping the backpack he'd carried slung over his shoulder. Setting it on the ground, he bent down and rummaged through it until he emerged with a binder, a notebook, and the same worksheet.

"You sure?" Oliver asked. "I don't mind, and it might be easier for you to spread all your things out—I mean, if it takes a while, won't you get tired?"

"It won't take a while," Luke said firmly. "Let's just get this over with."

"But—oh." Oliver's brain caught up with what Luke had just said. "Okay."

"Sorry." Luke's apology was quick and quiet, and it took Oliver completely by surprise. "I didn't mean—it's not." He sighed. "I just meant that I'm sure it'll be fast. You're the best student in Bowman's class, remember? You're probably a great teacher."

"Right..." Oliver trailed off.

He couldn't get a read on Luke. He didn't seem mad at Oliver for touching his hand or anything, but he didn't seem comfortable either. But it wasn't like Oliver could just ask Luke what he was thinking.

Right. That wouldn't be weird at all.

"Um," Oliver continued. "I guess we just start, uh, with the first problem then? Have you looked at these yet?"

Luke shook his head as he looked down at the paper.

"Okay," Oliver said slowly, trying to figure out how to start. He'd always been good at math, good at teaching himself pretty much anything, actually, but he'd never tried to teach anyone else. "So for this one, we have to find the limit. So, uh, do you... remember how we start that?"

Luke gave him an unreadable look but said nothing. Had that come off patronizing? Oliver flushed. Maybe Luke was uncomfortable because he thought Oliver thought he was dumb. Fuck, Oliver didn't want that—he didn't want Luke mad at him at all.

"Right, well, okay, so in this case, because we're looking at —" as soon as Oliver started talking, he was off running. He knew he talked a lot when he got nervous, but Luke wasn't helping matters, just nodding and giving the barest of *"yeahs"* in response, which only made Oliver more nervous and made him talk even more.

Luke seemed to be getting it, though, which was good. He wasn't just nodding and pretending—he was actually doing the math as they went along. In fact, it was almost kind of surprising. Oliver had seen other kids in their class struggle with certain problems, and they certainly didn't seem to pick things up as quickly as Luke was. Maybe Luke really had been studying harder, like he'd told Ms. Bowman he would?

"Oliver?"

Oliver jumped at the sound of his dad's voice downstairs. That was weird. His dad never got home before seven, and that was usually only for a quick TV dinner before he went out again for night work. What was he doing home now?

Luke looked at Oliver in confusion, his head cocked to the side.

"My dad," Oliver said. "He's uh—he doesn't usually come home this early. I'll go see—I mean, I'll be right back."

He stood up quickly and darted out of the room. It wasn't that there was anything to be afraid of—if anything, Oliver thought, his dad would probably be thrilled that someone as normal, as popular, as Luke was spending time with Oliver. But still, he hadn't told his dad that anyone was coming over, and he didn't want him to be surprised.

"Hey Dad," Oliver said as he made his way into the kitchen. His dad was bent over in front of the refrigerator, and when he straightened out, he had a beer in his hand. "What are you—why are you home so early?"

"We've got a job down at City Hall tonight," his dad replied. "Likely to take all night, so we cut out early for dinner before heading back in."

He gestured to a McDonald's bag on the counter. Of course. Oliver should have noticed—the whole house smelled like fries now.

"Dad, you know you shouldn't eat that," Oliver said, more out of habit than out of any belief his dad was going to listen to him. They'd had this discussion way too often.

"Kid, when you're as busy as I am, you'll understand," his dad said with an exasperated look. "Besides, it's cheap."

"I'm never going to be so busy that I'll eat crap all day just because it's cheap."

"Oh, the confidence of youth." His dad rolled his eyes. "Anyway, what's up? What's got you jumping around like a cricket?"

Oliver flushed and immediately schooled his feet to stillness.

"Nothing. I just, uh... I have a friend over, is all. I just wanted to tell you."

His dad nearly spit out his beer. "You *what*? Since when?"

Oliver might have been insulted if his dad hadn't been, well, so justified in his surprise. It was definitely a stretch, calling Luke a friend, but what else was Oliver supposed to say?

A boy I have a giant crush on is currently waiting in my bedroom for me to teach him calculus. Oh, yeah, by the way. I like boys and girls.

Not, he thought, that his dad would even really be that surprised by that last part.

"It's for a school thing," Oliver explained. "I mean, he's not really a *friend* friend. But I just, you know, thought you should know. Or something."

His dad shook his head in amusement. "*A friend over*," he repeated like it was the most amazing thing he'd ever heard.

"Is that—"

"No, no, not a problem at all," Oliver's dad said. "Just surprised is all." He took another swig of his beer. "Go, by all means. Do your school thing."

"Okay. Um. Thanks," Oliver said. "See you when you get back from work then."

"You'll probably be asleep by then," his dad said. He gave Oliver a stern look. "You *should* be asleep, anyway. Not up late on your computer."

"Yeah, yeah." Oliver turned and walked out of the kitchen, trying not to listen to his dad as he repeated, *"a friend over,"* again with a chuckle.

It wasn't *so* impossible to conceive of, was it?

Well, okay, maybe it was.

"Sorry about that," Oliver said as he walked back into his bedroom a minute later. "I was just—"

Luke, instead of sitting on the edge of his bed, was now slouching against it, sitting on the floor. He had his binder and the worksheet on his lap. His head was tilted down, hunched over it, but from what Oliver could see, it looked like Luke was... on the last problem in the set?

"Wait, what?"

Luke looked up, and his cheeks flushed—exactly the same color as his lips, which shouldn't have been as attractive as it was.

"I uh," Luke began, his eyes darting around wildly like he'd been caught doing something far more embarrassing than math homework. "I just thought I'd—I mean, I wasn't sure how long you were gonna be down there, so I figured I'd—"

"You just did it all by yourself?" Oliver asked, looking at Luke in consternation.

"I mean, it's probably all wrong," Luke said. He shifted, grabbing his backpack from where it rested next to him and beginning to put his things away. "It's fine though. I actually have to go, so I can just—"

"Wait, well, let me *see* it, at least." Oliver stepped into the room and bent down to take the paper from Luke.

"No, really, it's not a big deal," Luke said, shaking his head.

"Uh, it is if you don't want Ms. Bowman to yell at us. *You* might not care about pissing her off, but if the problems are all wrong, I don't wanna get in trouble for not tutoring you like I'm supposed to. Just let me see the—" Oliver finally wrested the paper out of Luke's hands. "Do you really have to go, or do you have time for me to at least look at these?"

"It's... whatever," Luke said. He sounded defeated.

Oliver tilted his head to the side. Every time he thought he had Luke figured out, he'd go and do something that didn't make any sense. If he really had to go, there was no reason he should let Oliver stop him—or even let Oliver look at his paper. But instead of seeming angry, he just seemed tired.

And it only got weirder once Oliver sat back down at his desk—Luke still standing awkwardly in the middle of the room—and actually looked at Luke's work. It didn't make any sense at all. Not that the answers were wrong. The opposite, actually.

"Luke, these are all..." Oliver turned to stare at him. "These are all right?"

Luke said nothing, just looked down and shoved his hands in his pockets.

"Are you... do you actually understand this?" Oliver continued. "Do you even need tutoring at all?"

"I don't know," Luke said finally, shrugging his shoulders again.

It was starting to make a kind of sense, Oliver realized, in a way. Luke had always been in honors and AP math before and had never struggled, as far as Oliver knew, until this year. And he'd been way too quick to pick up on Oliver's directions as they'd worked through the first few problems.

"But if you already know how to do all of this," Oliver asked, confused, "then why aren't you—why are you failing?"

"Forget it," Luke said. "Can I have my paper back, if it's all right?"

"You can," Oliver said, "but I don't—I don't get it."

"Don't worry about it, Oliver," Luke said, and that defeated tone was back, and the strangest thing happened in Oliver's chest.

Did he feel—did he want to *comfort* Luke?

How the hell had that happened?

"Look, we can still tell Bowman you tutored me," Luke said. "You won't get in trouble, I won't get in trouble, it's fine. And

I won't take up any more of your afternoons—I can just do the problems on my own from now on, Bowman doesn't have to know."

Right, because *that* was what mattered here—Luke was concerned about inconveniencing Oliver.

Honestly—what the *fuck*?

"Okay," Oliver said slowly.

"Good." Luke took the worksheet back and shoved it into his backpack, then headed towards the door.

"Wait, but—wait!" Oliver jumped up with a start when he realized Luke was actually leaving. He followed him out the door and down the stairs. "I don't understand. Why are you intentionally failing calc if you know all of this stuff already?"

"It's not—"

"Why would you agree to tutoring if you knew you didn't need it?"

"Oliver, it's not—"

"I mean, aren't you at least worried about your grades for colleges and stuff? I know they don't really look at your spring semester grades, but fall ones still count. Doesn't that matter to you?"

"Jesus, I'm not *going* to college, okay?" Luke burst out.

"You're not—what?"

"I'm not going to college," Luke repeated fiercely as they reached the bottom of the stairs. "I'm not worried about my grades, I agreed to tutoring because I don't want Bowman to call my mom and get her worried about something that doesn't really matter, and the reason I'm failing calc is my own damn business so maybe keep *out of it*."

Oliver stepped back. He'd never actually seen Luke angry before, he realized, and he'd never again mistake the normal intensity of Luke's eyes for... this. He was glaring daggers at Oliver, and his jaw had a stubborn set to it.

"Okay, okay, fine. Jeez, sorry." Oliver held his hands up in surrender. "Consider it forgotten."

Luke's gaze softened, and then he nodded, shouldered his backpack again, and walked to the front door.

"Hey, Oliver!"

Both Oliver and Luke turned around in surprise at the sound of Oliver's dad's voice and saw him standing in the doorway to the kitchen. Oliver hadn't even realized his dad was still downstairs, and he froze for a second in panic, wondering what his dad had overheard. Nothing too weird, right?

"Introduce me to your friend," his dad said with a smile.

"Oh. Um, right." Oliver shook himself. "Dad, this is Luke. Luke, my dad. Luke's actually just leaving, though, so we—"

"I thought you boys had a school project or something?" Oliver's dad went on. "Finished already?"

"Yeah, it uh—" Oliver stuttered, trying to think of what to say, his mind suddenly frozen.

This whole genial dad act was weirding him out. It wasn't that his dad was mean or anything, but he'd seemed to have given up on Oliver having a normal social life years ago and had mostly left him to his own devices.

"It went quicker than we thought," Luke said with a grin. What the fuck? How was Luke suddenly this calm, his posture relaxed, his smile fucking radiant, when seconds ago he'd been actually angry at Oliver. "We think we can finish the rest of it in school, probably."

"Oh. Okay, then," Oliver's dad said. He seemed to notice what Luke was wearing for the first time. "You play lacrosse?"

"What? Oh, yeah." Luke smiled again. "Yeah. Well, normally I do. I play soccer too, but I messed up my ACL, so I'm sitting the season out. I hope it'll be better by spring, though."

That was news to Oliver. Luke wasn't playing soccer this fall? Oliver hadn't known that—not that Luke was obligated to tell him anything. But it suddenly made more sense why Luke had been free this afternoon. If he were playing normally, he'd probably be at practice right now.

"That's rough," Oliver's dad said. "I used to play football until I busted my knee. You gotta take care of your body, you know, and it'll take care of you."

That was rich, coming from someone with his dad's lifestyle.

"Yes, sir," Luke said, that easy-going grin still in place. "Absolutely."

"Well, good luck with your project," Oliver's dad said. "Hey, maybe if you finish early, you can even get this one to do something athletic," he went on, gesturing to Oliver with his beer. "I can't remember the last time I saw him with a ball in his hands."

"Oh my God, *Dad*," Oliver said, burying his face in his hands. It was bad enough for his dad to say something that implied like Oliver and Luke were actually friends—did he have to go and accidentally slip in sexual innuendo too?

"What? I'm just saying."

"Yeah," Oliver said. "And Luke was just going. So. Bye, Dad!"

He turned, and before he could think of what he was doing, he put his hands on Luke's shoulders and marched him back towards the front door. It was only after he'd started that he realized how weird it was, but strangely enough, Luke let himself be marched.

"Uh, sorry." Oliver said once they reached the door again. He flushed. "About... uh, all that. My dad's just... he's a little..."

"It's fine," Luke said with a shrug. He'd dropped the *"gee whiz"* act now that they weren't in front of Oliver's dad anymore, but he didn't seem angry any longer, either.

"He's just—he's not really used to me, uh, having friends, you know?" Oliver blinked. That explanation only made things weirder. "I mean, not that like, you're my friend. I mean, I told him you were, just because it seemed easier, but I know we're not—I'm just trying to say, he doesn't think that we're like—that we were doing any—God, nevermind. Just—forget I started talking."

He buried his face in his hands again. Jesus, he couldn't stop making everything weird, could he? It was like a curse. Luke was in his house, *talking to him*, actually *being nice* to him, and Oliver found a way to ruin it by implying his dad thought they'd been up to something that *wasn't* schoolwork in his room.

"Really, it's fine," Luke said, and when Oliver finally dropped his hands—miracle of miracles—Luke wasn't looking at him like he was insane. In fact, he seemed almost amused. "At least your dad's around. And cares."

"I uh—yeah." Oliver didn't know what to say to that.

"Well, I should—I should go," Luke said after a moment, and Oliver realized he'd just been standing there, staring at Luke again.

"Right. Yeah." Oliver nodded, then leaned forward to unlock and open the front door. "I'll uh—I'll see you around."

"See ya."

And then Luke was gone.

7

LUKE

*W*hat the fuck?

I mean, honestly, not to sound harsh or anything but... what the fuck?

What the hell had just happened?

From the minute Oliver had asked me back to his hotel, I'd been completely confused—but willing to go with it. Maybe I shouldn't have been, but he was gorgeous and interested and offering. Was I really supposed to turn that down?

And it's not like he lived in New York, so I didn't have to worry about explaining the whole *"not looking for anything"* part. Hell, he was the one who'd told me—multiple times— that this was a one-time offer.

It had seemed... I don't know, harmless. Fun. And yeah, okay, maybe a part of me was curious about what Oliver was like now—the same part of me that had been grasping at straws, trying to keep him from leaving as we'd stood in the parking lot. But that was probably just because his reaction to me apologizing had been unexpected.

Maybe, I'd thought, maybe sleeping with Oliver was exactly what I needed to get him out of my system. It would be one night of fun, and then he'd go back to California, and I'd go back to my regularly scheduled life, and I'd stop waking up in the middle of the night dreaming about him.

So no, I'd never expected Oliver to invite me back to his hotel, not after he'd seemed so completely disinterested in even talking to me in the library—but I *definitely* hadn't expected anything that had happened after that.

Moments from the last few hours flashed through my mind like cards being shuffled, fleeting glimpses catching my eye, then disappearing back into the flow, only to be replaced by new ones.

Oliver's shape, silhouetted in the dark on the trip back to Manhattan, beautiful and brittle, the arch of his nose, the cut of his cheekbones, the pale curve of his neck caught in the occasional flash of a headlight. The feel of his fingertips as they'd skated across my skin, so hot I'd thought I'd see scorch marks left behind. The sound of his voice, of his breath, as he'd ridden my cock, his back arched slightly, his head thrown back, panting in pleasure.

Had that all really happened? It felt as though I'd lived a lifetime's worth of memories in the space of a night.

And now that's all they'll be. Way to fuck that up, Wolitzky.

Not that I wanted anything more. I didn't. One night was all I'd been looking for. It was all I ever wanted with guys. Just because it was Oliver didn't change that. But at least I'd wanted to make him feel as good as he made me feel, to see his face, to hear my name on his lips as he came. And somehow—somehow I'd ruined it.

I didn't know what had happened, but something clearly had, and the Oliver who'd peered out from under those dark lashes of his in the parking lot, stealing my breath, was not the same Oliver who'd been in bed with me by the end of the night.

You're still here?

Clearly, Oliver had wanted me gone. And since I'd fucked up everything else tonight, leaving when he'd asked me to was the one chance I'd had to do something right.

But the thing I couldn't stop asking myself was *how* I'd fucked everything up? All I'd tried to do was follow Oliver's lead. My stomach twisted at the thought that I'd hurt him or made him feel unsafe. I hated the idea of doing that to anyone, but especially Oliver. Not because this meant anything—we'd both been clear on that. But to mess things up this spectacularly, to hurt him again when I'd only been trying to apologize...

I shook my head as I walked through the lobby of my building and rode the elevator up to my apartment.

Oliver was the one who'd initiated everything. And I'd thought we were—well, I'd felt, anyway, even if my brain had been so blissed out with desire that it had trouble working properly—on the same page. Of course, it was Oliver's right to change his mind if he wanted to, to stop things from going further if he realized he didn't want to go through with it.

But then why had he tried to suck me off after? Why had he been so insistent the whole goddamn time? And why had he seemed *angry* at me while he did it? You didn't blow people you were pissed at, did you?

What the fuck did I do?

Well, aside from give myself a major case of blue balls, that is. That outcome was very apparent. I was still hard, uncomfortably so, and my cock was yelling at me for stopping things where I had.

But what was I supposed to do? Oliver was clearly upset about something, but if he wouldn't tell me, there was no way I felt comfortable letting things continue. Even if it meant feeling distinctly *less* comfortable in certain body regions right now.

I sighed as I got into my apartment, tossing my keys down on the table by the entryway. On top of everything with Oliver, I was exhausted. Too many late nights at the office with not enough sleep were catching up with me. I knew I should probably check and see if I'd gotten any more emails from Harvey but fuck it, I couldn't bring myself to look. That was a problem for Tomorrow-Luke.

I kicked off my shoes, shrugged out of my clothes, and promptly banged my shin on the corner of my bed frame. God, I hated my bed, but I'd never gotten around to getting a new one. Howling in pain, I decided that this was my subconscious, punishing me for leaving my clothes and shoes everywhere. Grumbling to myself, I put my shoes where they belonged and my clothes in the hamper. Dammit, I couldn't even be irresponsible and lazy in the comfort of my own home. It was ridiculous.

My cock was still hard as I got into bed, completely undaunted by my still smarting shin and rubbing insistently against the fabric of my boxer briefs. You'd think that getting turned down so decisively by a guy, having him stare at you in cold confusion as if he were wondering how the fuck you could be so dumb as to still be sitting in his living room after he'd abandoned you to take a shower for 30 minutes, would have some kind of dampening effect on my erection, but it didn't.

I glanced down at my groin and addressed it with a glare.

"Go to sleep."

I turned onto my side and decided to think of something different. Work, maybe. Or Tyler's lawsuit. Or how I needed to go out to my mom's tomorrow to help her prepare for her lessons next week. But my mind wouldn't stop thinking about Oliver, and my dick wouldn't either. I turned over onto my back again and sighed.

Fine. I was just going to jerk off quickly and go to sleep. And I wasn't even going to think about Oliver, I decided as I slid my hand down and freed my cock. Why should I waste brain space on a guy who clearly wasn't wasting any on me? Why should I fantasize about a guy who'd kicked me out of his apartment?

I wanted to be pissed at him—and then stop thinking about him. Only, as I started stroking my shaft, I couldn't. Because even though I'd managed to piss Oliver off, I wasn't mad at him myself.

Yeah, I could still see that cold look in his eyes when he'd kicked me out. But I could also see that vulnerable, almost hopeful look in his eyes when he'd finally dropped his guard around me. And I couldn't forget the flicker of something—something almost like fear—that had danced through his eyes right before he'd started getting mad.

Not that that made it any better—if I'd somehow scared Oliver, in addition to making him angry, I definitely shouldn't be jerking off to thoughts of him now. That was just gross. That was a thing gross people did. I wasn't a gross person.

Except...

There'd definitely been good moments there, mixed in with all that. Moments where I knew Oliver had felt good. Had felt safe and comfortable. Where he'd wanted to be there, right there, with me.

Dammit, I *knew* Oliver. Or at least, I *had* known him. I knew what he looked like when he wanted someone. And I knew what he looked like when he got what he wanted. And the way he'd moaned, the way he'd said my name, the way he'd taken control and fucked himself up and down on my cock —he'd *wanted* that.

Fuck, I was so close to coming. It wasn't like I'd been that far away to start with, after all, and as I stroked myself faster, I let images of Oliver cascade through my mind. The long, lean lines of his body as he'd pulled me towards the bed. The trust and desire in his eyes as he'd knelt in front of me and taken my cock in his mouth. The look of abandon as he'd straddled me and fingered himself. Fuck, I could have watched him do that for hours.

I wasn't imagining it. Oliver had wanted me. I'd made him feel good. And the way he'd licked my cock, the way he'd sunk himself all the way down onto it, the smile on his face as he heard me breathing his name—he'd wanted me to feel good too.

I came hard, cum shooting into my hands unexpectedly as Oliver's smile filled my mind. Jesus Christ, I'd missed that smile. I hadn't known I'd missed it till I saw it again, but there was no denying it now.

Only, what was I supposed to do with that? So I missed his smile—so what? It didn't change anything, not what had happened between us tonight, or what had happened all those years ago. It didn't change who I was.

It's over. It's done with. Just put it out of your mind.

Sure, it would have been nice if tonight had gone better. And yeah, maybe I'd still picture his smile from time to time. But none of this meant anything, and it was over now.

I turned back onto my side, and exhaustion rolled over me. It was time to let it go. And I certainly wasn't going to dream about Oliver tonight.

And yet, my last thought, before sleep overtook me, was a slight pain, thinking that I'd never see that smile again.

***

I woke up at 7:00 a.m. Late for me, even though it was a Sunday. Actually, very late, I thought as I rolled over sleepily to shut off my backup alarm clock.

I couldn't remember the last time I hadn't set an earlier alarm on my phone to wake me up for a run or a workout—or been woken up even earlier by an insistent stream of emails and texts from work. I reached out groggily to grab my phone. It was probably going to be clogged with—

Fuck.

I'd left my phone at Oliver's hotel. My eyes widened as I saw myself toss it onto his couch when we'd first walked in. I hadn't realized it wasn't with me when I left.

Double-fuck. Not only was it undoubtedly going to have a string of increasingly irate emails from Harvey waiting on it, I was going to have to bother Oliver in order to get it back. Oliver, who definitely didn't want to see me. Oliver, who, in the cold light of morning, I had to admit I should not have jerked off thinking about last night.

Jesus, how the hell was I even supposed to get in touch with him? It was probably too much to hope that he'd realized I'd left it there and emailed me, wasn't it? Of course it was— Oliver didn't even have my email, unless he remembered the one I'd used in high school, which I did technically still have, but only used as a dummy address at this point.

I groaned as I pushed myself out of bed and padded into the living room to grab my laptop out of my briefcase. Sure enough, there were nine emails from Harvey, and two from MacFarlane, but nothing from Oliver.

Dammit.

I pulled Facebook up on my browser, typed Oliver's name into the search box, and drummed my fingers on the arm of my sofa as I stared at what I could see of his profile. Despite my occasional late-night stalking, I wasn't Facebook friends with Oliver or connected to him in any way online. And it felt especially weird to friend him now.

I could message him without being his friend, of course, but I knew he'd have a better chance of noticing my message if it also came along with a friend request. And how the hell else was I supposed to get in touch with him?

I needed my phone back. And dammit, it wasn't totally insane to ask that Oliver acknowledge I exist online, considering my dick had been inside him less than twelve hours ago.

I took a deep breath, clicked *"Add Friend,"* and then opened up a message box to type before I psyched myself out.

Hi!

No. Too perky.

Hello!

Even more no. Too formal.

Hey, Oliver.

Ugh, even that seemed dumb. But the longer I hemmed and hawed over this message, the longer my friend request would go sitting in his inbox, unaccompanied by an explanatory message—and the weirder I would look.

Hey—I know things were a little weird last night but it turns out I left my phone at your hotel? Any chance I can come by and get it? I live close, so I can come anytime. Thanks!

PS—Feel free to ignore the friend request if you want. Just wanted to make sure you saw this.

I hit send before I could think about it anymore, and then immediately wished I hadn't. Who wrote a PS like that? Only someone who obviously *did* care about the friend request would draw attention to it by trying to play it off. I wanted to smack myself.

And as I went about my morning, it only got worse. The whole time I responded to Harvey's emails, went for a run, tried and failed to make my juicer work and ended up buying enough juices for the whole week and sticking them in my freezer, I couldn't stop thinking about it. And by the time I was supposed to sit down and actually get to work on the things Harvey had asked me to do, Oliver was the only thing on my mind.

Before I knew it, I was out the door, walking towards Oliver's hotel.

This was insane. This was definitely insane. Even if none of my previous behavior from the last night—or last seven years—counted as insane, this definitely did.

No chance of pretending you're not a stalker now.

But what was I supposed to do? Oliver still hadn't answered me. Hadn't accepted my friend request. For all I knew, he was dead, and I'd get to his hotel and find the whole thing cordoned off with police tape.

Knocking on a tree as I passed—that counted as wood, right?—to ward off that possibility, I tucked my hands back into my pockets and kept going.

I was just going to walk up to the front desk and ask if I could make a call to Oliver's room. And if Oliver didn't pick up, I could ask if they'd seen him, explain I was an old friend—which was sort of true, at least. And then, if I felt like being particularly creepy, I could just hang out in the lobby and use the hotel's wifi until Oliver came back.

Not that I was going to do that.

Probably.

Definitely.

Maybe.

I'd brought my laptop with me just in case.

It was cold, and I was walking so fast, my head tilted down against the wind, that I didn't see the person I ran into until it was too late, and we'd smacked against each other on the sidewalk. I looked up in shock, feeling stupid.

"Oh God, I'm so sorry," the other guy said. "Are you o—"

"Nick?" I blinked, realizing for the first time just who I'd run into. "What are you—"

"Luke!" Nick smiled broadly, like running into me was the most pleasant surprise he could have. But then he glanced over at the person standing next to him, a cute blond guy with an amused expression, and the smile on Nick's face faded. When he looked back at me, I swore I saw a flicker of worry in his eyes.

"Hey, man." I smiled, trying to put him at ease. God, maybe there was just something about me these days that scared people. "Really sorry, I need to watch where I'm going. It's just, I was in a hurry to—"

"Oh, no worries," Nick said, waving my apology away. "I know how it goes. Listen, it's good to see you, but if you're in a—"

"Yeah, I should probably—"

"Wait, you guys know each other, and you're not even going to introduce me?" the blond guy broke in, sounding half-annoyed, half-amused.

Nick flushed bright red and suddenly it dawned on me that maybe *I* wasn't the reason Nick seemed so nervous. The blond guy shook his head and laughed, then stuck his hand out to me.

"Hi, I'm Eli."

"I'm—Eli?"

"Wait, seriously? Your name is Eli too?"

"What? Oh, no, sorry," I said, shaking my head. "I'm Luke. I just..."

I trailed off, glancing at Nick, who still looked apprehensive.

"It's just... not a common name," I finished lamely. "Not one you hear a lot."

Eli wasn't a common name, it was true. Which was why it had stuck in my mind, the first time I'd heard it, months ago. Which had been when Adam and Ben had been giving Nick shit about some guy he was dating named Eli. Some mysterious guy who Nick didn't want to talk about, wouldn't let anyone meet, and claimed to not even really be dating, actually.

And here he was on the sidewalk, standing next to Nick.

"You know, I keep telling him how amazing and unique I am," Eli said, elbowing Nick in the side, "but he doesn't seem to appreciate just how rare and precious I truly am." Eli's grin was lopsided and enormous. "I'm glad *someone* gets it."

I raised an eyebrow and looked back at Nick. His face took on a pleading expression. Oh yeah, there was *definitely* something going on here. And even though I didn't know

Nick as well as Adam and Ben did, even though I hadn't heard about this mysterious Eli until later, I had to admit to some curiosity.

"Maybe I just don't want you getting a big head about it," Nick said, rolling his eyes at Eli affectionately.

"Too late." Eli's grin grew even bigger.

"It was always too late for me," Nick said in a tone that struck me as half-joking, half-morose. He looked back at me, an unspoken request in his eyes. "Did you say you were in a hurry to get somewhere? We don't want to keep you."

"Yeah, I, uh—I have to go meet someone," I said slowly. Not exactly true, but Nick clearly didn't want to draw this conversation out any longer than necessary. "I uh, I left my phone with them, and I—"

"God, I hate it when I do that," Eli said with a snort. "You don't know how many times I've left my phone in cabs or bars or one time even in the cheese section of a Westside Market. He hates it," Eli finished, jabbing his finger in Nick's direction.

"Only because then we have to spend entire Saturdays tracing your phone across the city," Nick retorted, his voice exasperated but warm.

"Fair," Eli said. He wiggled his eyebrows suggestively. "Especially when there are so many other fun things to do on a Saturday."

I still don't think I've ever seen anyone blush as hard as Nick did at that.

"I, uh, I should probably go," I said. Nick gave me a grateful look. "It was nice to meet you, Eli. Good seeing you, Nick."

"Yeah," Nick said with a smile that wasn't nearly as casual as I thought he wanted it to look. "See you around."

I had to stifle a laugh as I walked away. Adam and Ben were going to have a field day once they found out about this. Except, I supposed, Nick probably wouldn't want me to say anything to them about it.

If he'd been keeping things with Eli a secret till now, he probably didn't want me spreading around the fact that I'd actually met Eli and he *was* a real person, not a figment of Nick's imagination or, from what I could tell, a prince in disguise or a CIA operative undercover or anything equally hush-hush.

Which meant that if I was at all attached to the idea of not being a totally terrible person, I probably needed to keep my mouth shut.

Dammit.

If only things with Oliver had gone better last night. If only I weren't growing more and more convinced that I *was* just a shitty person. Or at the very least, a boring one who was lucky his friends even hung out with him. But as it was, I figured I should probably try not to add to my karmic debit account. I was just going to get my phone back from Oliver and start with a clean slate.

Only, that was beginning to look practically impossible because once I got to the hotel and gave them Oliver's room —the concierge gave me the strangest look when I told him it was a Fibonacci number—the phone just rang and rang.

And when I asked, the concierge said he hadn't seen him all day.

Which, fair enough—it was a big hotel. Maybe he'd just missed him. So I decided to wait.

It wasn't *that* weird a thing to do, was it? I mean, I needed my phone back. So I sank down into an uncomfortable lime-green leather armchair, pulled out my laptop and got to work. But after three hours there, Oliver still hadn't turned up.

I glanced at the time on my screen and sighed. Dammit, I had to get out to my mom's. I shot her a quick email, letting her know what train I'd be on and that I'd lost my phone, then closed my computer with a sigh. So much for my brilliant plan.

Where the fuck was Oliver? What if he'd flown home already? He hadn't made it sound like he was leaving today, but what if I'd somehow done something to convince him he needed to flee back to California immediately?

I knew that was pretty irrational, but as I rode the LIRR out to Garden City, I couldn't stop my mind from going to crazier and crazier places. But hell, even if Oliver were on a plane right now, the guy was an app developer—he probably lived on his phone. There was no way he hadn't seen my message, was there?

My mom was waiting in the beat-up old Honda she'd had since I was little when I got out of the station. She greeted me with a smile and a wave, and I tried to suppress a flash of guilt. I didn't get out to see her as much as I should. She never reproached me for it, but I knew I should be a better son. For so long, it had just been the two of us, and even with Tyler back now, I still wanted her to know I'd be there for her.

"Hi sweetie," she said, tousling my hair as I got in the car. My hand flew up to fix it automatically. "How are you?"

"Fine," I said. "Sorry, I meant to get out here sooner but, you know—work."

My mom sighed. "I hate that you have to work so much."

"I know." I gave her a halfhearted smile. "Hey, at least it pays well. That's good, right?"

She gave me a hard look. "You know I care more about you being happy than any amount of money you might make."

"Mom, I didn't mean that—"

"I know you want to help with my bills, sweetheart, and I appreciate that, but I'm fine. Your job is not to take care of me—it's to take care of you."

"I know." I sighed. "But I want to."

"I know you do." She reached out and squeezed my shoulder. "I just want your life to be filled with love, you know. Happiness. Money's not going to get you that."

"Well, I love *you*, so that counts, doesn't it?"

"Oh, you are a sweet-talker, aren't you? Always know what to say to make your mom smile."

We drove back to the house through town, and after a few minutes, my mom gave me a shrewd look.

"Is something else bothering you, aside from work? You seem tense."

"What? Oh. No, nothing."

I mean, what was I supposed to say?

"How was the reunion last night?"

"Fine."

I knew I sounded terse, but there was literally no way to tell her anything without telling her *everything,* and that sure as hell wasn't happening. My mom knew who Oliver was, of course—he and I had gone to school together from seventh through twelfth grade. And she knew that, well, that *something* had happened senior year. But she didn't know anything more than that, and it was going to stay that way.

What would the point even be of telling her? Oliver was leaving. He'd moved on. And so had I.

So when my mom changed the subject to her lesson plans for school that week, I let her. Apparently, the hundredth day of school would be on Friday, and since she was a first-grade teacher, that was a big deal. Each of her students would be bringing in one hundred of *something* that day, and the whole week leading up to it was going to be math- and numbers-themed.

It was kind of fun, actually, helping her cut up all the manipulables she needed for the week, organizing and sorting crayons and beads and pipe cleaners into color-coded piles. It was mindless and ended up being weirdly soothing. Plus, unlike my actual job, I felt a sense of accomplishment as we packed it all up and got it loaded into the back of the car for her to take to school. I'd just closed the trunk when I heard a skidding sound behind me and turned to see two kids, a girl and a boy, pulling their bikes to a halt at the end of our driveway.

"Oh, hi Caitlin, hi Neal," my mom said, smiling. I wondered if they were her students or if they were just kids from the neighborhood who knew her.

"Hi, Ms. Lang," they said—well, screeched, really.

Lang was my mom's maiden name, and she'd changed it back after the divorce.

"Who are you?" Caitlin, the girl, asked, staring at me with the kind of undisguised curiosity only a seven-year-old can muster.

I grinned. "I'm Ms. Lang's son. I'm L—"

"Mr. Wolitzky," my mom cut in. "This is my son, Mr. Wolitzky."

"Mr. Wo..." Neal said, clearly not sure he could get his mouth around my last name.

"You can call me Mr. W," I said, smiling. "It's nice to meet you, Neal and Caitlin."

"Nice to meet you, Mr. W," they chorused.

I could practically see the instructions they must have gotten from their parents on how to be polite to adults. I'd gotten the same ones from my mom. It was funny to realize I counted as a *"grown up,"* especially considering how often I felt like I was just flailing around, pretending to have my life together.

"Is that for school this week?" Neal asked, pointing to the boxes in the car. "Can we see?"

My mom laughed. "I can't show you all of it, but I guess I can give you a sneak peek."

Neal looked very excited at the prospect, and my mom opened the trunk back up. Caitlin, on the other hand, seemed more interested in something in her jacket pocket. She kept sticking her hand into it and eventually brought her hand out, clenched in a fist around something.

"Whatcha got there?" I asked, curious as to what could be more interesting than the veritable carnival of school supplies in my mom's car.

Caitlin looked up at me, then over to my mom, then back at me. "An alien," she said, her eyebrows drawn down very seriously.

"An alien! Whoa." I smiled. "Can I see?"

"Only if you promise not to tell," Caitlin said. "Not anyone."

For a brief moment of panic, I wondered what, exactly, I was promising, but whatever she had in her hand, it couldn't be that dangerous, right? She was only seven—her hand wasn't that big.

"I promise," I swore solemnly.

Caitlin slowly crooked her fingers open, and I had to stifle a laugh when I saw what she held. It was a ladybug, but one of the ones that was more orange than red. Hardly an alien, but I supposed it might look like one if you'd never seen it before.

"Very cool," I said as authoritatively as possible. "What are you going to do with it? Keep it for science? Do experiments?"

"No!" Caitlin closed her fist protectively. "No, I'm going to help him. I think he's lost. I found him on Neal's floor, and the dog was gonna eat him. I have to help him get home."

"That's a very noble and selfless act," I said.

Caitlin frowned. "Selfless?"

"It means you're thinking about other people and helping them, instead of just helping yourself. It's the opposite of selfish."

"Ohh."

"Who's selfish?" my mom asked as she closed the trunk again.

"Not Caitlin, that's for sure," I said with a grin. "She's on a very important mission."

"I see," my mom said gravely. "Then we'd better not keep you from it. Besides, I know your parents will want you home for dinner soon. I'll see you in school tomorrow."

"Bye, Ms. Lang!"

Caitlin and Neal got back on their bikes and flew down the street again. My mom smiled after them, but when she turned to me, her expression took on a sad tinge.

"You're so good with kids. It's a shame you're not—"

"Hey, I'm only 26. You're not going to start pestering me to have kids all of a sudden, are you?"

"That's how old I was when I had you, you know." My mom shook her head and laughed. "But no. I just think it's a shame you never thought about working with kids, instead of the job you have."

"Right." I snorted. "Because that would pay the rent. And the student loans. And let me help you out."

My mom sighed. "Money isn't everything, sweetheart."

I glanced at my laptop when we got inside, more out of habit than because I actually expected to see anything other than emails from Harvey, but there was a new email in my personal inbox. I clicked over and almost fainted with relief.

Oliver Luna had accepted my friend request—and had sent me a message in return.

Thank God. At least he's not dead.

Not that I'd really thought that was a possibility. But still. Not dead, and not completely ignoring me, either. I opened the message from Oliver, yelling silently at my heart to stop trying to beat its way out of my chest. Why the hell did I feel so excited?

Shit, sorry. I've been with my dad all day. Fishing. In February. Because he's determined to torture me and apparently thinks I spend too much time indoors with computers. I actually found your phone last night, but I brought it out to Long Island with me bc I didn't want housekeeping to do something weird with it. I'll be back in Manhattan tomorrow morning. So sorry it's so late!

The wash of relief I'd felt before seemed like a trickle compared the flood I felt now. Oliver wasn't just not ignoring me, he didn't even sound mad. And okay, so maybe it was a *little* weird that he hadn't addressed last night at all. But at least he wasn't avoiding me.

And if he were out on Long Island right now... Oliver's dad only lived a few minutes from my mom. I might not have been to that house in seven years, but I still knew the way to walk there from my place by heart. And suddenly, that was exactly what I was doing, telling my mom I'd be back in a few minutes and dashing outside.

Oliver was in Garden City, which meant I could see him, tonight. See him, and get my phone back, and finally stop thinking about him. The end. I was actually smiling by the time I got to Oliver's block, all the way up until I got to his house, put my hand on the gate—and stopped.

Oliver's dad was standing on the front porch, smoking a cigarette and frowning.

A frown that only deepened when we made eye contact.

"You?" he said, and I couldn't tell if he sounded more shocked or disgusted. "What are you doing here?"

8

OLIVER

"Hey, Dad," I called from the kitchen, where I stood in front of the refrigerator, assessing its sad and empty state. "What if I stuck around for dinner tonight and we maybe cooked? I could go to the store and get, I don't know, chicken? I'm sure I could find a recipe or something online."

I paused and waited, listening for my dad to respond. But he didn't say anything, which was weird, because I'd have thought he'd at least get a jab in about how he wouldn't trust anything I cooked. Which, to be fair, was maybe a good point. I really *didn't* cook. At all.

But there was nothing in the fridge but leftover pizza and beer, and I couldn't stand the thought of my dad eating more crappy fast food when I left. Granted, that was what I tended to eat, too, when left to my own devices. But I wasn't the one who'd just had a heart attack. And it couldn't be that hard to cook chicken, right?

Maybe I could just get some of that pre-cooked, frozen stuff, like chicken tenders or fish sticks. And lettuce. Make a salad or something. That still had to be healthier than fast food, didn't it?

Tilting my head to the side, I waited for my dad to reply, but no response came. Jesus, was he just freezing me out now? I was pretty sure the only reason he'd made us go fishing was that he hadn't wanted to spend the day with me in the first place and thought I'd give up and go home if he made me cold enough and bored enough.

Well tough luck, Dad. I got my stubbornness from you.

I sighed and closed the fridge door.

"Or if we don't cook," I said as I walked back out into the living room, "we could at least order from somewhere that makes, like, vegetables and stuff. Dad?"

I looked around, confused. Where *was* my dad? He'd been in here a few minutes ago. A thin thread of worry wormed its way up into my chest.

"Dad?" I called, a little louder.

Maybe he'd gone upstairs. I'd gone down to the basement for a minute to put his tackle away. I probably just hadn't heard him. Everything was fine. Probably.

"Dad—" I cut off when I noticed, for the first time, that the porch light was on. I crossed the living room quickly and threw the door open. "Jesus, Dad, you scared me, I thought you were—"

I stopped.

My dad was on the front porch. Smoking. But the fact that

he was still smoking after having a heart attack wasn't even the most shocking thing about the scene. No, the most shocking part was that my dad wasn't alone.

Luke was standing next to him.

"Um... hi?" I said, completely confused. "I thought you were—"

"Yeah, no, I know," Luke said quickly. "I was actually out at my mom's, and when you said you had it here, I just figured I'd—"

"Oh. Right." I shook my head. "Yeah, sorry. I just wasn't expecting—"

My dad turned to look at me. "You didn't invite this guy over?"

I flushed. "Well, no, but the thing is, I have—"

"Sounds like he doesn't want you to be here," my dad said, turning back to Luke. His gaze hardened. "Sounds like he doesn't want to see you."

"No, Dad, it's not—"

"Mr. Luna, I'm sorry, I just—"

"Sounds," my dad said, his voice even icier, "like you should get off my porch."

"No, Dad, listen," I broke in, putting a hand on his shoulder. "It's okay. I have something of Luke's. He just stopped by to get it."

My dad's eyes narrowed. "You hangin' out with this guy again?"

Of all the times for my dad to get overbearing and protective, he had to pick now? What had happened to the cold shoulder?

"We're not hanging out," I insisted. "He's just here to get his phone."

"Sounds like you're hanging out." My dad flicked ash off the end of his cigarette. "Don't know how you end up with a guy's phone if you're not hanging out."

"Well, I don't know how you're out here smoking when you *know* you're not supposed to be doing that anymore," I spit back. "But I don't question you about your life."

Okay, that last part wasn't entirely true, but we could let that slide.

My dad opened his mouth like he was going to respond, but then he closed it again without saying anything. He looked at Luke, then back to me, and then shook his head. And then, stubbing his cigarette out in the ashtray that lived on the porch rail, he walked back inside. He left the door open, and as I turned to watch him, he walked all the way back to the kitchen and grabbed a beer from the fridge.

Great.

I sighed and turned back to Luke—which wasn't much better. He might not be currently trying to give himself another heart attack, but his mere presence was giving me one. What the hell was he doing here? I wasn't ready for this.

Not, to be fair, that I was sure I'd ever be ready for this. Not after the stunt I'd pulled last night, which had only looked more insane when I woke up this morning. As I'd sat in bed, I'd realized that Luke must think I was a complete nut job. I'd ended up calling my dad, telling him I wanted to spend the day with him because I knew that the two of us bickering would at least distract me from the sinking humiliation I felt otherwise.

The worst part about it was that it didn't even *matter*. I shouldn't care what Luke thought of me. It shouldn't make the teeniest bit of difference. I was supposed to be over him. I *was* over him. I was going to go back to California in a week or two and never see him again.

So why the hell couldn't I stop thinking about him?

"I'm really sorry about that," Luke said, wincing. "I didn't realize—I guess I didn't realize how much your dad hated me?"

"Yeah, he's uh—" I shook my head, hugging my arms around myself. God it was cold out, and I wasn't wearing a jacket. "It's not really—he doesn't hate you. He's just protective sometimes, I guess."

Luke pressed his lips together for a second. "You told him? About... you know."

"I didn't mean to," I said, shrugging helplessly. "He was just there that night, when I got home. He could tell I was upset. It kind of just... came out."

Luke grimaced. "Yeah. That's—that's fair. I probably deserve that, to be honest."

I didn't know what to say to that. Telling Luke he did deserve my dad's ire seemed pointless—why bother, when five minutes from now, I was never going to see the guy again. Telling him he didn't deserve it, though—I wasn't sure I could do that.

Goddammit, why did I have to care about it so much?

"I uh, I really was with my mom," Luke said, and I blinked, remembering hazily that he'd said something about that when my dad was still out on the porch. "I was planning on coming out here to help her today for weeks, so I just happened to be here when I got your message, and I figured, you know..."

I snorted. "Don't worry, I'm not afraid you're stalking me."

I meant it as a joke, but Luke stiffened and gave me a weird look. Great. Now I'd made it awkward again. This was so—

"Motherfucker!"

The word rang out from inside the house. I turned my head in surprise and saw my dad tipping backwards in the kitchen, his arms windmilling, and then heard a *whump* as he fell behind the kitchen island.

"Oh, shit, was that—" Luke began, but I was already sprinting back into the house.

"Dad, are you okay?" I skidded to a stop on the kitchen floor, kneeling down and leaning over him. "Are you—can you breathe."

"I'm fine," my dad wheezed, despite the fact that he looked anything but. "Oliver, just—don't—don't hover."

"But Dad—"

"Oliver, please." Even breathless, my dad managed to put a heavy dose of anger into his voice.

I leaned back, giving him more space, and looked at him worriedly. His face was bright red, and he was struggling to push himself up into a seated position—but he waved off my attempts to help him. The step stool that we used to reach the highest shelves in the kitchen was on its back behind him, and a box of fishing tackle—the same box I'd just put away in the basement—was sitting on the counter. The cabinet above the fridge was open.

"Jesus, Dad, if you wanted to store that up here, you could have just told me. I would have put it up there."

"Didn't... know... I wanted it here... till just now," my dad said, breathing heavily as he finally pulled himself upright and leaned back against the fridge.

"Still, I would have moved it for you if you'd just asked."

"Didn't... want to bother you." At least his breath was starting to come back.

"It's not bothering me to ask me for my help," I said. "That's literally exactly why I'm here. That's why I came home."

"You didn't need to do that," my dad said adamantly. "I told you, I don't need your help."

"And what would you have done if you'd fallen and I hadn't been home?" I asked.

"Would have gotten up," my dad said. "Just like I'm doing now."

And before I could stop him, he grabbed on to the counter behind him and began pulling himself to his feet.

"I'm not sure you should be—"

"I'm *fine*, Oliver," my dad said, shaking his head. He fended off my offered hand and steadied himself against the counter. "It was just an accident. Not a big deal."

"It is a big deal," I said, hearing the frustration in my voice and then getting frustrated at that.

I hated that my dad didn't realize how serious this was, and I *really* hated how he made me feel like *I* was the crazy one for being concerned.

"It's not." My dad took a step away from the counter, then another, then started walking towards the sliding doors that led out to the back deck. He looked back at me as he went. "I'll be fine. Talk to your friend."

It was his grimace over my shoulder that made me turn and realize that Luke was standing in the kitchen doorway, looking concerned. I blinked, but by the time I looked back at my dad, he was out on the deck and he'd closed the door behind him. As I watched, he pulled a pack of cigarettes out of his pocket.

I could have killed him—if he weren't so apparently determined to kill his damn self.

"I um—I'm sorry," Luke said behind me. "I didn't realize—I should have called. This was probably a bad time to come over."

I sighed, too exhausted to feel anything other than, well, exhaustion.

"Don't worry about it." I barked a laugh. "Besides, how could you have? I've got your phone."

"Oh. Right." Luke gave me an apologetic look. "Still, though—"

"Anyway, it's fine," I said quickly. "Just give me a sec, and I'll grab your phone, and you can get back to your mom. I didn't mean for you to get sucked into all of... this."

I waved my hand vaguely around the kitchen, hoping Luke interpreted that well because I wasn't even sure what I meant by it.

This family drama. My dad being rude to you. The fact that my house is still falling apart and smells like cigarette smoke and looks even sadder than it did the last time you saw it.

"It's okay," Luke said, and then he smiled, and even though I was pretty sure it was a nervous smile, it still took my breath away. "Really, I don't mind."

It took me a minute to realize I was just staring at him instead of responding.

Jesus, because things aren't strange enough between you two. Just get his phone, give it to him, and let him go. He's probably desperate to get away from here.

"Um. Right. Okay, well, I'll be right back."

I sort of half-walked, half-ran through the living room and up the stairs to my old room. Why did I have to feel so nervous around him? I already knew I'd made an ass out of myself. You'd think at the very least I'd have reached rock bottom by now and stopped caring.

Luke was leaning against the arm of the sofa by the door when I came back down, the kind of semi-standing, semi-sitting perch that would have looked awkward and uncomfortable on me, but somehow came across as effortless on him, like he could stay in exactly that position until the world ended.

I held his phone out, and his fingers stroked mine as he grasped it. I shivered, then cursed myself for doing that. Jesus, getting the chills because he'd touched my hand—like we hadn't just—

"I uh, I know it's not really my place," Luke said, interrupting my thoughts, "but is everything, um, okay? With your dad, I mean?"

No. Yes. No, it's not. But yes, it is, because it's not, but if you tell him it is, he'll leave, he'll be gone, and you won't have to draw this out any longer.

"He—he had a heart attack." The words came out of my mouth slowly. "A couple weeks ago. And he's—he's not really—I mean, he's fine, I guess. But it's just..."

I had to stop talking. If I said anything more, I'd probably start babbling again, and that never led anywhere good.

"Whoa." Luke's eyes widened. "That's really scary. I'm glad he's doing okay."

"Yeah." My voice was tight. I didn't trust myself to talk at this point. "Thanks."

"How—how are *you* doing?"

"Like, tonight? Or about my dad?" I asked and immediately felt stupid. Of course Luke meant about my dad.

Luke cocked his head to the side. "Either."

My chest felt tight suddenly, like I didn't have enough air to get the words out. "I'm—it's—fine. I mean, not like, fine, you know. But it's okay. He's just... himself. And I—" I shook my head. "You don't really want the details."

"I do if you want to talk about them." Luke shrugged. "Really."

Dammit. Why did he have to go and be so... like that?

"It's just... he's not always the easiest to deal with." I sighed. "He has this whole thing where—I mean, he's right, in a way. It's his life, he can do what he wants. But he won't go to the doctor. He won't even call them. I don't know how I even got him to tell me that they recommended putting a stent in, soon, when they discharged him from the ER, because he's dead set against it. And he just—he's just ignoring it. Acting like it didn't happen, like he shouldn't have to change anything about how he lives, like he's just gonna go on eating crap and smoking and not taking care of himself, and I get it, it's his choice, but I just... he didn't even want me to come home. He wasn't going to tell me, I only found out because my mom found out, by accident, and called me. He doesn't want me to stay here, he's fighting me on everything, and I just—it's not—"

Oh God, I could feel a lump forming in my throat, which was not at all what I wanted. Tearing up in front of Luke for the second time in so many days—I was really going for gold here.

"That sounds really hard," Luke said, and his voice was quiet, warm, like someone pulling a blanket over your shoulders on a cold day. "I'm so sorry."

"It's—it's fine," I choked out. "It's really not that big a—I mean, people deal with this shit every day. It's not like I'm—

we're—special in any way. I just wish I could—I don't know how to—fuck—"

It was too late. The tears had spilled over, started rolling down my cheeks.

"Oliver—"

"No, no, don't—don't do that," I said, trying to wave away Luke's concern as I wiped the tears off my face. I turned around, braced my hand on the hall closet door, tried to ground myself. "It only makes it worse when you're nice about it."

"I'll... try to be more of an asshole... then?"

Luke's tone was so tentative, so unsure, that I started laughing, and once that happened there was no turning back. I pressed both hands to my face, trying to hold in tears as my shoulders shook with these half-sobs, half-laughs that racked my body.

And then Luke's hand was on my shoulder. I thought about shaking it off, thought I probably should because it would be safer, smarter, not to let myself let him be kind to me. Wasn't that what had set me off last night—him being good to me, and me not being able to handle it? But it just felt so stable, and moving of its own accord, my body turned and let him pull me close.

My arms pressed up against Luke's chest, crushed between us. I gripped his shoulders with both hands as his arms went around me, and I just sort of sniffle-sobbed into his neck. It should have been so awkward—it *was* awkward. I was an inch taller than Luke, and I was dripping snot down the back of his shirt while he held one arm around my waist and slowly stroked the back of my neck with his other hand. God, I was a mess.

I don't know how long we stood there like that—it could have been a minute, could have been an hour—before I could feel my body stop shaking. I extricated myself from Luke's arms with an embarrassed laugh.

"Sorry about that."

"Nothing to apologize for," Luke said. His voice sounded strange. "Really." He gave me a long look, then sighed. "Oliver, if you don't wanna talk about it, I completely understand. But I just wanted to say—last night, I didn't mean to push—I never would have—I mean, if I'd known about—" He shook his head. "Well, anyway, I just wanted to say I'm sorry I made things weird, I'm sorry I pushed. I didn't mean to make things harder for you."

Oh God, Luke thought I'd freaked out last night because I was upset about my dad? Jesus, that was... very sweet of him. And very wrong. Did he honestly think I was thinking about my dad during sex? He was giving me credit for being a way better son than I actually was.

Actually, Luke, my dad was the farthest thing from my mind last night because I'm kind of a terrible kid. My breakdown was entirely about you. And my inability to keep my walls up, even when I know I should.

"Uh, thanks."

I tried to laugh, but it turned into this weird thing where I just inhaled a bunch of the snot that had been sitting in the back of my throat and made this thick gurgling noise. Really attractive.

"Are you, um, are you going to be sticking around for a while?" Luke asked, looking down.

"I—yeah? I think so?" I sighed. "I don't know, it's weird. I only went to the reunion because my dad said he'd reschedule his doctor's appointment and let me come if I went. Not sure why he cares so much. But he still hasn't called them, so... I don't know."

"Oh. Okay." Luke nodded.

"Listen, I appreciate—well, all of this. I know—I know I've been kinda weird—"

"Okay, well, you haven't been, and even if you were, you'd be completely entitled to be. I'd be a total mess in your position."

"Yeah."

What else was I supposed to say? I felt like I needed to tell him something, but I wasn't sure what, or how, or why.

Luke, it's not about my dad? Luke, it's about you? It's always been about you?

Could I get any more pathetic?

"I, uh, I should get going, I guess," Luke said, glancing at the door.

Right. Of course. Because Luke didn't actually want to hear anything of the sort from me.

"Thanks, uh, thanks for the phone," he continued, hefting it in his hand. "I'll try not to forget it next time." He flushed. "I mean, not that there's gonna be—just—you know—you know what I mean."

I laughed, this sort of high-pitched, crazy-aunt-you-keep-locked-in-the-attic sound. "Yeah. No, I got it."

"I'll see you around, Oliver," Luke said, moving towards the door. "Tell your dad bye for me. Or don't, maybe. Whatever would make him happier."

"Right. See ya."

I watched Luke open the door, step out onto the porch. Why did it feel like I was watching him walk out of my life? Why the hell did I care, even if that was what was happening?

I put my hand on the doorknob, watched Luke walk across the porch and down the steps to the front yard. Time to close the door now. Letting the warm air out and all that.

Luke walked along the flagstone path to the sidewalk, his figure cutting determinedly through the dusk. It would be completely dark out in a few minutes. He reached the sidewalk, turned right, started to walk around to the far side of the—

"Luke! Wait!"

Luke stopped, turned. It was hard to see his expression, the light was so bad, but I would have bet it was confused as hell.

"What's—"

I flew out of the house and down the steps, leaving the front door wide open behind me. If possible, it was even colder than before. The air cut through the long sleeves of my shirt, but I barely noticed. I ran down the path and caught up to Luke on the sidewalk, grabbing his wrist.

"Oliver, what are you—"

I kissed him. It was a clumsy, graceless kiss, more teeth than lips at first because Luke's mouth was open, still trying to ask me what the hell I was doing when I crushed my face to his.

But he didn't pull away, and after a second's frozen confusion, I felt his arms wrap around me again—and it felt right. I held my hands to his face and pulled him close, his hot breath mingling with mine under the cool glow of the streetlights and the moon.

God, what had possessed me to do this? I could have kissed him forever, but I knew I was only making more of a mess of things. Luke probably just wanted to get out of here. But he'd been nice to me just now, even last night he'd been nice, and I'd done nothing but confuse him.

"It's not about my dad," I said, breaking away, but still not taking my hands from Luke's face.

"What?"

"Last night. The reunion, the hotel. When I freaked out—it wasn't about my dad." My words tumbled and thumped all over each other like sneakers in a dryer. "It was—it was me. And you. Us. I'm—I'm not over it. That's why—that's why I've been so—"

"Not over—"

"Not over everything." I shook my head. "I lied. When I said I was in the library just trying to get service, when I said it would be sad if I'd really spent the past seven years thinking about it. I lied. I, uh—I have. Thought about it."

"Oh." Luke didn't say anything else. Just stared at me.

Fuck, this was probably a terrible idea, telling him all of this. Why had I thought this was smart, again?

"I know it's pathetic. I just—when I came to the reunion. I wanted to prove how over you I was. Prove it to you, and to myself. But I—well, it's not—I'm not—it's—"

"Hey, hey," Luke said and oh God, kill me now, he was starting to look concerned, which was definitely not the expression you wanted to see on the face of the guy you were kissing. "You don't need to explain any of this."

You don't need to explain any of this. Fuck. That was just a polite way of saying, *"please stop talking,"* wasn't it? Luke didn't care about what was going on with me. He'd been kind to me just now because that was what decent human beings did, not because he wanted *me*.

"Right." I shut my eyes for a second, and when I opened them, I took a step back. "Yeah, no, sorry. I didn't mean to— you're right."

"You don't owe me anything," Luke said quietly.

"Yeah. Of course."

Fuck, I wasn't sure I'd ever felt more stupid, even including last night. Luke just stared at me, quietly, and I shivered in the cold, waiting for him to speak.

Say something. Put me out of my misery.

"Oliver, I—" Luke stopped and grimaced.

Here it comes.

"I wish—I just, you should know," he began again. "I never

meant for—I mean, everything that happened last night. Tonight. Just now. I didn't mean to hurt you and—"

"No, it's fine. Really." I held up a hand. "I get it. You weren't trying to—"

"I'm never going to not have *some* feelings for you," Luke said softly. "I'm beginning to realize that. But this is—I mean, we're not—*I'm* not... looking for anything." Luke grimaced. "And I don't—I don't want to hurt you even more..."

This was it. This was the rejection I'd known was coming all along, the rejection that some part of me had been bracing for since I'd first seen that stupid invitation.

You should have known better than to go.

Except, *no*. That was bullshit. *Luke* wasn't looking for anything? Neither was I! I didn't even live here. If anything, I should have been the one rejecting him.

"Oh, Luke, no," I heard myself say. "Did you think I—no, sorry, God, that's not what I meant." I laughed—this cool, almost derisive sound that wasn't my normal laugh at all. "Trust me. I live three thousand miles away from here. I'm not looking for anything either. I was just trying to explain, last night—I don't know, I guess I just had a lot of memories that kind of came back. But you don't have to feel bad about anything. Trust me."

"Okay?" Luke gave me a baffled look.

Which he was right to do. I sounded completely unhinged, throwing myself at him one second, then more or less telling him to fuck off the next.

"Anyway, I should probably..." I gestured towards the house.

"God, right. You must be freezing," Luke said. "Um, okay, I guess. I'll uh—" he paused. "You know, I just realized I don't have your number."

"Oh." I blinked.

Luke laughed wryly. "Maybe I should get it—in case tomorrow morning it turns out I left something at your dad's house."

That you were inside of for all of two minutes?

That didn't seem very likely. But Luke was asking. Was I really going to say no?

"Yeah, of course."

Apparently not.

I pulled out my phone, and we exchanged numbers.

"Cool, okay—"

"Yeah, well—"

We both started, then stopped, talking at the same time.

"You first," Luke said with a laugh.

"Oh, no, I was just gonna say, um—it was good to see you, I guess."

"Yeah, you too." Luke studied me for a second. "I'll see you around."

"Right. Yeah. See you around."

And as simple as that, it was over. I waved, Luke began

walking down the street, and as I watched his figure retreat into the gloom, I knew I was never going to see him again.

This was fine. This was always what was going to happen. This was exactly how things had stood for seven years, up until a week ago. I was just going back to where we'd been.

This was fine.

So why did it hurt so much?

9

LUKE

7 YEARS AGO

"*S*hit, she's so hot," Andy said appreciatively, wiggling his eyebrows at Kyle. "We should go back there today."

"Definitely," Kyle agreed. He elbowed Luke in the side as they walked through A Hall towards the front entrance of the school. "Don't you think she's hot?"

"Who?" Luke asked, completely lost.

"That girl who works at the CVS downtown," Kyle said. "You know, we saw her last week when we went down there on Saturday."

"I uh, I wasn't there," Luke said quietly.

"Oh. Shit man, sorry."

Luke shrugged and looked away, pretending to be very interested in the trophy cases they were passing. The shitty thing about being left out by your friends, he reflected, was that there was no good way to fix it.

You either said nothing, and so they kept forgetting to include you in things, and pretty soon you weren't friends anymore—or you said something, and then you became that whiny friend who made everything awkward, so no one wanted to hang out with you, and pretty soon, well, you weren't friends anymore.

Even when they did remember to include you, like Andy and Kyle had today after their practice got cancelled early, all they did was talk about things you hadn't been there for, people you hadn't met, reminding you of how little they'd missed your presence.

It fucking sucked.

"Well, you'll see her today," Andy said stoutly, "and you'll see—she's really fucking hot."

"Yeah, sure," Luke agreed. "Sounds—"

"Luke?"

All three of them turned at the sound of his name, to see Ms. Bowman standing at the edge of the lobby, next to the auditorium.

Oliver was standing next to her.

Fuck. Something's wrong.

It had been two weeks since that afternoon at Oliver's house. Luke still cringed, remembering it—the way Oliver had looked at him like Luke was just incomprehensibly dumb for the choices he was making. He'd known Oliver would never understand if he tried to explain—no one would.

But whatever, he didn't owe Oliver anything. And he certainly didn't care what Oliver thought of him. There was no reason for Luke to even think about Oliver at all. Which made the fact that Oliver kept popping into his mind all the time even more annoying.

Since that afternoon, Luke had just done the other worksheets Ms. Bowman had given them on his own and assumed Oliver was doing the same thing. They hadn't actually spoken since he'd left Oliver's house.

"Luke, can you come here, please?" Ms. Bowman asked.

"Uh, yeah." He turned back to Andy and Kyle. "One sec, okay?"

He walked over to Ms. Bowman, full of misgiving. Please let her just be trying to rope him into the decorations committee for the winter formal or something.

"Um, hi?" Luke said when he reached Ms. Bowman.

He consciously didn't look at Oliver. Oliver's eyes were dark and bright and had this weird habit of fixating on Luke in a way that made him feel... seen.

It was disconcerting. He didn't *want* Oliver to see him, didn't want to think about what Oliver saw.

"What uh—what's up?" Luke asked.

Ms. Bowman frowned. "Last Friday's test," she said, going directly to the point.

"What about it?"

"You got a D, Luke."

"I got a—" Luke shook his head. Even after a concerted month's effort to flunk calc, he still wasn't quite used to hearing someone connect grades that low with him. He'd never gotten worse than a B in his life, before this year. "I mean, okay."

"And yet your tutoring assignments seem to be going just swimmingly," Ms. Bowman said.

"Uh..." Luke frowned, not quite sure what she was getting at. "I mean, a D's actually an improvement over my last test, isn't it?"

Ms. Bowman rolled her eyes. "Tell me how it is that someone who's able to turn in flawless problem sets from tutoring is unable to get better than a D on a test covering *the exact same material*?"

"Uh. I mean." Luke flashed a glance at Oliver, who looked away quickly. "Oliver's a good teacher? But it's just—it's different, you know, when it's just me on a test. It's harder."

"Really." Ms. Bowman's voice was flat. "And that's the story you're sticking to. Not that you've perhaps been copying Oliver's answers from his worksheet? Making him do the work for you?"

"What? No," Luke spluttered, insulted by the accusation. "No, I've been doing the work. On my—well, not on my own," he corrected himself quickly. "But I've been doing it." He looked at Ms. Bowman, willing her to believe him. "I swear. I just—I don't test well. I get nervous, you know? And it's different when you have someone helping you and I—"

"And I will believe that," Ms. Bowman interrupted him, "when I see it."

"What do you—what do you mean?" Luke asked, suddenly unsure of his footing.

There was a promise in there somewhere, or maybe a threat, that he didn't understand yet. He looked to Oliver for some indication of what Ms. Bowman meant, but Oliver just gave him a silent, apologetic look.

Had Oliver told Ms. Bowman something?

"I mean," Ms. Bowman said, "that you and Oliver are coming back to my room with me this afternoon. Now, in fact. And you'll do your tutoring session there for the day. Where I can watch."

"But I—"

"Oliver told me that you already had a session scheduled for today," Ms. Bowman said with a blithe smile. "So I'm assuming this won't present any sort of a problem. Right?"

Luke looked at Oliver again, and Oliver's apologetic look turned to one of guilt. Goddammit. What had he told her?

But there was nothing Luke could do. Not unless he wanted to explain what was actually happening to Ms. Bowman. Whatever Oliver might have told her, it wasn't as bad as it would get if she found out Luke was deliberately failing. Luke just needed to keep this contained, keep the situation from spiraling so he could keep his mom from finding out.

"Yeah," Luke said after a moment, feeling himself give up. "Yeah, that's fine. Just let me—" he gestured over his shoulder to where Andy and Kyle were waiting for him. "Just give me a sec."

He turned and walked back to them quickly.

"What was that all about?" Kyle asked with a smirk. "She trying to get you to join a math squad or something?"

Luke rolled his eyes. Kyle had teased Luke about being in honors classes for as long as he could remember. But it hadn't been till this year, when Luke no longer had soccer in common with Kyle and the other guys, that it had started to rankle.

"No," Luke said angrily—angry at Ms. Bowman, at Oliver, at Kyle, and hell, even at himself. "As a matter of fact, she wants to talk to me about how I'm failing calc."

"What?" Kyle blinked. "You're supposed to be all smart and shit."

"Yeah, well, apparently not," Luke said, his voice heated. "And now I have to stay and do some tutoring thing."

"What? Come on, we were gonna hang out, man," Kyle said. He glanced over his shoulder. "And now you're ditching us for Ms. Bowman and Oliver fuckin' Luna?"

"Jesus, I'm not doing it because I *want* to," Luke said.

"You're doing tutoring with Oliver? God, he must be thrilled. Probably came all over himself when he found out he got that job," Andy said with a laugh.

Andy's voice was full of scorn—and distressingly loud. In spite of himself, Luke looked over his shoulder to see if Oliver had heard. Oliver was looking the other way, but Luke felt shitty anyway.

"I guess he's just—he's doing really well in the class," Luke said, trying to move things along. "Anyway, I don't think I can hang out today. Sorry."

"Oh, don't be sorry," Andy said with a grin. "We'd never dream of interrupting your *date*."

"It's not—"

"Yeah, no, we definitely respect your need for some alone time with Luna," Kyle added with a laugh.

"Jesus Christ guys, he's not—it's not... like that," Luke hissed.

Did they have to be so loud? Oliver had to be hearing this. Fuck.

"Just keep telling yourself that buddy," Andy said, shouldering his gym bag. "But remember, no means no, and just because he throws himself at you doesn't mean you have to let him suck your dick."

"Well, unless you want to," Kyle laughed.

And with that, they were gone, leaving Luke gaping after them.

He dreaded having to turn around again. He knew Andy and Kyle weren't serious—not about Luke being gay, anyway. At least, he was pretty sure.

It wasn't like they could read his mind, like they knew the thoughts he'd been having about Oliver, about guys in general, for the past... No. They didn't know. If they did, they'd never joke about it with Luke—because they wouldn't even be talking to him anymore.

But what Kyle and Andy had said about Oliver—that wasn't a joke. Or, at least, not the kind that was meant innocently. That was the kind of joke that was meant to hurt. The kind of thing they probably *wanted* Oliver to overhear.

Luke couldn't remember exactly when it had started— seventh grade? eighth?—but by freshman year, it was just one of those things everyone kind of agreed on without ever having talked about it: Oliver Luna was gay.

Why? Why not. Because he dressed kind of funny, because he talked with his hands, because he still lapsed into a lisp now and then when he got excited—all of that was somehow proof.

Or maybe it was just because Oliver was a loner, because he didn't seem to have any friends. It definitely didn't help that Oliver had never denied what everyone said about him. Though Luke had to admit, even if Oliver had, he doubted that would have been enough to deter people.

High school was just like that. Kids were assholes, and it was easy to pick on the misfit, to make fun of the outsider to make yourself feel better. It wasn't fair, Luke knew. But if he said anything, if he tried to fight against it, he could very easily become the next target of all the gossip and rumors. And he had no intention of letting that happen.

Only when Luke was absolutely sure that his face gave nothing away did he turn around again. If Oliver hadn't heard what Kyle and Andy had said, then everything was fine. And if he had heard... Well, it didn't make Luke feel good, but there wasn't much he could do about it now.

"Sorry about that," he said when he walked back over to Ms. Bowman and Oliver. "I'm ready now."

Ms. Bowman looked up from her phone. "Good," she said briskly. "Let's go."

Oliver and Luke fell into step behind Ms. Bowman as she walked back to her classroom and Luke remembered, suddenly, that he was annoyed at Oliver—though it was hard to bring that feeling back to the surface through all the shame and guilt Luke felt about what Andy and Kyle had just said. *Had* Oliver heard them? Would he even care, if he had?

"Remind me what I gave you this week," Ms Bowman said when they got back to her room. "Problem sets 8 and 13?"

"Yeah," Oliver said quickly. "We uh, we did 8 on Tuesday. So we were gonna do 13 today." He glanced at Luke for corroboration.

"Right," Luke said, trying to bring his focus back to the matter at hand.

"Alright, well," Ms. Bowman said, "get to it. I have grading to do, but I'll be here if you need anything."

She gave them an expectant look as she pulled out the chair behind her desk and sat down.

Luke followed Oliver towards the back of the classroom—not to their usual seats, but he guessed that Oliver was trying to put more distance between them and Ms. Bowman, and Luke could get behind that. He grabbed a desk next to the one Oliver chose and, in spite of himself, pulled it closer to Oliver's.

"This is ridiculous," Luke grumbled as he sat. "I can't believe she's making us do this."

"Yeah, well," Oliver said with a shrug. "Much as it might shock you to hear this, this wasn't my first choice of afternoon activity either."

There was a touch of bite in Oliver's voice. Luke heard it,

recognized it—but instead of doing the right thing and softening his own tone, he matched it.

"I actually had *plans*," Luke said, glaring down at the worksheet that he'd pulled out of his backpack, then glaring up at Ms. Bowman in the front of the room for good measure.

"Oh, hanging out with your friends?" Oliver's voice was cool.

"Yeah. Why? Is that a problem?"

"No, of course not," Oliver said levelly, pulling out his own worksheet. "I'm so sorry this happened. I definitely respect your need for alone time with your friends. I'd never *dream* of interrupting that under normal circumstances."

Fuck. Well, that answered that question.

"Listen, Oliver—"

"Honestly, Luke, don't bother," Oliver interrupted. "Let's just get this over with."

"That's not what I—"

"We just have to pretend that I'm tutoring you for, what, half an hour?" Oliver continued, glancing up at the clock on the wall. "Since you're so great at pretending, should be a piece of cake."

"Fine," Luke said, feeling exasperated, and then guilty about feeling exasperated. "Whatever."

"So on this first one," Oliver said, raising his voice a little, "we have to start by..."

The minutes ticked by slowly. It was excruciating. Oliver was clearly pissed at Luke, and other than the few times Oliver spoke loud enough about math for Ms. Bowman to hear, they worked in silence. Well, except for the times that Oliver muttered, *"not my choice,"* and, *"ridiculous farce,"* under his breath, just loud enough for Luke to hear.

"Negative seven," Luke said abruptly when he glanced over at Oliver's paper a few minutes later.

"What?"

"Negative seven," Luke repeated, pointing to the error in Oliver's equation on problem four. "That should be negative."

"No," Oliver said, shaking his head. "It shouldn't."

"Yes," Luke said, just as firmly. "It should. Here, look."

He walked Oliver through what he'd done wrong. It was just a tiny mistake earlier up in his calculations that had cascaded down through the problem. Garbage in, garbage out, as Ms. Bowman was fond of saying. That was all it was —a mistake that anyone could have made. But Oliver seemed incensed that Luke was pointing it out to him.

"This is absurd," Oliver muttered. "Why do you even care?"

"I *care*," Luke said, glaring at Oliver, "because as you've reminded me, if we're going to keep up this *farce*, our answers have to actually match. And if *you're* the one tutoring *me*, you probably shouldn't be the one with the wrong answer, should you?"

"It's not wr—" Oliver started to say, but for the first time, he actually seemed to look at the scribbles Luke had added to his paper and registered the mistake he made.

Luke could see the moment Oliver realized it, could see the flush creep up his neck and onto his cheeks. And suddenly, that weird, hot, tight feeling in Luke's stomach was back.

Go. Away. He yelled at the feeling silently. He was already figuratively hot and bothered over Oliver—he didn't need to literally feel that way too.

"Fine," Oliver said, and there was a touch of sullenness in his tone as he twirled his pencil upside down with his long fingers and began to erase what he'd written. "I still think this is ridiculous."

"If it's so ridiculous," Luke pointed out, "why the hell did you tell Bowman we had another tutoring session scheduled today?"

"Because she confronted me, point blank, with her suspicion that you were taking advantage of me," Oliver hissed angrily, "and making me do all the work for you. And when I lied and told her that no, we were still doing the sessions and you were doing your own work—something I only had to do because of the situation you put me in, I might add— she asked me when our next session was. I said the first day that came to my mind. I didn't know she was going to go hunt you down after that."

"Really?" Luke arched an eyebrow. "You're sure this didn't all start because you told her we weren't actually doing the sessions? You sure it didn't start because you were pissed and wanted to get back at me?"

"No," Oliver snapped. "It didn't. It started because you're the one who was dumb enough to do a shitty job on that test and not realize it was going to look suspicious after you were handing in these perfect problem sets."

Oliver's eyes blazed as he glared at Luke. "It started because you're the one who's intentionally failing this course for some insane reason he won't even explain and dragging me into lying for you to cover it up—something I can't even believe I'm doing when you clearly don't deserve my help or sympathy. I might be pissed at you now, but that has nothing to do with why we're here."

And that was it, really. They'd cut to the heart of it now, why Oliver was actually pissed, and how Luke knew he had every right to be, and how any pretense that Luke was bothered by something Oliver *might* have done was nothing compared to what they both knew Luke's friends had actually done—and what Luke had done nothing to stop.

The shame cut through Luke like a knife. He made himself look at Oliver. Made himself see the person in front of him who he'd hurt, by doing nothing. Because doing nothing didn't make him any better than Andy and Kyle when you got down to it.

"I'm sorry," Luke said quietly. He held Oliver's eyes, made himself keep looking even though the pressure in his chest was begging him to look away. "That was—I should have—I should have said something—done something."

"It's fine," Oliver said.

"It's not," Luke countered. "It's not fine at all."

"Look," Oliver said, casting a glance up towards the front of the room to make sure Ms. Bowman was engrossed in her grading. "I appreciate the sentiment, but really, don't worry about it."

"Don't worry about it?" Luke frowned. "Oliver, you're clearly pissed, and I'm trying to apologize. Will you just, you know, *let me*?"

"Oh, because I owe you that?" Oliver retorted. "You're the one in the wrong here, but somehow I'm the one who owes you, who's removing your inalienable right to an apology and a guilt-free conscience?"

"That's not what I meant."

"Forget it. It's really not that important."

"Except it obviously is." Luke gave Oliver a confused, annoyed look. "And honestly, if it bothers you so much, which it clearly does, whatever you say—why don't you just tell them to stop? Just say it's not true and tell them to shove it."

"Are you even—" Oliver stopped and looked at Luke like he couldn't believe how dense Luke was.

The same look, Luke realized, that he was giving Oliver.

"There's so much wrong with that statement I don't even know where to start," Oliver went on. "Like, A, are you implying that I only have the right to ask them to stop if what they say about me isn't true? But if it is true, I just have to put up with their homophobia? And B, I would refuse to do that on principle anyway, because telling them to stop calling me gay is tantamount to saying that there's something shameful about being gay, which there's not, so fuck that. Also, C, I don't owe anyone any explanations about my life. And D, do you really, honestly think that any of those guys would actually stop, just because I asked them to?"

Oliver's cheeks were heated with anger by the time he finished, and he was speaking so quickly that his lisp had crept out towards the end, but none of that took away from the fury, the power behind his words.

Luke knew he should feel ashamed, guilty. And he did. But he was also, weirdly, impressed. He'd never feel confident enough to express himself like that—and he was the ostensibly popular one.

Oliver glared at Luke, those bright eyes of his not the least bit dimmed behind his glasses, which had, admittedly, slipped down the bridge of his nose a bit as he'd talked.

Luke opened his mouth to apologize again, to tell Oliver he was right, that he hadn't been thinking straight when he'd spoken before.

"Wait, but... *is* it true? Are you, you know...?"

What?

That wasn't what Luke had meant to ask at all. Where the hell had that come from? Oliver's glare only intensified, and Luke couldn't blame him.

"Fuck you," Oliver said, and Luke flinched.

"No, sorry, I'm—fuck, that's not what I meant to say," Luke said hurriedly. "I—fuck, you just said you don't owe anyone any explanations, and you're totally right, and I'm sorry. I just..." He ran a hand through his hair. "I don't know, nevermind."

"What?" Oliver said, his voice hushed but sharp. "What were you going to say?"

"I don't know," Luke said, again, floundering, trying to feel his way to something that was honest and wouldn't accidentally offend Oliver or make Luke seem like an even bigger asshole.

"I guess I just was curious because if it's true, I think that's like, amazing. I don't know how you do it. Put up with what everyone says about you. And like, not let it get to you." Luke shook his head. "Like, this school is just... it sucks, you know? People are assholes. And I just—I'm just really impressed, I guess. That's all I was trying to say."

Oliver looked at Luke for a long time, chewing on his lower lip. He was quiet for so long that Luke thought he was just going to change the subject and go back to the problems in front of them.

"It's not entirely true," Oliver said finally, lowering his voice even more, though a glance over his shoulder told Luke that Ms. Bowman wasn't paying them the slightest bit of attention.

"I'm bi," Oliver continued. "Not gay. I like guys *and* girls. But that doesn't really matter—it wouldn't stop anyone from being assholes to me, and I refuse to correct them because that would sound like I'm trying to say that being bi is better than being gay, or like, less *gay* than being gay, you know? Which it's not. So fuck that."

"Oh," Luke said, trying to process the onslaught of words.

"And as for how I do it—I do it because I know that being who I am and not being ashamed of that, not letting douche-canoes like your friends make me feel bad about myself, is the one thing in life that I *can* do, the one thing I can control. So does it suck that my high school is full of homophobic morons? Yeah, it sure doesn't feel great. But it definitely helps to know that the people making fun of you are bottom-feeding sacks of shit. No offense."

"Oh," Luke said again.

God, *he* sounded like a moron. Come to think of it, Oliver might have been including him in the *"homophobic moron"* category. Luke couldn't blame him if he had.

"I uh—thank you for telling me," Luke said after a moment's silence. "I won't tell anyone."

"It's fine, honestly." Oliver waved Luke's words away. "It wouldn't make a difference if you did, and I really don't care. Not about that."

And then he was quiet and looked down at his paper. Luke wondered if Oliver assumed the conversation was over, or if maybe he just wanted it to be.

"I'm really sorry, though," Luke said. "I should have—I should have said something. Stopped them."

Oliver shrugged. "I mean, I get it. You stand up for me, then it's like, *'Oh, why's he doing that, he's probably gay too,'* right?"

Luke flushed. That had been exactly his chain of thought. He looked down at the problem set. Maybe they should just let this conversation die.

"I just don't see why you care what they think," Oliver said after a minute of silence. "I mean, if you know they'd say something like that, if you know they're assholes…"

"They're my friends," Luke said, knowing how pathetic that sounded.

"But if you can't tell them what you really think because

you're afraid they'll turn on you—"

"Look, I never said they were perfect." Luke flushed, feeling hot again. He couldn't tell if he was angry or embarrassed, but he didn't like it, regardless. "No one is."

"Yeah, but it sounds a lot like you feel like you have to be someone you're not around them," Oliver pressed.

"Okay, look, you don't actually know—"

"Just like you're doing with Ms. Bowman," Oliver went on, flicking a glance up towards the front of the room. "Just like you're doing with everyone. I mean, is there actually *anyone* you're honest with?"

Luke flinched again.

"Sorry," Oliver said. "Sorry, I shouldn't have—I didn't mean that."

Luke laughed bitterly. "You sure about that? Sure sounded like you did."

Oliver was quiet for a second. "You know, you may not have said anything to stop them—Andy and Kyle, I mean. But I know—well, you've also never said anything like that about me."

"Yeah, but I still should have—"

"I'm just saying—it makes a difference. I've noticed, you know?" Oliver gave him a small smile. "And for the record, I don't think you're a bottom-feeding sack of shit."

"Um, thanks?"

"I mean, don't get me wrong, I still think it's really fucking dumb that you're deliberately failing calculus but that's—I don't know, it's a different kind of dumb, I guess, than the way Andy and Kyle act."

"God, Oliver, you're gonna make me blush if you keep it up with these compliments," Luke snorted.

They went back to working in silence, but it was a better silence this time. Oliver didn't seem as mad now, and Luke felt a little bit better about that—though his mind was still spinning from everything else Oliver had said.

They handed in their papers to Ms. Bowman at the end of the hour, who looked them over, stared at the two of them for a disconcertingly long time, and finally told them they could go. Luke and Oliver walked back to the lobby and out to the front of the school together, but it wasn't until Oliver turned and started walking away from the parking lot that they spoke again.

"Wait, you're walking home?" Luke said in surprise.

"Yeah," Oliver said, sounding confused. "I live close. Why?"

"No—no reason. I just—I'm walking too," Luke said.

"Oh."

"Do you wanna, like, walk together?" Luke asked, not entirely sure he could believe his own ears.

Oliver barked a laugh. "You sure you wanna be seen with me in public?"

"If you don't want to, you can just say so," Luke said, flushing.

"No, no, that's not—" Oliver's cheeks were pink now, too. "That's not what I meant. It's—it's fine. Yeah. We can walk."

So they did.

The days were growing shorter, and the sun was already slanting low in the sky, turning everything a burnished gold. They walked in silence, but not an uncomfortable one. Maybe it was the walk that made it easier. Or maybe they'd run out of things to fight about. Luke wasn't sure.

After a while, though, Luke realized Oliver was giving him suspicious glances when he thought Luke wasn't looking, and finally Luke broke down.

"What?" he asked, the next time he caught Oliver doing it. "Do I have something in my teeth or something?"

"What?" Oliver blinked. "Oh. No. I was just—don't you have a car? I thought I remembered you having one last year."

Oh. That.

"Yeah," Luke said shortly. "I sold it."

"Shit, what for?"

Oliver must have thought there was some kind of interesting story behind that, Luke realized. Like he wanted the money for something cool. But the fact was, Luke had sold it to help his mom out because his parents' divorce had cleaned out her savings, and his dad was refusing to pay alimony, child-support, anything. His mom had gone back to work, but that was barely enough money to cover their regular expenses, let alone his school fees.

But he couldn't explain any of that to Oliver, and after a while, Oliver seemed to decide he'd offended Luke.

"Sorry," Oliver said. "Was that a weird thing to ask? I didn't mean to pry. I know you're not supposed to talk about money and stuff like that, I just—I thought I remembered you really used to like your car. I mean, you used it in that video project for German last year with Marisa and Tom, and it was really funny, so it just stuck in my mind, and I guess I just..." Oliver winced and bit his lip, looking at Luke. "Nevermind. Sorry."

And suddenly, it dawned on Luke that Oliver was nervous. Which struck him as odd. What did Oliver have to be nervous around Luke for?

He was the smartest person Luke knew and seemed light years beyond high school, way more grown up and mature than anyone else, and yet here he was, babbling because he was afraid he'd offended Luke.

It was just absurd, and so Luke started to laugh. Only now Oliver was looking at Luke like he thought Luke was laughing *at* him, which he was, but not in the way Oliver was worried about. But in typical Luke fashion, he'd managed to offend Oliver again, and the only thing he could think of to do to level the playing field was to tell the truth.

"Sorry," he said, trying to pull himself together. "I'm not laughing—it was just—"

"I'm not stalking you or anything," Oliver said defensively. "I just happened to notice."

"No, I know," Luke said. "I was laughing because, I don't know, because you seemed worried that you'd offended me and honestly, nothing could be further from the truth." He took a deep breath. "I sold my car to help my mom out."

Huh. That had been easier to say than he'd thought. But then, Oliver had been honest with Luke—more honest than

Luke deserved, and more forgiving—and maybe Luke returning that honesty was the least he could do.

"We uh—we don't have a lot of money," Luke added.

"Oh," Oliver said. "That's rough."

Luke was grateful for the way Oliver took his statement in stride. Strangely, it made Luke want to offer more.

"My parents got divorced this summer," he said. "And it wasn't, like, a good divorce. It was expensive, and my mom doesn't have any money left, and my dad won't pay what the court ordered him to, and he's basically kidnapped my little brother and won't let us see him, and it just—" he cut himself off. "Sorry, you didn't ask for all of that. I just don't talk about it much."

"It's okay." Oliver shrugged. "My parents are divorced too. My mom cheated on my dad, I guess, and left him for my stepfather when I was eight."

"Shit."

"Yeah." Oliver laughed, short and a little bitter sounding. "For a while, it seemed okay. They lived in Great Neck, so it's not like they were far away, and I got more presents at Christmas." His mouth twisted into a wry grin. "But then I got older, and my mom and stepdad moved to New Hampshire and just kinda... forgot me, I guess. The gifts kept coming—for a while, anyway—but eventually even those stopped."

"That sucks." It didn't seem like enough, and Luke wished he could think of something better to say, but Oliver didn't seem bothered by it.

"It does," Oliver agreed. "But I don't know, if my mom's the kinda person who can just forget her son... maybe I don't want her in my life anyway? I mean, I know my dad doesn't understand me at all, but at least he's there."

It was an echo of what Luke had said to Oliver two weeks ago, Luke realized, and then he realized that Oliver remembered that too as he gave Luke a strange smile.

"Anyway," Oliver said. "I get the money thing. My dad and I don't really—well, you've seen our house."

Luke had, though, to be honest, he hadn't really noticed anything other than Oliver himself that afternoon when he'd gone over there. Had the house not been nice? Luke couldn't remember.

When they'd gone up to Oliver's bedroom—Luke had definitely paid attention there, but it had been in this kind of mad quest to drink in everything he could see in the room, to tag and label it, analyze it, to try to use Oliver's things to make sense of Oliver the person.

When Oliver had first gone downstairs to talk to his dad, Luke had spent a minute pouring over every book in Oliver's bookshelf as though they held the secrets to the mystery that was Oliver Luna, the boy who twirled his pencil and distracted Luke and wouldn't get out of his head.

Luke felt like he should understand Oliver better, after today. He knew so many more facts about him, now. Child of divorce. Bi, not gay. Hadn't thrown Luke under the bus to Ms. Bowman—even though Luke probably deserved it. Forgave Luke when he *didn't* deserve it. Had more principles at age 18 than any adult Luke knew—certainly more principles than Luke himself had.

And yet, all Luke felt was an insatiable need to learn more. His curiosity hadn't been sated so much as whetted, and suddenly he had a million more questions.

How long have you known you were bi? How did you figure it out? Do you have other friends I don't know about? Do you have a whole life no one at school knows anything about? What's it like —being you? And how the hell are you brave enough to do it?

But those were the kinds of questions you could only ask a friend—questions Luke wouldn't even feel comfortable asking Andy and Kyle, let alone someone he barely knew, like Oliver.

And so Luke just nodded. "Yeah, us too. My mom's gone back to work for the first time since I was born, and she's doing so much, but it's just—it's hard—especially when it seems like everyone else around you has money." He tried to keep his smile from turning into a grimace.

Luke wasn't really sure what they talked about, after that, but five blocks later, they were standing on the sidewalk in front of Luke's house, and everything felt weirdly momentous, like this was the end of a week spent together instead of just an hour.

"I guess I should—" Luke gestured back towards the front door. "My mom's a teacher, so we usually eat dinner kind of early. She goes to bed at like, 8 p.m. Gets up at like, 4."

"Shit," Oliver laughed. "That's when I go to bed some nights."

He paused, and gave Luke another one of those inscrutable looks that seemed to see right through him.

"Do you wanna um—I mean, if you wanna come in..." Luke

heard himself say.

Where the hell did that come from?

"No, I uh—thanks, but I should get back."

Oliver bit his lip again, and Luke wondered what he was nervous about this time.

"Yeah. Okay." Luke said, trying to ignore the fact that his chest still felt full, charged, like everything that was happening right now was somehow very, very important. "I'll uh, see you tomorrow then."

"Yeah." Oliver nodded. "See you tomorrow."

He turned and walked away.

Luke started to do the same but stopped before he'd even made it two steps towards his front door. He turned around, and instead of moving, instead of doing anything, he just watched Oliver walk down the sidewalk.

He felt like an idiot, not even sure why he was doing it, and he realized how stupid it was, because if Oliver were to turn around now, there was no way Luke could pretend he'd been doing anything but staring at him.

But Oliver didn't look back. He just kept walking, his figure receding in the distance until, finally, he turned a corner and was gone. Luke heaved a sigh of relief—and felt a pang of something in his chest at the same time.

It was good that Oliver hadn't looked back. Very good.

Because how could Luke explain what he'd been doing, what he'd been feeling, to Oliver when he couldn't even explain it to himself?

10

LUKE

*I*t was fucking cold on the West Side Highway this morning.

Even after running my usual six miles—well, five and three quarters, I wasn't *quite* at the end of my run yet—and working up body heat, I was still cold. It didn't matter how many layers I'd put on this morning, the wind was determined to slice through them.

I was sprinting as hard as I could. It was still dark—not even 7 a.m. on Friday morning—and I had the path mostly to myself. The frigid air knifed into my lungs and my legs were on fire as I pushed, flinging myself towards the end of my run.

I couldn't think anymore, was barely aware of where or who I was, which was exactly my goal. This past week—since seeing Oliver, since saying goodbye—had been really weird, and I just wanted to forget everything for a while.

Not weird because anything had happened. The opposite—

nothing had happened. Which was exactly the way it was supposed to be.

So why the hell couldn't I stop thinking about Oliver?

I mean, it was probably just because he'd kissed me, right? That had been a little weird—but apparently not weird enough to stop me from kissing him back, which—fuck, even just remembering that moment made me shiver. It had felt so good, so *right*, to have Oliver back in my arms.

But then he'd told me he wasn't over us, that he still had feelings for me, and suddenly everything got complicated again. I should have known better than to kiss him. I should have been smarter than to give into something just because it felt good.

I didn't want to make things harder for Oliver. But I hadn't known how he felt when he kissed me. I should have guessed, maybe. But I hadn't been thinking. That was kind of a recurring problem with me, I was beginning to realize. I had trouble thinking straight around Oliver.

So I'd tried to tell him the truth. To just be honest. He deserved that from me. And the truth was, yeah, maybe I did still feel something for him. But I *definitely* wasn't looking for anything—not with anyone. And especially not with someone who lived three thousand miles away.

So you'd think that when Oliver had told me he wasn't looking for anything either, that he'd just gotten caught up in the moment, that he wasn't actually interested—you'd think that was exactly what I wanted to hear. You'd think I'd be happy about that, happy we were on the same page.

I wanted to be happy about it.

And yet...

And yet standing there, knowing it was time for me to leave, knowing this would be the end of everything, it had felt like something was stabbing through my chest. I knew it was the right thing. For me, certainly, and probably for Oliver as well.

But I'd asked for his number anyway.

And every day since then, Oliver had lurked at the edge of my thoughts, like he was just hanging out in my brain, watching me. And my chest constricted every time I let myself see his face, any time I closed my eyes and remembered the feel of his lips on mine. In fact, pretty much the only time I could get Oliver out of my mind was when I was so stressed about work or so physically exhausted that I was practically brain-dead—hence this run.

I couldn't call him. I couldn't see him again. I'd already tried sleeping with him, in the hopes that would get him out of my system, and look how well that had turned out.

Contacting him again, suggesting we see each other... that would be a terrible idea, for both of us, and only make things more confusing. Maybe I still had some feelings for him, but they'd pass if I gave it enough time. They had to.

Suddenly, it occurred to me what I was doing. Thinking about Oliver again—even in the middle of an all-out run. Dammit. I needed to stop doing that.

"Luke?"

I stumbled when I heard someone say my name and caught myself just before falling. When I turned, I saw Nick, sitting on a bench, bundled in a peacoat, scarf, gloves, and the hat-equivalent of the puppy dog Snapchat filter, with little ear tabs at the top and a nose knit right above his brow. It was a little incongruous for Nick. I would have pegged him as too reserved for that hat—but what did I know?

"Shit, sorry," Nick said, wincing at my stumble.

"It's—alright," I puffed "I just—wasn't—expecting..." I trailed off and turned around, walking back to where he was sitting. "Hey."

"Hey," Nick said. "Sorry, I didn't mean to interrupt your run. But Ben said this was your usual route, so I figured—"

"No worries." I shrugged as I bent over and began stretching.

Ben and I ran together on the weekends sometimes, but for some bizarre reason, he wasn't on board with getting up before dawn on a weekday to voluntarily run in freezing temperatures—couldn't imagine why.

"He's right—I do usually stop just up there." I gestured to a traffic light a couple blocks north of us, then glanced down at my watch and grinned. "Besides, I still PR-ed today, so it's all good."

"Damn." Nick arched an eyebrow. "I knew you were like, 'healthy,' but I didn't know you were *that* into fitness."

"It's the only way to know if you're improving."

Which was true, though not the whole, or even really any of the reason I'd been throwing myself so hard into my run this morning. But Nick wasn't here to hear the emotional vomit running a spin cycle through my head right now.

Though come to think of it... why *was* Nick here? We were

friends, sure, but not so close I'd expect him to stake out the end of my run on a particularly bitter morning.

"Anyway," I said, switching legs as I stretched. "What's up?"

"Not much. Just—" Nick paused. "Well, I wanted to talk to you about something, but we don't have to do it here. I don't want you to freeze."

"Well, I usually walk home from here," I said, "by way of a cool down. So we could…"

"Sure, sounds good," Nick agreed.

I tried to quiet the nerves I felt in my stomach now that the run was over. Most of them were nerves that had been there all week, but the fact that Nick wanted to talk to me now— my brain had actually panicked for a second, imagining that Oliver had dispatched Nick to tell me I was an asshole or something before I remembered that Oliver didn't know any of my friends.

Still—*I wanted to talk to you about something*" was an ominous phrase, if you asked me.

"You want my hat or something?" Nick offered as we started walking. "It's really cold out."

"I'll uh, I'll survive." I tried not to laugh. It was a kind offer, but I was pretty sure I could die a happy man never having worn a puppy hat. "Besides, I'd just get it sweaty."

Nick nodded absently as we crossed the street, clearly turning something over in his mind. I waited for him to speak, trying to tell myself that everything was fine.

"So, I'm sorry for being a giant creep," Nick began, "accosting you this morning. I just—I figured it'd be easier to talk in person. I'm sure you know why I'm here and are probably laughing at me for making such a big deal of this, it's just—"

"Nick, I have *no* idea why you're here," I said. I was laughing a little, but it was only out of nervousness. He was being so serious. "Not that I'm not flattered you care enough to want to talk to me before the sun's even up, but..."

"Oh." Nick blinked. "Oh, I thought it was obvious. I wanted to talk to you about Eli."

Eli? Why did that name sound so...

"Shit, yeah." I grinned at Nick. "I totally forgot."

Nick snorted. "Glad I've been freaking out for the past four days, then. I feel really cool now."

I laughed. "To be totally honest, man, I completely forgot I ran into you that day. Things have been..." I cocked my head to the side. "Complicated."

"Oh," Nick said again. "Okay, well, um. Yeah."

"So—Eli." I glanced at Nick. "I'm guessing you'd rather I *not* tell anyone else that I met him and have proof that he actually exists?"

"I mean, I know that's kind of a weird request but... yeah. If you wouldn't mind. Things with Eli are just... well, complicated."

If there was one thing I understood, it was complicated feelings about a guy that you didn't even want to be having yourself, let alone want to have to explain to anyone else.

"No worries," I said, trying to put him at ease. "You got it."

"I really would love for you guys to meet him," Nick said as we came to another intersection. "Properly, I mean. He's..." A smile flitted across Nick's face. "He's..."

"He seemed great," I offered as we crossed, since Nick seemed to be having trouble coming up with the word. "Funny, cute—clearly obsessed with you."

Nick flushed. "He's amazing," he said. "And if it were his choice, he'd have met you guys months ago. It's just... I just need a little more time."

I nodded. Introducing your boyfriend—which is what I assumed Eli was to Nick, even though Nick hadn't said as much—to your friends was a big step. Or... so I understood. I'd never actually done it, since I'd never actually had a boyfriend, or been inclined to see a guy more than twice.

I just wasn't the relationship type. I'd accepted that. In theory, it sounded great. But invariably, by the second date, all I could see were a guy's flaws, the millions of little ways we were incompatible, the inevitable down-in-flames ending. And God help him if a guy suggested a third date— all my alarm bells would start going off, shouting, *"Clingy! Clingy! Clingy!"* at me like a tornado warning.

I knew it wasn't fair. I knew it made me an asshole. But then —I'd kind of always known I was an asshole. Ever since things with Oliver... happened the way they did. That had made it clear. I just wasn't meant for relationships, and I'd only hurt someone by trying.

"Got it," I said. "My lips are sealed."

"Thanks." Nick cocked his head to the side. "How are things

with you these days? You said something about it being
'complicated?'"

"Yeah, but it's..." I sighed. "You don't actually want to know,
trust me."

"Dude, I asked."

"I know but—" I shook my head. "It's stupid, for one thing.
It's definitely going to make you think I'm a jerk, for another.
And there's like, way too much boring backstory. It's not that
interesting, and it'd take us the rest of the walk back to my
apartment."

"Hey, if you don't wanna talk about it," Nick said, "I'm not
pressing. No worries. But if you do..." he shrugged. "I don't
have to be anywhere till 10, and I seriously doubt it's going
to make me think you're *that* terrible a person. Unless you've
got a refrigerator full of severed heads or something, but I've
always gotten the impression you're a bit of a neat freak, and
I kinda think that would offend your sensibilities."

I laughed, in spite of myself. I wasn't convinced Nick's mind
wouldn't change *after* he heard my story, but I supposed in
comparison with a serial killer, I wasn't *that* bad.

And it might actually feel good to talk to someone about it?
I'd been trying so hard to forget all the feelings I had for
Oliver that were swirling around inside me, making me feel
seasick. But maybe if I actually said them out loud, it might
help take some of the pressure off?

I screwed up my face as I thought about it, and Nick must
have noticed because he laughed and put his hand on my
shoulder.

"Don't worry about it," he said easily. "Forget I—"

"It's about that reunion I went to," I burst out.

"What? I thought you—you went to that? I thought you'd decided not to."

"Yeah, so did I," I said darkly. "And if I had just stuck to that plan, I wouldn't be in this mess."

"So... what changed your mind?" Nick asked.

I didn't answer immediately. This was going to sound so stupid. This whole story just made me sound like an idiot. But Nick was looking at me expectantly, and I'd already started telling him, so I couldn't very well stop here.

"A guy," I said, finally.

"Okay," Nick said.

And that was it. Nothing else—no surprise, no shock, no laughing at me and telling me how dumb that was. No reminding me that I was always getting into trouble with guys, hooking up with them and then hurting them.

Those were all the reactions I'd have given myself, but Nick just nodded and waited for me to keep talking. It was disconcerting, which made me feel kind of silly. Was I really that thrown off by *not* being judged?

And if Nick really was going to withhold judgment... maybe that meant I could actually *say* all the things I was thinking?

"It's just... so... ugh, it's just so stupid," I exploded. "It's this guy—Oliver—who I kind of—well, we had a thing in high school. And it ended badly. Really badly. And it was my fault, completely. And then we just... didn't talk for seven years, which, I mean, is also my fault, even though there's no reason he would have wanted to talk to me, not after the way I... anyway, when I heard about this reunion, I wasn't going to go because I just—I mean, I don't talk to anyone from high school, and I didn't care, but then I saw his name on the guest list, and he hadn't even replied, and he lives in California, so it's not like I thought he was coming, but then I—I kind of couldn't stop thinking about him. Like, a lot. And there have definitely been some times I've thought about him in the past—you know, the way you would about any ex, I guess. But this was different, this wasn't like, the every-few-months-you-google-him kind of thing, this was like, I couldn't stop checking the RSVP list for the stupid reunion every day, just in case his response changed. And then... well, then it did."

Oh God. That had been a lot. Probably way more than Nick had expected. It felt weirdly good to get it out, but I was sure he hadn't wanted that much detail when he'd asked.

"Sorry," I said, turning to him. "I just uh—I haven't talked about this with anyone and I—"

"No need to apologize," Nick said with a smile. "Trust me, I know what it's like, not feeling like you can talk to people about something that's important to you." He paused for a moment. "So, Oliver decided to come to the reunion?"

"Yeah," I said, sighing as I thought back on everything that had happened. "And before I knew it, I'd decided to go, too. I just wanted to apologize to him, really. I never had, for what I did back in high school, and I thought that was why I couldn't stop thinking about him. So I go, and I see him, and I try to apologize, and he basically won't even let me, because he says he's completely over it, and then he just, well, invites me back to his hotel for the night."

"Huh." Nick blinked. "So I'm guessing that's... not the response you expected?"

"Not at *all*," I complained. "And I don't know, I should have said no, right? That would have been the smart thing. But he said everything was fine between us, he said it would just be a one-night thing, and I figured—I mean, he's hot, right? And I kinda thought—I don't know, I kinda thought maybe if we hooked up, it would help me ... get him out of my system?"

I winced, waiting for Nick to laugh, but he just gave me an expectant look, like he was waiting for the next part of the story, and said, "Okay."

"Well, so, I go back there and we, you know... start... but then he kinda freaked out? In the middle of it? So I left because he definitely didn't want me there, but then I forgot my phone, and I ended up not being able to get it back from him until the next day when he was at his dad's house, and he's got some health stuff going on—his dad, not Oliver— and I thought maybe that was why he—Oliver, that is—had kind of freaked out, but then he told me that wasn't it, that he wasn't over us, and then—and then he kissed me."

Again, I waited for Nick to say something, but while his eyes widened a bit in surprise, he just nodded.

"And I... I kind of... kissed him back?" I made a face. "I know it was dumb, I know I shouldn't have, but I just felt—God, I don't know. He said he wasn't like, looking for anything to happen. I mean, he lives on the other side of the country. And I'm not either. So this should be good, right? Except now I can't stop thinking about him, and all I want to do is see him again, but I can't, because that would be such a bad idea, and I feel like I'm going crazy because I just—I can't—it's like —" God, putting this into words was excruciating "—it's like my body misses him. *I* miss him. I just, I can't help feeling— can't help wanting him. But that's dumb because it's not real. It's just because I can't have him. I mean, look at me. Look at my track record. I'm terrible with guys. And I've already hurt Oliver once. I couldn't live with myself if I did that again."

I felt completely emptied out. I crossed my arms in front of my chest as we turned up 7th Ave., partly because of the cold, but partly because I just felt... raw.

"Well, you're right," Nick said finally. "That is definitely complicated."

"I know," I said bitterly. "And I don't know what to do about it. It's entirely my fault, and anything I do next is probably going to backfire and be my fault too, and I just... I'm so fucked."

Nick gave me a considering look. "I'm guessing you've probably considered a bunch of worst-case scenarios here, right?"

"Uh, yeah." I snorted. "I don't think there's a way in which I see Oliver again that doesn't end terribly, with me hurting him."

"And if you don't see Oliver again..."

I closed my eyes for a second. Those words—the same ones that had been bouncing around my brain for the past week as I'd tried to convince myself to do just that—those words hurt.

"If I don't see Oliver again," I began. "If I don't see him again —I think that's even worse."

Nick gave me a sympathetic look.

"Except worse for whom?" I went on. "Worse for me, maybe —but is it fair to ask Oliver to see me again just to make *me* feel better?"

"Well, you can't force Oliver to do anything," Nick said reasonably. "All you can do is ask—it's still up to him if he says yes."

"Right but I still don't want to hurt—"

"I have another question, though."

"Yeah?" I asked, feeling a little mutinous. How dare Nick cut off my train of self-pity?

"What's the best-case scenario here?"

"What?"

"What's the best possible outcome?" Nick said. "And not the most likely outcome, not the thing you think is guaranteed to happen no matter how much you wish it wouldn't. You've told me about all that. But I want to know—unlikely as it might seem, scary as it might be to want it—what's the best-case scenario?"

"I don't—" I stopped myself before I could finish what I was going to say. *"I don't think there is one."* Because I didn't, but that wasn't what Nick had asked. And since he was being nice enough to even listen to me whine in the first place, the least I could do was try to answer him honestly. "I don't know."

"Okay," Nick said. "That's fair. But let's spitball here for a minute. You know not seeing Oliver again feels worse than seeing him again. So let's start there. You see him again and... what? What would you want?"

"I don't know," I said, exasperated, 99% with myself and 1% with Nick for making me realize how ridiculous I was being. "I want—I want—I just want... him."

"There we go," Nick said, his voice encouraging. "That's a step in the right direction."

"Is it?" I asked desperately "Is it, really? I don't have any clue what the fuck I want after that."

"Okay, so let's look at your options. You could see him once?"

I frowned.

"More than once?"

"But I—"

"Meet for coffee? Drinks? A seven-course dinner with wine pairing? Rip each other's clothes off immediately or keep a five-foot bubble in between you at all times? Write each other chaste and respectful letters for the rest of your lives? I'm just saying... there are lots of options."

"But none of them are realistic!" I said—okay, practically shouted, which really wasn't fair to Nick when the person I was mad at was myself. "I don't do relationships, he doesn't live here, he's not going to want to just hook up with me again, I don't want to just hook up with him again, I just— oh." I stopped short, looking around. "This is me."

How had we reached my apartment already?

Nick stopped and gave me an apologetic look. "Sorry," he said. "I didn't realize—I think I just made things worse, didn't I?"

"No. No, you..." I shook my head. "You didn't. This was—this was helpful. I'm just frustrated—with myself."

"It's easy to feel trapped," Nick said slowly. "Trust me, I've been there. Usually there is a way forward—but we can't always see it from where we stand. Sometimes we have to take the first step on faith."

"So how am I supposed to figure it out? How do I know which direction to take?"

Nick shrugged. "You don't. Not really. I think the best you can do is try to be honest—and kind. Not just with Oliver, but with yourself. Whatever step you take, if it's honest—it'll be the right direction."

"Honest, huh?" I grimaced.

Nick laughed. "I know. It kinda sucks. But it's the only thing I've ever found that works."

Nick's words rattled through my mind the rest of the day. They were there when Harvey told me to get him a report three days earlier than he'd originally asked. They were there when MacFarlane dropped by for *"help"* with a sector analysis. They were there when my phone buzzed and my stomach turned a somersault, hoping the text might be from Oliver.

It wasn't—it was from my mom, asking if I could help her out at a school fair tonight because her student teacher had called in sick. But I still couldn't stop thinking about what Nick had said.

Honest. And Kind. I wasn't sure I knew how to be both of those things—either to Oliver or myself. It was probably kinder to both of us, in the long run, to let this run its course. To resist the urge to contact him. To let it go.

But if I were being honest?

My heart in my throat, I texted my mom back, and then pulled up a new message to Oliver.

My future self was probably going to wish he could time travel back to this moment and slap the phone out of my hands, then throw it out the window for good measure.

But to be honest...

LUKE: Hey—maybe this is weird, but is there any chance we could see each other again?

OLIVER

*T*his time, it was my phone that woke me up—and, for the record, I wasn't even asleep at a desk.

Granted, that might have been because my hotel suite's desk came with the least comfortable chair on the planet, so I'd been working on my laptop in bed. And yeah, okay, so maybe I *had* fallen asleep in the middle of working around 3 a.m. last night, but I'd at least woken up around 7 and moved my laptop to one side before promptly passing out again.

That had to count for something, didn't it?

After spending the past week with my dad, doing everything I could to annoy him with my presence, I'd finally gotten him to cave and reschedule his follow-up—probably just to get me out of his hair. Annoyingly, they couldn't take him immediately, but it was better than nothing.

My dad had rather pointedly suggested that I could book my return flight to California for right after the appointment. He'd even offered to drive me to the airport himself. I had no intention of booking any flights anywhere until I knew for certain what my dad's prognosis was, but it was easier to just nod and say that sure, I'd let him know. He'd almost been in a good mood by the time I'd left his place yesterday evening—probably overjoyed at the prospect of having me gone, even though I had promised to come back for dinner tonight.

Honestly, I should have wanted to get back to San Francisco. It was silly, spending all this money to stay in a hotel just so my offers of help could be continually, gruffly refused. And it wasn't like I had any other reason to be in New York.

Right?

I didn't. I knew that, deep down. And I'd made my peace with it. Things with Luke had ended weirdly, but they'd ended. Just because he'd asked for my number didn't mean —well, anything, really. I was going back to California, one of these days, and everything would go back to normal.

I'd worked hard to get myself into that mindset, but I'd gotten there, finally.

Which was why I wasn't at all ready for the text that woke me up.

LUKE: Hey—maybe this is weird, but is there any chance we could see each other again?

Um.

What?

I stared at my phone for a solid five minutes, just trying to process what I was seeing—trying to convince myself I wasn't actually still asleep and dreaming this. Luke wanted to see me again? Now? After a whole week of having my number? He was texting me now?

And what did *"see each other"* even mean, exactly? How was I supposed to answer that question if I didn't know?

Though, to be honest—would it actually make a difference to my answer?

Groaning, I tossed my phone down on the bed and stood up, rubbing my eyes as I walked to the bathroom to brush my teeth.

I was a mess. I knew it. I clearly wasn't over Luke, which would be pathetic enough if it were just a truth I held in the silent recesses of my heart or whatever, but was like, ten million times worse now that I'd accidentally blurted it out to Luke himself. He'd said he wasn't interested. Well, fine—I wasn't interested either! Except... Well, except that my heart was dead set on making this as hard for me as possible.

Because let's be honest—it was pretty dumb to still have feelings for Luke. And what was I even interested in? None of this made sense. But I'd been content to just deal with that on my own. Time and distance would either help things heal or make them fester even more, but either way, Luke wouldn't be involved.

Except now he wanted to see me?

I couldn't deal with this on my phone. I needed reinforcements. I glanced at the time and texted Micah.

OLIVER: ALCOHOL. I NEED ALCOHOL NOW

OLIVER: *Please tell me you're working. I need panic beers and maybe someone to help me drown myself in a vat of whiskey?*

Micah, thank God, was surgically attached to his phone and responded quickly.

MICAH: Oooh

MICAH: Interesting

MICAH: Tell me more

MICAH: I thought you were with your dad all week

OLIVER: I thought so too. But he ended up breaking down and calling the doctors sooner than expected. And then...

OLIVER: Things got interesting

MICAH: Say no more

MICAH: As it happens, I'm babysitting, not working, but that just means I can drink with you instead of just watching you drink. Meet you at Maggie's in an hour?

OLIVER: Perfect

Micah sent me the address, and I ate an energy bar while I threw on fresh clothes and grabbed my jacket. It wasn't far away, so less than 15 minutes later, I was standing outside a dark-fronted building with a neon sign that said *"Maggie's"* on the door. It had a retro feel as I walked in, full of thick velvet curtains and old industrial seating, but I didn't see Micah.

Frowning, I started to pull my phone out to make sure I had the right place when one set of velvet curtains moved, and a woman walked through them and then past me, out to the street. Curious, I stepped forward and poked my head through, then stopped in surprise.

The room on the other side was much bigger—a huge, open

space that let out onto an interior courtyard, currently closed off behind sliding glass garage doors. There were potted citrus trees everywhere, strung with twinkle lights. Climbing jasmine twined along the walls and—were those *motorcycles*, hanging from the ceiling? Even though it was February, I felt like I'd stepped onto a lanai, somewhere warm and tropical.

I saw Micah waving at me from a seat at the bar—and blinked when I realized he had a baby on his lap.

"Hey!" I said as I walked over, giving him a one-armed hug. "What's with the kid?"

"Babysitting," Micah said. "I told you, didn't I?"

"Yeah," I said, shaking my head as I pulled out a stool and sat down next to him. "But I thought you were joking. Or like, babysitting some beers."

"Well, I'm doing that too," Micah said, grinning. He pushed a pint glass towards me. "Hope you like porters because that's what we're drinking until this keg kicks and I can change it out. We need to get the new IPA from a local brewery on tap before a neighborhood party thing tomorrow."

"So you're giving me reject beer?" I laughed. "Thanks."

Micah snorted. "I'm giving you *free* beer. Are you really turning it down?"

"Well when you put it like that..." I raised my glass to him in thanks and took a sip, then pointed at the baby who was currently staring at me, drooling. "So what, you're not making enough as a bar owner, you've got to babysit to make some extra cash?"

"Sadly, I do this for free," Micah grinned. "Well, also because I like hanging out with this little button." As I watched, he booped her on the nose with his finger, and she giggled. He took one of her arms and stretched it out towards me, "This is Bea. She's my friend Caro's daughter."

"Hello, Bea," I said, shaking her hand formally. "Pleased to make your acquaintance."

"She's charmed, I'm sure," Micah laughed.

"Caro..." I said, casting my mind back. "I know that name, right? She's your friend from..."

"From everything," Micah said. "Since forever. But she and her husband Chris got married last year and had Bea a few months ago. And they roped me into being one of Bea's godfathers before I realized that that honor also came saddled with weekly babysitting duties."

"*One* of her godfathers?" I asked, raising an eyebrow.

Micah gave me a dark look. "Yeah. There's another— Hunter. Chris's brother." He shuddered. "I'm pretty sure he just feeds her buffalo wings whenever he babysits, so I have to counteract his influence."

"Micah, she doesn't have teeth yet. I don't really think she's eating wings."

"Well, that just means he's probably feeding her blue cheese sauce from a spoon. I *know* he's making her watch football," Micah said mutinously. "So I'm trying to get her hooked on musical theater instead. After this, I'm taking her home to watch *Singin' in the Rain*."

"Oh, do you need to go? I asked. "I didn't mean to—"

"What I need," Micah interrupted, "is for you to tell me why you're panic drinking. It'd better be good, too. My life is way too boring right now. I need to live vicariously through someone."

I sighed. "Okay, well... it kind of starts with a confession. Remember that invitation I got? To my high school reunion?"

Micah's eyes widened. "Holy shit, you little liar. You said you weren't going to go to that—"

"I know, I know." I sighed. "I just—I kind of panicked and somehow it felt like if I told anyone I was going to the reunion, I would jinx it. Ridiculous, I know. Especially because I think I more or less jinxed it anyway."

"Oh no, I'm sorry," Micah said, looking fascinated and not the least bit sorry at all. "What happened?"

I grimaced. "Well, remember the guy I told you about?"

Micah laughed. "Your long-lost high school fling that you've obsessed about for years but you've never even told me the name of, out of some weird sense of shame or guilt? No, don't remember him at all, I've completely forgotten and lost all interest."

"Okay, cute, but also, fuck you."

"I'm kidding, Oliver. Of course I remember him, and I actually think it's really noble of you to still be like, respecting this guy's desire for discretion after all these years."

"You?" I blinked. "Applauding someone for discretion?"

"Hey, just because I have none of my own doesn't mean I can't admire it in others," Micah said with an impish grin.

"Anyway, please tell me this story involves you dragging him into the art supply closet and—sorry, Bea—fucking his brains out."

"Well..."

"Oh my God, you *did*?" Micah said, his eyes huge. "Jesus, Oliver, since when did you become so fun?"

"No, no, before you go complimenting me, it's... way more awkward than it sounds. I ran into him, and he wouldn't stop trying to apologize to me, but instead of playing it cool and walking away with my head held high, I kinda, um, invited him back to my hotel room with me?"

"Holy shit."

"Yeah, so um, we started hooking up—"

"Well, I assumed you didn't just play *Boggle* all night—"

"—but then I kinda, um, had a nervous breakdown and started crying in the middle of it—"

"No—"

"—and so I kind of had to like, stop, but then I felt bad, so I tried to blow him as like, a *mea culpa*, which I realize now was a really weird thing to do, but it seemed like a good idea at the time, except then *he* made *me* stop—"

"Jesus—"

"—so I ran into the bathroom and hid for half an hour."

"Holy shit," Micah repeated. "Really? That's—"

"Incredibly embarrassing and messed up?"

"I was gonna say... intense. How are you—how are you feeling? What happened? Did he—did you talk about it after or—"

"Oh, yeah, it gets worse. Because he was still there after I realized I needed to stop being a complete fucking lunatic, crying in my shower, but then I kinda accidentally kicked him out. Only, he left his phone with me, but by the time we got in touch, I was out on Long Island at my dad's, but then it turned out he was too, so he *came over,* and my dad more or less threatened to murder him, but then proceeded to almost kill *himself* by trying to lift something too heavy, and I kind of had another breakdown, which he—the guy, not my dad—proceeded to console me through like I was a child... and then when he was trying to leave, probably desperate to change out of the shirt I'd just gotten snot all over, I kissed him."

"You *what?*"

"Yeah." I blushed, remembering the way I'd thrown myself at Luke, basically forcing him to kiss me by hurling my lips at him. *Real fucking smooth, Oliver.* "Yeah. It was... not my finest moment."

"Did he—I mean, did he kiss you back?"

I looked down, feeling my cheeks heat up again as I thought about Luke's arms around my waist, the scratch of his stubble on my cheek, the heat of his lips on mine. "Yeah. He —he did."

"So what's the problem then?" Micah blinked. "You kissed him, he kissed you. Seems like it all—"

"He asked me if I wanted to hang out again," I blurted out.

"So? Don't you?"

"I don't know!" I looked at Micah, helplessly. "I mean, yes, kinda. I do. Obviously. But then I also don't? Because I don't know what it means? And I don't trust myself to not—well, to not start liking him again. And I can't be that guy, can I? The guy who never got over his high school crush?"

Micah gave me a long look. "Oliver, I hate to tell you this, but I don't really think you get a say in the matter. I think you've basically admitted you already *are* that guy."

That stung. But he was right.

"But what if he..."

"What if he what?"

"What if he still—what if I—" I gave Micah a plaintive look. "I don't wanna get hurt again. He's cute, and he's funny, and I wouldn't mind being his friend, maybe, or like, just hooking up—but I don't think I can do both? And I don't know what Luke wants, and I don't know how to ask without looking like an idiot, and I don't even know if I know what I want, except that I can't *fall* for him again. I won't do it."

Micah cocked his head to the side and gave me a long look.

"Did you say... Luke?"

Fuck.

Now that Luke and I were friends on Facebook, I'd spent more time than I cared to admit this week scrolling through old photos of his. Look, I wasn't proud of it, but honestly, who wouldn't do the same thing if they suddenly got the chance to see what an old—and then new again—hookup had been up to for the past seven years?

Luke was clearly out—there were pictures of him with guys hanging all over him—exes, I assumed—from years ago, and there were way too many pictures of him in tiny shorts —and not much else—at Pride parades for him to be hiding anything. And it wasn't like Micah was ever gonna meet him. But still, I was so used to keeping Luke's identity a secret—keeping everything that had happened senior year a secret—that I still felt like I'd betrayed Luke just by saying his name.

"Shit." I winced. "I didn't mean to say that. I mean, I guess it doesn't matter but—"

"Luke... Wolitzky?" Micah asked, his voice a little funny.

"Wait. What?" I blinked. "How do you—"

"Holy shit," Micah said, an exceptionally pleased-with-himself smile spreading across his face. "I can't believe I never—I thought I'd heard something about Luke having a reunion coming up, but I'd never put it together until—holy shit." He pointed a finger at me and jabbed it in the air to emphasize each word. "You. Hooked. Up. With. Luke."

"Well you don't have to sound like the Spanish Inquisition about it," I said, shifting uncomfortably.

"Sorry," Micah said, bouncing Bea on his lap. "I'm just..." He shook his head. "That's crazy. Good crazy," he added with a placating smile. "Just... I can't believe you've known him this whole time and I never knew."

"But how do *you* know him?" I asked.

"Through friends." Micah shrugged. "He's friends with these guys, Ben and Adam, who are friends with my friend Gray—the guy who owns the bar with me. And Gray's dating Tyler, Luke's brother, so it's all kind of this tangled mix. I don't know Luke super well or anything but—" he snorted "—I know him well enough for this to be very fun gossip."

"Well, keep it to yourself for now," I said, looking over my shoulder. Suddenly it felt like Luke might be here, hiding behind a potted lime tree, listening to every word I said.

"Ugh, you're no fun," Micah pouted.

"I don't have *time* to be fun, I'm too busy falling apart for that."

"Drink your beer," Micah said. "That'll help."

I rolled my eyes but followed his advice, then paused as a thought occurred to me.

"Wait, so if you know Luke..."

"Yeah?"

"Okay, not to be totally weird but... what's he—what's he like?"

"What do you mean, '*what's he like?*'" Micah asked, confused. "You know him better than I do."

"Yeah, but I only know *old* Luke. And old Luke was... I don't know, kind of a contradiction. You know what he's like *now*. Is he—" I flushed, hating myself for how pathetic I sounded. "Does he like... you know, have a lot of—fuck, that's not what I meant, I just mean, is he like... the kind of guy who... fuck, I don't know what I'm saying. Is he—"

"A player?" Micah said with a laugh, finally putting me out of my misery. "Or a dick?"

"Either?" I said helplessly. "Both?"

"He's..." Micah pursed his lips and was quiet for a moment.

"Well that's not good. If you have to take that long to think about it—"

"No, no, it's not that," Micah said. "It's just... well, take all of this with a grain of salt because like I said, I don't actually know Luke *super* well but... I do kind of get the impression that Luke is, um... popular? With other guys? And he hasn't had a serious relationship in the time I've known him. But —" Micah said, reaching out and putting a hand on my arm "—but I don't think he's a dick. I don't think he's trying to play games. Luke's a good guy. If he said he wants to see you, he wants to see you. Unless he's a total sociopath and really good at hiding it, but if that's the case, you're probably screwed no matter what."

"Ugh," I said, burying my face in my hands. "I feel so pathetic."

"Why?"

"Because I—because I care! I don't want to care. I really don't."

"Right, but..." Micah gave me a patient look. "You *do*, so..."

"What am I supposed to do?" I asked.

"Uhhh... hang out with him? Unless, of course, you don't want to. In which case... don't?"

I glared at Micah. "You make it sound so easy."

"I know," Micah said sadly. "It's an annoying habit of mine. I'd say I'm trying to work on it but... I'm not."

I sighed. "I do want to see him. That's the problem. Against my better judgment. But I don't want to get hurt again."

"Have you considered... telling him that?"

"Ugh, stop. I came here for booze and commiseration, not practical, reasonable advice."

"You haven't even finished your drink," Micah said with a significant glance at my still-mostly full beer.

"Hey, I never said I was perfect," I grumbled. "What am I supposed to say to him? 'I do want to see you again, but we have to keep things strictly platonic, or we can fuck, but then you're not allowed to be nice to me?' How do I say that without sounding insane?"

"Oliver?"

"Yeah?"

"Have you considered the fact that if everything that you said happened and Luke *still* said he wants to see you again, that maybe he likes whatever version of insanity you're serving? Because I'm pretty sure he's seen it all by now. Why don't you just say you'd like to see him, but you want to talk first and lay down some ground rules?"

"And that's not weird?"

"No. It's not." Micah laughed. "I'm not saying other parts of you aren't weird, but hey, we're all a little weird, right? All that matters is that Luke likes your flavor of it."

"I don't even know how to word it," I protested, feeling incredibly whiny.

Micah sighed. "Okay, here. Give me your phone, you take

Bea, and I'll compose the text for you. Hey, what's that look for?" he said, looking outraged. "You can still be the one who sends it. You get veto power."

Glowering, but completely unconfident in my own ability to write something passable, I put my phone on the bar and took Bea from Micah. She squirmed a little at first, but then she discovered my sleeves and happily began gumming them.

"Here, how's this?" Micah said after a moment, showing me what he'd written.

OLIVER: *Yeah, I'd like that. But could we talk first, just to sort of clear the air?*

I looked at Micah. "That's not very specific."

"No, but it lets him know you want to talk, and this way you don't have to spill your entire soul via text message."

"Good point."

I bit my lip as I thought about it. When I hadn't been in the middle of a meltdown, it had actually been fun to see Luke. Almost like—well, *old* old times, before everything went to shit.

And I couldn't deny that part of me wanted a chance to finish what we'd started the night of the reunion, and *not* lose my mind in the middle of it. If I was just careful to set some parameters, I could still walk out of this with my heart intact.

"Alright," I said, nodding. "Hit send."

***

"Dad? You home? I brought dinner!"

I walked through the front door and shut it behind me, grateful to be in out of the cold. I'd stopped to pick dinner up from a vegetarian place in town that Yelp said had great food. I'd had no idea what to order, since I wasn't all that great at eating healthily myself, so I'd just gotten one of everything.

I set the bags of food down on the coffee table and started to take off my coat. I forced myself *not* to check my phone for the twenty-millionth time that afternoon. Luke had responded to my text, saying, *"Sure!"* and then... nothing else for the rest of the day. I was doing my very best not to obsess over what that meant.

"I wasn't sure what you'd want," I continued, yelling towards the stairs since it was clear at this point my dad wasn't on the main floor. "So I figured I'd just get—wait, are you going somewhere?"

My dad had just appeared at the top of the stairs, jacket on and keys in hand.

"Oh. Oliver. What are you doing here?"

"Um, I told you I was coming for dinner?" I stared at him. "Did you seriously forget I was coming? I told you last night I'd be back."

My dad shrugged as he reached the bottom of the steps. "I don't know. I hadn't heard from you today. Figured you had other things going on."

"Dad I'm not just going to—" I stopped and took a breath. I could hear myself starting to get worked up, but that wasn't going to help anything. "Anyway, I'm here now. And I brought food. I thought it might be nice if we ate something healthy for once."

I gestured to the bags on the table. My dad looked at them suspiciously.

"What is it?"

"It's from that Lettuce Feed You place, downtown."

"So it's rabbit food?" My dad shook his head. "I appreciate the gesture, Oliver, but I'm not gonna eat that. I'll pick something up on my way home."

"Where are you going?" I asked, taking a step closer to the door.

"Bill was doing a job over at Eaton Elementary and left his toolbox in the utility room. Asked me to pick it up for him, since he's out in Paramus tonight."

"I can get it," I said, reaching out and snatching the keys from my dad's hand. "You should be taking it easy anyway."

"I don't think a five-minute car ride is gonna kill me, Oliver."

"Yeah, but getting more fast food might," I said. I marched over to the coffee table and grabbed the first container I could reach in the bag. Some kind of rice dish with broccoli and peppers, which normally wouldn't have been my first choice, but the sauce smelled amazing.

"Here," I said, depositing the container into my dad's hands. "Eat it while it's hot. I'll be back in a flash."

"This is ridiculous." My dad glared at me. "I'm not eating this. And you don't even know where—"

"I'll find it," I said as I opened the door. "And you are *too*

eating that unless you want me moving back in and super-
vising all your meals."

"You wouldn't."

"Don't test me, Dad," I said, smiling darkly at him. "Don't
test me."

I figured the school would be empty. It was dinner time on a
Friday—who would still be there? So when I saw the
parking lot half-full, I thought maybe some kind of PTA
meeting had run long. What I did not expect was for the
gym—which the utility room was connected to—to be in
complete pandemonium.

It was some kind of... something. A fair, maybe? Elementary
school had been a long time ago, and my dad had always
been too busy working to come to school events, but I had
some vague memories that things like this existed. The
whole room was filled up into booths with games, tables
with crafts, and children—very loud children—everywhere.
Even just standing in the doorway to the gym, I almost got
pelted as two kids ran past me throwing some kind of slime
at each other.

Yikes.

I worked my way around the edge of the room, trying to
avoid contact with the messiest substances I could see—
though I did get caught in an unavoidable cloud of glitter
underneath one of the basketball hoops, where a group of
kids were making... well, I wasn't sure what it was, but it
involved googly eyes, glitter, and a whole bunch of rocks.

The bleachers had been pulled down for people to sit on
and eat, and I was almost to the end of them when I heard—

But no, that couldn't be right.

What I'd heard was Luke's voice saying, "How's your alien?"

But that didn't make any sense—neither that string of words nor the fact that Luke would be here. It was probably just my subconscious, still wondering if he was going to text me again, making me hear things.

I swung around, though, curious to see if I could figure out who I'd misheard—and stopped.

Luke was standing 15 feet away, crouching down and talking to a kid—a girl with curly brown hair and a bright blue t-shirt. Luke, funnily enough, was also wearing blue, and despite the fact that his face was painted and someone had put a confusing amount of sparkly barrettes in his hair, he still looked gorgeous.

"He went back to his home planet," said the girl—if I was hearing her right, which I still wasn't entirely sure about.

"Really," Luke said, sounding riveted. "What happened?"

"I couldn't find his spaceship," the girl said. "So I put him on my nightstand so he could sleep next to me, and when I woke up in the morning, he was gone."

"Whoa, that's crazy."

Clearly there was some kind of backstory here, and even though I knew I was supposed to be going to the utility room, even though I knew it was pretty weird of me to just stop and eavesdrop, I couldn't help myself—I sat down on the second row of bleachers and listened, fascinated.

"His spaceship is invisible," the girl continued. "That's why I couldn't find it. But I figured it out later."

"Ohhh," Luke said. "That makes a lot of sense."

To him, at least. I was lost—but then again, I was the weirdo listening, uninvited, to a conversation between the guy I'd kinda-sorta hooked up with and a seven-year-old, so it wasn't like I could really complain about the lack of narrative clarity.

"Oh, hey, Neal," Luke said, turning to look at a boy who'd just come up to join them. "Caitlin and I were just talking about rocket science. What's up?"

Neal held up what looked like a foam football. "Can you teach me to throw this? My brother says he doesn't think I can."

Luke gasped as if very affronted. "Well, we'll just have to show him he's wrong. Yeah, I can try to teach you."

"Ooh, me too, me too?" the girl, Caitlin, said, tugging on Luke's sleeve.

"Sure," Luke said, smiling. "Why don't you go grab another ball from the bin over there, and then we can practice in the corner where we won't accidentally hit anyone."

Okay, well, now I *had* to sit and watch this play out because the corner Luke was referring to was the one where the utility room was located. Since there was no chance of me not looking like a creepy stalker, if Luke saw me at this point, my only option, as I saw it, was to wait for the football lesson to conclude and for them to move on.

So when Caitlin came back, holding another foam football triumphantly, Luke got to work teaching them how to throw, and I got to work watching Luke. He started by having them each throw the ball at the wall a few times, to analyze their form, he said. I knew as much about proper football throwing technique as the kids did, but according to Luke, Neal was releasing too late and Caitlin was taking her eye off the target at the last second and stepping forward with the wrong foot.

What happened next was quite possibly the most heart-warming 10 minutes of my entire life. Slowly, patiently, Luke actually made progress with both Neal and Caitlin. It was really sweet to watch him talk to them seriously, crouching down to listen to them as they asked questions, cheering for them when they hit their targets and pretending to be mortally wounded when they hit him with the ball instead.

Between working on their athletic form, and also their vocabulary, because he had to explain what "analyze your form" and "releasing" even meant, Luke helped both kids get better. And between his general hotness and the overall gentleness working with Caitlin and Neal, Luke helped *me* get perilously close to doing the one thing I'd sworn not to do.

I was *not* going to have feelings for Luke. I mean, yeah, fine, I guess I still had some residual ones. But I certainly wasn't going to develop any new ones, thank you very much.

It was almost a relief when a woman with short, dark hair called for Caitlin and Neal from across the gym and they took off running in her direction. Luke plus kids was a dangerous combination for my heart. It was way too easy to get caught up in how sweet Luke was and forget my better—-

"Oliver?"

—judgment.

Case in point, I was so far gone in la-la land that I hadn't even realized Luke had turned around, and was now staring right at me.

"Uh... hi," I said, straightening up and feeling my cheeks turn red. There was no way to pretend I'd been doing anything other than what I'd been doing, was there?

"What are you doing here?" Luke asked. He sounded surprised, but not *too* creeped out. Or he was just very good at hiding it.

"I uh—I had to—to come and get something," I said, shifting awkwardly. "For my—for my dad. I wasn't just—I mean, I was, uh, watching you. Sorry. That was... probably kind of weird. But I wasn't like, *here* for you. I know that's kind of splitting hairs when it comes to like, the finer gradations of creepiness, but I really did come here to pick something up for him, and then I saw you, and I just—"

"Oliver, Oliver, it's okay." Luke smiled and fuck me, even with a poorly drawn Yankees logo on one cheek and what was *maybe* a raccoon... with boxing gloves?... on the other, that smile was still lethal. He seemed to remember the barrettes in his hair for the first time and began removing them. "Honestly, if anyone's embarrassed here, it's me. I must look like an idiot."

"You look," I said, standing up and walking down the bleachers to the ground, "like someone who's really good with kids."

Luke shook his head. "I wouldn't say good with them. I mostly just let them make me look ridiculous."

"Well, whatever you're doing, it's working." I smiled. "And I think you do more than that, anyway. You're a pretty good teacher, from what I saw."

"Eh," Luke said. "It's just nice to concentrate on someone else's problems, for a change. It gets me out of my own head. And teaching someone how to throw a football is a lot more satisfying than turning in yet another quarterly report for my boss three days earlier than he said he needed it.

"Ick." I grimaced. "That sounds awful."

"Yeah, it's not great," Luke said. "But it's not—"

He cut off, cocking his head to the side and giving me a funny look.

"What?" I asked.

"Nothing," he said, but he grinned. "I was just remembering that I still owe you a dodgeball lesson. You distracted me pretty efficiently the last time I tried, if I remember correctly."

I flushed. He did remember correctly.

And so did I.

"Yeah, well, from what I recall, you weren't exactly complaining about that at the time."

Luke snorted. "You know, I really wasn't, was I?"

He smiled, and in spite of myself, I smiled too. And then I just stood there like that for a minute, smiling at him before I realized what an adoring idiot I looked like.

"Well," I said, clearing my throat, "I'm sure you'd have done a great job with your dodgeball lesson. You're a natural teacher."

"Maybe." Luke shrugged. "Anyway. Hi."

"Hi." God, why was my brain working so slowly? Why couldn't I think of anything else to say, anything else to do but just stare at him?

Great job not developing feelings, dumbass.

"Um, so—"

"So I—"

We both laughed.

"You go," Luke said.

"Ugh, no fair," I grumbled. Because I was really emotionally mature.

"You're the one who said he wanted to talk," Luke pointed out.

"Yeah, but it's a lot easier to say that and a lot harder to actually do it." I looked down and took a deep breath. "Okay, so um, I've been thinking about it and... Luke, I don't know. I want to see you again, I do. But I—I'm not sure I can—I mean, stuff with my dad—I don't know if—I just—I don't know if I can do, like, a whole—"

"No, no, it's fine," Luke broke in. "We can just—I mean, ball's totally in your court. If you wanna hang out, it's totally fine. But if you don't, that's fine too. It was just—it was really great to get to see you, and I just didn't want you to go back to California without—but it can be totally casual, I promise. I'll keep my hands to myself and everything, I just—"

"No, no, Luke, that's not what I—" I stopped. Fuck, what was I saying? I mean, *"hands to myself"* wasn't exactly what I wanted from Luke, but I hadn't intended to be quite so... eager about telling him that.

Way to play it cool.

I looked over my shoulder to make sure there weren't any impressionable ears around before speaking again.

"I'm not like, averse to, you know... hands... not... being to ourselves? I just—I can't—I don't wanna—I mean, I don't live here. So I don't think I can... you know... I just—keeping it... casual... would be good?"

I sounded moronic. And in addition to barely being able to string a sentence together, I'd come within milliseconds of just spilling my guts out to Luke.

I'm afraid you'll hurt me again. Because Micah's right, I'm that guy. I'm that pathetic guy whose high school ex still has the power to do that to him, and I would really, really, like the chance to leave you with a better impression of me, and God it would be good to get off with more than my own hand for once, but please, please, be careful with me, or I will break. Again.

Because that would go over well.

"Oh." Luke blinked. "Oh, yeah, no, totally. I thought—I'm sorry, I should have made that clear. That's definitely what I —yeah. That's perfect."

"Oh."

"Yeah."

"Yeah."

And now I was just staring at him again.

What the fuck was wrong with me? Luke had said exactly

what I wanted him to. Exactly what I should have expected, given what Micah had told me about him. Luke didn't date. And even if he did, he certainly wouldn't pick someone like me.

But that was fine. This was good. This was what I wanted.

"Okay," I said slowly. "Okay, then, um... great. I guess. Cool. This is... this sounds good."

"Definitely." Luke smiled. "Um, feel free to say no, but what would you say to coming over to my place for dinner on Monday? I have to work pretty much the whole weekend, but because of that, Monday might actually be a light day for me. And I promise, there would actually be food involved, it's not just a ploy to, well—" he glanced around. "You know."

I snorted. "That sounds great."

It did sound great. We'd have fun—and we'd *have fun*—and then I could leave, no strings attached.

This was perfect. Not-Oliver would be proud. All I had to do was just manage not to fuck it up, not to get too emotional or weird or, you know, have a mental breakdown.

Should be easy, right?

12

OLIVER

*L*unch was the worst.

During most of the school day, it was easy enough for Oliver to ignore the fact that he didn't have a ton of friends. Or, really, any, if you got down to it. Sure, not everyone in school was a total dick to him, but even the nicer kids had never really made overtures of friendship.

But during class, at least, it didn't matter much. He mostly just kept his head down and did his work. Sometimes there were group projects, and Oliver participated in those as much as he was asked to—but otherwise... well, the fact of the matter was that most of his classes were boring, so Oliver just kind of tuned them out. And even in those moments just before the bell rang or when the teacher's attention was somewhere else, there was always some coding problem for Oliver to turn over in his mind, or a book to read, rather than talk to his classmates.

Lunch, though... There was no avoiding the fact that Oliver didn't have friends at lunch. The tables in the cafeteria were divided up by friend group, and Oliver didn't belong to any, so finding somewhere to sit required running a gauntlet of people's cold shoulders and blank-faced stares as he approached their tables. Even the kids who were nice to him closed ranks at lunch, subtly circling tighter around their tables.

Oliver knew he shouldn't care—and he didn't, once he got home and had time to let the social pressure drain out of his system. But in the moment, when all he wanted was somewhere to sit and eat—it usually left him red-faced and incredibly uncomfortable.

So Oliver avoided the whole situation as much as possible. When the weather was nice, he ate in the courtyard wherever he could find a patch of grass to himself. Once the season turned, though, as it had now, he had to get more creative. Mondays and Wednesdays, he ate lunch in the library, piling books around him. Tuesdays and Fridays, when the library was being used for club meetings, he did independent studies with Ms. Bowman in calculus and Ms. Mayer in chemistry—not because he was that desperate to study more, but because it gave him a reason to skip the cafeteria and eat in their rooms.

But Thursdays, there was nothing for it but to brave the cafeteria and try to find some group of kids who didn't mind him sitting at their table. He always brought a book with him—more as a prop than anything else. It gave him something to focus on while he ate, and, he thought, it provided a bit of security for whoever let him sit at their table. *"I won't try to talk to you,"* the book said. *"Please ignore me."*

Today, though—today Oliver had gotten held up talking to Mr. Garcia, his English teacher, and by the time he got to the cafeteria, it was like every student had gotten there ahead of him. Oliver couldn't see a single open seat. He scanned the room carefully, holding his brown paper bag and copy of *The Stranger* in front of him like armor.

Maybe there'd be more room in the back? Oliver hated having to venture to the back of the lunchroom. Since teachers on lunch duty usually stayed up at the front of the cafeteria, it was generally acknowledged that the cool kids— and the kids who seemed to get off the most on making Oliver's life hell—sat in the back, as far from adult supervision as possible.

Oliver walked across the cafeteria slowly, looking left and right for any empty seat he might find. There was one over there with the drama kids—oh, no, nevermind. A pretty girl in a choker necklace with black lipstick had just grabbed it. Was that another seat at Tony's table? Oliver walked over, trying to appear casual, but then Tony saw him coming and casually moved his backpack onto the empty chair, the message clear.

God, Oliver hated this. Maybe he should go back to Mr. Garcia's room and pretend to have questions about *Hedda Gabler*? But no, Mr. Garcia had said something about leaving early for the day. Fuck.

But then he saw it—a lone table, in the far corner of the room, completely empty. That was weird, to say the least. It was too late in the lunch period for that to be open. And there was something tickling Oliver's memory about that table—he couldn't remember what, exactly.

He bit his lip as he studied it. Maybe someone had spilled something over there, and that was why people were avoiding it? But he needed somewhere to sit. He might as well go investigate.

He crossed the room quickly this time, threading his way through the crowd until he reached the table in question. It looked normal, smelled normal. Nothing seemed wet. Oliver couldn't for the life of him figure out why no one was sitting there, but at this point, he didn't much care. He set his book and lunch bag down on the table, slung his messenger bag off his shoulder, and began to sit—

"Luna, what the fuck do you think you're doing?"

Oliver jumped and turned at the sound of the voice behind him. Kyle Richardson was standing there, regarding him with shock and disgust—and, Oliver realized to his chagrin —amusement. Andy was there too, and what looked like half of the soccer team. The only person missing was Luke.

They all had their uniforms on, and that was when Oliver remembered why he knew this table. This was the jocks' table, and they occupied the very top of the social pyramid. It looked like they were all coming in late from some team thing, but of course, the rest of the student body had known instinctively to leave their table empty.

Not Oliver, though.

"I was just—" Oliver began, but he knew as soon as he started speaking, it was pointless.

"Just hoping you could sit with us?" Andy said with a malicious grin. "No one else wants to sit with the gay boy so you were hoping we'd take pity on you?"

It didn't even make sense, Oliver fumed as the guys swarmed around him and sat down at the table—Andy shouldering Oliver out of the way roughly. They didn't care why he was there. They were just going to insult him anyway—for shit that wasn't even logical. It wasn't worth his time to try to explain.

Oliver shouldered his bag, preparing to leave.

"Or were you here to confess your love?" Kyle said, dropping his Adidas bag with a thump on the floor as he pulled out a chair across the table from Oliver. He sat down and folded his arms behind his head, grinning widely. "Hoping if you asked nicely, we'd let you suck us off?"

Oliver stiffened, turning bright red. He hated this—hated that they talked this way, hated that it still got to him when he knew how dumb it was. He made it a policy not to dignify shit like that with a response, but he wished for once he could think of something suitably cutting to say in return. Everyone was always telling him how smart he was —teachers, anyway. Why couldn't he think faster on his feet?

Glaring, Oliver picked up his lunch and his book and turned to leave.

"No, I know what it is," Andy said. "He's looking for Luke. His boyfriend."

Oliver froze.

"Oh, shit, you're right," Kyle laughed. "It all makes sense now. Did you want to ask him to eat lunch with you? And hold your hand? And go steady?"

Oliver could barely breathe. It wasn't what they were saying, exactly. That was just more of the same dumb shit, more that he should have been able to just ignore—if they hadn't brought Luke into it.

They couldn't actually *know* how he felt about Luke. Hell, he and Luke still never even spoke in school. Besides, Oliver had had his hopeless, ill-advised crush on Luke for years, but Kyle and Andy had never said anything about it until this tutoring thing started.

No, the thing that worried Oliver was what Luke would think if he heard this. Would *Luke* think that Oliver had come over to the table looking for him? Would *Luke* think that Oliver had a crush on him? That, Oliver realized, was the one thing he couldn't handle. He had to stop this before it got worse.

"For your information," he said, whirling back around, "I was only coming over here because the table was empty. I'd literally rather starve than eat lunch with assholes like you and—"

"Ooh, touched a nerve there, huh?" Kyle said, looking disgustingly pleased with himself.

Oliver rolled his eyes.

"Oh, Luna, don't get your panties in a twist," Andy said. "Look, Luke's here now. You don't have to leave unsatisfied. You can still get down on your knees and beg him to let you sit here—"

"Or beg him for something else," Kyle added. "While you're down there."

Oliver's stomach dropped to the bottom of his shoes. Slowly, wishing to God this weren't happening, he looked over his shoulder to have his worst fears confirmed. Luke was entering the cafeteria, backpack slung over one shoulder. He wasn't in his uniform, but he was walking straight towards the rest of the team, wearing that intensely focused expression of his—one that melted into confusion as he got close and saw Oliver standing there.

"Hey, Wolitzky, your boyfriend's here," Andy said with that shit-eating grin of his.

"What?" Luke stared at the tableau before him in surprise. "What's going—"

"Luna has something very important he'd like to ask you," Kyle said.

Oliver shook his head vehemently. "No, Luke, I'm not—I thought the table was empty, I wasn't—"

"Oh, don't get shy now, Luna," Andy smirked. "Not when you're so close to getting what you want. Go on, tell Luke everything you were just telling us, about all your locker room fantasies and what you want to give him—"

"Or what you want him to give to you," Kyle added.

"I swear, I wasn't trying to—" Oliver began, but Andy cut him off again, louder this time.

"*Oh God, yes, Luke, please,*" Andy said, making his voice high and breathy, imitating Oliver as he thrust his hips forward repeatedly. "*Give it to me. Harder, harder. I need it, I need—*"

"Jesus Christ," Luke said. His voice was cold and hard. "What the fuck is wrong with you guys?"

"What's wrong with *us*?" Kyle said, his eyes wide. "Nothing. But you might want to ask Luna what—"

"Can't you fucking leave him alone?" Luke said. He glared at the entire table but saved the worst of it for Kyle and Andy. "What the fuck did he ever do to you?"

"Nothing," Andy said unrepentantly. "But not for lack of trying. I'm sure there's plenty he'd like to—"

"I can't believe it," Luke said, shaking his head in disgust. "You guys are such assholes—"

"Luke, come on, we were just jo—" Kyle began, but Luke cut him off.

"I can't believe how long it took me to realize that."

"Dude, what the fuck?" Andy said. "Since when do you give a shit? This is Luna we're talking about."

"God." Luke looked at Andy in disbelief. "You really are just a shithead, Andy, you know that? Christ, I'm so done with this."

His cold glance swept across the table from Kyle to Andy before coming to rest, finally, on Oliver. It was the first time he'd actually looked at Oliver since he'd walked over to the table. And in spite of himself, in spite of knowing how *not the time or place for this* it was, Oliver could feel tears forming behind his eyes.

Luke had stood up for him.

But Luke's glare didn't soften as he looked at Oliver. It was just as cold as it had been when he'd looked at Andy and Kyle. And despite his words, despite what he'd said, Oliver was sure, suddenly, that Luke was just as mad at him as he was at everyone else.

"Luke, I'm sorry," he said, knowing how pathetic he

sounded, hating the way his voice was cracking, but desperate to tell Luke how much this meant to him. "I didn't mean to..."

"So done," Luke said, interrupting Oliver. And with a final shake of his head, he turned and walked away.

***

Oliver watched Luke out of the corner of his eye for the rest of the day, trying to make sense of what had happened. Thank God he didn't have any classes with Andy and Kyle and the rest of those guys—after making his own exit from the cafeteria, Oliver didn't have to see them again. But Luke... Luke was in most of the same classes as Oliver, which made the afternoon particularly painful.

True, it wasn't like they talked in school, so there was nothing different about Luke's silence today. But since that afternoon in Ms. Bowman's classroom the week before, it had felt like something had shifted between the two of them. Oliver wasn't sure why, exactly, but he could have sworn he'd caught Luke staring at him sometimes.

Not today. Luke looked straight ahead in all their classes and didn't just not speak to Oliver—he didn't speak at all. Which Oliver could understand, in a way. He kept catching the edges of whispers, conversations paused hastily as he walked by, all about Luke and what had happened in the cafeteria. Which meant that, in a way, the whispers were about Oliver, too.

It wasn't like Oliver wasn't used to people talking about him. But this was the first time that those whispers hadn't felt derisive, or cruel. Just curious, and maybe a little bit stunned. That, in and of itself, was almost as disconcerting as if the whispers had been meaner.

All in all, it was a relief when the final bell rang and Oliver could go home.

He didn't know what to think. What to make of the fact that Luke had stood up for Oliver, told off his friends, finally said what should have been said years ago. If Oliver had said things like that, people would have just laughed. But when someone like Luke said it—Oliver had heard respect in those whispers, too.

But then why had Luke looked at him like that? Why had he acted so cold? Was he mad at Oliver for creating the whole situation in the first place? Did he think Oliver had done it on purpose? And what the hell was Oliver supposed to do, now?

He didn't have any answers for those questions, so he did what he always did when he was anxious or stressed—or bored, or tired, or really just had any free time, for that matter. He buried himself in code.

There was something calming, to Oliver, about immersing himself in lines of code, in white and black commands and concrete, solvable problems. Even the most complex problem in programming could be broken down into smaller, simpler units. Everything could—that was the beauty of it.

Everything had a solution if you gave your brain room to roam, twisting and turning ideas over in your mind. There was logic, there was trial and error—and sometimes, there were those sublime moments of inspiration where an answer came to you like a gift from the universe.

The world didn't make a lot of sense to Oliver. People were so needlessly cruel, and even when they weren't cruel, they were callous. Everyone said it got better after high school, and he sure as hell hoped so because at this point, high school was mostly an exercise in enduring the worst of humanity.

Well, it had been until Luke had come along. Only, now... now he didn't know what to think. So he resolved not to, doing his best to push everything with Luke out of his mind. It worked too—at least, until the doorbell rang.

That was weird. They weren't expecting anyone—at least, Oliver wasn't, and he assumed his dad wasn't because his dad wasn't home. Maybe it was just a delivery guy? Oliver slid off his bed, where he'd been flopped down and considering a particularly finicky issue in the JavaScript program he'd been writing, and loped down the stairs to check.

He opened the front door to see Luke standing on his porch.

Oliver stared at him, dumbstruck. What the hell was Luke doing there?

Oliver cocked his head to the side. "Um. Hi?"

"Hi."

Oliver waited for Luke to say something more, to explain his presence, but he didn't. He just stood there, smiling at Oliver as though it were the most normal thing in the world for him to be there right now.

"Uh... what are you doing here?" Oliver asked, aware of how rude he sounded but unable to help it.

Was Luke here to apologize? Or yell at him? Or—

"Tutoring, right?" Luke said brightly. And then he opened the screen door and marched inside.

Oliver turned to stare at him, his hand still on the doorframe. What the fuck was happening?

"I thought—I thought we weren't doing that anymore?" he said. "Ms. Bowman hasn't said anything since last week, so I think we're okay."

"Yeah, but what if you get more questions wrong?" Luke said with a laugh. "Figured I might as well come by to help you out."

And with that, he turned and started walking up the stairs towards Oliver's bedroom while Oliver just stood and gaped after him. Luke Wolitzky had come over, voluntarily, to... help him with math homework? In what world did any of that make sense?

A world that is definitely about to disappear if you don't get up there and stop being weird.

So Oliver shook his head and followed Luke up the stairs. Luke was digging through his backpack, sitting at Oliver's desk when Oliver got to his room.

Okay, then. I guess we're just... doing math.

Luke must have sat at Oliver's desk because, Oliver realized, his bed was a disaster area. Sure, Oliver might not have any trouble lying on top of a pile of laundry and textbooks while he worked, but Luke evidently had standards.

His whole room was a mess, Oliver realized. He wasn't used to having anyone over—much less someone he'd pined over for years showing up on his doorstep unexpectedly. But

Luke didn't seem to think any of this was weird, so Oliver couldn't think of anything else to do but find his own bag and rummage around for his calc notebook.

He looked back at Luke once he got the worksheet out.

"So I guess we're doing derivatives now," Oliver began. "Are you—"

He stopped when he caught a glance at Luke's worksheet— already completely filled out.

"Yeah, I did them already," Luke said with a shrug.

"Are you serious? Why did you come over, then?"

"I told you, to help you," Luke said, as though this were the most reasonable explanation in the world. "I can watch, and if you get stuck—"

"I'm not gonna get stuck." Oliver stared at Luke in incomprehension. "Are you seriously just going to sit there and watch me do math problems?"

"Do you want me to... sit and stare at the wall instead?"

"I don't want you to do anything. I didn't even invite you here!"

"Oh." Luke stiffened before Oliver's eyes. "Okay. Sorry. I thought—nevermind. I'll go."

"No, no, wait." Without thinking, Oliver reached out and grabbed Luke's arm. "Wait, sorry. That's—that came out wrong." Oliver shook his head. "I just—I don't get it."

"Don't get what?" Luke asked. But when he met Oliver's eyes, he looked like he was afraid of Oliver's answer.

Afraid! Luke, afraid of something Oliver might say, afraid of anything Oliver might do. It was ridiculous—and suddenly, Oliver found himself getting mad.

"I don't get you!" Oliver exploded. "Anything about you. Why you're failing calc when you clearly get it, why you're here right now when you don't have to be. Why you—"

He paused. Was he really going to bring this up? God, this was going to make him look so completely pathetic. But fuck, he'd already done nothing but make an ass out of himself in front of Luke. And Luke had stood up for him, even if he had looked at Oliver like he was less than nothing right after. He couldn't hate Oliver completely, could he?

And if Luke did, maybe that was for the best. Good for Oliver to really get that through his thick skull before he started fantasizing about a world in which he wasn't the butt of every joke in school, a world where he wasn't a complete pariah. A world where he and Luke were actually friends. Fuck it—he was just going to say it.

"Why did you say all of that, at lunch," Oliver began, "but then when I tried to talk to you, you just—you looked at me like—" he cut off. No, even now, he couldn't quite bring himself to say that. "You just walked away."

Luke flinched, and Oliver had the strangest experience of feeling both anger at Luke and guilt over hurting him at the same time.

"I'm just... I'm just trying to understand you, I guess," Oliver finished.

Luke looked down and was quiet for a long moment. "I'm

sorry," he said finally. "Andy and Kyle shouldn't have said that stuff. They really are assholes."

Well that didn't answer *any* of Oliver's questions, but somehow, Oliver wasn't surprised. He got the feeling Luke had no intention of actually telling him anything useful. And still, somehow, when Oliver looked at Luke, it was like something squeezed his heart, and his anger started to melt away.

Oliver sighed. "Well, yeah. But I—I appreciate what you said. I know they're your friends."

"I don't think they are anymore," Luke said softly.

And he sounded so defeated that somehow, Oliver found himself wanting to make Luke feel better, which made no sense, and yet there it was.

"I'm sure you guys can get through it," Oliver said. "It was one fight. They'll get over it."

Luke shook his head, and when he looked up, he was staring into middle distance as if he could see something there that Oliver couldn't.

"It's more than that," Luke said. "They've been—it's been a long time coming, I think. I'm not sure they ever really were my friends. I don't think—I don't think they ever really knew me. Or understood me, anyway. Or me, them."

Oliver watched Luke in fascination—in wonder. Why was Luke telling him all of this? Why would he open up to Oliver, of all people?

"What are you going to do, now?" Oliver asked.

Luke closed his eyes. "I really don't know."

Oliver's breath caught.

"I could—" No. No, Oliver wasn't really going to say this, was he? He couldn't. It was too embarrassing, too desperate sounding. But somehow, the words came out of his mouth anyway. "I could be your friend." He laughed lightly. "I mean, I'm not saying I'm in like, high demand or anything, but you know. If you wanted."

Oliver sucked in a breath of air and held it. Luke still hadn't opened his eyes, and he didn't say anything. God, Oliver had probably just made the biggest mistake of his life.

You fucking idiot. You complete fucking idiot. This is why you don't have any friends. Because you have no idea how to not be a giant weirdo, and literally any chance you ever had of getting Luke to even tolerate you, you just ruined by opening your stupid mouth.

"Sorry," Oliver said quietly. "I uh—just—nevermind. Forget I said that. That was weird. We can just do math and forget I said anything."

Luke opened his eyes, and Oliver almost fainted with relief. Luke didn't look angry, or distant, or hard. Just incredibly sad.

"Okay," Luke said.

And, Oliver, who didn't know what else to say, just nodded and looked down at his worksheet. Somehow, he felt sadder now than he ever had before about anything with Luke, or school in general. Maybe it was because he'd never let himself hope, before, that anything could change.

Oliver picked up his pencil and stared at the first problem in the set. He knew it wasn't difficult. He'd glanced over the worksheet when Ms. Bowman had handed it to him. But somehow, this afternoon, nothing made sense. He couldn't even figure out how to start the problem, which was just embarrassing.

It wasn't until the numbers began to swim before Oliver's eyes that he realized he was crying.

"Are you—shit, Oliver, are you okay?"

Out of nowhere Luke's hand was on his shoulder. Oliver looked up in shock—and then pulled his eyes away quickly. He wasn't even sure *why* he was crying—why this conversation with Luke had somehow gotten to him the way nothing else had—but he didn't want Luke to see him like this.

"Yeah, no, I'm fine," he said, turning away roughly. He wiped the sleeve of his shirt across his eyes. "I just—I think there's some dust in here or—"

"Oliver, I'm sorry, I didn't mean to—"

"No, really, it's fine," Oliver said, trying to clear the thickness in his throat, wiping at his eyes again. This was humiliating —more, even, than the scene in the cafeteria had been.

"Oh, God, I'm so sorry. I really—"

"I said I'm *fine*," Oliver snapped. He turned back and glared at Luke, not sure where this sudden anger was coming from, but more than willing to let it fill him if it meant he got to stop feeling so sad and pathetic. "I'm fine. You don't have to worry about me, and you don't have to apologize to me. You don't even *like* me. And honestly, as far as I'm concerned, you can stop pretending. Just make it easier on both of us. I don't know why you came over here, but you can just—"

And then he stopped talking.

Because Luke was kissing him.

Oliver froze. This wasn't happening. There was no way this was happening. He must have finally snapped and lost it—or maybe he'd hit his head on something and was passed out and hallucinating this whole thing. There was no way that—

No way that Luke's lips were on his, soft and strong, pressing against Oliver's. No way that Luke's hands were on Oliver's shoulders, holding onto him like he was the only thing that mattered. No way that Luke was leaning over in Oliver's desk chair, perilously close to falling on the floor, all because he wanted Oliver, because he was kissing Oliver.

There was no way that Oliver was kissing him back.

Except.

That he was.

Not sure if he was asleep or dreaming, alive or dead, Oliver leaned forward, meeting Luke halfway, his own hands going to Luke's arms, pushing ever closer, his lips moving with Luke's, his mouth opening ever so slightly to—

"Holy shit," Oliver said.

He fell off the bed with a thud.

Well, he definitely wasn't kissing Luke now, because now he was sitting on the floor, somewhat dazed, staring up at him instead. Had that really...?

"What the fuck?" Oliver whispered, scrambling up and back onto the bed.

He stared at Luke in confusion.

"Fuck, sorry, I shouldn't have—" Luke cut off, shaking his head. "I didn't mean to—I just—you were so—fuck." He ran a hand through his hair and gave Oliver a helpless look. "I just... I *do* like you, Oliver. I like you... a lot. And I know I shouldn't have kissed you, but I just couldn't stand the idea that you—fuck, I'm sorry. I'll go."

For the second time that day, Oliver grabbed Luke's hand.

"Don't."

Luke stopped, his gaze traveling from Oliver's hand to Oliver's face, his eyes the blue of a storm-tossed sea.

Oliver wanted to say something—to say everything. To tell Luke how he felt. But he was paralyzed. He didn't want Luke to go, but he still wasn't quite sure this wasn't all a dream.

It briefly flitted through his mind that maybe all of this was some kind of practical joke. Or a misunderstanding. Or something—anything—that explained what was happening instead of what Luke had said. Because that couldn't, just couldn't be real.

And so he looked at Luke, who looked at him, and time slowed down until Oliver could hear the spaces between the seconds, could feel the wild pulsing hope in the silence between every heartbeat—his, and Luke's, and the whole world's. Luke still hadn't moved. Hadn't flinched, hadn't shaken Oliver's hand off of him. Could this actually be happening?

Oliver bit his lip. He'd never kissed anyone before, but slowly, he leaned towards Luke, who leaned towards him, and Oliver stretched his neck, and Luke did too, and then all at once they met in the middle, their lips crashing together, and they were kissing again. They were kissing, Oliver was kissing Luke, and holy shit, how was this real? He felt so full of everything—nerves, disbelief, excitement, relief, but then Luke was pulling away again.

"What's wrong?" Luke asked, looking at Oliver with concern.

"What?" Oliver blinked. "Nothing."

Never in his life had anything ever been less wrong than right now.

"You're shaking."

Luke put a hand on Oliver's shoulder, and it was only then that Oliver realized he was.

"Nothing's wrong," Oliver insisted. "I just—I can't believe this is happening. This isn't—I never thought—"

"Me neither."

"And this is, it's just—it's the first time I've, uh—" Oliver blushed. "This is new to me."

"Me too," Luke said, his face breaking out in a smile.

"Yeah, but you—" Oliver shook his head, trying to make his brain work. "You were going out with Grace Tighe last year, weren't you?"

"Yeah, but things with Grace were—" Luke's cheeks flushed a rosy pink. "I don't uh, don't really think I like girls? And I've never—never done anything with—with a guy."

"I've never done anything with anyone!" Oliver said, and

then clapped a hand to his mouth as soon as he heard the words. "Oh God, forget I said that."

"No, no," Luke laughed. His hand was still on Oliver's shoulder, and he gave it a little squeeze. "It's fine. It's—I—I like it."

"I like you," Oliver blurted out. "I'm sorry, is that weird? I don't know if you're not supposed to say things like that, if you're supposed to play it cool."

Luke laughed again. "Well, I just told you that I liked you, so... I think it's okay."

"But how though?" Oliver asked. Luke looked at him in confusion. "I mean how do you—how do you like me? I thought you hated me. The way you looked at me today in the cafeteria—"

"I thought you were going to tell me how pathetic I was in front of everyone. For ever being friends with those guys," Luke said. "I thought—the things they said—I thought you were going to call me out for what a piece of shit I've been." Luke shook his head in wonder. "Maybe—*maybe*—I told myself, you might be willing to be my friend. If I could make it up to you somehow. But I never thought you'd want anything more."

"Are you insane?"

Luke squirmed. "I'm not—I mean, you're—you're you, you know?"

Oliver's jaw dropped. "Yeah. Precisely. What about me suggests that I wouldn't be into the hottest guy in school who also happens to be the one person who's nice to me?"

"The part where you're so beyond high school that you

don't even pay attention to the rest of us? The part where you don't give a shit what anyone thinks, the part where you're smarter and more principled and braver than anyone I've ever met and objectively like, a way better person than I am, and you're—you're—why are you laughing?"

"I'm not—I swear, I'm not trying—" Oliver could barely get the words out, he was laughing so hard. Giggling, really, hysterically, because it was just so absurd. "No—no offense," he gasped. "But that's the dumbest thing I've ever heard."

"What? But I—"

"Luke, I'm not a monk, you know."

"Well, yeah, but it just seemed like—I don't know, like you probably dated older guys who like, lived in the city and wanted to talk to you about French philosophy or whatever."

"French philosophy?" Oliver repeated, still giggling. "Are you serious?"

"You were carrying Camus at lunch," Luke protested.

"Luke, I just grabbed that book at random from the library on Monday," Oliver said. He gestured to his ridiculously sci-fi-filled bedroom. "Look around this room. Do I look like someone who knows anything about French philosophy?"

"I don't know," Luke said, laughing. "I just... you always seemed so, cool, you know?"

"This is actually insane." Oliver shook his head in wonder. "This can't be happening. Luke Wolitzky is not telling me I'm cool."

"Shut up, now you're just making fun of me," Luke grumbled, but he was still laughing.

"I mean, look at you—" Oliver said, gesturing up and down Luke's entire, perfect body. "You're all perfect, and you think I'm—"

But then he wasn't talking anymore, because Luke had kissed him again, and this time—this time, there was nothing hesitant about it. This time, Luke moved to the bed and sat down next to Oliver, tugging him closer. Oh God, this really was happening, and it was perfect—absolutely fucking perfect.

Oliver's hands gripped Luke's shoulders like he was drowning, and he had to fight the urge to let them roam everywhere, to touch every part of Luke he'd ever daydreamed about touching. He wanted that—more than anything—but he already felt like he was in free fall.

Luke's tongue traced along Oliver's bottom lip, and Oliver opened his mouth ever so slightly, letting Luke inside. The way Luke tasted, the way his tongue felt as it slid against Oliver's, was better than any daydream he'd ever had.

Luke tangled one hand in Oliver's hair, and Oliver had to stop himself from letting out something that sounded suspiciously like a moan. His heart began to race as they inched backwards on the bed, his breath coming in shorter bursts. Their chests were touching, and he was sure that Luke could feel his heartbeat, the way it was doing jumping jacks on a trampoline.

Oliver felt himself bump up against the headboard and gasped in surprise. How had they moved from one end of the bed to the other so quickly? He'd been so caught up in the feel of Luke, the taste of Luke—the everything of Luke, to be honest—that he hadn't even noticed. Luke leaned in further, pressing more of his body up against Oliver's and oh God, that felt way too good, that felt—

"Wait, wait, stop—" Oliver said, forcing himself to break the kiss.

He put a hand on Luke's chest to create a separation, and his fingers wanted to roam over everything they felt there. He pulled the hand away like it burned.

"I um—is it okay if we—if we take this, um, slow?" Oliver could feel his cheeks burning with embarrassment—well, embarrassment, and also desire. He didn't actually want to go slow at all, and that was what scared him. "It's not that I don't want to like—I just—I mean, I've never—"

"Oh, yeah, no, me uh—me neither," Luke said, and Oliver was relieved to see him blush, too. "I've never like—I mean, Grace and I did some—"

"You don't have to tell me. It's none of my business."

"No but I—I want you to—to know. We didn't have sex. I wasn't—I mean, I wanted to, kind of. But I think I kind of already knew that I didn't actually want to? It was more like —like I wanted to want to? Does that make any sense?"

"Yeah," Oliver said. "Yeah, no, totally."

"But we don't—" Luke scooted back on the bed a bit, making room between him and Oliver. "I didn't mean to make you think—I'm not trying to like—like, we don't have do anything."

"No, but I—" Oliver found himself blushing again. "It's not

that I *don't* want to like... do other stuff. Someday—I mean, if you still... I just—can we just do more of... this? For a while?"

"Yeah," Luke said, a smile spreading across his face—one that matched the giant, goofy grin Oliver knew he was wearing himself. "Yeah. That sounds perfect."

13

LUKE

I should have known that the mere act of making plans with Oliver meant everything was going to immediately fall apart.

The problem, honestly, was that I was looking forward to it too much. That's what jinxed it. From the moment I'd seen Oliver at Eaton Elementary, any doubts in my mind had faded. Nick had asked me what I wanted, and what I wanted was Oliver.

Granted, I still had doubts about... everything else. Which you'd think would have been put to rest after Oliver had told me he didn't want, well, anything. *I* didn't want anything. And now I didn't have to be worried about leading him on. But then why, when Oliver said that, had it felt like a punch to the stomach?

So yeah—doubts faded... and then back for round two, with a vengeance. Peachy.

But I knew I wanted to see Oliver—that much was rock solid. And it was the knowledge that I'd get to spend

Monday night with him, even if we didn't hook up at all, that helped get me through a truly hellish weekend of work.

Harvey had a trip the following weekend—hobnobbing with some of our richest clients in Jackson Hole—and he'd asked me to come along. Obviously, I wasn't going to turn that down—not when he'd hinted he'd be making the announcement about who he was naming to the VP position afterwards. Even if it meant I'd have to get up at 3 a.m. this Friday morning to catch my crack-of-dawn flight, it was worth it.

But the trip did mean we were extra slammed with work trying to prepare for it. Hence my weekend of basically living at the office. It was distracting as hell, finding myself thinking about Oliver's eyes, or his lips, or his laugh, or, well, his everything, while I was supposed to be working, but I was also pretty sure it was the only thing keeping me sane.

So naturally, it all had to come crashing down.

Monday started, the way all my bad days started now, because it had apparently been decreed in some cosmic ledger that it would ever be thus, with my juicer crapping out on me. The damn thing did this semi-regularly now—it just stopped working for a day or two, and then right when I was ready to chuck it in the trash and buy a new one, it would magically decide it felt like macerating spinach again.

But not this morning—no, because today, absolutely nothing was going right. I still hadn't figured out what was wrong with it and—surprise, surprise—I made no more progress during the 15 minutes I spent fiddling with it and yelling at it this morning, threatening to toss it in the East River with rocks tied to its shoes.

Somehow, I got the feeling it wasn't treating my threats with the seriousness that they deserved. It just sat there on the counter, cheerfully refusing to work, so I was annoyed as well as hungry as I walked to the office. And things only went downhill from there.

Tyler called when I was a few blocks away from work, which was strange. It was way earlier than anyone usually called me. I picked up, trying to squelch the thin thread of worry I felt in my stomach.

"Hey," I said, cramming the phone between my ear and my shoulder as I pulled my gloves on. The forecast was calling for below freezing temperatures tonight, and the sky was a leaden gray, blanketed with clouds. "What's up? Everything okay?"

"Yeah. No. I don't know," Tyler said. He sounded distraught. "Dad won't stop calling me. He called me five times last night—literally in the middle of the night—and he's been leaving me all these messages. He sounds drunk in most of them. And I know I'm not supposed to do anything about it, I know I'm not supposed to contact him, but I just—Luke, why won't he stop?"

"Oh, Tyler, I'm sorry," I said, slowing my pace a bit. "I'm so sorry. I wish he would stop doing that."

"Why can't he just leave me alone?" Tyler asked, his voice ragged with panic.

"I don't know," I said sadly. "It's clearly one of his problems because he's only making things worse for himself when he does this. You've been sending your lawyer all of the messages, right?"

"Yeah." Tyler sounded defeated. "Yeah, I have. I just want this to be done."

"I know," I said, feeling useless. "It will be soon. I promise. Have you told Gray?"

"Yeah, he knows. But he had to leave so early this morning for shooting that I didn't get a chance to mention the worst parts of last night to him. And I know I should let it all go, but I'm so fucking frustrated. I just hate this. I hate Dad."

"I do too," I said fiercely. "Believe me." I paused, thinking through my schedule in my head. "I've got a thing tonight, but wanna hang out tomorrow? Trash talk Dad a little?"

Tyler laughed. "Gray's off tomorrow night, so we were gonna have a date night—which honestly just means pizza and Netflix. But soon?"

"Definitely."

"What's your thing tonight?"

"Oh it's... nothing really. Just a dinner thing..."

It wasn't that I wanted to keep Oliver a secret, exactly. Hell, Oliver was the fucking tech genius who'd already made a fortune developing and selling two companies. He was the one who should be ashamed of me.

But I knew Tyler would have questions if I told him. Questions I had no idea how to answer.

"Work," Tyler pressed. Or something else?"

"No, just a friend."

"Which friend?"

"I don't know, does it matter?" I grimaced, mostly at myself for how much of an idiot I sounded like.

"Uh, it does now that you clearly don't wanna tell me who it is," Tyler said with a laugh. "Come on, who is it?"

"You don't know them."

"Luke, duh. I don't know *most* of the people you know, I've only lived in the same city as you for six months."

"Right but—"

"Wait. Wait a second." Tyler's tone grew sharp. "Is it... a boy?"

"What are you, 13? Who says that? *'A boy'*... You sound like you're in middle school."

"And you sound like you're avoiding the question. Which means I'm right."

"It's not—it's just—ugh," I said, exasperated.

"I'm so right. You don't even have to say anything. I know I am."

"Well if I don't have to say anything, I'm ending this phone call. You sound in better spirits, at least."

"Yeah, intrigue does that to me."

"You're impossible."

"It's my job as your little brother. Have fun tonight. With your *boy*."

Tyler said it all sing-song-y, in a way that pretty much begged for at least an eye-roll, if not something stronger, only I couldn't exactly project that through the phone, so I settled for a growled thanks and let him hang up.

It was a small price to pay for cheering him up, I supposed. Mildly annoyed at Tyler, medium-annoyed at myself for being such a terrible liar, and extremely annoyed at my father, I walked into the office.

Harvey called me into his office before I'd even gotten my coat off, which was strange. Harvey was hardly ever in the office before 10 a.m., and it was barely 8:05.

"Hey," I said, poking my head into Harvey's office. "You wanted to see me?"

"Yeah," Harvey said, glancing up from his computer. "I need you to redo these reports." He gestured to a stack of papers on his desk. "They're not at the quality level we need."

Fuck. Heart sinking, I stepped forward and picked them up. What had I done wrong? Harvey had never taken issue with my work before, and this close to the promotion, it wasn't a good sign that—

"Wait." I blinked as I shuffled through the papers. "These are MacFarlane's."

"I know," Harvey said, his attention already back on his computer screen. "But he's not in right now, and I need them fixed by tomorrow."

"Where is he?" I asked, realizing too late how accusatory that sounded.

Harvey narrowed his eyes. "He's not here."

Which wasn't an answer—it was a rebuke. But there wasn't

anything I could do except take the reports back to my office and get to work. So I did.

I supposed I should be grateful I even had my own office— no one did, aside from Harvey, MacFarlane, and me. Harvey claimed that as a smaller hedge fund, an open floor plan would keep us cutting edge and foster innovation. Privately, I thought he'd just been too cheap to pay for the build-out. Though, to be honest, I might have forgone the private office if it meant my overall work life were more pleasant.

Don't think about it. Just do the work and don't think about it. Dwelling on it isn't going to make it any better, but getting it done might.

I decided to do my own work first, which I had enough of already, just to make sure it was done right. But I got called into a conference call at 10 and a last-minute meeting at 11, so by the time lunch came around, I had to keep working and didn't have time to run out and get something. I had to raid my stash of dried fruit and nuts that I kept in my desk drawer for emergencies.

It wasn't that it was unhealthy—I kept them there precisely because they were. But I could practically feel the lack of green nutrients in my body, and I couldn't help worrying that I was going to get sick. I *hated* getting sick. And I was already exhausted. Was that a tickle I felt in the back of my throat?

I decided to try to combat the exhaustion with coffee from the office kitchen—only I'd cut out caffeine a year ago in an effort to reduce my physical dependencies on stimulants, so the coffee had me wired. Fair enough, I figured. Maybe I'd at least have the energy I needed to tackle MacFarlane's reports. Steeling myself, I pulled them to the center of my desk.

And almost broke down crying.

They were even worse than I'd realized this morning. I'd always known MacFarlane wasn't very good at his job, but since I usually ended up doing his work *for* him, I'd never actually seen how truly incompetent he was on his own until now.

He clearly had no idea what he was doing. No wonder Harvey was asking me to redo this—as they were, the reports were useless. Only, they were for sectors I didn't cover, and there was no possible way I could get up to speed on everything before close of business.

Even if I worked late, I wasn't sure I'd get them done before morning. And I couldn't work late, because I was supposed to have Oliver over. Not just supposed to—wanted to. I shouldn't have had to give that up.

My personal phone buzzed, and my stomach turned a somersault. What if it *was* Oliver? What if thinking about him had somehow manifested him, and now Oliver was calling to cancel on me or something, in some kind of karmic retribution? I picked up my phone, preparing for disappointment.

But it wasn't Oliver.

It was worse.

DAD: Luke, I need to talk to you and Tyler. This is getting ridiculous. You can't shut me out. We can resolve this like adults.

Great. Because I didn't feel shitty enough yet today. Apparently my dad was back on the *"pretend I have my shit together and am not a lying sleazeball"* train, so he was trying to reason with me instead of just calling me an ungrateful disappointment and a liar. Good to know.

Angrily, I forwarded the message to Tyler's lawyer, slammed my phone down, and glared down at my computer. This fucking day. Why couldn't it just be over? It was already 2 p.m.

But then again, MacFarlane's reports still weren't done, and what I actually needed was to stop time so I could work on them for longer. So, feeling jittery from the coffee, worried I was getting sick, antsy because I'd only gotten to run three miles today due to unexpected construction along my route, and angry at the world in general, I got back to work.

By 3 p.m., though, it was clear I wasn't going to finish by the end of the day. I mean, it had already been clear, but I'd kept at it, hoping somehow I'd been wrong, that maybe I'd turn out to be a fucking genius who just magically knew everything there was to know about the fucking commercial fishing industry and the various other sectors MacFarlane covered.

Uh, spoiler alert: I didn't.

Feeling only like, 64% sure I was about to vomit, I forced myself to take a deep breath, stand up, and go talk to Harvey.

"Hey, uh, Harvey? Do you have a second?" I asked, knocking on his door and already kicking myself for how deferential and scared I sounded.

Don't get me wrong—I *was* deferential and scared. But I didn't want to sound it.

"What?" Harvey barked, his eyes glued to his computer, per usual. Sometimes I wondered if he was actually looking at work when he did that, or if he just did it to make me feel off-balance.

"I've been looking at MacFarlane's reports," I said. "And I—I'm not sure I'm going to be able to get them done by tomorrow."

"Not sure?" Harvey repeated. He finally moved his eyes from his screen to my face, and I immediately wished he hadn't. "What does that mean? Either you can or you can't."

"I can't," I forced myself to say. "I just—there's too much background work, this isn't my area. At best, I can get you an overview by like, 6 or 7 tonight, but I just can't—"

"Luke, I didn't hire you to make excuses, I hired you to do your job."

"With all due respect, sir, this isn't my job, it's MacFarlane's. I *do* do my job, but you didn't hire me to do two people's."

Harvey just stared at me, and I could feel my face turn bright red. Why the fuck had I said that?

"I mean, I can still—" I stumbled. "I'll try. But I'm just—"

Harvey cleared his throat, and the sound alone was enough to shut me up.

"Luke, I'm not going to lie, I'm a little disappointed to hear that attitude coming from you. A vice president doesn't come to me with excuses—he finds a way to get things done.

Now, you can only do your best, of course. But I have to say, I expected more out of you."

I didn't say anything stupid in response to that. In response to that, I just gaped at him, my mouth open in a silent "o," like a fish.

"Close the door on your way out, would you?" Harvey said. "I'm expecting a phone call."

I walked back to my office feeling worse than before—and my throat definitely felt funny. Why hadn't I laid up a supply of vitamin C pills along with the rest of my stash?

What the hell was I supposed to do now? This was going to take forever. Should I cancel on Oliver? I didn't want to, and on top of that, I wasn't sure it would make a difference even if I spent the night at the office. The fact was, this wasn't my brief, these weren't my reports, and it wasn't reasonable to expect me to be able to get them to Harvey by tomorrow.

A vice president doesn't make excuses.

Well fuck that—a vice president was still allowed to have a personal life, wasn't he? I worked all the time. Harvey knew that. At this point, I was beginning to wonder if he was just stringing me along for some sadistic reason of his own, giving me crazier and crazier assignments just to see what would break me.

Tough luck, Harvey. It's not going to be this.

I'd just leaned forward and peered at my computer screen, trying to remember where I'd left off when my office phone rang. It wasn't a number I recognized, but that was normal enough. It was a little weird that the caller ID didn't say who it was registered to, but then again, some of our clients had unlisted numbers. Some of our wealthiest clients probably had their own area codes.

I picked up the receiver, trying to squelch the frustration in my voice—whatever I was feeling, it wasn't our client's fault.

"Luke Wolitzky, Mortimer Bancroft.

"Luke, we need to talk."

Fuck.

It was my dad.

"Dad, I really can't—"

"Don't hang up. Don't hang up," my dad said quickly. "Just— just hear me out."

"Dad, no, I can't—I can't talk to you. This is my work number. And I know Tyler's lawyer says we're not supposed to talk to you, and I'm *sure* your lawyer's told you the same thing."

"I don't care about what some nerd in a bad suit says, you're my sons," my dad said belligerently. "I can talk to you whenever I want."

"Oh, so now I'm your son? After you took my brother away, put our mother through hell, and abandoned the family entirely?"

Oh, and stole millions of dollars from Tyler for over 12 years?

But I didn't say that. I wanted to, and I had to physically bite my tongue until I tasted blood, but I didn't say it. I didn't want to say anything that would prolong this phone call—or give my dad any kind of ammunition.

For once in my life, I wished I cared a little bit less about being perfect. Unfortunately, my dad seemed to take my silence as permission to keep speaking.

"Listen, Luke, you have to tell Tyler to talk to me. I know we can work this out."

"I'm not going to do that," I said, shaking my head even though I knew he couldn't see it.

God, I was so angry, I could feel it flooding my body. He was not actually saying this all, was he? My dad couldn't really think something like this could just get *"worked out."*

"Luke, we're family."

I snorted.

"What? We are."

"Right. Sure," I said, working hard to keep my voice even. "Sure, we're family. But that's still not happening."

"Don't you take that tone with me," my dad said.

So much for keeping my voice even. But you know what? Fuck it. Why bother, honestly? My dad was an asshole, through and through. Why even bother?

"Um, I'm sorry, I don't think *you* get to take *that tone* with *me*," I shot back, quivering with rage. "You lost the right to call me family when you abandoned me and Mom. When you made her life hell with the divorce. And you never fucking *had* the right to do what you did to Tyler. So no, we're not family. We're complete strangers who you've lied to and defrauded, who you just happen to share some DNA with."

"Oh don't you get self-righteous with me," my dad spat. "Everything I did was for Tyler's own good. You think you're so much better? What do you do all day? Move rich pricks' money around for them. Don't act like you're so pure. I was taking care of my family. What the fuck are you doing?"

"You weren't taking care of your family, you were stealing from them."

I drew a shuddering breath. I had to stop. I wasn't supposed to be talking to him, and this was why—it was impossible to be rational, to not get emotional, if I did. When I thought about what he'd done to Tyler—what he'd done to all of us.

"This conversation is over," I said, drawing another long breath. "Goodbye."

I hung up before he had a chance to respond.

I felt completely drained. My heart was beating 10 million miles an hour, and I hadn't even moved from my desk, but I felt like I'd just run a marathon. So much for not getting my full workout in. Jesus.

Why had I picked up? Okay, well, I knew why, but why hadn't I hung up immediately? Why had I let my dad suck me into conversation?

I tried to run through the conversation in my mind. Had I said anything problematic? I hadn't accused him of anything that we hadn't already accused him of formally in the suit. But still, I knew Tyler's lawyer wasn't going to be happy.

Ugh, today was such a shit show.

And now I was left with two options—continue to dwell on this situation with my father—not just the phone call, but the fact that he'd been harassing Tyler, the fact that I couldn't protect Tyler—or I could buckle down and... do work that wasn't mine, on a task that was basically impossible.

I glanced up at the clock on my wall. Still only 3:30. I had to keep working. There was no other option, not really.

Except by 5 p.m., I wasn't done. I wasn't done by 6 p.m. either. Or by 7. And at that point, I had to make a decision. Call Oliver and cancel—or accept that this wasn't happening.

Maybe I should make one more pitch to Harvey. Show him my work so far and explain that I wasn't going to get it done, not tonight, not by 8 o'clock, which was when I was supposed to meet Oliver back at my apartment.

Maybe I could do dinner with Oliver and then—ugh—go back to the office? Or at least set myself up with my laptop at home for the rest of the night? Which pretty much precluded the possibility of Oliver staying over, which yeah, wasn't necessarily going to happen anyway, but this would guarantee that it wouldn't.

I hated the thought of having my night with Oliver colored with the dread of going back to work after. But if I wanted to impress Harvey...

I stood up and stepped out into the hall. The walk back to Harvey's office was slow—I was not looking forward to this conversation. I stopped a few feet away from his door, breathed deep, and then walked the final distance, sticking my head into his office.

It was empty.

Where the hell was Harvey? It wasn't like he wasn't allowed to leave early—he did most of the time, actually. But if getting these reports was so important, even if he wasn't going to work on them himself, couldn't he have, you know, stayed and actually *acted* like he cared?

"Goddammit," I muttered.

"Luke? You okay?"

I turned around to see Sandra, Harvey's assistant, come walking down the hall from the bathrooms. She gave me a concerned look as she picked her coat up from the back of her chair and pulled it on.

"Yeah, no, I'm fine," I said. "I just—"

"You're here late," Sandra said as she pulled her purse out from under her desk. "Harvey left hours ago. Why are you still here?"

"Harvey what?"

"Yeah." Sandra nodded. "He had a 4 p.m. tee time with Gerlach from Goldman-Sachs, and then I think he had something at the Met tonight."

"He—he left to go golf?"

Sandra gave me a concerned look. "You sure everything's okay? I can call him, if you need him to—"

"No, no, don't—don't do that," I said quickly. "It's—it's fine. Thanks. Good night, Sandra."

For the second time that day, I walked back to my office feeling more discouraged than I had when I'd left it. Harvey had left. To go play *golf*. While I sat here and sweated over—fucking hell.

I'd put up with a lot of shit at this job—shit that was probably worse than this, actually—but for some reason, today —I just couldn't. I grabbed my coat, shoved my laptop into my briefcase, and stalked out of the office. Fuck it.

My self-righteous anger carried me all the way home, even with the nagging voice in the back of my mind telling me I'd better set my alarm for 3 a.m. this morning to get up and get some more work in before Harvey arrived in the morning.

That was a problem for Tomorrow-Luke. Today-Luke was done with that. I coughed to clear a scratch in my throat and pushed open the door to my apartment building.

I was still fuming when I got into my apartment, so when my gaze fell on my juicer, I pounced. I knew I needed to run out to the store. Pick up ingredients for the zucchini noodle and quinoa stir-fry I was planning on cooking. I knew I needed to shower because even if I hadn't gotten an evening workout in, I wanted to wash all the ick of the day off of me. And I knew I needed to find some way to decompress and not have all of this shit swirling around in my head when Oliver got here.

But the sight of the juicer taunting me from the kitchen was enough to make my blood boil, and dammit, I was going to fix it before I did anything else.

I set my briefcase down in its usual spot next to the door with slightly more force than necessary, hung my coat up in the closet with a vengeance, and stomped over to the kitchen, pulling the juicer out of the sink where I'd left it. Somehow, some way, the juicer was refusing to grate, pulse, grind... whatever. And I was going to figure out what was wrong.

Glaring at it, I pulled the machine apart piece by piece. I washed each component thoroughly, by hand, and inspected them for damage. I knew I was taking up time I needed for other chores, but dammit—I was going to figure this out. Painstakingly, I put it back together, plugged it back in, and turned it on.

Nothing.

Goddammit, this juicer was *going to work*. Nothing else in my life was working today, but so help me, I was going to fix this juicer or die trying. I growled and dismantled the thing again, this time finding a spare toothbrush and scrubbing at all the tiny nooks and grooves of the machinery until they shined. I was sweating by the time I was done—and definitely in need of a shower—but please, God, let this thing work when I put it back together and pressed...

"Fuck! You!" I shouted at the juicer when it failed to work yet again. "You are Going. To. Work. I have cleaned you too many times for you not to fucking work."

I grabbed a handful of kale from the refrigerator and shoved it into the juicer before jamming the power button again.

"Work, goddammit!"

And—miracle of miracles—I heard a faint stirring in the juicer's motor. It wasn't working—no, far from that. But it was making noise, at least. It hadn't done that the past few times I'd tried.

"Come on," I pleaded with it, wiggling the kale at the top of its spout. "Come on, you can do this."

I pressed the power button and heard the motor again—stronger this time—but still, nothing moved.

"Please," I begged it, aware of how insane I sounded now, pleading with a piece of machinery like it had the power to save my soul. "Please. Just work. I just—I need you to work."

I pushed the power button again—and the juicer exploded.

With a loud pop, fragments of plastic, chunks of metal, and macerated splashes of kale flew out from under my hands, clattering, clunking, and splatting against the walls and cabinets.

"Fucking hell," I cried, slamming my hand down on the counter before slowly sinking to the floor, balling my fists up and shoving them against my eyes. "Fuck my life."

"Luke?"

My head snapped up in confusion at the sound of Oliver's voice. There was no way he could be—it wasn't—my gaze darted to the wall. Fuck. It was 8 p.m.

"Are you—is anyone home?" Oliver's voice called again. "The door's open, so I—"

"I'm um—I'm in the kitchen?"

It sounded like a question, the way I said it, which felt fitting since I was no longer sure of anything today. My ability to fix a juicer. My ability to do my job, or be a good brother. My ability to not be a complete failure as a human being. With any luck, the juicer explosion had knocked me out, and I was currently talking to a figment of my imagination.

But no—I heard my apartment door close, then heard foot-steps crossing the floor in the living room, and then Oliver's head appeared around the corner of the peninsula that separated the kitchen from the rest of the apartment.

"Jesus, what happened?" Oliver said, looking at me in surprise. "Are you bleeding? Fuck, your face is all—"

He stopped talking and gave me a worried look. He was so beautiful. Long and lean, his dark hair peeking out from under a hat, his eyes bright, his lips so—fuck, I wanted to kiss him. Had he always been this beautiful?

Yeah. Yeah, he has. You're just the fucking moron who ruined every chance you ever had with him.

"I'm fine," I said, trying to wave away his concern. "It was just—my juicer is—"

I stopped when I caught sight of my hands for the first time. Amid the thin coating of green kale remnants, there were splashes of red. Fuck. I must have cut myself on something, when the juicer exploded.

Oliver bent down and peered at my face. Some kind of warm shiver rushed through my body—I hoped it was from Oliver and not from blood loss.

"Oh God, you *are* bleeding." Oliver looked at me in dismay. "Luke, what happened? Are you sure you're okay?"

"It's just my hands," I said, holding them out for him to inspect. "I must have gotten it on my face when I—" *When I lost my mind over a damn juicer.* "Really, I'm sure it looks worse than it is."

"Why do I get the impression you'd say that even if you were dying?" Oliver arched an eyebrow doubtfully.

"Clearly because you don't trust me enough." I laughed—

and then stopped awkwardly. Oliver had plenty of reason not to trust me, actually. And yet, here he was, crouched down on the floor of my kitchen, worried about me anyway. "I really am glad to see you. You're the only good thing that's happened all day."

"What happened with your day?" Oliver asked, his eyes concerned.

"Ugh, what didn't?" I glanced around my kitchen despairingly. Not only was everything a mess, I still hadn't showered, hadn't gone to the store—hadn't done anything to actually prepare for Oliver's arrival. "Sorry, you don't want to hear about that. Just give me a second, and I can get cleaned up and—"

"Luke, Luke," Oliver said, leaning forward and putting his hand on my knee to keep me from rising. "It's okay. I'd love to hear about your day, if you wanna talk about it. But we don't have to do anything if it's gonna stress you out more."

"Yeah, but you came all the way over here, and I really wanted to make you something nice, and I haven't gotten anything ready, and I might have to go back to the office, and I don't wanna ruin your night—our night—and I just —" something caught in my throat. I hadn't realized just how frayed I felt until that moment. "I'm sorry. I'm kind of a mess."

"You," Oliver said, leaning forward and glaring at me, "are perfect."

The words caught me off-guard, and I looked up at Oliver in surprise. I caught the tail end of a smile as it slid off Oliver's face. His cheeks turned pink, as if he'd just realized what he'd said. And we just stared at each other, quiet for a moment, as though the whole world had stopped. Three tiny words, completely innocuous, said by accident. And somehow, it felt like the fate of the world hung on what happened next.

No, I wanted to say to Oliver. *I'm not. But you are.*

But I couldn't say that. True though it felt, it also felt too important, too weighty, to toss off like that. Saying those words would cross a line that I wasn't sure could be uncrossed. And as much as part of me wanted to hurl myself across it with abandon, another part of me urged caution.

"I mean—my point is, you don't have to worry about anything," Oliver said abruptly, clearing his throat. He stood up, his long legs unfolding, but pressed down on my knee again when I started to get to my feet. "Stay there. First things first, we'll get you cleaned up. Then we'll figure out what to do about dinner."

Oliver walked over to the sink while I sat there, somewhat bemused by what was happening. I could hear Oliver run some water, and then he was back, a damp paper towel in his hand.

"No, let me," he said when I tried to reach out and grab it.

I rolled my eyes but complied, letting Oliver dab my face clean. I felt ridiculous, but it was kind of sweet, I had to admit, how focused Oliver was on being gentle. Honestly, though, I wasn't going to complain about a chance to be this close to him.

When Oliver finished with my face, he moved on to cleaning up my hands, then gave me a fresh paper towel and instructed me to squeeze it until the bleeding stopped.

"I feel like an invalid," I grumbled. At least he had finally let me stand up, though he wouldn't let me help clean up the juicer explosion.

"Humor me," Oliver laughed. "My dad still refuses to admit he just had a heart attack and won't let me help him with anything. Please, just let me be useful."

So I did. I perched on the one clean patch of counter and regaled Oliver with the saga of my juicer while he wiped down all the surfaces, gathered up the juicer parts, and generally got my kitchen to stop looking like the site of some kind of alien slime experiment gone awry.

And what was weird about it, I realized, was how not weird it felt at all. I mean, sure, I hadn't exactly wanted Oliver to see me when I felt like such a mess, but it felt surprisingly natural, having him here in my kitchen, talking about stupid stuff like juicer warranties and where I kept my sponges.

I could get used to this.

The thought came out of nowhere and knocked me completely off-balance. I'd never thought that about anyone. And besides, Oliver *didn't* live here, so, no, I couldn't get used to this. What was wrong with me? Maybe I'd lost more blood than I thought.

"There, all done," Oliver said finally. "And I might even be able to take a crack at that juicer, later. I think it might be a circuitry problem." He hung up the dish towel and turned to smile at me, but I must have still been staring, stricken, because his smile turned to a frown after a moment. "What? What's wrong?"

"N-nothing," I said, shaking my head and trying to clear it.

"Just still feeling a little guilty you cleaned my whole kitchen while I just stood around and watched."

"It really wasn't that bad," Oliver said, laughing. "But sure, if you want to feel like you owe me, go for it."

"Well, I can start making up for it with dinner," I said with a smile. "Do you have any dietary restrictions I should know about before I run out to the store?"

"Dietary restrictions? You really know how to sweet-talk a guy," Oliver snorted. He gave me a considering look. "Do you really have to go back to work after this?"

My heart sank. For a few minutes there, I'd actually forgotten about work, about my shitty day, about everything except how badly I wanted to press Oliver up against the counter and kiss him.

I sighed. "Yeah. Probably. I mean, I guess I could just work from my laptop here, but I might be more—"

"Then that's what you should do," Oliver said decisively. "And we can just get takeout. Faster, less stressful, you know?"

"Takeout?" I blinked.

Oliver laughed. "Yeah. You have heard of the concept, yes?"

"Yeah, but I—I mean, I wanted to do something nice for you."

"*This* is nice, Luke."

"Cleaning up my juicer and bandaging my wounds?"

"Yes," Oliver said. He smiled. "I promise. I'm having a good time, and I'll have an even better one if I know you're not stressing out. So come on. Wanna see what glories Seamless has for us? Or are you more of a GrubHub guy?"

"I—I um—" I flushed. "I've actually never used either of those?"

"Really?" Oliver blinked. "What do you do for takeout? UberEats? Don't tell me you still use old-fashioned paper menus and actually talk to a human being on the phone to order. This isn't the Dark Ages, Luke. You never have to interact with another human being—or even leave your apartment—if you don't want to."

"Yeah, no, I know, I just..." I snorted. "I don't know, takeout never seems all that healthy, so I just... I kinda tend to make my own food."

"Are you one of those real adults who cooks and every-thing?" Oliver gave me a horrified look. "I might need to rethink this entire *'let's see each other again'* thing."

"I mean, I don't cook *all* the time. A lot of what I eat is actu-ally raw."

"Oh my God, this just gets worse and worse," Oliver groaned. "Raw? Luke, what do you actually eat?"

"I don't know," I said, shrugging uncomfortably. "A lot of juices. Smoothies with protein powder. Fruit, nuts. Home-made jerky, that kind of thing."

"Homemade jerky?" Oliver stared at me, aghast.

"It's not that weird," I protested. "I got this dehydrator thing, and you can use it to dry almost any food, and the jerky you can get at a store is always pumped full of additives—you wouldn't believe the amount of sugar in it—so it just seemed easier to—"

"That's it," Oliver said. "We're ordering the greasiest, sauciest, most unhealthy option we can find." He shook his head at me despairingly. "It's no wonder you lost your mind today if you've been living on a diet of nothing but kale."

"It's not just kale," I said defensively. Oliver raised an eyebrow at me. "It's not! I add like, beets and stuff, too."

"Oh my God." Oliver buried his face in his hands. "What am I going to do with you?"

What he was going to do with me, it turned out, was order half of the entire menu of a Chinese restaurant that I'd apparently lived around the corner from for a whole year without ever patronizing. And I had to admit, as we sat on my couch half an hour later and ate egg rolls, pan-fried dumplings, crab rangoon, sweet and sour chicken, and a bunch of little donuts covered in sugar, that it was delicious —even if I thought my body might go into shock from the amount of salt and the utter lack of leafy greens.

"You'll be fine," Oliver said, popping another donut into his mouth. "I mean, I suppose I can't endorse eating like this *all* the time, but you gotta live a little."

"Says you. My body is a finely tuned machine, I'll have you know, and if it doesn't get its daily servings of fruits and vegetables, terrible things could happen. I already have a sore throat."

"Here, eat this," Oliver said, dipping a donut into some sweet and sour sauce that was swimming around with leftover chicken in one carton. He held it out to me, dripping. "It'll help."

"That is the single most disgusting thing I've ever seen." I eyed it with misgiving. "It could kill me on the spot."

"No, I'm serious," Oliver laughed. "Look, it's sweet and sour sauce, right? So that's like, fruit. Then there's probably some kind of dairy in the donut, plus grains. That's three food groups right there. There's probably little chicken enzymes floating around in the sauce by now, so that's four. And look —I think that orange speck is a tiny piece of carrot. That's five food groups in one bite. How can you say no to that?"

"With shocking ease," I said, shaking my head. "I'm not letting that monstrous concoction anywhere near me."

"Suit yourself," Oliver said, popping it into his mouth and licking his fingers. "You have no idea what you're missing out on."

"Somehow I think I'll survive."

"What if you *are* getting sick and that was the one thing that could have cured you? Huh? And you're lying there on your deathbed, breathing your last breaths, wishing you'd just listened to my advice so many months ago."

"I don't think I want to live in a world where eating something like that keeps me from dying," I said. "Besides, I'm pretty sure food like that just gives you a heart attack, so—"

I cut myself off abruptly. Fuck, I hadn't been thinking at all. I winced at Oliver.

"Shit, sorry," I said. "I didn't mean—I wasn't thinking."

"No, it's fine." Oliver gave me a weak smile. "Honestly, you're right. Eating this kind of food all the time is pretty disgusting. And things with my dad are still... what they are. But you're fine. "

"Do you wanna talk about it?" I asked. "About—you know, how things are going with him?"

Oliver paused for a second, wrinkling his face in thought before shaking his head.

"You know? No, I don't think I do." He smiled again, and this time it reached his eyes. "Tell me about your day. "

"I meant it when I said you didn't want to hear about it. It's incredibly boring, and it's gonna sound so self-indulgent. My problems aren't like, real problems."

"They're real to you." Oliver leaned back against the end of the couch and pulled a pillow across his lap, then stretched his legs out so his feet almost reached me as I sat cross-legged on the other end. "I wanna hear about them."

"You think that now. But I promise. A lot of it's work stuff. Most people fall asleep when I talk about work."

"Try me."

So, I did.

I told him about the promotion, about the Jackson Hole trip, about MacFarlane, and Harvey, and the ridiculous assignment, and my dad's phone call and everything that was going on with Tyler. And somehow, Oliver actually seemed interested, and asked questions, and laughed.

He slouched down a little further on the couch, and I found myself wanting to pick up Oliver's feet and put them in my lap, which was strange. I didn't consider myself an overly affectionate person—outside of sex, that was. But that was always in the bedroom, and whenever sex was over, I wasn't really a big cuddler.

But here Oliver was, and suddenly I just wanted to be touching him, any part of him—just wanted the warm, comforting weight of Oliver's body on my own.

Jesus, get a grip.

"Your boss sounds like a complete asshole," Oliver said with a serious look when I was finally done. "I mean, that MacFarlane guy does too, but your boss is the one enabling his behavior."

"It's not that bad," I said. "I mean, from a business perspective, he's stuck with MacFarlane, but he knows he can get more work out of me. It's just the practical thing to do."

"It *is* that bad," Oliver disagreed. "Not only is it just a shitty thing to do to you, it's dumb in the long run because that kind of treatment is what makes people quit." He shook his head. "I wouldn't put up with it, anyway."

I snorted. "True, but you work for yourself. Some of us have to work for other people."

"But you can still choose *who* you work for."

"Anywhere else I go could be just as bad." I shrugged. "I don't know. Finance kinda sucks, but that's just how it is. It's a shitty job, so they pay you well to do it because no one would otherwise."

"Yeah, but if you hate it—" Oliver stopped, then shook his head repentantly. "Sorry, it's not my place to tell you what you should be doing with your life."

I laughed. "I don't know, maybe it is. You seem happy, at least. Maybe I should listen to you."

"You're not happy?"

He asked it so casually, and I'd already opened my mouth to speak before I realized I had no idea what to say. *Was* I happy? How could you even tell? I mean, sure, some things could be better. And yeah, maybe, all other things being equal, I could be happier, but...

My problems weren't all that big, in the grand scheme of things. It seemed a little selfish to complain. I had no one to blame but myself for where I was anyway. Besides, I had to do *something* to make money.

"I'm not really sure," I said, finally. "I mean, is anyone?"

Oliver shrugged. "I don't know about anyone else. But I think we can all try to be, right? That's the only thing we can control anyway—our decisions, our actions."

"But not all of us can be brilliant and talented multi-million-aire geniuses like you," I said with a laugh. "Selling companies and winning 'Young Developer of the Year' awards three years in a row."

"Wait, what?" Oliver said, giving me a strange look.

"I didn't mean it as a bad thing," I said quickly.

"No, no," Oliver interrupted. "I just meant... you know about that?"

Way to out yourself, you creep. "Oh yeah, I've been meaning to tell you about that, Oliver. Googling you is actually my favorite 3 a.m. pastime." Because that's not weird at all.

"I might have read something about it. Once." I flushed. "It's not like a big deal or anything, I just always thought it was cool, how you knew exactly what you wanted to do back in high school and then you went out and did it. It was inspiring. Anyway," I added with a nervous laugh. "You're the one who stalked me over at Eaton Elementary. What's seven years of cyber-stalking in comparison?"

"Seven years?" Oliver shook his head. "Luke, why didn't you ever, you know, talk to me? During all that time?"

Why did Oliver have to keep doing that—asking questions that seemed simple but led to deeply uncomfortable answers? Uncomfortable to me anyway. I thought about what Nick had said.

Be honest, huh?

"I wasn't sure you'd—I mean," I took a deep breath. "I was scared. I thought you'd still be mad at me. And your life seemed so perfect. I guess maybe I thought if I talked to you, it might put my own life into perspective—in a way I wouldn't like."

Oliver smiled sadly. "That's so—"

"I know." I shook my head. "I know it's pathetic, I'm not denying that. It was just—I don't know, I felt like if I could convince enough other people I had my life together, maybe I could convince myself. But if I talked to you... I knew you'd see through that."

"Oh, Luke," Oliver said. "I probably just would have thought what I always thought about you."

That I'm an entitled, cowardly asshole, I filled in in my head—but before I had a chance to say that out loud, my phone began to ring. I'd set it down on the coffee table, and it was closer to Oliver, so he picked it up and offered it to me. I waved it away.

"No, don't bother," I said. I didn't care who it was—I didn't want anything to interrupt tonight. "It's not important."

Oliver glanced down at it. "It says '*Dad.*'"

"Oh, God, then definitely don't pick it up."

"You sure?"

"Yes. 100%. You know what, maybe just to be safe, we should burn the phone too."

"We could drop it out your window," Oliver said with a laugh as he set the phone back down.

"Yeah," I agreed. "Actually, better yet—submerge it in the sweet and sour sauce. That should fry its circuits for good."

"Hey," Oliver said, shoving me with his foot. "I thought we just agreed that was probably a universal cure to all human ills."

I laughed. "Um, I think *you* agreed that. And don't kick me. I'm sick and weak."

"Oh yeah?" Oliver shoved me again lightly with his foot. "How you gonna stop me?"

I grabbed Oliver's feet and held them tight. "Like this."

Oliver laughed and tried to wrench his feet free of my grasp. "No fair. I thought you were supposed to be weak."

"This *is* me in a weakened state. You should be terrified of me at my full powers."

Oliver arched an eyebrow. "Oh yeah?"

"Yeah."

"Why? What would you do to me?"

I tugged on Oliver's feet quickly, and he yelped as I pulled him so he was lying down on the sofa instead of sitting up. I let go then, but before he could do anything, I moved forward and straddled him. I brought my face down close to his.

"This."

I leaned in and kissed him—something I'd been waiting all day to do. And God, was it worth the wait. Oliver's lips were soft and yielding—and covered with a light dusting of sugar from that last donut. I licked them clean.

My hands found Oliver's, and I brought them slowly above his head as I deepened the kiss. Oliver gasped, but let my tongue inside, swirling his against mine as he arched up off the couch, pressing his body against mine as well. Fuck, I'd been half-hard all night and feeling Oliver underneath me, it didn't take long to get the rest of the way there. Feeling Oliver's own erection pressing against me didn't hurt, either.

I ground my hips down onto Oliver, and he whimpered with pleasure. I could have fucked him right there. I wanted to— wanted to make Oliver make all sorts of delicious sounds, wanted to memorize every inch of his skin, wanted to become a connoisseur of everything *Oliver*.

I knew I should wait—knew I should get things clearer in my mind before we did anything rash. But then, Oliver had told me he wasn't looking for anything more than this—and he'd definitely told me he didn't want me to keep my hands to myself. So really, the only thing standing in the way here was me. The only problem was if *I* wanted more than this.

I squelched the hot, nervous feeling I got in my stomach at that thought. I couldn't want more than this. I didn't do relationships, and even if I did, Oliver deserved better than me. This was all it could ever be.

Still, my heart was racing when Oliver finally broke the kiss, smiling up at me, his eyes dancing.

"No fair," he said, and I was pleased to hear his breath was just as ragged as mine.

"Oh?" I nipped at his bottom lip. "How was I unfair?"

"I wasn't ready."

"Oh yeah? And what would *you* have done if you were?"

"Something like this," Oliver said, grinning as he wrapped his legs around my body and thrust up against me, his cock rubbing against mine. Even through all our layers of clothing, it was driving me wild, like Oliver was inviting me in, begging for more.

You thought that last time, too. And he wasn't.

But Oliver had agreed to see me again. And he was pushing things just as much as I was, wasn't he? Fuck, I didn't want to stop now.

"Will you stay?" I whispered, kissing Oliver's neck. "Will you stay over tonight?"

"Luke, I'm not sure that's—"

Fuck. Fucking fuck. I should have known better.

"It's okay," I said, pulling back. "That's fine."

"No, that's not—"

"I just thought—but no, no, it's totally fine." I knew I sounded like an idiot, but I couldn't stop. I tried to scramble off of the couch. "Do you want to call a cab or—"

"Luke, will you shut up and listen to me?" Oliver said, reaching up and touching my cheek. I froze. "All I was going to say was that I thought you had to work." He smiled. "That's all. I'd love to spend the night. I just meant that if you had to work, maybe that would be a little, um... distracting?"

Something I didn't even know was clenched released in my chest at those words. Oliver wanted to stay. He wanted to be here. Which made sense, I realized, logically. But the thought that he might not want to had thrown me into a panic. The thought of losing him... I was so fucking wrecked when it came to him.

"Fuck work," I growled, leaning back down. "I'll deal with it tomorrow."

"But I thought you said—"

"I know." I shook my head. "I know what I said. But I changed my mind. I don't want anything to take me away from—from this."

"From you" was what I'd almost said. And I would have meant it. I knew that I wasn't thinking straight. I knew I was very possibly making a decision I'd regret tomorrow when I didn't have those reports done. But right now, nothing seemed more important than Oliver.

"Are you sure?" Oliver gave me a long look. "Because even if I don't spend the night, that doesn't mean we can't..." He trailed off, but the blush in his cheeks finished his sentence for him.

I laughed. "I'm positive. It's not like it's life or death, anyway. I'm not a surgeon. All I do is just—"

I stopped short as I heard the words I'd been about to say out loud.

"What?" Oliver asked, looking worried.

"It's—it's nothing." I shook my head, trying to make the thought go away.

"Luke, you look like you're about to throw up. What's wrong?"

"It's just..." I looked down at the couch cushions in disgust. "It's something my dad said earlier. About my job."

"Okay, but from everything you've told me, you shouldn't listen to a word your father says—"

"But he's right." I backed up onto my heels and looked at Oliver, my eyes wide. "He told me today that all I was doing was moving rich people's money around, that it was no different from what he did. I brushed it off at the time, but God, he's right."

"Well, no, he's not right." Oliver pushed himself up on his elbows to look at me. "Because what he did is illegal and what you do isn't just legal, it's something you get paid large amounts of money to do."

"But still—what good am I doing in the world?" I said, feeling disgusted with myself. "Maybe I'm not actively committing crimes, but am I really doing anything worthwhile? Hell, I was planning on going back into the office tonight to work overtime all so that—what—some rich guy who already has more money than he knows what to do with can get *even more*?"

Oliver frowned at me. "Okay, for the record, I still think your dad is completely wrong. So let's get that clear. And if you were happy, if you loved your job, then that would be what mattered. I don't think you're hurting anybody by doing it. But," he said, biting his lip, "Luke, if you're not happy... maybe it's not insane to think about if there's something else you'd rather be doing."

"But how do I know what that *is*?" I said helplessly.

"I don't know," Oliver gave me a sad smile. "But I don't think you're gonna find it if you keep worrying so much about being perfect for other people, or looking like you have your life together, or just picking what's gonna make you the most money."

"But those things matter, Oliver. Making a decent living matters. And maybe I spend too much time worrying about what other people think of me, but that matters too. I'm not a genius. I'm not brilliant. I'm just... me. If people don't like me, it could actually hurt my career, hurt my future. I know it sounds shallow but—"

"But if you spend all your time trying to get people to like you, to think you're perfect..." Oliver shook his head. "Then they'll never actually get to know you. Not the real you, anyway."

"Who says they'd like the real me? Who says the real me is anything to be proud of?"

Oliver's eyebrows shot up, and his mouth dropped open. "Are you... actually being serious right now?"

"I mean..." I could feel my cheeks heating up, and not in a cute, *"we're both thinking about sex"* kind of way. I didn't want to talk about this. "Forget it."

"No," Oliver said vehemently. "No, I'm not forgetting it. Are you serious? You really think that about yourself?" He pushed up into a full sitting position and glared at me.

"I'm not saying I—I mean that's not what I—" I shook my head angrily. "This is stupid, that's not what I meant."

"It's what you said."

"Well it's not what I meant," I insisted, hating how petulant I sounded. "Please, can we just drop it and go back to you telling me how I'm gonna die because I'm not eating enough MSG? Remember how fun that was?"

Oliver tried to keep a stern expression on his face, but I could tell he wanted to laugh, so I pressed my advantage, leaning in and grazing Oliver's cheek against my own as I whispered, "What if I promised that I would eat some sweet and sour sauce if I could lick it off your body? Would that work?"

Oliver erupted into giggles, and I glared at him.

"Thanks. That's just the reaction I'm usually looking for when I suggest sexy foreplay to someone."

"If that's your idea of sexy foreplay..." Oliver said. He gave me a long look and then nodded judiciously. He stood up, then held his hand out. "Come on."

"Why, what are you doing?"

"You'll see when you take my hand. Come on."

Giving Oliver a suspicious look, I sighed and let him pull me off the couch.

"Where's your bedroom?" Oliver asked. "Back that way?"

"Yeah, but—" I started to protest. "Shouldn't we put the food away f—"

"The food can wait. This cannot. It's very important."

"Yes, but what *is* this?" I asked as Oliver led me into my bedroom.

I didn't have to wonder for long. As soon as we were inside, Oliver spun around and pushed me up against the wall.

"This," he said, brushing his lips lightly across mine, "is me helping you feel better about yourself."

"But I—"

"This is you *letting me help you* feel better about yourself," Oliver continued, his hand stroking down my chest and coming to rest exactly where my cock was pressing up against the fabric of my pants.

"Yeah, but—"

"This is you *shutting up* now," Oliver said sternly, and then he kissed me again.

And okay, I'm not a robot. I still wished Oliver would just let this all go, but at least he wanted to kiss me now instead of making me *talk* about it. So yeah, I gave in. Who wouldn't?

"You may not think you're anything special," Oliver said as he maneuvered me towards the bed, somehow also managing to take my clothes off at the same time like he'd grown an extra set of hands, "but I happen to think you're amazing—and as you keep reminding me, I'm very smart. So you should probably listen to me."

"You don't think I'm amazing," I said as he pulled my shirt off, then his own. "You think I'm an asshole."

Oliver gave me a look that said I didn't understand anything. Then he leaned in and nipped at my lower lip.

"Correction. I thought you *acted* like an asshole." His hands went to my belt and unbuckled it. "And for a long time, it made me feel a lot better to believe you were an asshole." Now his hands were on my zipper. "If I believed you were one, it meant what happened didn't hurt so much." And now my pants and boxer briefs were on the floor. "If I convinced myself you were never that great in the first place, then what we had wasn't anything to miss, you know?"

"Oliver I'm so—fuck!" I banged my shin on my bed again as I stepped out of my clothes. "Goddammit, I hate this bed."

"Want me to kiss it and make it better?" Oliver asked, wiggling his eyebrows suggestively.

"What I *want* is for—"

"Shh," Oliver said, hastily stepping out of his own pants and stripping his underwear off. "Upon further reflection, I've decided that that was a sign from the universe telling you to shut up. So you can apologize to me another night, okay? But not tonight."

He straightened up, and I sucked in a breath when I saw how hard Oliver was. But I barely had time to look before Oliver closed the distance between us. I wanted to put my hands around his waist, to stroke his back, his ass—any part of him he'd let me touch, really—but Oliver pulled me onto the bed instead.

It wasn't until he'd gotten me into exactly the position he wanted—lying on my back, painfully hard—before he put me out of my misery and straddled me just the way he had the night of the reunion. God, that seemed so long ago.

Oliver reached down, and I thought he was going to stroke his cock, or maybe mine, but instead, he took my right hand and brought it up to his mouth, kissing the backs of my fingers.

"Tonight," Oliver said quietly, "I want to tell you something. You are not actually an asshole, Luke Wolitzky. You might think you are. And I certainly wanted to think so, for a long time. But everything you've said, everything you've done since I've been back—it proves otherwise."

He unfolded my index finger and brought it to his lips, sucking it slowly in and out of his mouth. My stomach did a somersault. Fuck, that was hot.

"You are kind," Oliver said, releasing my index finger and going to work on my middle finger instead. "And sweet." Ring finger. "And caring." Pinky. "And good."

My cock was throbbing by the time Oliver finally dropped my hand and bent down to kiss my lips, then my jaw, my neck, and my chest.

"You're smart," he continued as he moved his way down my body. "You're funny. You're a good brother and a good son. You make other people's lives better. You care about making the world a better place. You're hot as fuck." He pressed a kiss to my groin and paused, looking up and catching my eyes. "And you've got the world's most gorgeous cock."

I twitched at that, and Oliver laughed lightly, running his finger up the underside of my shaft to my slit where precum was already leaking out. He swirled his finger around the head, then brought it to his mouth, licking it clean. It was pornographic, and insanely sexy.

"Well, you," I started to say, "are the most—"

"Nope!" Oliver said, pressing the finger he'd just licked clean to my lips. "Shush."

I glared at him and tried to catch his finger in my mouth, but he just pulled it away and laughed.

"Come here," I said, trying to grab it back, but Oliver shook his head, shooting daggers at me.

"Stop that," he said. "Shh. You're breaking the rules."

"And what are these rules that I'm supposedly breaking?" I asked, rolling my eyes and reaching up to put my hands on Oliver's waist. "You never actually explained them to me, you know."

"Well, I'd explain them now if you'd ever stop talking," Oliver said with a laugh, swatting my hands away. "That's the first rule, by the way. You don't get to talk. You don't get to distract me. You just have to lie there and enjoy this."

"But—"

"Hey, what's rule number one?"

"Bossy," I muttered mutinously.

"Trust me—you can boss me around all you like next time. Just not tonight, okay?"

Next time? Forget somersaults, my stomach was going bungee jumping. I'd never wanted a *"next time"* before in my life, but now I felt like I'd die if I didn't get one.

So I nodded. What else could I do?

Oliver smiled like I'd just given him a present, then leaned in to kiss me once before sliding back down to return his attention to my cock. Or rather, to the area around it, on my stomach, my hips, my inner thighs. I gripped the sheets in frustration as Oliver teased me, letting his chin or neck brush against my cock sometimes but never touching it with his mouth until I was writhing on the bed.

And when he finally did bring his hand to my cock and press a kiss to the base, I honestly think I could have come on the spot if I'd let myself. It felt so good. Oliver licked my cock up and down like he was savoring it, swirling his tongue around the tip each time. And when he began sucking me in and out of his mouth, so hot and wet, I felt like I was going to lose it. Which was wrong—I couldn't come when I hadn't done anything for Oliver tonight at all.

I reached out tentatively, put my hand on Oliver's shoulder. He looked up, his mouth still wrapped around my cock, which only made it twitch again.

"Come here," I said.

Oliver shook his head silently, steadying the base of my cock with his hand so he could lick all the way around it.

"Please," I begged, my voice cracking. "I'm gonna—I'm gonna come if you keep doing that."

"Luke, what do you think the point of all of this is?" Oliver said, looking at me like that was the dumbest thing he'd ever heard. "I'm not trying to get you to sing *'I'm a Little Teapot.'*"

"But I want to make you feel—I want to—you haven't even —fuck," I groaned as Oliver took me in his mouth again. "Dammit, Oliver." My voice was completely broken. "Are you trying to kill me?"

"I'm trying to do the opposite, dumbass," Oliver said with a snort. He gave me a firm look. "Listen. Let *me* make *you* feel good for once. You don't have to do anything. You don't have to please anyone or make anyone else happy, okay? You don't have to try to be perfect. Just you—like this—is enough."

By the time he was done talking, he was glaring at me. I still didn't like it—the whole thing seemed unfair to Oliver. But there was a fierce look in his eyes, and he had his hand around my cock, so it didn't really seem like a good time to argue. I nodded wearily and let Oliver press my shoulders down until I was flat on my back again.

Enough? This was enough? *I* was enough? It didn't feel right. Not that it didn't feel good—it felt fucking fantastic. But it felt weird, wrong even, to not be doing anything right now, to just concentrate on my own pleasure.

Not only were my hookups not usually this slow, this tender, but I'd always prided myself on making sure whoever I slept with had a good time. I knew I was good at getting guys off, and even though I rarely slept with anyone twice, never three times, I always wanted them to remember how good I'd made them feel.

But now I was supposed to ignore all that and what—let Oliver take care of me?

Take care of me?

Could I trust Oliver like that?

I lifted my head up, my eyes wide as thoughts raced through my brain. Oliver looked gorgeous, even though I could only see the top of his head, and suddenly I felt ridiculous, worrying about trust. It was just a blow job, wasn't it?

Only, Oliver happened to choose that moment to look up. I don't know what he saw when our eyes met, but he reached out and took my hand with one of his own, lacing our fingers together, and then nodded. It was like something inside me unlocked.

If I couldn't trust Oliver—a guy who had every reason in the world to hate me, a guy who had never been anything other than good to me despite that—then I'd never be able to trust anyone. I had to try.

I let my head fall back, my breath growing ragged, but I kept my fingers locked tight around Oliver's, holding onto him for dear life. I could feel my orgasm building up inside me as Oliver continued to work my cock. I was so close. And when Oliver licked a long stripe up the sensitive underside and then sucked my head in again, I couldn't hold back any longer.

"Fuck, Oliver—I'm gonna—I'm gonna come," I gasped, trying to give him some warning.

But instead of moving away, or finishing me with his hand, Oliver just sank down around my cock, pushing me over the edge. I came into his mouth as Oliver's tongue caressed me.

My body shook with pleasure, and it seemed like hours before I came back down to earth.

"Fuck," I whispered, and I heard Oliver laugh. "Come here."

I pulled Oliver up fiercely until he was face-to-face with me —apparently, I was allowed to use my hands now. I kissed him deeply, and I could taste myself on his tongue.

"Good?" Oliver asked.

"Good? Fucking..." I laughed weakly. "I can't remember the last time I came that hard. Maybe never."

Oliver nodded with satisfaction. "Good." He gave me a scrutinizing look. "I meant it, you know."

"Meant what?" I asked, confused.

"All that stuff. It wasn't just some weird trick to make your orgasm better. It makes me really sad to hear that you think so little of yourself."

And suddenly, I could feel tears pressing at the back of my eyes. I pulled Oliver in and kissed him, hard, then snuggled him to my chest in the hopes that he couldn't see me crying.

We lay like that for a long while, and even though tears were rolling down my cheeks, I still felt better than I had in... in I couldn't remember how long. I didn't want the moment to end.

But then Oliver pressed up on an elbow.

"Are you sure you don't need me to go? I still can, you know, and it's not—"

He stopped when he saw the tears.

"Hey, hey, what's wrong?" Oliver asked, stroking a finger along my cheek.

"Nothing," I said helplessly.

And I meant it. God, I was crying like a little kid, and it should have been so embarrassing, but somehow it wasn't, because with Oliver, for the first time in my life, I felt... safe.

"I mean it," I said, smiling through the tears. "Nothing's wrong. I know I'm crying, but this is—this is the best I've felt in—God, I don't even know."

"Okay," Oliver said simply. He found my hand and laced our fingers together again. "Is there anything I can do?"

"Just stay with me," I whispered. "Is that okay?"

"Of course," Oliver said. "Anything you want."

"That's what I want." I pulled him close, wrapping my arms around him. "Just stay."

I slept better that night than I had in ages. I didn't think about work, or my dad, or any of the million things that usually filled my dreams or woke me up in a panic. And somehow, even though I was the one holding Oliver, it felt like he was holding me.

It was a deep, dreamless sleep.

Warm, and safe.

And when I woke up the next morning, my throat was on fire.

14

OLIVER

I woke up feeling snuggly and washed in sunlight. I wasn't sure where I was, exactly, but it was bright and clean and soft, and I liked it. The sheets smelled like sun-warmed cotton, the comforter was crumpled around me like a waterfall and the arms around me were strong and warm.

Arms.

Around me.

Holy shit, those were Luke's arms. I was lying here with Luke. In his apartment, where I'd spent the night after—

Oh, holy shit. It all came flooding back to me. The juicer and the takeout and the *everything* that came after. Luke had been more vulnerable last night than I'd seen him in... well, a very long time. So long that I'd begun to wonder if I'd only ever imagined that side of him.

It had been so strange, listening to Luke talk about himself. For so long, I'd assumed I was the one who was messed up, the overly emotional, erratic, too-sensitive weirdo, and Luke was the one who had it all together. That I was the broken one, and Luke the one who was strong. It had never occurred to me that it might be the other way around. Because while I never expected anyone else to like me—at least I liked myself.

Luke didn't even seem to have that.

Which was baffling. Luke was amazing, and I couldn't understand why he didn't see that. He was the same guy I'd fallen for all those years ago—the kind of guy I needed to be careful not to fall for again.

And yeah, okay, Luke wasn't perfect. This didn't erase what had happened back then. But he was sweet and kind, and he'd carved his way into my heart years ago, made himself a home there, and I'd never quite been able to evict him.

And yet, Luke seemed to believe he was worthless, seemed to hate himself in a way I'd never even managed to hate him when I was most angry with him. And something had come over me, this need to show him he was so much more than that. I'd wanted to show him what I thought, what I felt. And I'd thought it was good, that maybe I'd gotten through to him.

But then he'd started crying. I blinked, remembering that. I'd thought he'd play it off or push me away. Never in a million years would I have dreamed he'd pull me closer instead.

Had I made a difference, somehow? And was any of it going to last?

I knew I was right—deep down, Luke was good. But I'd been

burned by him before when he'd let his fears get the better of him. What if the same thing happened now?

Well, and...? What if it does? Who said he owes you anything? You told him you wanted to keep this casual.

Still, I could appreciate the last few minutes of this morning, couldn't I? Before it ended? It had been so long since I'd gotten even this simple pleasure—waking up in bed with someone I... well, I didn't want to say "someone I *liked*" because I didn't want to *like* Luke. But someone I was happy to be waking up next to, anyway.

I closed my eyes and snuggled deeper under the covers, and Luke's arms tightened around me. I couldn't decide which idea I liked better—that Luke was awake and pulling me closer consciously, or asleep and not able to help himself. And then I felt Luke press a kiss to the back of my neck, so, okay, definitely not asleep, and I *definitely* wasn't complaining.

I couldn't help myself. I arched my back a little, rubbing my ass against Luke's body. Luke kissed my neck again and let one of his hands trace down my side and rub my thigh.

"Morning," I whispered, smiling like an idiot. God, I should not feel this happy, it was embarrassing. At least Luke couldn't see my face right now.

"Morn—" Luke stopped mid-word and coughed, then groaned. "Fuck."

My stomach turned over. *"Fuck?"* That wasn't what you wanted to hear someone say while you were still lying in their bed. At least, not in this context.

"What's wrong," I asked quickly, my body already tensing.

Luke probably wanted me gone, now that he was fully conscious. He probably regretted letting me stay the night, was probably desperate to get back to work.

"Do you need to—I mean, I can go," I said, steeling myself. I pushed myself upright. "So you can get to the office. Sorry, I shouldn't have—"

"No," Luke croaked, and for the first time, I looked behind me and realized that he hadn't moved. He was lying in bed with a pained expression on his face. Literally pained, I realized as Luke grimaced, cleared his throat, and then brought his hand to it.

"No, it's not—" Luke stopped and shook his head, then looked at me, bewildered. "I think I really am sick."

Shit. I blinked. When Luke had said something about that last night, I'd assumed he was just being dramatic. I'd never thought it was actually real.

"Is it—it's your throat?" I asked.

"Yeah," Luke whispered. He nodded gingerly. "It feels— fuck, it hurts. Ugh, and my head."

"Okay," I said, feeling myself snap into problem-solving mode. "Okay, does anything else hurt? Are you stuffy at all? Here—" I sat back down on the bed "—let me feel your lymph nodes."

"No," Luke said, backing away as I leaned in. "No, I don't want to get you sick too."

I snorted. "Luke, I think we're a little bit past that point, don't you? After last night? Either I'm not going to get sick, or I am, and it's already too late to do anything about it. But I feel fine now, so just let me—"

"What are you gonna do?" Luke asked, and he looked at me so suspiciously that I couldn't help laughing.

"I'm not going to kill you, so you can stop looking at me like that. I'm just gonna feel your lymph nodes, those little bumps in your neck. They swell when you get sick."

Luke was still eyeing me skeptically, but he sat up and let me touch his neck. I found his lymph nodes quickly. Years of living with my dad as a child had taught me how to self-diagnose. He'd never taken a sick day in his life, or so he claimed, so he'd decided I wasn't going to either. And since he avoided doctors like the plague, I'd had to learn how to be my own doctor. Luke's lymph nodes were really swollen, and even though I kept my touch feather light, I could tell he was in pain.

"Well," I said, pulling my hands back. "You're definitely sick."

"But I don't get sick." Luke shook his head. "Never."

"Never?" I arched an eyebrow.

"Well, almost never," Luke said mutinously. "This is the second time I've gotten sick this year, but before this, I hadn't been sick since middle school. It doesn't make sense. Why is this happening now? I'm not the kind of person who—"

"Luke," I said, giving him a firm look. "I don't think whatever virus or bacteria you've got swimming around in your system cares what kind of person you are. And you *are* the kind of person who gets sick because you're human." I reached out and felt his forehead. "I think you have a fever, too. And since you don't seem to be stuffy, my guess is strep throat."

"Strep throat? That's something kids get," Luke scoffed.

"Adults too. I used to get it all the time, actually, until I finally got my tonsils out when I was 21." I shook my head. "It was awful. My dad never took me to the doctor, and I had to just wait it out and try to treat it myself with honey and stuff. It was painful and really unpleasant. I think you should just go to the doctor."

"But I have to go to work," Luke protested.

"Not today, you don't. You're clearly in no shape to go. And if you do have strep, you could be contagious."

"But I can't—"

"Luke," I said sternly.

"What?"

"Who's your doctor?"

Luke looked away and mumbled something.

"What? I didn't hear—"

"I said I don't have one," Luke said louder, and then winced, touching his throat again.

"You don't have—"

"I don't get sick," Luke said. "I never got around to needing one."

"But don't you have someone you go to for your physical each year?"

Luke shrugged. "What's a doctor gonna tell me about my health that I don't already know? I take care of myself."

"Oh my God." I clapped a hand to my face in exasperation. "You're literally the same as my dad."

"Oh good, that's sexy," Luke grumbled. "Thanks for the compliment."

"Right, because you were so sexy before, with all the streptococcal bacteria teeming in your mouth." I rolled my eyes. "Want me to look up an urgent care place?"

"No. No, that's gonna take too long. I have to get to work."

"You're not going to work," I said, starting to get annoyed. "You're sick, and you're not going to get better if you don't rest."

Luke glared at me, was quiet for a moment, and then tossed his head. "Fine," he said airily. "I'll work from home."

"You still need to—"

"It's probably just a cold. That's what it was the last time I got sick. I don't need to go to the doctor."

"I am absolutely positive that you do."

"Come on, you just said you knew like, herbal remedies and stuff, didn't you?" Luke asked. "Can't you teach them to me?"

I glared at him. "The point you were supposed to take away from that story was that they were a lot slower and less effective than antibiotics would have been."

"Please?"

"You're being ridiculous."

"And you're being cold and uncaring." Luke batted his eyelashes outrageously. "I'm just a poor, sickly creature, and you're being sooooo meeeean to me."

"Oh my God," I groaned, running a hand through my hair. "Fine. You get one day. If none of your symptoms have improved by tomorrow, you're going to the doctor."

"One day?" Luke scoffed. "That's like, no time. Don't colds last like, a week?"

"Ugh, fine, two days," I grumbled. "But you don't get to work from home, you have to actually sleep and rest."

"Four days," Luke countered. "And I do get to work. Oliver, I have to. My promotion is on the line."

"Three days and you don't work today," I said. "You call in sick. I mean it, or I'm withholding any and all of these herbal remedies you're so desperate for."

"You're mean."

"Tough luck. Now pull out your phone and tell them you're not coming in."

"You're gonna *watch* me?" Luke asked incredulously.

"Damn right. And then I'm taking your phone away while I go to the store and pick some stuff up for you."

Luke glared daggers at me, but he did eventually write an email to his boss and then hand me his phone. He sighed vociferously the whole time.

"Hey, you wanted my help," I reminded him.

"I'm beginning to regret asking," Luke said darkly.

"Great, you'll be charming company today, then." I rolled my eyes. "Okay, I'm going out to the store. Try to be asleep when I get back."

***

What the hell are you doing?

The question reverberated through my mind as I wandered the aisles of the Whole Foods a few blocks from Luke's apartment. Though, at the moment, I was standing—and had been standing for five minutes—in front of the honey section, trying to decide if the supposed healing powers of raw, imported Manuka honey superseded those of the raw, local honey.

It was ridiculous to spend so much time on something so trivial. Why did I care so much? Luke probably just wanted me to make him a hot toddy and then leave. I shook my head in disgust, put the local honey in my basket, and the Manuka honey back on the shelf.

I only made it three steps down the aisle before I turned around and grabbed the Manuka honey too.

I wasn't entirely sure what I needed to buy, since I didn't know what the contents of Luke's kitchen were. I got extra of everything just to be safe. Maybe I'd have time to see if I could get Luke's juicer to work when I got back, but in the meantime, I bought a cheap, plastic citrus squeezer just in case.

Honestly, what the fuck is wrong with you? Planning on fixing his juicer? Why don't you offer to add your name to the lease while you're at it?

I walked back to Luke's apartment, carrying two bulging

reusable grocery bags, thoroughly mortified. Maybe I could hide all of this in Luke's fridge before he saw me, and then convince him he bought it via a grocery delivery service last night and didn't remember because of his fever. Maybe he'd be asleep when I got back, so he wouldn't see how fucking insane I was.

But, of course, Luke wasn't asleep when I walked back into his apartment. He was sitting on the couch, hunched over staring at his—

"Is that a second phone?" I asked, staring at him in shock.

Luke at least had the grace to look ashamed. "You just said I had to give you my phone, singular. You didn't ask if I had more than one."

"You," I said, setting the grocery bags down with a thud, "are ridiculous. Go back to bed."

"Oliver," Luke said, clearly trying to sound reasonable— which would have worked better if he weren't whispering and grimacing with every word, "I appreciate what you're doing. And how much you care. It's sweet. But I can't just stop working because I have a little cold. I should have gotten those reports done yesterday, and with this trip at the end of the week, I really can't afford to let Harvey down now."

"Oh."

"What?" Luke asked.

"Nothing." I shook my head and tried to ignore the sinking feeling in my chest.

I should have known better than to think that anything

Luke had said last night *meant* anything. We'd had some nice moments, but I should have remembered who I was dealing with. Luke was the king of meaning well, but not quite being able to follow through.

"No, really, Oliver," Luke said. He even put the phone down. "I can see you're upset. What's wrong?"

"Ugh, it really is nothing," I said, hating how defensive I sounded. "I just thought—I mean last night, you practically sounded ready to quit your job. You said you didn't care about those reports. And now you're—I mean, I get it. We all say things in the heat of the moment, I didn't expect you to upend your life, but I just—"

I cut myself off. I was babbling. I hated that. I picked the grocery bags up again and started walking towards the kitchen. "Nevermind. I'll just put these away, and then I'll get out of your hair."

"What? You're leaving? Oliver, wait, no—" Luke sprang up off the couch. "Oliver, no, I'm sorry."

He grabbed my hand. "Hey, come on. I didn't mean to—" Luke took a deep breath, winced, and ran a hand through his hair.

"Last night was—it meant—I meant what I said. And I appreciate everything you did—and everything you're doing. But I can't just up and quit my job because I realized it's not my passion, you know? That would be a huge decision, and huge decisions take time. And in the meantime, I still have to, you know, make my salary. Get paid."

I frowned, not sure what to say. When Luke put it like that, it made sense. And now I felt stupid, taking everything too seriously.

"Please stay," Luke said. He squeezed my hand. "I'll be good. I promise, I'll go back to bed, and I'll let you keep both phones. Please? Stay?"

Why? Why do you want me to stay so badly? What does it mean?

But of course I couldn't say that. Because I knew the answer. It didn't mean anything—it just meant that Luke was stressed, and anxious, and wanted a friendly face around. It didn't mean he thought of me as anything other than that— a friend, with both sexual- and citrus-related benefits.

"Are you just saying that because you know you have an ancient flip phone hidden in a shoebox under your bed?" I asked finally, making myself smile.

"Maybe," Luke said with a grin. "But you can search my room from top to bottom if you stay. You can search me, too, if you want."

"You're incorrigible," I said, smiling for real this time. "Fine. Go to bed. I'm gonna make you some juice."

***

Adorably, though, when I came back into Luke's bedroom a few minutes later, my hands surprisingly tired from squeezing a shit ton of oranges into a glass for Luke, he was already asleep. I stood there and watched him for a minute.

I'd never actually seen Luke sleep before, I realized. We'd slept in the same bed last night, but I hadn't really *seen* him.

Not, of course, that I was complaining. But it was sweet, some-how, seeing Luke like this. His brow was furrowed, like even in sleep he was concentrating very hard on being perfect.

Well, if he'd fallen back asleep that easily, he definitely needed the rest. I padded across the room silently and deposited the juice on his nightstand. I had the strangest urge to brush away a stray hair that had fallen onto Luke's forehead, but I didn't want to wake him up.

I pulled my phone out when I got back out to the living room, flopping down on the couch. I realized that I hadn't called my dad last night to check in. Not that I'd promised to or anything, but I'd kind of made a habit of it on the days when I didn't see him, and since he seemed to only tolerate my presence every other day at most, those phone calls had become a pattern.

Sighing, I pulled his number up and hit *"call."*

"Oliver," my dad barked by way of a greeting when he answered. "What's wrong, why are you calling?"

"What? Dad, nothing's wrong. I'm just calling to check in. I realized I hadn't last night."

"Oliver, you don't have to do that, I've told you."

"No, I know but—"

"And Jesus, now you scare me half to death, calling me in the morning when you're usually not even awake. What are you trying to do, give me another heart attack?" He laughed, this loud, booming sound, but it faded, I think when he real-ized I wasn't laughing with him. "Come on, kid, it was a joke."

"It's not funny, Dad," I said. "Don't joke about shit like that."

"Oh, come on, Oliver. I was just messin' ar—"

"I know what you were doing, but it's not funny. Don't you get that? The whole reason I'm home is because I'm scared to death of what happens if you get sick again, if you have another heart attack and this time you're not so lucky. All I want to do is make sure that *doesn't* happen, and you won't even admit there's a problem, but then you make jokes about it?"

I was on the edge of tears, and I needed to rein it in. I knew emotions made my dad uncomfortable—that was exactly why I'd never told him how scared I was. But apparently, today was my day for having emotional reactions that were massively disproportionate to the things that had provoked them.

"I'm sorry," I said once I was sure I had my voice under control. "I didn't mean to—"

"No, no," my dad cut in. "I'm the one who's sorry, Oliver. I shouldn't have joked about it."

What? Since when did my dad apologize? Since when did he admit I was right? About anything, but especially about his health.

"I—I mean—it's okay," I stuttered, completely thrown.

"So," my dad said after a moment. "We've established that I'm okay and you're okay. So that's good. How, uh, how's everything else?"

Had I entered an alternate universe? Was my dad actually trying to make small talk with me?

"It's, um, it's good," I said, trying to stifle the thread of laughter that was bubbling up at the thought of actually telling my dad about the *"everything else"* he'd asked about. I didn't know who that would embarrass more, him or me.

"Good, good," he said. "You uh—you go out last night or something?"

"I—yeah. I did." I blinked. "How did you know?"

"Eh, you usually call around 8 or so. By 9 p.m., I hadn't heard from you, so I figured you must have gone out with friends or something."

"Uh. Yeah." I shook my head in wonder. My dad *paid attention* to that kind of thing? "Yeah, I did. With some friends. We got dinner and just, you know. Caught up and stuff."

Not true, but given my dad's feelings about Luke, I certainly wasn't going to tell the truth.

"Late night?"

"Kinda." What the hell was I supposed to say?

"Well, good. Good. I'm glad you're reconnecting with people. Glad this isn't a total waste of a trip for you while you're stuck out here because of me."

"Dad, I'm not *"stuck here"* with you. And it's not a waste of a trip. I wanted to come. You know that, right?"

"Yeah, yeah." My dad cleared his throat. "Anyway, I, uh, I should probably go. Gotta get back to work. But we'll talk soon."

"Um, okay."

"And let me know next time you wanna come out. I know

you're busy working, but we can try that vegetable place again or something."

Yeah, I was definitely dead. Either that or someone had body-snatched my dad.

"Right. Yeah, definitely."

"Okay. Sounds good, then. Bye, Oliver."

"Bye."

I hung up and stared at the phone in my hands. That had been completely unexpected, and I felt weirdly at loose ends now. I didn't feel bad for lying to my dad, exactly. But suddenly, it felt weird to just be sitting in Luke's apartment, staring at the walls while my dad thought I was *"busy working."*

How long did Luke want me to stay for, anyway? He hadn't said. Maybe he'd only meant for the morning. Only, now that he was asleep, I couldn't exactly ask him.

Maybe I should actually do some work. I didn't have my computer with me, but...

My eyes drifted to the door where Luke's briefcase was propped up. My coat lay in a heap on the floor next to it. Luke's laptop was just peeking out of the top of the briefcase. What were the chances it wouldn't be password-protected?

30 seconds later, I'd pulled the laptop out and set it on the coffee table. Dammit, it did need a password. I stared at it for a second and then typed in Luke's birthday. No dice. I tried his mom's address. Also wrong. I paused for a second. What if...

On a whim, I typed in *"FrederickCabotCoolidge3"* and hit enter.

The screen flashed—and suddenly, I was staring at the desktop of Luke's computer. Holy shit. That had worked? I'd just typed it in to amuse myself, not because I'd actually thought for a second that it was right. Shit.

And what the hell did it mean that that was Luke's password?

Suddenly, it occurred to me what I was doing. This was an incredible breach of privacy. Luke had asked me to stay over because he was sick. That wasn't an invitation to break into his computer. Even if all I wanted to do was access GitHub on a bigger screen than my phone, it still felt... wrong.

I closed the computer with a snap, then pushed it away from me for good measure.

You're such a fucking creep.

My phone pinged in my pocket, and I jumped. A sudden vision of Luke texting me from the bedroom, having watched me break into his computer, flashed into my mind before I remembered that I actually *had* both of Luke's phones. Still, I looked over my shoulder guiltily to double-check that Luke's door was closed before I pulled my phone out and saw a text from Micah.

MICAH: Soooooooooo

MICAH: How'd the date go?

MICAH: I'm assuming from your complete radio silence that Luke either murdered you and is disintegrating your body in vats of acid or you're still fucking like rabbits in bed

MICAH: Really hoping it's the latter but... figured I'd check

I snorted.

OLIVER: Jesus, you're pushy

MICAH: I know, it's one of my charms

OLIVER: If this is you charming, I'd hate to see you when you're not trying

MICAH: Hilarious

MICAH: I'll repeat my earlier question

MICAH: Soooooooo?

OLIVER: Hmm, I'm not sure what you mean

OLIVER: That only has 8 o's. Your first question had 9. How am I supposed to make sense of this? What do you mean???

MICAH: I mean I'll come over there and murder you myself if you don't answer the fucking question

MICAH: Do you have any idea how slow it is at the bar right now?

MICAH: Entertain me, pleeeeeeeeease

MICAH: (10 o's so you know i'm serious)

OLIVER: You're ridiculous

MICAH: Uh huh

MICAH: Yep

MICAH: True

MICAH: ... i'm waiting

I laughed. It wasn't that I didn't want to tell Micah, exactly. It was more that telling him, telling anyone, meant actually having to think through what I was feeling, think about what had happened in the past 24 hours, and what, if anything, it meant.

OLIVER: *Ok well, since you've been so patient and polite...*

OLIVER: *It went well, I think? Luke had had a bad day and seemed really stressed when I got here so we just ordered takeout and hung out*

OLIVER: *That was it, really!*

I hemmed and hawed over that exclamation point. Using it seemed so weird and perky. But not using it made me sound depressed, which I wasn't. It took Micah longer to reply than I expected, but when he did, I almost dropped my phone.

MICAH: *YOU'RE STILL THERE?*

What? How the hell did he know that.

MICAH: *YOU SAID "HERE." THAT MEANS YOU'RE STILL THERE. RIGHT?*

MICAH: *TELL ME IT MEANS YOU SPENT THE NIGHT*

OLIVER: *Jesus, caps much?*

MICAH: *I will not apologize for my excitement. Also you're avoiding the question*

OLIVER: *Fine, yes, I'm still here*

MICAH: *I KNEW IT*

MICAH: *Sorry, I just get capsy when I'm excited*

MICAH: *So it was a good night then? Ehh??*

I rolled my eyes.

OLIVER: *Yeah, but then he woke up this morning super sick and he won't go to the doctor, but he asked me to stay with him, but I don't know if he meant for the morning or the whole day or what and now he's asleep again so I can't ask so I'm just sitting in his apartment like a weirdo*

OLIVER: *Does that answer your question?*

MICAH: *Uh yes, by giving me a million more*

MICAH: *He asked you to STAY WITH HIM?*

OLIVER: *I KNOW! I don't know what the fuck it means*

MICAH: *I... have no idea either*

MICAH: *That's not like, his typical MO, from what I understand*

OLIVER: *I'm sure it doesn't mean anything. I just...*

OLIVER: *IDK it's weird*

OLIVER: *I think I'm gonna try to fix his juicer and try not to think about it*

MICAH: *Is that what the kids are calling it these days? "Fix his juicer?"*

OLIVER: *Fuck you. His actual juicer is broken*

MICAH: *Sure*

MICAH: *Right*

MICAH: *Whatever you say*

OLIVER: *Ugh, we're not friends anymore*

MICAH: *Have fun.... * wiggles eyebrows **

OLIVER: Go away

Talking about Luke's juicer had reminded me I actually did want to try and fix it, so I spent the next 30 minutes searching Luke's apartment from top to bottom before I finally found a tool set—stored in his oven, of all places—and set about putting his juicer back together.

It was clear the problem wasn't mechanical, so the electrical was the next logical thing to check. It had been a while since I'd messed around with any hardware, but the digital components of the juicer didn't look too complex, and I'd built countless computers from scratch. I felt pretty confident handling it. I was just about finished putting the wiring back together when I heard Luke's voice behind me.

"What are you doing?" Luke asked, sounding sleepy.

"Uh.... fixing your juicer?" I said, feeling my cheeks heat up a bit. Suddenly this seemed less like a friendly gesture and more like the kind of thing that said, *"Also, I thought a June wedding would be nice."*

"You're—" Luke stopped and smiled. It was like the sun breaking through the clouds. "I can't believe you're doing that."

"Is that... a good *'can't believe'* or a bad *'can't believe?'*"

"Good," Luke said, still smiling as he rubbed the sleep from his eyes. "Definitely good."

"Oh. Okay." I smiled back. "How are you feeling? Any better?"

"Worse," Luke said, looking morose. "Thanks for the orange juice."

"No problem." I brushed my hands off and grabbed a mason jar from the fridge, another drink I'd prepared for him when I'd first gotten back with the groceries. "Here, drink this, too."

Luke took the jar and gave the brown liquid inside it a dubious look. "What *is* this?"

"Apple cider vinegar, local raw honey, cayenne pepper, cinnamon, and water."

"And you want me to *drink* this," Luke said skeptically.

"Yup." I grinned. "But, actually, first, I want you to eat some raw garlic. Then shake that jar up and drink it to get the taste out of your mouth."

"*Raw* garlic?" Luke repeated.

"Hey, you're the one who wanted my home remedies. I still think you should go to the doctor."

"Fine," Luke said. "If you let me check my email after this."

I narrowed my eyes as I thought for a moment. "Deal."

Luke eyed the garlic I pressed on him with some misgiving, but he dutifully chewed and swallowed it down, making a face the whole time. But he brightened a little as he drank the tonic.

"That's actually not bad," Luke said. "I thought it was going to taste way worse." Then he smiled brightly. "Computer?"

"Nope." I shook my head. "You're going straight back to bed."

"But you said—"

"I said I'd let you check your email after this." I grinned. "I never said how long after."

"You're such a sneak," Luke protested.

"I know." I smiled heartlessly. "And you're such a sick person. Bed. Now."

"But I'm not sleepy," Luke whined. He gave me a speculative look. "Come with me. We can watch Netflix or something. Please?"

"Is this a ploy to get *me* to fall asleep so you can use the computer?"

"Maybe," Luke said with a grin. "Are you scared it'll work?"

"No," I said with a snort. "But I'm bored enough to agree to it."

So that was how we ended up in bed together, mounds of pillows propped up behind us, arguing about what to watch. I won, which meant I picked a documentary about the inter-library-loan system and the fate of public libraries in the digital age. I was kind of shocked that Luke agreed to watch that—though maybe that was just another sign of how sick he actually was.

I averted my eyes as Luke typed in his password, another wave of guilt rolling through my body. Once Luke cued up the movie, he pulled me towards him, tucking my head just under his chin. He did it so naturally that my breath caught for a moment. God, it would be easy to get used to this.

I knew Luke was just feeling needy, but this was way too nice. Luke wanted me here. He hadn't asked why I was still around, he didn't think it was weird that I'd tried to fix his juicer, and he wanted me to stay.

And I'd hacked into his computer. Fuck.

Within five minutes of watching the documentary, I felt so guilty I couldn't stand it. I glanced up at Luke—his eyes were open, focused on the screen, but they looked drowsy. Dammit, if I was going to tell him, I should really do it now before he inevitably fell asleep again.

"Hey Luke?" I said after a moment.

"Yeah?"

I couldn't look him in the eye as I talked—I stared straight ahead instead.

"I, um—okay so this is going to sound really bad. And I'm not saying it was great. But I didn't actually do anything. I just wanted to tell you because I feel really shitty for doing it, and like, you should know. So anyway, I um kinda accidentally hacked your computer password earlier today?"

"You what?"

Luke sounded surprised, and in spite of myself, I looked up at him.

"Yeah," I said. "It was just—I didn't mean to. I mean, I kind of did—but I didn't really, you know? You were just sleeping, and I was thinking about doing some work, but I didn't have my computer, and I shouldn't have done it, but I was just kind of wondering if your password would be something really simple like your birthday, and then I uh—well, I guessed it just by accident, I didn't think it would work."

I winced. "I closed your computer as soon as I realized what

I'd done. I didn't, like, look at anything. But uh, yeah. If you want to change your password, I understand. And if you think I'm a horrible person with no regard for privacy or trust I uh—I understand that too."

Luke didn't say anything—he just stared at me.

"I uh—I know it was a shitty thing to do," I said when I couldn't bear the silence any longer. "And if you want me to leave—"

"Oliver, what? No," Luke said. "No, I'm sorry. I was just... I'm not mad."

"But you were quiet for so long—" I began, but Luke cut me off with a laugh.

"I was thinking," Luke said, "about how embarrassed I was that you know what my password is now. That's all." He shook his head. "Trust me, my life's pretty boring—there's nothing all that interesting to find."

"Really? You're not mad?"

"I'm not mad," Luke said with a grin. "Hell, I'm impressed."

"Well," I smiled. "I did have kind of a leg up. Doppelgänger and all."

"Yeah. I guess you did." Luke held my eyes for a moment, and I blushed. Luke cleared his throat. "Anyway, you can work on my computer any time you want. It's fine."

As if mentioning the computer woke it up from a nap, there was a whooshing sound of an email arriving, and we both turned to look at the screen. Before I could say anything, Luke grabbed the laptop, minimized the Netflix window, and opened his email. His face drained of color.

"Oh, fuck," he whispered. "Oh, fuhhhhck."

"What's—what's wrong?

"I wrote—" Luke shook his head and looked at me in disbelief. "That email I wrote this morning—telling them I wasn't coming in today?"

"Yeah?"

"The subject line was, *'Luke out sick today'*—so they'd know what it was about without having to open it."

"Okay."

"But I didn't write *'out sick today.'*" Luke looked horrified. "I wrote *'out dick today'* by accident. And MacFarlane just emailed me about it."

He turned the screen to me so I could see.

How's your dick day going, buddy? Gotta say, didn't think you were ever gonna be brave enough to tell Harvey about your extracurriculars, but I guess it's only fair to be honest with him before he made his VP decision. Don't worry, I'm sure he'll be open-minded about all those dicks you're getting when I tell him it wasn't just a typo. Rest up—sounds like you're gonna need it!

"What a fucking asshole." I stared at Luke in shock. "I mean, I know you told me he was an asshole, but that's evil. Threatening to out someone. That's fucking—you could go to HR for that."

"And deal with whatever retaliation comes? MacFarlane's related to Harvey—he can't fire him."

"You could sue."

"I'm already involved in one lawsuit," Luke said, shaking his head helplessly. "I can't—I don't—whatever. I honestly don't have the energy for this right now."

I gave him a pained look. "Luke, this is fucked up. Everything you've said about work, really."

"I know," Luke sighed. "I know. Maybe I really should quit. Just write them back and be like, sorry, too busy out getting dicks. See you never."

"On a permanent dick vacation?" I grinned.

"Yeah," Luke said, answering with a wan smile. "It's very serious business, all this dick. Gotta devote yourself to it full time."

"A bizz-cation then," I said, trying to cheer Luke up.

Luke snorted. "A jizz-cation, I think you mean."

"See?" I was actually giggling now. "You don't even have *time* for this finance job, not when you've got a full-time side-hustle rustling up dicks."

"Good point," Luke said with a smile. He closed his email app. "Whatever. I don't want to think about it anymore."

I eyed him with misgiving. "You sure?"

"Yeah," Luke said. "Either MacFarlane says something to Harvey, or he doesn't. There's nothing I can do about it now."

"That's... a very different attitude from the one you had this morning," I couldn't help observing.

"Yeah, well, maybe you inspire me."

"That, or dicks do," I replied archly.

"Yeah," Luke said, pulling me back down onto his chest. "Both, really."

He hit play on the documentary again as I snuggled down against the pillows and him. Luke's arm curled around my shoulders, and it wasn't long before the rise and fall of his chest grew steady and slow.

I knew Luke had probably fallen asleep again. Knew I should get up and go, take the computer out of the room so Luke could rest more easily. Knew I should maybe do some work or go back and see my dad.

There was so much I should do, really. But doing any of it meant leaving this spot, this moment. It meant ending this and having to figure out what happened next.

So I didn't. Instead, I just watched the movie through to the end and let the screen grow dark until, eventually, listening to the rhythm of Luke's breathing and warm in his arms, I fell asleep as well.

15

LUKE

7 YEARS AGO

"*J*esus Christ, it's freezing this morning."

Luke's head snapped up as Tony Hooper came into the locker room and pulled his hat off. Tony grabbed a locker on the same row as Luke and continued talking to no one in particular.

"Chambers had better not make us go outside today. That should be, like, illegal for zero period."

Zero period gym took place before school technically even started. And since gym was a required course all four years, the idea was to give the kids who were taking both AP Bio and AP Chem their senior year enough space for all their classes.

Luke was doing what he always did in the locker room, which was attempting not to look at anyone else too closely. Not just because he didn't want to be creepy, or have anyone call him out on it, but because it was 6:45 in the morning and not really the right context for thinking about sex.

He did, however, catch Oliver out of the corner of his eye as he pulled his sweater off and put a t-shirt on before forcing himself to turn away. Even though Luke and Oliver were spending a lot of time together outside of school now, they still didn't talk in any of their classes.

Luke felt shitty about that. He had the feeling Oliver was trying to make things easier for him, which made him feel gross, and he appreciated it, which made him feel grosser.

"Not if we vote for dodgeball again, he won't," Justin Stewart said from the other end of the row of lockers. "You know Chambers loves that because he doesn't have to do anything."

"Oh God," Tony moaned. "I suck at dodgeball."

"Dude, we all suck at dodgeball," Justin replied. "Get over it —we're all equally terrible. Well, except maybe Luke."

Luke flushed as he pulled on his gym shorts. "I'm not *that* good at it."

Tony snorted. "Your *'not that good'* makes the rest of us look like thumbless babies, so, thanks for that."

Luke didn't really know what else to say, so he just kept changing.

Zero period gym was mostly made up of the *"honors kids"*—a group of 30 or so seniors who were in all the same honors and AP classes. Luke was in most of those classes, but he'd never felt like he fit in with them. So, for that matter, was Oliver, though he didn't seem to fit in either—he just inhabited a world of his own.

Guys like Tony and Justin were nice though, Luke thought.

They didn't seem to care that Luke was popular and treated him like anyone else. Though Luke wasn't actually sure how popular he was anymore. Not since his falling out with Kyle and Andy.

For a moment, Luke tried to picture his life if it were entirely different. What would it be like to be friends with these guys instead of Andy and Kyle? Would Tony and Justin care if Luke was gay? Would they want to be friends with Oliver, too? Would they care if he and Oliver were together? It was tempting to lose himself in that fantasy.

But it *was* just a fantasy. In reality, this was high school. No one wanted to be friends with the school misfits.

Look how everyone treated Oliver. No one in zero period was *mean* to Oliver, but no one went out of their way to be friendly, either. Including, Luke realized, himself. He was just as much of a problem as every other guy in their grade. Only where everyone else was just an asshole, Luke was an asshole and a hypocrite.

Luke's eyes cut over to Oliver as everyone finished changing and filed out into the gym. God, Oliver was so gorgeous. Luke found himself fascinated by the smallest pieces of Oliver, found himself wanting to stare at him for hours and contemplate the curve of Oliver's earlobe, or the spray of freckles on the back of his neck.

So much for 6:45 being too early to think about sex. Luke wanted to pull Oliver out of line, stay in the locker room and press him up against the wall, kiss him right where—

Fuck.

Luke's eyes shifted from the freckles on Oliver's neck to a

spot one inch above them where an angry red circle stood out clear as day on his pale skin.

"Hey!" Luke said, grabbing Oliver's hand before he could slip out the door and into the gym proper.

Oliver turned around in surprise—and so did some other kids in line who, Luke realized, might have thought he was talking to them.

"Uh, I need to ask you something about that last problem on the tutoring set," Luke said, dropping Oliver's hand quickly. "It'll only take a sec."

It was common knowledge by now that Luke had apparently forgotten how numbers worked this year, so everyone else drifted away, uninterested.

"What?" Oliver asked, his tone worried. He glanced towards the door to make sure it had closed after the last of the guys walked out. "Did you—"

"Your neck," Luke said quickly, panic rising in his chest. Who else had seen Oliver this morning? Had anyone else noticed?

"What about—"

"You have—I gave you—" Luke could barely get the words out, he was so embarrassed. "You have a hickey on your neck."

Oliver's face turned bright red—matching the color of Luke's own, Luke was sure.

"Holy shit," Oliver breathed. "I had no—oh God, is it really noticeable?"

Luke winced. "Didn't you look in the mirror this morning?"

Oliver flushed even harder. "Not, uh, not really."

And for some reason, that was the detail that took Luke from panic to hysterical amusement. Only Oliver could have ended up in this situation because only Oliver cared so little about his appearance to have not bothered to look in the mirror.

Luke had spent 20 minutes in the bathroom this morning getting ready, getting his hair to just the right style, even knowing he was going to mess it up in gym immediately. Only Oliver could care that little and still look perfect.

"Do you have a scarf or something?" Luke asked.

Oliver shook his head in dismay.

"I forgot to put one on this morning, and I was five blocks from my house when I realized." He turned and regarded himself in the mirrors on the wall. "Shit, it's really obvious isn't it?"

Luke racked his brain, trying to come up with something Oliver could—

"Oh," he said. "I know. You can wear my sweatshirt!"

"Your what?"

"My sweatshirt. It's a hoodie. Maybe the extra fabric will bunch up around your neck and sort of hide it. Or something."

"You can't give me your sweatshirt," Oliver protested. "It's— it's yours. What if someone asks why I'm wearing it?"

Oliver made a good point. Luke really didn't want to have to explain that to anyone. But if Oliver didn't wear the hoodie and someone noticed his neck, it'd only be weirder. Everyone would wonder who'd given it to him. And given what people already thought about Oliver, given the fact that Luke's fight with Andy and Kyle was gossip everyone in the school knew about, including the topic of the fight... Well, there was only one person who'd been spending time with Oliver lately, and that person was Luke.

"Just say you forgot your coat and I lent it to you," Luke said.

"But that's—"

"Can you think of any better options?"

Oliver frowned, drawing his eyebrows down in thought, and finally shook his head.

"I guess not."

"And you're a genius," Luke pointed out. "If you can't think of anything else..." He walked back to his locker, grabbed his sweatshirt, and tossed it at Oliver. "Here."

Oliver pulled it on quickly. It wasn't a perfect solution, but as long as he pulled the drawstrings tight, the hood bunched up around his neck and helped to obscure Luke's handiwork.

"Can you still see?" Oliver asked. "Does it look okay?"

Oliver bit his lip—and despite the fact that they were alone in the locker room together, despite the fact that everyone probably wondered what they were talking about, despite the fact that Luke still felt panic pulsing through his body— there was nothing Luke wanted to do more at that moment than to kiss him.

"You look perfect," Luke said.

He did, Luke realized. Oliver, with his messy hair, his wiry glasses, standing there swimming in a sweatshirt that was way too big for him, chewing on his bottom lip, looked perfect. And he always had.

You are completely fucked.

He was. Luke was wrecked over Oliver. And terrified of what would happen if anyone found out.

***

The rest of the school day was agonizing. Luke kept waiting for someone to say something about Oliver wearing his shirt, or to notice the hickey, or—the thought occurred to him in fourth period and drained his face of color—for someone to notice both the sweatshirt *and* the hickey.

But if anyone noticed, no one said anything, and the school day ended with Luke still completely on edge. He and Oliver walked home separately, like they always did, and Luke waited for Oliver to text him to come over, trying to figure out what to do with all his excess energy.

He had homework, but every time he sat down to do it, he was up again in five minutes, unable to concentrate. Besides, since he was no longer able to fail calc as thoroughly as he'd tried at the beginning of the year, Luke had shifted strategies and was now trying to moderately suck in all his classes.

Eventually, Luke gave up and went downstairs. His mom was in the dining room, school supplies for her first-grade classroom spread out across the table.

"Hey sweetie," she said, smiling warmly at Luke when he walked in. "How was school?"

"Fine, I guess," Luke said.

He felt a flash of guilt at the disappointment he saw in his mom's eyes. His guidance counselor had finally called home last week to talk to her about his grades, and he knew she was worried. But what could he tell her?

I know I'm torpedoing my grades this year, but I'm doing it for you. I know I'm never around anymore, but it's because I'm falling for someone. He's the most amazing guy, but he's a guy, and I'm nowhere close to being able to tell you about that.

"What are you working on?" he asked instead, pulling out a chair and sitting down opposite her. "Anything I can help with?"

His mom smiled, surprised but delighted, and Luke tried to focus on how good her happiness made him feel.

"We're working on shapes this week," his mom said, holding up a picture of a perfectly round sun with oval eyes, a square nose, a half-moon smile and little triangular rays coming off of it. "You could help me cut out stencils—but don't you have that science lab?"

"That science lab" was Luke's current excuse for why he was spending so much time elsewhere after school—which he realized didn't track with his most recent grades in either bio or chem, but it was the first thing he'd thought to say when his mom had asked where he was going every afternoon.

"Um, yeah." He winced. "But I can stay for a little while. Let me help."

"Okay," his mom said, still sounding surprised. "If you want to." She cocked her head to the side. "Is there anything you wanted to talk about?"

"What? No," Luke said quickly. "I just—I know I haven't been around much lately. I don't know, I just wanted to help."

"You're sweet," his mom said, smiling. Then she laughed. "And I've got enough to do that I'm not going to turn down free labor. Here, you can start with this."

She passed him a piece of cardboard with different-sized shapes to cut out, and a pair of scissors, and set him to work.

Luke tried to concentrate, but even something as simple as cutting up squares and diamonds was apparently beyond his capacities today, and after the third time he cut straight through a shape his mom had drawn, she laid her hand on top of his on the table and gave him a worried look.

"Sweetie, are you sure there's nothing you want to talk about?"

"Yeah," Luke said, a bit more forcefully than he meant to. "Sorry, I'm just really—"

He cut off when his phone finally buzzed. He pulled it out of his pocket and looked down to see a text from Oliver. And then another. And then another.

OLIVER: Hey, apparently my dad's off today? I didn't realize it but he's gonna be home all night

OLIVER: Sorry to cancel at the last minute :(

OLIVER: I mean, not to imply that like, you don't have a life or like, other things to do

OLIVER: Or like we have to see each other every day

OLIVER: Obviously you have better things to do

OLIVER: I just meant like, I would have told you if I'd known and I didn't want you to think I wouldn't have—ugh sorry I'm babbling

OLIVER: I can just give you your sweatshirt back tomorrow

OLIVER: Sorry for being uh

OLIVER: Me

Luke tried and failed to stifle a laugh. It was so like Oliver to worry what Luke would think about him, as if Luke could ever think he was less than amazing.

His mom gave him an inquiring look.

"School stuff," Luke said. He paused as an idea occurred to him. "Hey, would it be okay if my friend came over here? We were gonna work at his place, but I guess we can't so—"

"Of course, honey." His mom looked delighted. She must have been really worried about him if the mere fact that he was inviting someone over had her this overjoyed. "Not a problem at all. Who is this, again?"

"Oliver," Luke said. "Oliver Luna? He's in a bunch of my classes and we—"

"Oh, he's the one tutoring you in calculus, too, right? That's so nice that you've become friends."

Luke blinked. He hadn't realized how detailed his mom's conversation with his guidance counselor had been. God, if his mom knew he was getting tutored, did she know exactly how bad his grades really were?

"Uh, yeah," he said, shoving that complex welter of emotions down to deal with another time. "Okay, I'll, uh, tell him to come."

"He can stay for dinner, if he wants," Luke's mom added as he stood up from the table. "It's just leftovers but—"

"I'll ask him," Luke said, with no intention of doing anything of the sort.

It wasn't that he thought Oliver would judge him, exactly. But though the house he and his mom lived in was big, and nice looking, it felt so cold. They'd had to sell a lot of the furniture, now that Luke's dad had saddled his mom with tons of debt, and it was like the ghost of the divorce itself had taken up residence. The whole place just felt empty and sad. Oliver's house, even if it was smaller and shabbier, felt lived in. Warm. Luke's was just depressing.

Wanting to see Oliver was enough to make Luke bite the bullet and invite him over—but he didn't think he could stomach Oliver eating whatever depressing dinner he and his mom were going to eat tonight, leftover casserole made with minute-rice and whatever cans of soup were on a ten-for-ten-dollars deal at the supermarket that week.

Somehow, waiting for Oliver, Luke got even more nervous. It seemed like he should be used to the idea that he and Oliver were... well, whatever they were, now. But it still felt unreal. Kissing Oliver that first afternoon—Luke still couldn't believe he'd done that.

Or that Oliver had kissed him back.

They were spending most afternoons together, and Luke still couldn't get enough of it, couldn't get enough of Oliver.

Yesterday, for example—they hadn't even done anything in particular. They'd just laid around on Oliver's bed, watching some documentary on birds of the Arctic and then making out when Luke got bored, at which point Oliver had accidentally kicked the computer he was in the process of building off the bed, which had led to Luke asking him how it worked, and somehow that turned into Oliver writing a program that spit out messages on the screen telling Luke to try harder in calculus, and hours had gone by in what felt like minutes.

There had definitely been some *intense* make-out sessions, but they'd never gone any further. And considering the way Luke's heart thumped and his stomach somersaulted every time he tasted Oliver's lips or felt Oliver's hand on his chest, maybe that was a good thing. Luke wasn't entirely sure he could handle anything more without hyperventilating.

He and Grace had dated last year, but they'd never gotten any further than second base—partly because Grace was a strict Catholic, and partly because Luke hadn't found himself really wanting to. He liked Grace a lot and was generally in awe of her competence, but he'd always had the nagging suspicion he was supposed to be more attracted to her than he was.

Things with Oliver had cleared that up quickly—and while Oliver himself might be bi, Luke was pretty sure now that he was gay.

Which was a weird thing to think about himself. He'd spent his whole life thinking of *"gay"* as an adjective that described other people, and now it described... him. But Luke didn't feel any different now—he *wasn't* any different, really—and that was what showed him just how many stereotypes he'd had about what it meant to be gay.

It was liberating, in a way, and gave him this heady, top-of-a-roller-coaster feeling. Except that Luke didn't have Oliver's strength. He didn't know how to not care what everyone else thought about him. He could only imagine the things everyone at school would think about him if they knew.

He didn't think he could handle that.

But he didn't want to think about that now, didn't want to think about how he wasn't strong enough, good enough, to deserve Oliver, and definitely didn't want to think about how depressing and empty his life had been this year until Oliver had come into it.

So when Oliver arrived, Luke brought him inside to say hi to his mom—who was clearly holding herself back from asking Oliver a million questions—and then, on impulse, brought Oliver out to the back porch. It was warmer outside than it had been this morning. Besides, the porch wasn't as depressing as the rest of the house.

Plus, it was out of view of the dining room.

"Hey," Luke said, smiling, once they got outside. Oliver was still wearing his sweatshirt, and it made Luke feel weirdly proud, and a little possessive, seeing Oliver in his clothes. He liked it in a way he couldn't quite explain.

"Hey," Oliver said, smiling around the lip he was biting. "I'm sorry about that insane wall of texts. I was just—I don't know. Just being weird."

"You're not weird," Luke said.

He took a step closer. The afternoon sunlight was falling on Oliver's face, lighting it up in gold. The whole afternoon felt golden, and Luke had a sudden urge to freeze the moment in amber, from the crisp blue sky to the orange leaves rustling in the trees, to the look in Oliver's eyes. He didn't want to forget this.

"Umm okay," Oliver snorted. "That's objectively not true but uh... thanks."

"Fine then." Luke laughed. "You're weird, if you want to be. But I like your weird.

Luke leaned in and kissed him. Oliver's lips were so soft, and Luke swore they tasted sweet. Oliver stepped backwards, tugging Luke with him, and they bumped up against the side of the house with a *thump*.

Luke broke the kiss, and for a full minute, he and Oliver stood chest to chest, staring at each other in silence with wide, nervous eyes. Finally, Luke decided his mom must not have heard, and he kissed Oliver again. But when he let his body do what it was desperate to do, let it grind up against Oliver, Oliver pulled away.

"We should probably be more careful," Oliver said, breathless.

Luke flushed. "Yeah. Yeah, you're right. See, told you you were the smart one."

He laughed lightly, but he worried that he'd pushed Oliver too far. The last thing in the world he wanted was to make Oliver uncomfortable, especially when Luke was just as afraid as Oliver and had just as little idea what he was doing.

Yes, it felt amazing to finally get to kiss someone—kiss a guy

—kiss *Oliver*. To *want* someone in a way he never had before. But if that was all they ever did, Luke still counted himself lucky.

Luke gave Oliver a sheepish smile. "I have to admit, I didn't actually think much past the point of inviting you here. I'd say we should go up to my room, but my mom would just come up every 15 minutes and ask if we wanted a snack."

Oliver's eyes went wide. "Does she know about—"

"No, no," Luke said quickly. "At least, I don't think so." He snorted. "I think she's honestly just excited I'm not doing heroin down by the train tracks or something."

Oliver laughed. "I mean, I guess we could actually do school stuff. Out here, maybe?"

"Ugh, do we have to?" Luke groaned.

"What, are you just on general strike now?" Oliver said, poking Luke in the chest. "You just don't do school at all anymore?"

Luke shrugged uncomfortably. "It's not that. It's just... nevermind."

There was no way he could explain it so that Oliver would understand.

"Okay," Oliver said, giving Luke a skeptical look. "But—"

"Yeah, I know," Luke cut him off. "You've registered your conviction that I'm an idiot. It's been recorded for posterity."

"That's the thing though," Oliver said, sounding frustrated. "You're *not* an idiot. If you were actually bad at school, that'd be one thing. Like, I suck at dodgeball, right, but I'm never going to get any better at that. But you're already good at this stuff, and you're deliberately trying to suck at it, and I don't understand—"

"I can't afford to go to college," Luke burst out.

"Wait—what?" Oliver blinked.

"I can't afford to go to college," Luke repeated. "My mom had to sell most of our stuff just to pay all the bills after the divorce, and my dad won't pay child support or alimony, even though he's been ordered to, but my mom can't afford to take him to court again. She's already taken out huge loans just to pay for this last year at Astor Hills, even though I told her I could go to public school, and I know she wants to do the same thing for college, and she wants me to go wherever I want and not just SUNY or somewhere cheap. She shouldn't have to take on more debt when she's already done so much, but I can't make her understand that."

"So you're just..."

"Making it so that most schools don't want me," Luke said defiantly. "There. Now you know. You happy now?"

Oliver just stared at him. "Oh."

Luke felt abashed. "Sorry, I shouldn't have yelled. I just—it's hard, you know? No one understands, and I'm just trying to do the right thing, but I keep fucking up. No matter what I do, I'm letting her down one way or another."

"Couldn't you get a scholarship?" Oliver asked. "Or could you take out the loans in your name?"

"Scholarships wouldn't cover enough," Luke said, feeling deflated. "I'm smart, but I'm nothing special. There are thousands of me's applying to every school. And loans—I've seen what debt's done to my mom. I'm not doing that to myself. Besides, she'd just try to pay for it anyway."

Oliver didn't say anything to that, and Luke looked at him expectantly.

"Come on," Luke said. "I'm sure you're dying to tell me how dumb an idea this is. I mean, I will go to some college. Eventually. Stony Brook, probably. But I'll probably try to work for a while, first." He paused again. "Oliver, you're killing me. Give me the lecture I know you want to give me."

"I don't know what to say." Oliver gave Luke a sad look. "I just think that you spend a lot of time worrying about being perfect. Don't you ever get tired of pretending all the time?"

Luke felt like he'd been punched. It wasn't a lecture at all. But it hurt more than any lecture could have. Because it was true.

"I'm sorry," Oliver said quietly. "Even if I don't agree with what you're doing—I get it. I mean, it's clearly coming from a good place."

Luke tried to laugh. "I feel like I can see you reconsidering right now if you can bear to talk to someone who's going to go to SUNY Stony Brook."

"Shut up," Oliver said, smiling. "You act like I'm such a snob."

"Not a snob. Just really, really annoyingly smart." Luke grinned. "And by the way—your original premise is completely flawed. Because you could totally get better at dodgeball. I could teach you right now."

Oliver laughed. "Luke I appreciate your enthusiasm, but some things are hopeless."

"Bullshit. I definitely could. Here, come with me."

He dragged a spluttering Oliver off the porch and into the garage. They'd sold off pretty much anything of value, and there was an empty space where his car used to be, but they still had all the sports equipment he and Tyler used to play with when they were younger. Before his dad and Tyler had left.

Luke rummaged around, ignoring Oliver's arched eyebrow until he finally found what he was looking for—a perfect red rubber ball, exactly the right size for dodgeball. Amazingly, it was still fairly inflated.

"Get ready to have your mind blown," he said, wiggling his eyebrows at Oliver and pulling him back out into the yard.

"Let's start with the basics," Luke began. He pointed at the maple tree, its leaves a beautiful mix of orange and red, right up against the neighbor's fence. "Try to hit that tree."

Oliver shook his head. "Luke, this is mortifying. I'm terrible."

"No, you're not."

"Well, you clearly haven't been paying enough attention to me in gym, then," Oliver retorted. "I suck."

"Um, in gym, you always deliberately get hit with the ball, so that you get out and never have to throw it," Luke countered. "So how could I even know if you suck?" Luke barked a laugh at Oliver's shocked look. "See, I pay plenty of attention."

"You... really do. I never—"

"Believed me when I told you that I'd been paying attention to you for years?" Luke said with a wry smile.

"But *why*?" Oliver asked. "Why would you be interested?"

"Why not? I don't know. I just..." Luke felt himself flush. "I just like you."

"But you're not supposed to like me!" Oliver wailed. "You're hot."

"How am I not supposed to like you? You're all dark and mysterious and beautiful. You look like a fucking oil painting."

"Yeah, right."

"I'm completely serious."

"An *oil painting*? Who even says that?" Oliver laughed. "Like, I'm flattered but—"

"There's legitimately an oil painting hanging up in the school library," Luke said, "that looks like you. Have you seriously never noticed it? It's literally your doppelgänger. Well, if you lived in the 1890s and were like, a prince or the son of an oil tycoon or something. Frederick Cabot Coolidge III, it says on the plaque. I think he was an early donor. I swear to God, it's there."

"No, it's not."

"Are you calling me a liar, or just crazy?" Luke asked, exasperated, but amused. "Just trying to get things straight."

"Show me," Oliver said, narrowing his eyes.

"What?" Luke blinked. "I mean, I can tell you what corner of the library it's in. I swear it's there, Oliver."

"Prove it. Let's go right now."

"We can't go now. The building's probably locked. And stop trying to change the subject, anyway. You're just trying to get out of your dodgeball lesson."

"There's a window in the maintenance room that's never locked," Oliver said, ignoring Luke's dodgeball comment. "My dad does plumbing work at the school sometimes, and when he forgets his key, that's how he gets in. He showed me one time."

"Your dad does plumbing for the school?"

Oliver had never mentioned that before.

Oliver flushed. "I mean, not like, as a regular thing. But he knows the headmaster from CCD when he was a kid." He looked down at his shoes. "That's uh—that's how we can afford to—"

"Hey," Luke said, stepping forward and taking Oliver's hand. "That's not—trust me. I don't care about that."

Oliver flushed even harder. "Thanks. I know money stuff isn't supposed to matter. It's just... I don't know, your house is so nice, and I just—"

"If it makes you feel any better, we can't afford the property taxes, and I think my mom's going to have to sell it."

"Oh," Oliver said. "Shit, I'm sorry."

"Don't worry about it." Luke smiled. "Come on, let's go

break into the school so we can go to the library and look at art like the degenerates we are."

The school was dark when they got there, and Oliver led them around to a door Luke had never noticed before, back by the science hall.

"One second," Oliver said, peering through the window to make sure the coast was clear before shimmying it up and sticking an arm in. "It's a little... tricky... to get," he went on as he reached for what Luke assumed was the doorknob, "but my dad showed me... the way... to... yes!"

"I can't believe Oliver fucking Luna knows how to break and enter." Luke said, grinning. "Of all people."

"Hey, I've got hidden depths."

It was odd, walking through the halls together. Luke had been on campus at night before, but always for official reasons. Tonight felt illicit, stolen. Even though there were probably some teachers around somewhere, it felt like they had the school to themselves.

"Alright," Oliver said, grinning when they reached the library. "Show me this—"

Luke held a finger up to his lips. "Shh," he hissed. "We're not supposed to be here. What if someone's inside?"

Oliver laughed—but he did at least do it quietly. "Are you serious, Luke? Can you think of two kids who'd be less likely to get in trouble for doing anything on school property? You're Mr. All American, and I'm as geeky as they come. Even if there were someone in there, I highly doubt they'd think we were planning to vandalize the place."

"Yeah, but what the hell are we going to say we're doing here instead? *'Sorry, Headmaster, but Oliver doesn't believe me that he looks like a hot old dude in a painting, so I had to prove him wrong.'* Because that's believable."

Oliver rolled his eyes but mimed zipping his lips. Luke opened the door to the library quietly, sticking his head in slowly to make sure it was empty before motioning Oliver to come in after him.

The library consisted of three rooms, and the painting Luke was thinking of was on the wall in the third one where the rare books were stored. No one ever used those books, but Luke studied there sometimes when he needed somewhere quiet.

The first, main room of the library was the biggest, and it was filled with long tables for students to study at. The first table they came to tonight was covered with boxes of tinsel and snowflakes and a stack of papers that Luke peered at as they walked by. They were flyers for the Astor Hills Winter Wonderland Dance.

"Shit," he said, glancing at Oliver. "You don't think they're like, having a planning committee meeting for that in here or anything, do you?"

"Right," Oliver grinned. "Because the lights are off and there's no one here—just the way most committee meetings go."

"Fuck you."

Oliver took his hand and squeezed it as they walked through the room. "I wouldn't actually know, to be fair. I've never been on a committee meeting. And I've definitely never been to a school dance."

"Gotta work on those extracurriculars, Mr. Luna," Luke said, laughing.

"What do you call this?" Oliver replied.

Luke couldn't remember when, exactly, he'd first noticed the painting, or its resemblance to Oliver. As far back as tenth grade, certainly. Maybe ninth, even. But ever since he'd made the connection, he'd had a soft spot for this particular corner, and that was where he brought Oliver now, still holding his hand as they passed across the thickly carpeted floor and through the musty old stacks.

"There." Luke pointed up at the painting.

The lights were off, and the room was dark, but there was enough light lingering in the sky outside to make the painting visible. The guy, Frederick Cabot Coolidge III, *did* look like Oliver if you asked Luke. His dark hair curled around his ears, and he had those same thin, wire-framed glasses, with dark eyes that seemed to see inside of you. His red lips were quirked up in an expression that suggested secret amusement.

Granted, it would have looked even more like Oliver if Oliver wore a pocket watch and cloak. Honestly, Oliver could probably get away with doing that now and make it look good, though.

"See?" Luke said.

Oliver looked at the painting, then turned to stare at Luke in shock.

"You thought this looked like me?"

Luke was confused. Sure, it wasn't a perfect match, but there was enough similarity between the painting and Oliver that he thought the resemblance was obvious to anyone who looked.

"I mean..." he stalled. "I didn't mean it in a bad way or anything. I just—I think—I know it's old fashioned, but I meant it as a compliment. He looks good, you know? And I just thought—"

Oliver launched himself at Luke, so hard that he pushed him back into a stack of books. Luke threw his arms out to steady himself—and to keep from knocking any books off the shelves—and it took him a second to realize what was happening. Which was that Oliver was kissing him. Hard.

Luke pulled back, confused.

"Um, is everything... okay?"

"I can't believe you thought—" Oliver began, then stopped again. "It's just so—"

"I really didn't mean—"

"It's so nice!" Oliver finished.

Luke blinked at him, completely at sea.

"What?"

"He *is* good looking. You're right. And you thought I looked like him, which means that—that you think that I'm good looking."

Luke started to laugh. "Because I've only told you that like, five trillion times."

"Hey, shut up," Oliver said, punching him lightly, but this time Luke just gave in and slid to the floor.

Still laughing, he looked up at Oliver and shook his head. "Oliver, I *told* you."

Oliver glared at him, then sat down and faced him on the ground.

"I know. But I didn't know you meant it."

"What do you think I'm doing with you? I *like* you. I *want* you. I think you're fucking hot, and if you think for one second that I haven't jerked off every night thinking ab—" Luke stopped and winced. "Uhhhh, or... you know... forget I said that last part."

A tiny smile appeared at the corner of Oliver's lips. "What if I don't want to forget it?"

Before Luke could say anything, Oliver leaned forward and kissed Luke again and somehow, Oliver ended up in his lap. Luke's felt like it was about to explode. This was way more intimate a position than they'd ever been in, and he was marginally concerned he was going to die of excitement, but there was no way he wanted this to stop.

Luke could feel himself getting hard, and flushed. Not that he hadn't been half-hard all afternoon, all day, really, but Oliver hadn't been in his lap all day. Now, though, there was no way Oliver could fail to notice.

But then again, Oliver was the one who had thrown himself at Luke now, twice. And he'd said he didn't want to forget about Luke jerking off to him. And his hands were fucking everywhere, one tugging at the neck of Luke's shirt as Oliver kissed his collarbone, the other sliding down to Luke's waist and then up underneath the fabric of Luke's shirt and Jesus, that was good.

Whenever they'd made out before, Luke had been careful to follow Oliver's lead, to keep his hands on Oliver's shoulders or above. But now, Oliver's hands were everywhere, at Luke's waist, under his shirt, and Luke could let his hands roam across Oliver's body the way he'd wanted to for weeks now. He stroked every vertebra down Oliver's back, traced his hands up Oliver's slim sides, slid them underneath Oliver's shirt to find a nipple, which he thumbed experimentally.

Oliver gasped, but when Luke looked up at him, he was smiling. Whatever was happening, Oliver was definitely into it because his hips were rolling, grinding down onto Luke's lap. Oliver *had* to feel Luke's hard-on now, since he was basically rubbing himself across it and, fuck, that might actually feel a little too good.

Oliver's lips found Luke's again, and Luke moaned into the kiss, trying to be quiet and failing. He bit down on Oliver's lower lip as Oliver's hips stuttered against his.

"Fuck," Luke whispered, forcing himself to pull back. "Oliver, Oliver—wait. You have to—wait."

"What?" Oliver looked worried. "Does that—did I do something wrong?"

"No," Luke said, trying to catch his breath. "No. No, nothing's wrong. It's uh—actually the opposite of that."

His hands tightened on Oliver's waist as he forced himself to take another deep breath and focus.

"What do you mean?" Oliver asked, confused. "Does it... does it not feel good?" He bit his lip again.

"Fuck, Oliver, it feels too good," Luke said. He flushed. "I'm gonna come if we don't stop."

Oliver's eyes widened, and Luke wondered if he'd freaked Oliver out.

But then Oliver smiled.

"What if I don't want to stop?"

Very deliberately, Oliver dropped his hand to Luke's crotch, stroking the bulge in Luke's pants. Luke inhaled sharply. Fuck, even through fabric, it felt good. It felt good just knowing that Oliver was doing that on purpose, that Oliver wanted him.

"Are you sure?" Luke asked. "We don't have to—"

"I'm sure."

And before Luke could say anything else, Oliver was kissing him again while both hands went to work on Luke's belt. Luke could barely breathe.

He'd never felt anyone else's hands on him other than his own, but now that Oliver was stroking Luke's cock through his boxers, then sliding his hand underneath the waistband and—oh, fuck—actually touching Luke's cock, it was only through bombarding himself with the saddest images of three-legged dogs and one-eyed kittens in cages at high-kill shelters that Luke managed not to come on the spot.

He groaned into the kiss, his hands clenching around Oliver's waist. Oliver guided Luke's cock out and began stroking him. His movements were hurried, erratic and unpracticed, but it didn't matter. Luke tried his best to hold on, but he was fighting a losing battle.

And when Oliver pulled back from the kiss and looked at Luke, his pupils blown wide with desire, all Luke could think was that Oliver had the most beautiful eyes he'd ever seen, that Oliver was the most beautiful *person* Luke had ever seen, and fuck, fuck, he couldn't—

"I'm gonna come," Luke gasped, and Oliver pressed his lips to Luke's again, keeping his strokes steady as Luke released into his hand.

Luke panted, his body shuddering as he clutched Oliver to his chest, riding out the high of his orgasm. Fuck, he'd never come that hard. But then, he'd never gotten a hand job before—a hand job from quite possibly the most perfect guy on the planet, he mentally amended.

"Holy shit," Luke breathed as he caught his breath. "I don't think I've—" He stopped, and they both froze.

Two rooms away, he could hear the sound of the library door opening. Two voices spilled into the room.

"Just put them here," said a female voice. Ms. Bowman's, Luke realized.

"Are you sure it's okay to just leave them here?" the other voice replied.

Shit, that was Grace Tighe, Luke's ex.

"I'm positive," Ms. Bowman responded. "Trust me, Grace, nobody wants to steal tinsel and cardboard snowflakes that are older than you are. They'll be fine until morning."

Grace said something in response, but it was faint, and then the door closed again, cutting all sound off entirely.

"Fuck," Oliver whispered, looking down at Luke. "Oh God."

"Told you there was a committee meeting," Luke said, fighting the wild urge to laugh that bubbled up inside of him.

Oliver scrambled off his lap, and Luke cleaned himself up as best he could with a tissue from his pants pocket, pulling himself together as quickly and quietly as possible, in case Ms. Bowman and Grace came back in.

"Jesus," Oliver said. "I don't think I've ever been so scared in my life. What if they'd seen us?"

Luke heaved a sigh of relief. "I don't even want to think about it."

They approached the next room cautiously.

"How do we know if it's safe to go out?" Oliver asked.

"Beats me," Luke said, still on the edge of panic. "I'm still trying to process the fact that my ex-girlfriend and my math teacher almost walked in on the first hand job I ever got."

Oliver glanced back at him, and Luke could see he was fighting laughter too. "I mean, if you want, we could do it again and I could try to be louder. I'm sure we could get them to actually walk in if that's what you—"

"Don't you dare," Luke said, poking Oliver in the side.

Oliver danced away, then looked back at Luke with a crazy grin, and it hit Luke again, just the way it had this morning in the locker room.

He was completely helpless when it came to Oliver.

Luke caught up to Oliver quickly, tugging his hand before Oliver could walk back into the main room.

"I think they're gone," Oliver said. "And it didn't sound like they were coming back."

"I know." Luke blushed. "That's not why I'm—" He cleared his throat. "I uh, I just wanted to tell you. Um..."

He stopped, unsure of how to word it, exactly—this realization that Oliver was more important to him than anyone ever had been. He wanted Oliver to know that. Luke didn't want to scare him away, but he never wanted Oliver to doubt for a second what Luke felt for him.

"What?" Oliver asked, looking at Luke in confusion.

"I just..." Luke paused. "Remember how you asked me if I got tired of pretending all the time?"

"Yeah?"

"I don't," Luke said. "Pretend all the time, I mean. I don't pretend when I'm with you."

16

OLIVER

*D*espite the fact that Luke was sick and amazingly whiny for most of it, the rest of the week turned out to be, well, amazing.

Luke was still sick on Tuesday, and his throat was so inflamed that by Tuesday night, he was weak enough to let me take him to an urgent care facility. I tried really hard not to say, *"I told you so,"* when his quick strep test came back positive, but Luke's glare told me he knew what I was thinking.

Still, we got his antibiotic prescription filled, and by Wednesday, he was feeling—and sounding—enough better that I felt comfortable leaving him and going out to Long Island for dinner with my dad. Luke made me promise to come back, though, and spend the night at his place, and I also tried really hard not to feel too happy about that.

Neither one of us mentioned the fact that I was basically living at Luke's apartment that week, just like neither of us mentioned the fact that that would end on Friday when

Luke flew out to Jackson Hole. It felt a little like a lost week, somehow, something precious that we could only ruin by talking about it. So we didn't.

I tried not to let myself think about what it would feel like when it was over. That was a problem for Friday Oliver. Today was only Thursday—barely Thursday, at that. Luke's alarm had gone off at 6 a.m.—I was getting used to that, too, which was scary—and we were both still lying in bed. We'd been sleeping together but not, you know, *sleeping* together, the whole week, and it was disgustingly warm and cozy, being curled up next to Luke, watching snowflakes float down outside in the early morning light.

"How are you feeling?" I asked as Luke stroked my shoulder absently.

"Better," he said, sounding surprised. "A lot better, actually."

"Funny how antibiotics will do that," I said with a laugh. And then, forcing myself to be mature, I added, "you're probably dying to go back to work, huh?"

"You know what?" Luke said. "I don't think I'm going to. Not if you don't want me to, anyway."

"Me?" I propped myself up on my elbow and looked at him. "What do you mean?"

Luke shrugged. "Oliver, aside from the fact that I nearly died this week—"

"Okay, that's a little bit dramatic—"

"—*aside* from the fact that I looked death in the eyes and only barely escaped with my life, this has been the best week I've had in a long time. And you've been so wonderful, and I've barely been functional, and I just want to show you—"

"It's really not that big a—"

"-*show you* how much I appreciate it," Luke said. He grinned at me. "So tell me to take the day off, and I'll do it. And then we can spend the day doing whatever you want."

"Are you sure that's a good idea?" I asked.

What's wrong with you? He's offering. Take him up on it, you idiot.

Except what if Luke regretted it later? What if he blamed me?

"Come on," Luke wheedled. "I have to get up at three in the morning tomorrow to go to the airport. Let's make this last day fun."

This last day. Right. Because that was what this was.

If I were smart, I'd cut it off now before things got any worse. The sooner I started crawling out of the feelings-hole I'd dug for myself this week, the better. But Luke was smiling at me and I, sucker that I was, still hadn't built up any resistance to that smile.

"Okay," I said with a grin. "Call in sick again. Or dick, I suppose."

"I mean, there is a bunch of white stuff splattering down on us from the sky," Luke snorted. "Seems appropriate."

Luke didn't check his phone all day—didn't even take it with him. He let me make all the decisions as we wandered around the city and seemed happier than I'd ever seen him.

It felt like being inside a snow globe, the light all diffuse and silvery, the city more beautiful than I'd ever seen. When we ran into some kids having a snowball fight, I couldn't stop smiling, watching Luke instruct a group of ten-year-olds in the finer points of proper snowball packing.

He just seemed relaxed. Goofy and carefree—that furrow in his brow was gone. It was the same Luke I'd gotten to know back in high school, when we were alone together, when he wasn't worried about popularity or impressing his friends or being anyone other than himself.

It's the Luke you fell in love with.

I pushed the thought away. None of that. Not yet. No feelings until tomorrow. I was just going to enjoy this—while I still could.

"Hey Luke," I said, bending down to scoop up some snow before tapping him on the shoulder. "Think fast."

I dropped it down his back, then ran away laughing across the park, Luke chasing after me. I felt like a kid again. I let myself be caught.

We walked back to his apartment as it grew dark, holding hands. Luke was really quiet, and I wondered if he was thinking the same thing I was. This was it. We'd say goodbye tonight. It didn't make sense for me to stay, not when Luke had to get up so early.

But I didn't feel ready, so when Luke suggested we order more takeout, challenging me to find the greasiest thing in the city, all I could do was laugh.

"Greasy takeout?" I said, doing my best to sound outraged.

"I'm sorry, Luke, but my body is a Ferrari, and in case you haven't noticed, I'm very careful about what I put in it."

"Is that so?" Luke said, pulling me in and kissing me. "Shame. I was going to offer to put something else in it too, but I guess if all you'll accept is kale, I'll have to refrain."

"I don't make the rules," I started to say, but Luke's work phone rang and cut me off.

"You were saying?" Luke prompted.

"It can wait. You should answer that," I nodded at the phone as it tap-danced and sang on Luke's kitchen counter. "It could be about the trip."

"God, I thought you were supposed to be a *bad* influence on me," Luke said with a grin. "I'm so disappointed."

But he grabbed the phone and swiped it on, bringing it up to his ear.

"Harvey? How are you? Is there anything you —wait—what?"

Oh God, I wanted to sink into the floor for the next three minutes. It wasn't a long conversation, but it was excruciating, watching Luke's face change from curiosity to surprise to... what's the word for disappointment, anger, and acceptance? *Disacceptager?* What's the word for watching someone you lo—someone you *care about* go through that?

Heartbreak.

I could only hear half the conversation, but that was all I needed. Finally, Luke nodded, thanked Harvey for letting him know, and wished him safe travels. He hung up and turned to me in shock.

"That was Harvey," Luke said, sounding dazed. "He said—he said he doesn't need me for the Jackson Hole trip. He's taking MacFarlane instead."

"Oh, Luke, I'm so sorry."

"God, I'm so stupid." Luke squeezed his eyes shut. "I should have known—I *did* know—better than to do this. God, why did I have to get sick this week? Why did I take today off?"

I felt myself shrink inside.

"There's no way," Luke continued, opening his eyes again and looking at me plaintively, "there's no way I'm getting the promotion after this, is there?"

"Oh, Luke. I'm so, so sorry. I knew you were up for that promotion. You told me. I shouldn't have encouraged you to stay home, I should have told you to—"

"What?" Luke looked at me in confusion. "You don't need to apologize, Oliver. This is on me."

"Yeah, but I'm the one who—"

"I know I told you to tell me to take the day off, but it was my decision." A decision Luke seemed to regret with every fiber of his being.

"I know, but earlier in the week, you wanted to go to work, and I told you not to."

"You were looking out for me." Luke shook his head again. "Trust me, you are not the problem here. Harvey's the problem. MacFarlane's the problem. *I'm* the problem, for letting them treat me this way and not doing anything about it."

"Hey, you're not a problem," I said, closing the space between us. "Don't think that. You never have been."

Luke laughed mercilessly. "I don't know what I ever did to make you think I'm not an asshole, Oliver, but my God, am I grateful for it. Because most days, I'm pretty sure I am. In fact, I know I—"

"You're not an asshole," I said, but Luke didn't seem to hear me. He was staring into space, his eyes darting back and forth, clearly thinking about something else.

"Luke?" I said gently after the silence had stretched on long enough for me to get nervous.

Luke blinked, and then turned towards me, looking at me like he'd never seen me before.

"I'm grateful for you." Luke sounded stunned.

"Okay," I said slowly. "Um. That's nice of you to say."

"No, Oliver, listen." Luke took my hand, then he took the other for good measure. "I've been an idiot—a complete idiot. But the thing is—I just, I need you to know that—"

"Don't," I whispered, my voice raw. "Please. Don't."

"Don't what?"

"Don't say it." I swallowed hard. Oh God, this was awful. This was so much worse than I'd imagined. "Whatever it is, please—just, don't say it.

"But I—"

"I can't handle it, Luke. I can't do this." I started to shake. "I should have left days ago."

"But why would you—"

"Because I like you, you idiot," I said, practically spitting the words at him. "I didn't want to, and I kept telling myself I wouldn't, kept telling myself I could hang out with you and not let my feelings get involved. I knew you weren't looking for anything, and I told myself I wasn't either. But I can't keep doing this—I never could, and I was stupid for ever thinking so. And I know this isn't what you wanted, it's not what *I* wanted for God's sake, but I just—I need you not to say nice things to me. It's just going to make this harder."

Luke stared at me, baffled. "Oliver, I don't—you're not—"

"Look, it's fine. This was never even supposed to last as long as it has. And I get it, I do. Micah told me you never date anyone, and that's fine, because—"

"Wait, Micah?" Luke blinked. "How do you know Micah?"

"He's—we're friends from way back," I stammered, not prepared for that question, not prepared for any of this. "I didn't realize he knew you until a week ago. It doesn't matter. The point is, I'm not trying to change the rules on you, I know that's not fair. But I just—this week was so unexpected, and I got caught up in it and let myself pretend —let myself feel like things were—like they could be... different." I sighed. "It's stupid. I should just go."

I waited for Luke to let go of my hands. To say he'd never meant to hurt me. Instead, he just looked at me for a long moment.

"No," he said finally. Firmly. "No, it's not stupid." He tugged on my hands a little. "It's really not. I don't know what Micah told you, but—well, he's not wrong, exactly—"

"So then—"

"But listen. It's true I don't really date. Or like, know how to. Or, well, honestly have any experience with it whatsoever," Luke said with a small laugh. "But Oliver, I don't want you to go. Not tonight. Not—oh God, this sounds completely crazy but fuck it—not... ever?"

I blinked. I tilted my head to the side and stared at him. I blinked again. He couldn't possibly be saying—

"Shit." Luke let go of my hands and ran his own hand through his hair. "Okay, that made me sound like a serial killer. I'm just—what I'm trying to say is, I *know* you don't live here, and I know you have a million reasons in the world not to want to start anything with me and trust me, I get why you wouldn't want to do this, but I want—I want this to *not* end."

I just stared at him. There was no way this was happening. No way this was real. *Luke* wanted *me*?

"Oliver, I really need you to step in here and say something," Luke said, "because at this point I feel like I'm about to vomit. This doesn't make any sense, and I know it's complicated, and I get that but I just—I want you to—"

I kissed him. Because yeah, I could have said something, and maybe, honestly, I should have. I still didn't know what he meant, exactly. But unless I'd suddenly started hallucinating, Luke was at least saying he wanted more than what we were doing currently. Wanted—maybe—something like what I'd been trying and failing to not want.

Luke's arms swooped around my waist. I smiled into the kiss, and our teeth clacked together. Luke started laughing, and so did I, and then he actually picked me up and spun me around—twice—before setting me down.

"Or you could do that," Luke said, breathless. "That works too."

"This is crazy."

"I know."

"I don't live here. I live three thousand miles away. In California."

"I know."

"I've only been back a few weeks. And we've barely left your apartment for one of them. It's way too soon for us to make any kind of—it just, it doesn't make—I mean, it would be stupid for us to—"

"I know," Luke said. "I know. But I—I want this. I want you. Please just... just say you'll give it a chance."

"Okay," I whispered.

"You mean it? You wanna do this?" Luke grinned and poked me on the arm. "You wanna date me? Because you *like* me? And you wanna *kiss* me? You think I'm *cute*?"

"Well not if you're gonna be like that." I rolled my eyes. "Besides, you're the one who said he doesn't know how to date. Shouldn't I be asking you those questions?"

"It's true," Luke said thoughtfully. "I'm not too clear on what '*dating*' means. But if it means that we get to keep seeing each other, and you keep making me eat gross fried food, and breaking into my computer, and dumping snow down my shirt, and choosing terrible Netflix documentaries—"

"Hey, it wasn't *that* bad. You slept through most of it!"

"Why do you think I slept?" Luke said with a grin. "But if dating means we get to keep doing this—that I get to keep seeing you—then yeah. That's what I want. I mean, if—if you do, that is."

I snorted. "Yeah, no, I actually just put you through all of that because I'm a secret sadist. I don't really want to date you at all, and I'm on a flight back to San Francisco in two hours."

"Fuck you."

"Please," I said. "I've been waiting for you to suggest that all week."

"Pardon me for not wanting to infect you and get you sick. If I'd known you cared so little about your health—"

"Luke, you've seen me eat. Does it look like I care about that?"

"Well fine then." Luke arched an eyebrow. "Get in the bedroom. Stat."

"Pushy."

"Hey, you told me last time that I could be pushy in the future," Luke said, stepping close. "I'm just taking you up on your offer. Now, get."

And then he smacked my ass.

I yelped, and by the time he'd chased me into the bedroom and pinned me down on the bed, I was breathless with laughter.

"No fair," I said, trying to catch my breath. "If *this* is what dating you means, I might need to reconsider. I didn't have all the information I needed to make an informed decision."

"You still don't have all the information you need," Luke said. "You realized that we've hooked up twice now and you haven't come either time? You don't know what you're missing out on."

"Um, I know I'm not the biggest stud on the planet, Luke, but I'm pretty sure I've had an orgasm before."

"But never with me. Not in seven years, at least."

I laughed. I couldn't help it. And okay, maybe it was more of a giggle, but shut up. Luke just looked so serious when he said that, and it was maybe the most adorable thing on the planet.

"Hey, why are you laughing?"

"Because you said it like—I don't know, like you making me come is gonna be like winning the lottery."

"Okay, well maybe it's not *that*, but you don't have to make it sound like getting an appendectomy either," Luke said, pulling back and making a face at me. "Jeez, glad to know you think so highly of me."

"That's not what I meant," I said, still laughing. "Come on, you know that."

"How do you know it's *not* like winning the lottery," Luke asked, still offended. "I happen to be very good at making people come—"

"I just meant that I—"

"But fine, if you'd rather just have some fun with your hand tonight," Luke said, pushing up, "I guess I can just go—"

"Oh, get back here." I pulled him so hard that he *whumped* down on top of me. "Don't even think about going anywhere."

"Yeah?" Luke kissed the tip of my nose and gave me a small smile.

"Yeah." I smiled back. And blushed. "Definitely."

"Good. Because it's important to me. *You're* important to me." Luke grinned. "And so, for that matter, is getting you naked."

It didn't take very long for him to prove his point. We pulled off our remaining pieces of clothing so quickly and carelessly that my boxers ended up hanging off of a floor lamp in the corner of the room. Luke blinked when he saw them land there, which made me laugh.

"It makes you twitch, doesn't it, having all this clothing everywhere? Even at my hotel that first night, you folded all my clothes up neatly."

"I'm not twitching," Luke said primly. "I'm just noticing so I remember where everything is and it's easier to neaten up later."

"God, you are too perfect. It's really a problem."

"*I'm* too perfect?" Luke snorted. "Look who's talking."

"Um right. Okay."

"No, I'm serious." Luke looked into my eyes so long that I blushed—though that might have had something to do with the fact that I was naked and my cock was throbbing, pressed up against Luke's stomach, and I could feel his own erection on my hip.

"Sure," I agreed, wanting to move things along to the part where I got to touch said erection. "Fine. I'm perfect."

"Fuck you," Luke said.

"Uh, what do you think I'm trying to get you to do here?" I said, wishing to God Luke would drop this line of thought.

"No. Hey, listen to me," Luke said. "You don't get to do this. Especially not after you've been so fucking perfect to me. You don't get to go crawl into a hole where you think you're somehow anything less than amazing."

"Okay, well, the sentiment's very nice," I said dryly, "but it's patently untrue."

Luke appeared unmoved, and I sighed. Why was this so hard for him to get? And why did he insist on dragging this out?

"Luke, I'm a dumpster fire of awkwardness, I've sold both my companies because the thought of actually working with other people gives me hives, and despite the fact that I feel like, ten million emotions all the time, I only have one friend and he lives on the other side of the country from me. I am a giant nerd, I'm messy, I eat like a garbage disposal, and before you, it had been almost two years since I hooked up with anyone. Now can we please move on and get to the fun part?"

"That's the dumbest thing I've ever heard," Luke said. "All of that. You're so smart, and you're so funny, and you're insightful and thoughtful and kind, and I love your mess. And you're sexy as hell, so don't even start with that."

"I'm... okay." I barked a laugh. "I'm not fishing for compliments here, Luke. I just know what I'm working with. I definitely look better than I used to but—"

"You were always gorgeous. Always. Even back in high school."

"Sure. With my shitty haircuts and my old man glasses and the lisp and the clothes that didn't fit because I was literally too skinny for them, and how I was always stuffy and nasal and had the world's biggest buck teeth—yeah, I was really beating them off with a stick." I shook my head, hating how desperate I sounded. "Look, I'm not trying to make this about me or throw a pity party. Can we just—"

"No." Luke glared at me. "No, we can't. Is that really what you think about yourself? What you thought about yourself back then?"

"Luke, it's what everyone thought about me. It was objectively true."

"It's not what *I* thought about you."

"Right, which is why you were so willing to be seen with me. Why you wanted everyone to know about us. Because you were so proud of it?"

Luke flinched, and I winced. I hated it—hated how pathetic I sounded. But dammit, it wasn't like Luke could go back and rewrite history.

What had happened had happened—he didn't get to change it now because it made for a nicer story.

"That's not why—" Luke stopped and took a deep breath. "Oliver, I know I fucked up there. Badly. But how you looked never had anything to do with it. It was because I was scared, not because I didn't think you were beautiful." He shook his head, staring at me in amazement. "I can't believe you didn't realize that. I can't believe I ever let you *doubt* that."

Goddammit. Everything had been so happy and fun, such a relief, just a few minutes ago, and now it was all serious and awkward and ugh, why had I ever opened my mouth, why hadn't I just said *"thank you"* when he'd first called me sexy?

Luke scrutinized my face. "Okay, you clearly don't believe me, so, um, here's a list."

He pushed up onto his elbows and bent down to kiss me right above each eyelid.

"I love your eyes," he said softly. "They're so dark and beautiful, and they always seem like you're thinking about thoughts the rest of us idiots can't comprehend, and then you look at me, and I feel like you're seeing right inside of me."

Luke brushed his lips across mine.

"I love the way your lips quirk up into this little half smile when you're laughing at something that none of the rest of us have noticed, and the way they spread into this big lopsided grin when you can't hold back your laugh anymore."

He brushed a piece of hair off of my forehead, and I tried not to blush. This was sweet, but was he really going to document every part of me?

"I love the way that your hair keeps falling into your eyes, even with this new cut. Every time I see you, I want to brush it out of the way and kiss your forehead where it just was."

Luke kissed my neck, and okay, so maybe this wasn't an entirely terrible experience, though I still could have done without the narration.

"I love the way your neck curves where it meets your collarbone. I love how soft your skin is."

He slid down a little, kissing my chest, and fine, that part didn't suck either.

"I love your body. I love how long and light it is—you always remind me of a ballet dancer."

I struggled not to snort at that, because ridiculous as that sounded, somewhere along the way, I'd gone from being annoyed at Luke to touched, and I didn't want to ruin things by laughing. Luke picked up my right hand and kissed it.

"I love your fingers and how strong and delicate they are."

Luke kissed my elbow. "I love all your angles and corners, the way you refuse to smooth down and fold yourself in for anyone."

He slid down even further and kissed the top of my thigh, and I had to stop myself from shivering because fuck, apparently I was into this now and had become putty in Luke's hands?

"I love your legs and the way they look like you could take anything in stride. I love the way they curl around me."

And then he leaned in and placed his hand on my cock—

still throbbing, in case you were wondering—and pressed a kiss to the base before looking up.

"And I love your cock. In case you forgot that part."

I didn't know what to say. What *could* I say to something like that?

It wasn't like I went around all day just thinking about how unattractive I was—but I'd never thought, never felt like— well, like someone wanted me. Like I was someone to be desired. Because yeah, yeah, it's what's on the inside that counts and all, but when you've gone your whole life being told how weird you look—

"Fuck you," I whispered, trying to hold back tears. "Fuck you for making me cry."

"My pleasure." Luke slid back up and kissed my cheek. "And it's always been true, you know. I've loved all those parts of you since the first time I saw you." He gave me a wry smile. "Well, maybe not the part about your cock—but only because you weren't, you know, naked the first time I saw you."

I snorted.

"I don't know how to convince you," Luke continued, "but all that other stuff—all the things you seem to think make you undesirable? I never saw that stuff. All I ever saw was you."

"God, okay, okay," I said, groaning and wiping tears from the corners of my eyes. "I get it."

"Do you?" Luke's eyes wouldn't let me go—and whatever he

wanted to say about mine, it was his that were the real danger.

"I mean, I guess if you *want* to keep complimenting me for the rest of the night, you can," I said, trying to lighten the mood a little. "But you know what they say, actions speak louder than words."

"Oh, so now you *want* me to make you come, huh?"

I nodded. "Very sincerely much so."

"Say it," Luke said with a grin.

"Say what?"

"Say that you're gorgeous. Say you're gorgeous, and that you know it, and I'll make you come so hard you forget your name."

"Luke—"

"I mean it."

"This is ridiculous."

"Maybe. But hey, I'm not the one who hasn't gotten to come yet. Maybe it's just not that important to you. Do you want me to go get my computer? I'm sure we could find a fascinating documentary on the history of Allen wrenches."

"Oh my God," I groaned, putting my hands over my face. "I hate you so much. I'm gorgeous, and I know it, and will you *please* fuck me now?"

"Hmm. I probably should have inserted a clause about how you're not allowed to hide your face from me while you say that—"

"I swear to God, Luke—"

"—but since I don't actually want you to spontaneously combust—"

"Or murder you—"

"—I *guess* we'll save that caveat for next time."

"Next time? You've got to be kid—"

But I didn't get to finish my sentence because Luke was kissing me, and suddenly everything else seemed very unimportant.

Luke's mouth was hot and hungry, and he seemed determined to make up for a week's worth of lost kisses tonight. I moaned as he kissed his way across my jaw and flicked his tongue inside my ear before sucking on the lobe. Fuck, that felt good—everything about tonight felt good, to be honest. Well, except for maybe the talking part.

I arched my back, pressing up against Luke, and was rewarded with the hot, slick feeling of our bodies touching, our cocks sliding against each other. God, it had been too long.

"Fuck, Luke," I breathed as Luke bit at my neck. Maybe he really did like that part of me—he certainly couldn't seem to keep his lips—or teeth—off of it. "I'm going to have a hickey in the morning."

"Wanna borrow a sweatshirt?" Luke said with a grin, and it felt like something cracked open inside of my chest at those words.

He remembered.

"Hey, what's—what's with the—" Luke began, and I realized I was crying again. "I can stay away from your neck—whatever you want, just tell me, and I'll—"

"No," I said, shaking my head. "No, it's not that at all. It's—fuck, this is embarrassing."

"Hey, it's not embarrassing." Luke smiled at me. "I already cried in front of you, remember? This is just balancing the scales. It's all good."

"Yeah, but this is the second time I've cried tonight. So now they're weighted in my direction."

"Nah. Just think of tonight as one long, on-going cry, and we're still one for one."

"Because that makes it better," I grumbled, but I couldn't help laughing a little too. "Just what I wanted for tonight—to sob constantly. That's really what I'd like you to take away from the experience. *'Oh Oliver? Yeah, sex with him was good. Crying got a little weird, though.'*"

"Hey, maybe I'm into it."

"You're into making people cry during sex?" I raised an eyebrow. "Not that I'm trying to kinkshame, but I can't say I expected that."

"No, dummy. I meant that I'm into you. And whatever you need to do. But if you *want* me to make you cry—" he nipped at my earlobe "—just say the words. I'm more than happy to explore that with you. Or whatever else you want."

My stomach flipped over—and my cock twitched at the same time.

Jesus, did Luke just tell me he wanted to get into BDSM?

And Christ on a cracker, was I into that?

Thank God, Luke didn't give me any time to dwell on that thought because he was already moving on to kiss my chest and fuck, I did *not* remember him being so interested in my nipples before—but then, I didn't remember myself being very interested in them either. Now, however... Luke swirled his tongue around one, then the other, licking, sucking, nipping gently, and who the fuck knew you could have so much sensation in such a forgettable part of your body? I gasped as Luke bit down hard and he looked up at me with questioning eyes.

"Good gasp or bad gasp?"

"Good," I said. "Definitely good." He did it again, and I moaned. "Fuck, keep that up and you really will make me cry. And I'll probably like it."

"Duly noted." Luke said, kissing my stomach, stroking my cock.

"Please, Luke," I gasped as his fingers teased the tip. "Please, I need it."

"Need what?" Luke asked, looking up from where he'd been mapping the skin of my stomach with his tongue.

"Need you to fuck me," I moaned. "Please."

"Oh yeah? That's what you want?"

"Yes," I nodded frantically. Why was Luke drawing this out? "Yes, fuck, that's what I want. That's all I want. Isn't that what you want?"

"Oh," Luke said with a lazy grin, "I want lots of things." He smiled at me through heavy-lidded eyes. "But for starters..." He cocked his head to the side. "Repeat after me."

I frowned at him.

"I'm beautiful."

My frown became a glare.

"I'm beautiful," Luke prompted again.

"I thought you said we didn't have to do this again till next time."

"Changed my mind," Luke said with an unrepentant shrug.

He sat back, straddling me with his legs, resting lightly on his knees. He took my cock in one hand and his own with the other. He stroked us both up and down once and gave me a questioning look.

"Or have you changed your mind, too? Because really, I actually *would* like to learn more about Allen wrenches so—"

"I'm beautiful." I closed my eyes and grimaced, but I said it.

"Good." Luke stroked my cock again. "Hmm, let's see. I'm incredibly smart."

I gritted my teeth. "I'm incredibly smart."

He stroked me again. Fuck, that felt good.

"I'm kind and caring and always see the best in people."

"Jesus, Luke—" I began, opening my eyes, but at those words, he took his hand off my cock and gave me a disappointed look. I took a deep breath and closed them again. "I'm kind and caring and always see the best in people."

He stroked my cock again. He was totally fucking with me, wasn't he? Trying to make this some kind of Pavlovian response. And I, God help me, wasn't putting up much of a fight.

"I'm wickedly funny."

"I'm wickedly funny," I ground out through clenched teeth —frustrated both with Luke and with how fucking hard I was, how fucking good his hand felt, and how torturous the whole situation was becoming.

"And if anyone thinks I'm weird, they're just an idiot for not seeing how fucking special I am."

"Oh, come on." I opened my eyes and glared at him. "What is this, an after-school special?"

Luke didn't say anything. He just smiled and watched me, stroking his cock all the while. Probably because he knew, even before I did, that I was going to give in.

"Okay, at least say it again slowly," I said, rolling my eyes. "I can't remember all that."

"You should be trying harder, Oliver," Luke said, giving me a serious look. "I mean, if you really want me to fuck you—if you really want any goal, actually, you have to apply yourself. With hard work, and determination, and—"

"Fuck you. If anyone thinks I'm weird, it's because they don't see what a special, unique snowflake I am, okay?"

Luke snorted and shook his head, but he didn't correct me. Instead, he just leaned down until his lips were right above mine and his hand was stroking both of our cocks together.

"And sexy," he whispered.

"And sexy," I breathed.

"And stunning."

"And stunning."

"And incredibly fuckable."

"And incredibly fuckable," I groaned. "Fuck, Luke, I can't—I can't keep this up that much longer, I'm gonna come soon no matter what we're doing, so unless *you* want me to just lose it in the middle of a hand job—"

"Point taken." Luke nipped at my lip. "Besides, you did well. I'd say you earned it."

"I'm so glad I've won your approval."

"So I'll let you choose," Luke said, grinning at me as he pulled back and then leaned over to his bedside table. He pulled out a condom and then held up a bottle of lube. "Do you want to do the honors? Or should I?"

I flushed, flashing back to that night together two weeks ago. I'd been so determined to sleep with Luke, so determined to convince him—and myself—that I was okay, that I'd rushed through every step. God, just remembering how desperately, how eagerly, I'd fucked myself open with my own fingers was enough to make my cheeks turn scarlet.

"You, uh—you could do it," I said, my voice embarrassingly small. "If you want, I mean."

Luke's smile, if anything, grew bigger. "Oh, I want. Trust me."

I started to turn over, but Luke stopped me. "No. No, I wanna—I wanna see your face."

"Creepy. You just wanna be able to look at me so you can make me say more weird shit, don't you?"

"Because making you acknowledge how fucking amazing you are is weird?" Luke lay down on his side and turned me to face him.

"Oh, very weird," I said solemnly. "In the list of the top 10 weirdest things in human history, it's like, Stonehenge, JFK shooting, and then you making me say nice things about myself is number three."

"You would know, too, wouldn't you?" Luke said with a laugh. "You guessed my password. You've probably hacked into all the secret government files that explain those supposed conspiracies as just commonplace, everyday occurrences."

"Whereas you, on the other hand—" I placed my fingertips on his chest lightly "—you are a complete mystery."

"Oh yeah?"

"Yeah." *Like why the fuck do you want me?* But I didn't say that. Instead, I just smiled back. "Yeah, you are."

"Well get ready to be fucked by a mystery," Luke said with a laugh. "I'll do my best to make it a very spooky, very other-worldly experience."

"You'd fucking better. I'll be taking notes and uploading my findings tonight to that secret government file."

Luke leaned in and kissed me again—slow this time, and sweet, like honey. No rush, no urgency—like we had all the time in the world. I liked the thought of that.

What if he really does want this to be something? What if he really meant it when he said he wanted you to stay?

Luke's lips were soft and smooth and so distracting that I almost missed the sound of the lube bottle flicking open. It was a little awkward at first, me bending my knee and drawing my leg up to make room for Luke between my thighs—but then Luke's other hand began pumping our cocks together, and I decided that maybe this position wasn't awkward at all. Maybe it was perfect.

I gasped when I felt him touch my hole.

"Okay?" Luke whispered.

God, how was it possible for his eyes to be so blue?

"Okay," I whispered back.

Luke slid his finger inside of me and fuck, that felt good. He moved it slowly, steadily, opening me up. I moaned into the kiss, my nails digging into his back as Luke's finger sank all the way into me. When it finally stilled, I needed a second to catch my breath. Luke pulled back a bit and brushed his nose across mine.

"Like I said," he smiled. "Perfect."

He waited for me to nod—and okay, it was more of a nod combined with me thrusting my ass back onto his hand before he began to move, stroking in and out of me smoothly. We moved in tandem—almost like we'd done this before, even though we definitely, definitely hadn't. There was no way in hell I would have forgotten this.

"More," I gasped, and Luke obliged, adding a second finger, and, after a minute, a third.

Fuck, it was a stretch, but a good one, and I knew that the preparation now would be time well spent. Luke's cock wasn't exactly *small,* and since Luke seemed intent on taking his time, on looking into my eyes, there was no way I'd be able to hide the slightest shred of discomfort from him.

"Please," I breathed. "Luke, I'm ready. Please."

Luke smiled and shifted me onto my back, moving in between my legs. It felt sweet, but also strange, to let Luke take over and guide me to just where he wanted me. It made me feel vulnerable. Luke moved to tear open the condom, but I reached out and placed a hand on his wrist.

"Luke," I said, surprising myself. My voice was hesitant, nervous. Because, I realized, I was.

"Yeah?" Luke smiled and ran the pad of his thumb along my lower lip, freeing it from the bite I hadn't even known I was holding.

"You're not gonna disappear on me after this, right?"

"I'm not going to disappear," he said gently. "I promise. I'm not going anywhere."

He leaned in and kissed me, then pressed something into my hands. I looked down in surprise as he pulled back— he'd handed me the condom.

"What do—"

"I want you to do it," Luke said. "Put it on me."

Why should *that*, of all things, make me blush harder than anything else that had happened tonight? Why did it make me feel—I didn't even have words for it. Something very big and warm was expanding in my stomach like a balloon as I took the condom from Luke and tore open the wrapper. Why the fuck were my hands shaking?

Jesus, get a grip.

Somehow I managed to get the thing unrolled onto his cock, but by the time Luke handed me the lube, my hands were shaking so much I couldn't get it uncapped. He took it back from me, flicked the top open, and then squeezed some into my hand.

"I want to feel your hands on me," he whispered, leaning in close and pressing a kiss to my temple.

That, at least, I could do. Maybe it was because he wasn't looking at me anymore, those blue eyes staring like they saw into my soul. Maybe whatever weird thing that had come over me had passed. But as I began to stroke Luke's cock, he whispered encouragement in my ear, kissed my neck, and soon enough, I was writhing underneath him, desperate to feel him inside me again.

"Please," I gasped, and Luke pulled back to look at me.

"You sure?"

"Very sure," I smiled. "And didn't I tell you you weren't allowed to ask me that anymore?"

"Make an exception for me just this once."

You *are my exception, Luke. The fact that you want me is an exception. You are the amazing exception to the long, awkward, uncomfortable rule that is my life.*

"Anything," I whispered. "Anything you want."

"You," Luke said. He caught my chin and tilted it up until I was looking right at him. "I want you."

I shifted, spreading wider, opening up to him. I felt the head of his cock touch my hole. Luke caught my eyes, I nodded again, and he pressed inside me.

Luke moved slowly, and I concentrated on breathing and just taking him in. It felt good to be filled, to be connected to Luke. He slid into me smoothly and kept his eyes locked on mine the whole time. When he finally stopped, deep inside me, I let out a long breath. This felt right—this was what I'd needed.

We moved together, building our pace slowly, steadily. Luke hadn't been lying—he was good at this. He could read me like a book and somehow knew exactly what rhythm, what angles, I needed before I could even ask. I started to stroke myself as Luke fucked into me, but after a moment, Luke's hand closed around mine.

"Let me," he whispered, leaning close.

I surrendered to Luke completely. Not that I'd been holding back before, exactly, but there was something freeing in letting Luke take control. His hand moved in time with his cock as it pumped into me. Somewhere along the line, I'd started moaning and, mortifyingly, I couldn't seem to stop.

"Fuck, you look so good like that," Luke said. "So fucking good."

"God, Luke." My voice was getting breathier, higher, as I got closer to the edge. "Fuck, it's so—oh God."

"Let me take care of you," Luke breathed, kissing my forehead. "Let go."

My body melted into the mattress, and as Luke started to speed up, thrusting into me faster, I knew it wasn't going to be long. I could feel something inside of me coming undone, and when I looked up and saw the tenderness in Luke's eyes, that something exploded.

My orgasm rippled through me, knocking me over like the surf at high tide. For a moment, all I could see were stars. I could feel Luke coming, hear his gasps, feel the stuttering rhythm of his hips as his cock released into the condom.

I want to feel that without a condom, I realized. *I want all of him.*

It was minutes before either of us was ready to move, to talk, to do anything other than breathe. Luke collapsed down on top of me, our bodies still connected, tangled together. I didn't want this moment to end. Luke's head was tucked into the crook of my neck, and his body was a comforting weight on my chest.

But it did have to end, eventually. Luke got up to throw the condom away and clean up, coming back with a washcloth and two glasses of water.

"What, no fresh-squeezed juice?" I said with a lazy smile.

"I thought about it," Luke said, shrugging. "But I didn't want to be away from you that long. I told you I wasn't going anywhere, remember?"

I blushed.

Luke climbed back into bed and pulled me close. It was a feeling, frankly, that I was getting way too used to. I'd gotten used to so much, so quickly.

"How're you doing?" Luke asked, pressing a kiss to my forehead.

"Good," I said, laughing lightly. "You might even say spookily good."

"Glad to hear it."

"Don't worry, you'll go down in the annals of history as an otherworldly fuck."

"Annals, huh?" Luke laughed. He kissed the top of my head. "I like the sound of that."

"I'm sorry I ruined it the first time," I said suddenly.

"What?"

"I'm sorry I freaked out and—well, you know." I squeezed Luke tighter. Even though I knew I could trust Luke not to judge me, I was still kind of happy he couldn't really see my face right now. "If I hadn't, we could have done this weeks ago."

"Huh," Luke said. "I guess. I'm not sorry though."

"You're not?" In spite of myself, I pushed up to look Luke in the eye, confused.

"No." Luke smiled. "If you hadn't *'freaked out,'* if I hadn't thought you were kicking me out, if I hadn't left in a hurry— well, I might not have forgotten my phone. You might not have picked it up or brought it to your dad's place. We might never have seen each other again."

"Oh."

I'd never thought of it like that. I didn't like it. The thought that this—everything that had surged between us in the past few weeks like it had been waiting seven whole years just for the chance to do so—might never have happened was disconcerting.

What did that mean? That Luke could have so easily slept with me and forgotten me? What did that say about us now?

Is he going to forget me again?

"Hey, where'd you go?" Luke stroked my cheek with his index finger. "You okay?"

"Yeah." I shook my head. "Yeah, I'm fine. Sorry."

"You sure?" Luke asked. Then he laughed. "Shit, I'm not supposed to say that anymore, am I?"

"Good point. But yeah," I said firmly. "I'm sure. I was just thinking about how crazy these past few weeks have been."

That was close enough to the truth.

Luke smiled. "Tell me about it. I wouldn't change it though," he added as I lowered myself back down, curling up on Luke's chest again. "Wouldn't change a single second."

"Yeah," I said fiercely, trying to push the doubt out of the corner of my mind. "Yeah. Me neither."

17

LUKE

"*A*nd so then the doctor was like, *'Oh, what prescriptions did the hospital give you when you were released?'* and you know what he said? He said he didn't remember because he never got any of them filled! How fucked up is that?"

Oliver looked at me, eyes wide, and I had to bite back a laugh. It wasn't a funny story, not really, but he was so appalled at his dad's behavior and somehow, even staring at me with his eyes all wild and his mouth slightly open, he made my heart skip a beat.

It was myself, really, that I was laughing at, and how stupidly, completely gone for Oliver I was.

"That is seriously messed up," I agreed, stepping around a cluster of kids and their very harried-looking dads on the sidewalk. "I'm glad you were able to be there with him."

"Me too," Oliver said darkly. "Though now, my dad's doctor really wants him to get a surgery consult, and he already told me he doesn't want to. Because who cares if the medical consensus is that my dad needs a stent—he knows better, and if half a century of smoking and fast food got him into this situation, then more smoking and fast food can apparently get him out of it."

"Well, if he's anywhere near as stubborn as you are," I said as we reached an intersection, "he might just manage it. He's lucky to have you, though."

Oliver's dad had had a doctor's appointment in the city this morning, so I'd asked him if he wanted to get coffee afterwards. I didn't know his dad all that well, but from everything Oliver had said, I had a feeling Oliver might need to vent. So after seeing his dad back onto the train to Garden City, Oliver had swung by my office, and we'd stepped out to walk to my favorite coffee shop a few blocks away.

Well, I say my favorite coffee shop, but to be honest, I mostly went there for their wheatgrass shots. But I'd heard their coffee was good too.

It had been a busy week. Despite the fact that Harvey and MacFarlane were still gone—the weekend in Jackson Hole had turned into a very *long* weekend—I'd been working a ton. Or hell, maybe it was *because* they were gone. It was only Wednesday, but I felt like I'd worked the whole week and then some. Harvey kept calling, asking for additional reports, and MacFarlane had apparently decided to just... not *do* any of his work, now that he was out of the office.

Well, not that he'd ever done much in the office, either.

Yesterday, though, Harvey had mentioned over the phone that we'd be having a company dinner this Friday when he and MacFarlane returned. A chance to hobnob with our east coast investors who hadn't made it to Wyoming. And he'd intimated that he'd be making a big announcement that day too.

It had to be about the promotion, right? And then the dinner afterwards was to celebrate?

So yeah, this week had been hellish so far. And particularly hard, getting over the frustration of getting cut out of the Jackson Hole trip. Hell, the past six months had been hellish when you got right down to it. But I could handle it. All I had to get through was today and tomorrow. Harvey would make his announcement, we'd go to the dinner, and the promotion would be mine.

One more day. I could handle that.

The upside to Harvey being gone was that I could pop out of the office for midday dates with Oliver. And since I'd literally slept at the office two out of the past three nights, these midday breaks were the only thing keeping me sane. So walking with him now, in the pale, metallic blue of the late afternoon, felt special. The air was frosty, and it felt like it might snow again.

"Anyway," Oliver said. "The whole thing was kind of eye-opening. I know *you* don't believe in going to the doctor either," he said, poking me in the side, "but it's like, really a mess. From both the patient's point of view and the doctor's. There's so much room for miscommunication, for things to slip through the cracks. The incentive structure is all fucked up, and that's not even touching the issue of insurance. It just really got me thinking, like, this is an area that's kind of ripe for disruption, don't you think?"

He screwed up his face in thought. "I don't know, I need to do a ton more research, but I'm kind of wondering if that might be an area where you could make some really useful changes with the right technology. And if I could scale it right, it could be the kind of thing that would be accessible to anyone, no matter their income. I could really make a difference."

I stared at Oliver in wonder.

"What?" he asked. His cheeks were flushed, but I couldn't tell if he was embarrassed or just cold.

"Just you," I said, finally giving into the laugh I'd been fighting. "I'm just amazed. You're helping your dad go through a legitimately scary, confusing situation, and you're somehow also coming up with your next app development project and thinking about the greater good at the same time." I shook my head. "You always were an overachiever."

Now Oliver was flushing for sure. "You know, I don't really think it's fair for *you* to call *me* the overachiever. Last time we talked, you were dead set on working for a year and then going to SUNY Stony Brook. But no, then you end up going to school in Boston and becoming vice president of your fancy-pants hedge fund by age 26."

"Okay, not vice president yet—"

"It's only a matter of time," Oliver said. He gave me a side-long look. "But I guess as long as you're not laughing at me because you've decided I'm too much of a nerd to be seen with in public, we're okay."

He smiled as he said it, but something told me there was a bit of a question in there.

"Definitely not." I took Oliver's hand and squeezed it. "I love how much of a nerd you are. I just happen to think you're adorable when you get excited about something. Your eyes do this—this glowy thing when you get really passionate. It's cute."

I tugged Oliver's hand to stop him from crossing as the light changed, pulled him close, and kissed him. But I must have startled Oliver because he stumbled backwards in surprise. I caught him, pulling my arms around him to keep him upright.

"Careful there," I whispered. "Can't have you falling on your ass. Then I'd definitely be embarrassed to be around you in public."

Oliver snorted. "I'd just pull you down on top of me."

"Ooh. I think I might be on board with that," I said as we crossed the street. "Go on."

"Shush you," Oliver said. "We're like, three blocks from your office. Shouldn't you be standing a minimum of 12 inches of platonic distance away from me at all times?"

"I live on the edge," I said with a laugh. "That, and Harvey and MacFarlane don't get back until late tonight.

Oliver rolled his eyes, but then darted a worried look at me.

"I know, I know," I said. "Trust me. I know."

"You know what?" Oliver asked.

"That I shouldn't feel like I have to hide who I am at work, that Harvey takes me for granted, that it's a thankless, pathetic existence that I lead." I laughed wearily. "I know. But in 36 hours, this is all over."

Oliver frowned. "Not that I disagree with any of the things

you just said—because they're all true—but for all you know, maybe I was just thinking about how handsome you look in your finance bro suit."

"A likely story."

"Maybe I was thinking about how your eyes light up whenever you talk about setting up a regular IRA and then rolling those contributions into a Roth to avoid taxes. Maybe I was thinking about the way they dance when you talk about the advantages of being taxed as an S-Corp." Oliver grinned at me as we approached the coffee shop.

"Please don't let that be true. It's bad enough I have the most boring job—but if I ever start truly believing it's interesting, please just kill me. I can't be that guy."

"What kind of guy do you want to be instead?" Oliver asked as we stepped inside.

The coffee shop was still decorated with green boughs and twinkle lights, despite the fact that it was February. It was crowded, so I leaned in to whisper my reply into Oliver's ear.

"I'd like to be the kind of guy whose eyes light up when he's fucking you."

Oliver turned a satisfying shade of scarlet, and I laughed lightly, pressing a kiss to his cheek.

"Hey," Oliver said, clearly trying to glare at me and also clearly failing. "It's not *me* who's been too stressed and busy to make that happen this past week."

My stomach sank. I did feel guilty about that. I was the one who'd asked Oliver to be my... well, to date me, whatever that meant, and then I went and disappeared on him right afterwards.

The fact that this had all been my idea was still something I had trouble wrapping my mind around. I'd been telling the truth when I'd told Oliver I'd never done this before. But I'd known, with a lightning bolt of clarity, when Oliver said things had to end between us, that he couldn't get hurt again —I'd known I'd do anything in the world to stop that from happening.

I couldn't lose him again.

I didn't regret the decision. Didn't regret any of the things I'd said. They were all true. It was just...

Maybe there was a tiny part of me that was relieved when I'd gotten slammed at work. Relieved that I didn't have to dive, immediately, into figuring out what dating Oliver meant. Because I had a suspicion that dating Oliver was going to require my full attention, my full focus, everything I had to give. He deserved nothing less.

And I was terrified I was going to fuck it up.

Because let's face it—I was, as Oliver had put it, just another finance bro. He'd been joking, but honestly, it was true. Oliver had sold two companies by now. Oliver wanted to revolutionize the healthcare industry. Oliver had passions, and things to be proud of.

The only passion in my life was kale. The only things I was proud of were my quads. There was no way I was going to be enough for Oliver. Even if I did give him everything, he'd realize it soon enough. There was nothing special about me. And he'd end up disappointed.

"Hey," Oliver said, looking concerned. "Luke, I was just kidding. Really. You've been busy. You don't have to—I mean, we only just started... doing whatever it is we're doing. We've got time."

"Right," I said, trying to push my grim thoughts away. "Yeah, of course."

We've only just started. We've got time.

I repeated the words like a talisman and took Oliver's hand, but he was quiet as we ordered our coffees, and then told me he needed to go use the bathroom right after. Had I made everything worse—already?

"Hey, Luke!"

I turned around to see Adam and Ben waving at me from the door. As was typical now, they got some double-takes—Ben in particular. But after a few smiles and waves, everyone left them alone as they walked over to me. The pleasures of being famous in New York, I supposed, where everyone was too busy or too self-absorbed to care much about you.

"Hey," I said as they reached me. "What are you guys doing here?"

"We're on the way to the studio," Adam said with a grin, "and *someone* says that his throat hurts but a latte is gonna fix it somehow."

"Hey, my vocal cords are delicate things," Ben said defensively. "Besides, my body, my choice. Don't you trust me to know best what they need?"

"Not when what they need is an iced mocha frappuccino."

"Ugh," Ben shivered. "If you're gonna make fun of me, at least get it right. It's too cold for a cold drink."

"Poor thing," Adam said with a laugh. "You really are delicate."

"Very," Ben agreed. "Which is why we should blow off the studio entirely and run off to somewhere warm. How 'bout that? I'll skip the latte if we can go somewhere with palm trees."

"You have work to do," Adam said with a laugh. "So do I. We can't just take vacations willy-nilly."

"You're only saying that because you get to go to LA next week," Ben grumbled. He turned to me. "You see what I have to put up with? Maybe you have the right strategy, Luke. Stay single— at least that way, no one makes fun of your coffee orders."

"Oh shut up, you love it." Adam said, worming his way under Ben's arm. Ben rolled his eyes but kissed Adam on the cheek.

"You feeling any better?" Adam asked me. "Sounded like you were kinda sick there for a while."

"Yeah," I said. "Much better, actually. Though in my case, it was antibiotics that made the difference, not coffee."

"What?" Ben looked at me in surprise. "Antibiotics? You?"

"Yeah, shit," Adam said. "I would have expected you to try to exercise yourself back to health."

"Thanks," I said drily. "I'm not completely insane. I wasn't sure it was strep at first, so we tried some home remedies but eventually I saw the light and went to the doctor."

"Wait." Ben gave me a hard look. "We?"

Fuck.

"I didn't—"

"Holy shit, you totally said '*we*,'" Adam crowed. "Who's '*we?*'"

"It's not—"

"Who's '*we*,' Luke?" Ben wheedled.

"Well, if you'd let me get a word in edgewise, maybe I'd be able to tell you," I said, exasperated.

It wasn't that I didn't want to tell them about Oliver, exactly. But everything with him was so new. It felt... not fragile, maybe, but delicate. Like something I wanted to protect.

And what if I told them about Oliver only to have things fall apart? Then I wouldn't just be devastated, I'd feel like an idiot besides.

"Anyway," I continued, "'*we*' is—well, there's this—this guy."

"Oooh," Ben said, wiggling his eyebrows suggestively. "A guy."

"Go on," Adam put in, smirking and enjoying himself immensely.

"And he's—I'm—we're—" I stuttered. "We're figuring things out. But it's..." I blushed. "It's good."

"Well that's about the least explanatory explanation ever," Adam griped. "What's his name? How do you know him? When's the wedding? I have so many questions."

"And I'll answer them," I said. "It's just... complicated. I mean, it's not actually complicated, but I guess it feels complicated, and I just... can you give me a little more time?"

"Booo," Adam said. "Respect your boundaries and give you space? Boooooo."

"Yeah, yikes. Asking for to be treated with basic respect and kindness is *kind of* asking a lot, but I guess we can *try*," Ben said with a smile.

I barked a laugh. "Honestly, if you didn't, it would just be par for the course. My job's run over my boundaries about ten times with a tractor trailer. I'm not even sure I have any anymore."

"Ick," Ben said. "It's still bad?"

"Worse," I sighed. "But I only have to hold out through tomorrow. Harvey basically told me he's making the announcement then, so hopefully my life will get better after that."

"Sorry, man," Adam said. "That sounds rough."

"Anyway, as you both love to remind me, my job is horribly boring, so let's stop talking about it. What's up with you guys? I haven't seen you in forever."

Adam snorted. "Not a whole lot is up with us. I'm going to LA soon to do some recording, but other than that, I think we might actually be giving you a run for your boring money. We should hang out soon, though."

"And actually do it," Ben put in. "Not just say we're going to. February might be depressing, but we don't have to be."

"Oh, shit." Adam's eyes lit up. "I just remembered—Nick's birthday brunch. You have to come to that."

"Hmm?" I asked.

"Yeah, we're throwing Nick a surprise party," Ben said. "Except it's not so much a party as just going out for *dim sum*. It'll be a surprise, though, and you should come."

"But I'm not really—I mean, I like Nick," I said. "But if it's just close friends, I'm not sure he'd want me—"

"Oh shut up and say yes, you self-effacing weirdo," Adam said. "It's not some secret illuminati club. Gray and Tyler are coming. Micah too. And Nick said he ran into you the other day and you're inspiring him to get back into running. I'd say that counts as close enough."

"He... said that? What uh—what else did he say?"

I felt a sharp stab of panic. Would Nick have mentioned Oliver? I knew it shouldn't matter if he had. But I wasn't sure I could handle more questions about Oliver just yet. And now that Adam and Ben sort of knew about him, and Nick and Micah definitely did, a brunch with all four of them, plus Tyler and Gray felt like... a lot.

"I don't know, nothing, really," Adam said. He gave me a strange look. "Why?"

"No reason. I was just surprised. Anyway, I'd love to come, but I'm not sure I can—"

"We haven't even told you when it is yet," Ben said, laughing, "and you're already trying to get out of it."

"I'm not—"

"The day after tomorrow," Adam said. "Saturday at noon. And you just said your life gets easy again after tomorrow night, so it's perfect."

"You can even bring your *'it's not complicated but it's complicated'* guy," Ben added with a grin.

"Yeah, come on," Adam put in. "Let that be your birthday gift to Nick—we'll all focus on your love life for a change."

"Ooh, why are we focusing on your love life?" Oliver's voice said behind me.

I jumped, then turned to see him coming back from the bathrooms. I wondered how much he'd overheard—and then felt guilty about that. Oliver, I noticed, was giving me the *"12 inches of platonic distance"* as he came to stand next to me, for which I was grateful—and then immediately ashamed.

I shouldn't worry about what Oliver overheard. I shouldn't want him to give me space. I *didn't* want that, really. It was just a hard habit to break.

But I'd told Oliver that I wanted him to stay, that I wanted him to be with me. And even if I still had the nagging suspicion I was going to fuck everything up somehow, I owed it to him to at least try to do this right.

Taking a deep breath, I handed Oliver his coffee—and then slipped my arm around his waist and kissed him on the cheek.

"We're focusing on my love life," I said with a smile, "because my friends are horrible people who love to torture me. Oliver, this is Ben and Adam. Ben, Adam, this is Oliver."

My... something.

"Oh," Oliver flushed, and I wondered if he was surprised

that I'd kissed him. I hated that he probably was. Oliver smiled. "Torturing you sounds fun, though. Can I join?"

"Actually, yes," Ben said, grinning enthusiastically. "We were just talking about that. We're having a birthday brunch for our friend Nick, and we were telling Luke to bring you along."

"Oh," Oliver said again. He glanced at me uncertainly.

Fuck me.

Why was I so hung up on this? I'd already told Adam and Ben I was dating Oliver. They knew, and Oliver knew they knew. Why the hell did this still feel so scary?

"That sounds fun," Oliver continued. "But if it's a friends thing, I'm sure he'd rather not have a total stranger there."

"Well, it's a surprise party," Adam said. "So technically, he doesn't have any say in who comes—only we do. And we say we want you there."

"Okay." Oliver laughed nervously. "I mean, yeah, sure then. I can try to come."

He looked at me, and I could tell he was still looking for reassurance.

Say something, you asshole.

"Definitely," I said. "It sounds fun. We'll be there."

Because *that* was convincing. I'd never sounded more like a robot in my life. Thankfully, Adam and Ben let it pass, and a few minutes later, Oliver and I said goodbye to them and headed back outside.

"Oliver—" I began, but he cut me off.

"You probably need to get back to the office now." Oliver's voice was bright, too bright. "Before you turn into a pumpkin. And I should probably check on my dad so he can yell at me about refusing to set up that surgery consult. So I should probably actually get out to Long Island and spend the night with—"

"Oliver, Oliver, wait." I took his hand. "Wait, no, we need to talk."

Oliver's eyes took on a wary, skittish look.

"The thing is—" I started to say, but Oliver interrupted me again.

"It's fine." He shook his head quickly. "Really. Don't worry about it. You're allowed to change your mind. And we both knew this didn't really make sense. It's probably easier for us both if we just admit it now and not try to—"

"Wait, what?" I stared at him in confusion. "Are you breaking up with me?"

"Aren't you... breaking up with *me*?"

"What? No. God, no." I squeezed his hand. "The opposite of that. I was trying—and apparently failing—to apologize for being such an ass in there. I shouldn't have—"

"Luke, it's really fine. I don't have to go to the brunch thing, we only just started doing... *this*, and that's a big step, and it's—"

"Oliver, will you please let me talk for once instead of assuming I'm going to say the worst possible thing and cutting me off?"

"I wasn't—" Oliver paused, then flushed. "Okay, I guess I was kinda doing that."

"It's cute," I said. "But it's also giving me whiplash. What I was trying to say was that I know I kind of freaked out in there about this whole brunch thing, and I know you could tell. And I'm sorry. To be completely honest, a part of me was—*is*—very scared about the idea of you coming to brunch. But it's not because I'm unsure about you. I'm just..." I closed my eyes for a second and gathered my nerve. "I'm just scared that the more I let you in, the more it's going to suck when you realize you don't want to be with me."

"You think *I* wouldn't want to be with *you*?" Oliver shook his head and stared at me. "Oh, Luke. You sweet, dumb idiot."

And then he was wrapping his arms around me, right there on the street, and everything felt a little bit better.

"That's not gonna happen, okay?" Oliver said. "If anything, I'd think it'd be you who would run away from me. So, as long as I don't get all dressed up in a suit and tie and go to the Astor Hills gymnasium and jinx us, I think we'll be fine."

"Oh God, I didn't—"

"Joking, Luke, joking." Oliver pulled back and smiled at me. "I know you're sorry about that. And I like you, okay? A lot. I'm not gonna suddenly discover a part of you I don't like and peace out."

"You sure?" God, how was it that I was the one who needed reassuring after all of this?

"I'm positive," Oliver laughed. "I think maybe we're going to have to set up a rationing system on your *'are you sure'* questions, though. You get to ask me if I'm sure once per day. It was unreasonable to expect you to quit cold turkey."

"That's very generous of you," I snorted.

"I promise I'm not saying this because I still think you secretly don't want me there," Oliver said as he finally released me. "But still, if you think it would be weird for me to go to this brunch, it's fine. I wouldn't know anyone there, and I don't want you to feel like you have to babysit me. I mean, I can meet your friends any time."

"No," I said. "Come. I mean it. I think it'll be good. Besides, you won't not know anyone there—Micah's coming too. And if it'll make you feel any better about me babysitting you, I can promise to ignore you all afternoon instead.

"Perfect."

"I want you," I said fiercely. "I want you. In my life. In fact," I paused, an idea occurring to me, "why don't you come out tomorrow. Be with your dad tonight but come in, and we can get dinner and then spend the night. We can go to Nick's thing together on Saturday."

Oliver laughed. "Luke, I believe you. You don't need to offer to sew yourself to me surgically to convince me."

"Yeah, but still."

"You have that work dinner anyway tomorrow."

"Oh." How had I forgotten about that? "Okay, well, come after that. Or better yet, come to the restaurant and just hang out at the bar. I'll get there, make the requisite chit chat for like, 15 minutes, and then duck out early. Then we can meet up and go eat all the gross takeout food you want."

"I don't know. Don't you feel like you'll have to stay if you've just gotten the promotion?"

"I'll just run to the bathroom and say I have food poisoning. Come on, please? Knowing I get to see you at the end of the day will make me so much less nervous tomorrow. Please?"

Oliver laughed. "You're ridiculous. You know that, right?"

"Absolutely," I said. "If that means you're saying yes."

"I guess I am." Oliver grinned.

"Then I guess I'm ridiculous. And I've never been happier about it."

18

OLIVER

7 YEARS AGO

"*J*ust think about it, Oliver, okay?" Ms. Bowman said.

Oliver sighed and nodded. He didn't really want to think about it, but Ms. Bowman might have a point.

"Okay," he said. "I will."

"Good." Ms. Bowman smiled. "I'll let you go, then. Just remember, I'm always happy to review your essays or anything else, okay?"

"Yeah." Oliver smiled, hoping he didn't look as conflicted as he felt. "Thanks."

Oliver sighed with relief when he got out of her classroom. It wasn't that he didn't appreciate Ms. Bowman's interest. But he wasn't sure how he felt about her advice. He walked towards his locker, turning it over in his head.

When Ms. Bowman had first called him into her classroom fifteen minutes ago when the final bell rang, Oliver had assumed she'd wanted to talk about his coursework, or maybe, possibly about tutoring Luke. So he'd been completely at sea when she'd asked him how his college applications were going, instead.

It had taken him longer than it should have to understand what Ms. Bowman was getting at when she'd delicately suggested he consider sharing more of himself, *"beyond the numbers,"* in his personal essay. Sure, schools wanted diversity, but there wasn't much Oliver had to offer there as a white male. But Ms. Bowman had insisted that he had lots to offer, and that schools were looking for students of all different races, socioeconomic backgrounds, genders, sexualities...

She'd let that word linger, and that's when Oliver had understood. Ms. Bowman thought that if he wrote about being bisexual in his essay, it might help his chances.

Oliver wasn't sure how he felt about that. He thought he might be against it on principle—it felt a little gross, using that part of himself just for college admissions. Sure, people had bullied him for that, but had he really suffered on a grand scale? Did he deserve extra recognition from an admissions committee because of that?

But on the other hand, if he really wanted to get into his top schools, could he really turn down anything that might help him? Caltech and Stanford were so competitive, and he really wanted to get into one of them. Not just because they were good schools, but because they were on the other side of the country, somewhere Oliver could start fresh.

Only, now, right before he needed to turn his applications in, Oliver had a reason *not* to want to put everything to do with high school behind him. The thought of being on the other side of the country had always been tempting. But being on the other side of the country from *Luke*?

Oliver knew it was stupid. He and Luke weren't even anything, not really. They hadn't talked about what they were, anyway. What could he call Luke? *Boyfriend*? Surely not. *Friend*? He wasn't even sure that fit—they still only hung out in private.

But at the same time, Oliver was sure, on a gut level, that they were something more. Something deeper. Luke knew parts of him no one else did—Luke pulled out goofy, silly, actually hopeful sides of him that Oliver hadn't even known he had.

And Luke was determined to stay in New York.

It was ridiculous, the way Luke was sabotaging himself. But Oliver couldn't say anything. Luke was so sensitive about it, trying so hard to be perfect for everyone. He didn't want to make Luke feel worse.

He should just enjoy what he had with Luke. Who knew how long he'd have it, after all? It would be just like Oliver to ruin it by overthinking, over*feeling*.

Oliver smiled, thinking about that night in the library. He still couldn't believe any of that had happened. It was like he'd been possessed by some bolder, wilder version of himself. Jerking Luke off—in a fucking library—was the single hottest thing that had ever happened to him.

And okay, yeah, so he'd been feeling a little vulnerable since then, irrationally afraid that Luke wouldn't want him anymore. But he didn't want to let that hold him back. Not when he had no idea how long this would last.

Maybe, when Luke came over this afternoon, Oliver could show him just how much he *didn't* want to hold back.

Grinning, Oliver reached the junction of D hall and F hall. He was about to turn the corner to his locker when a familiar voice stopped him.

"Hey, what are you doing this afternoon?"

It was Kyle Richardson's voice. Luke's friend.

Ex-friend? Oliver wondered. Luke said he hadn't hung out with Kyle since they'd fought in the cafeteria. But Oliver knew they'd been friends for years, and he was pretty sure Luke missed those guys, even if he wouldn't admit it.

Oliver barely had time to wonder who Kyle was talking to before he heard the response.

"Why?"

It was Luke's voice—and it was surprisingly cold.

Oliver froze. He couldn't go around that corner now. Not when Kyle and Luke were actually talking for once, not when Oliver was part of the reason they hadn't spoken in weeks.

So he did what any perfectly normal, totally not creepy person would do, and flattened himself against the wall between two banks of lockers.

"Um, because practice got cancelled, and we're all going over to Andy's, and I thought you might want to come," Kyle said. "Jeez, you don't have to bite my head off."

"I wasn't—" Luke stopped, then tried again. "It doesn't matter. I'm busy."

"Doing what?" Kyle's voice held a note of challenge.

"Homework. Why?"

"Aren't you like, failing all your classes or something, though?" Kyle asked.

"What the fuck does that matter?"

"I'm just saying, you've always been like, the smart one, and now everyone says you're failing tests and stuff, and I haven't seen you in like, months—"

"And why do you think that is, Kyle?"

"What? I don't know, man, that's what I'm trying to say. I don't know why you've suddenly become an asshole, but I'm *trying* to tell you that I—"

"I'm the asshole?" Luke laughed angrily. "That's hilarious."

"I'm just saying—"

"Don't," Luke said. "Don't bother. Just don't fucking bother."

Oliver heard a locker door slam, and then heard Luke's footsteps approaching the intersection of the hallways. He held his breath. He was going to look completely ridiculous if Luke saw him.

But luckily, Luke's footsteps turned left instead of right and faded away down the hall. Oliver waited until he heard Kyle's move away, too, before he finally exhaled.

Holy shit.

He felt kind of guilty, overhearing all of that. But underneath the guilt, and way bigger, he felt... happiness.

Luke really was mad at Kyle. He sounded done with him—

like all those things he'd told Oliver about how his friends didn't really know him, didn't understand him, were true. Oliver knew he shouldn't be happy about the fact that Luke was going through a friend breakup. But he was.

Besides, those guys were assholes anyway, weren't they? Oliver was sorry if Luke was hurting. But Luke seemed to realize he was better off without them, didn't he? And Luke didn't need them. He had Oliver.

***

"Oliver, Luke's here!"

Oliver's dad's voice called up the stairs, and Oliver jumped. He'd been waiting for Luke to ring the bell, but his dad wasn't supposed to be home.

Oliver shut his laptop and pushed it underneath his—for once in his life—*made* bed and ran downstairs.

"Hey," he said, both to Luke and his dad. "I didn't know you were gonna be home."

That was directed to his dad, obviously, but he hoped Luke understood it was an *"I'm sorry this is awkward, and you had to talk to my dad"* message, too.

Because it *was* awkward. His dad being home could... complicate matters.

"I'm not, really," Oliver's dad said. "Just stopped by to grab my backup toolbox and saw Luke at the door. You boys working on homework again today?"

"Yeah," Oliver said quickly. "We're just—"

"Eh, I don't need to know," his dad said with a grin as he

walked through the living room. "Wouldn't understand it anyway, I'm sure. Have fun."

"Sorry about that," Oliver said to Luke. "Do you wanna...?" He nodded towards the stairs.

"Yeah." Luke smiled, his eyes crinkling. "Definitely."

Luke had barely closed the door to his room when Oliver turned and kissed him, pushing him up against it. He didn't even care that his dad might still be in the house—he'd be gone soon, and Oliver felt like he was going to jump out of his own skin. Luke's hands went to his waist, and Oliver pushed his tongue into Luke's mouth—but then Luke pulled away and gave him a look.

"Not that I'm not happy to do this," Luke said. "Trust me, I am. I had a kind of shitty afternoon. But is everything okay?"

"What?" Oliver blinked. "Yeah, definitely. Why?"

"I don't know," Luke said.

He was still holding Oliver's waist, but he was looking down now, frowning. Somehow it felt like space had opened up between him and Oliver, and Oliver didn't like it. But then Luke looked up and smiled.

"You know, nevermind, actually. Forget it."

He leaned forward and kissed Oliver again, and Oliver heaved an internal sigh of relief. He wasn't even sure what he was afraid of Luke saying, but whatever Luke didn't say, Oliver was glad. He kissed Luke back, then took a step towards his bed, then another and another until he felt the bed at the back of his knees. He sat back, pulling Luke down with him.

Luke laughed as he fell down on top of Oliver, but then climbed off of him—trying to give him space, Oliver realized. But Oliver didn't want space, he wanted *Luke,* and he wanted Luke to *know* that. So as Luke scooted over on the bed, Oliver followed him, pressing himself up on his hands and knees, unwilling to break the kiss.

A loud *thump* finally broke them apart. Oliver realized with surprise that Luke had hit his head against the wall above his bed.

"Jesus." Luke rubbed the back of his head with a pained expression.

"Sorry," Oliver winced. "I didn't mean to, you know, maim you."

"You're fine," Luke said with a laugh. "Hey, maybe if I get a concussion, I can retroactively justify my grades this year."

"Sounds like a plan." Oliver leaned forward again. "In that case, maybe I should investigate the situation more closely."

He crawled on top of Luke and kissed him again, letting his hands trace down Luke's chest to his waist. He could feel Luke getting hard, which was just what he wanted, but when Oliver's fingers went for Luke's zipper, Luke stopped him.

"Hey, hey," Luke said, pulling back slightly—and promptly banging his head on the wall again. He grimaced.

"What?" Oliver asked. "Do you not want to—"

"I... do," Luke said slowly, looking down. "But I'm just... I mean, you've been a little distant this past week, ever since —I just thought maybe..." He finally looked up and met

Oliver's eyes. "I thought maybe you'd changed your mind. But now you're all... I don't know, I'm just confused."

"You thought *what*?" Oliver said loudly and then clapped a hand over his mouth in consternation. Hopefully his dad had left. "I'm sorry," he said, more quietly. "I just—oh God, this is so stupid."

"It's not stupid," Luke said. "I promise. Just—tell me what's going on?"

"It *is* stupid." Oliver buried his face in his hands. "I'm such an idiot. I just thought—I was afraid that you, you know, that you weren't going to like me anymore after we—I mean, since the library. I just—I wanted to show you that I still want to—"

"Wait, what?" Luke pulled Oliver's hands down from his face. "Why wouldn't I like you anymore?"

"Because you—because you got what you wanted?" Oliver whispered.

"That's insane." Luke sat up straighter and looked indignant. "I didn't *'get what I wanted.'* I mean, not that I don't want that, but that's not *all* I want. I want *you*."

"Really?"

Luke shook his head and smiled. "You know, for a genius, you're actually kind of dumb sometimes?"

"Okay, okay, I get it—"

"Do you, though? Do you actually get that I like you? Because I do. And as for *'getting what I wanted,'* well... I didn't."

Oliver looked at Luke, confused, and Luke smiled.

"Because what I wanted," Luke said, "was a chance to return the favor. And then we got interrupted, and then you've been kinda, you know, distant, and so I haven't been able to —to show you how I, you know—to make you feel as good as you make me feel."

Oliver wanted to tell Luke everything. How much Luke meant to him, how much Luke had changed his life. How much he wanted Luke to come to California with him because Oliver couldn't imagine having to say goodbye.

But he was so afraid of ruining this, of saying more than he should, that the words caught in his throat. And so he was silent as Luke brought his hands to Oliver's waist, then thighs, and then slid one of them upwards and inwards. Luke paused, right before he reached Oliver's cock where it was pressing against his pants and looked at Oliver with his clear blue eyes, and Oliver realized that Luke was asking permission.

Oliver nodded, wordlessly, and swallowed hard as Luke's hand stroked over his cock. Fuck, that felt good, too good, because if this was what it felt like when all of Oliver's clothes were on, he wasn't sure he'd be able to stand it once his clothes were off. But God, he wanted that, so when Luke's hands moved to his fly, Oliver helped shimmy his khakis down off his hips and then pull them off completely.

When he moved to straddle Luke again, Luke smiled and guided him instead to lay down on his back.

"Kind of convenient your bed isn't covered in circuits and wires for once," Luke laughed, lying down next to Oliver and kissing him.

He ran a hand lightly up and down Oliver's chest, and even just that touch drove Oliver crazy. His cock was tenting his boxers, and he felt a little bit exposed, but he tried to remind himself that Luke wanted him, that Luke was kissing him right now, and that everything was going to be okay.

"That was... kind of the idea," Oliver said, breathless.

"Can I—" Luke paused and closed his eyes for a second "Can I blow you?"

Oliver gulped, hard.

Could Luke blow him? The question made him want to laugh. As though Oliver would ever say no to that. As though Oliver hadn't fantasized about that exact scenario for weeks, months—hell, years. Though, to be fair, he'd also fantasized about blowing Luke.

At the same time, though, it was terrifying to have the chance to get something he'd wanted so badly, for so long. It forced him to confront himself. To see if he was really as brave as he wanted to be.

What if Luke didn't like it? What if Luke didn't like *him*? Oliver wasn't small, exactly, but he wasn't as big as Luke, and what if once Luke saw Oliver, he changed his mind? What if he blew Oliver, but then wished he hadn't, and *then* he changed his mind?

"I don't—we don't have to," Luke said. "It's fine. We can just—"

"No, you can—you can do it," Oliver said. God, his heart was beating so fast now.

"Are you sure?"

"Yeah," Oliver said. He was 70% sure, at least, and he was rounding up. "I want, um—I want that."

He did want it. He was terrified of what might happen after, but he still wanted it.

Luke smiled and kissed Oliver again, then slid on top of him, straddling him and deepening the kiss. His tongue tangled with Oliver's just as his fingers tangled in Oliver's hair, and he ground his hips down. Oliver moaned at the friction and hipped up, meeting Luke's thrusts.

Luke's hands made their way down to Oliver's waist, and Oliver sucked in a breath as Luke palmed his erection again. He could feel Luke's cock, just as hard, pressing into his leg, though, and that made him braver, somehow.

So when Luke hooked a hesitant finger under the waistband of Oliver's boxers and said, "Can I, um...?" Oliver nodded and whispered, "Yes."

It felt distinctly odd to be lying on his bed, seconds later, with his boxers on the floor, naked from the waist down while Luke was still fully clothed. Oliver watched Luke's eyes for any sign of regret as he moved closer to Oliver's cock. He didn't see anything, but it wasn't until Luke glanced back up at Oliver and smiled that Oliver considered, for the first time, that Luke might actually want this as much as he did.

That didn't seem right, but the evidence was right there in front of him. And then, fuck, Luke wrapped his hand around Oliver's cock and stroked his shaft once, and Oliver didn't have time to worry anymore about Luke liking this because he had to concentrate all his attention on not dying.

Luke's hand was warm, his touch firm, and Oliver shivered as Luke stroked him and pressed a kiss to his stomach. The kiss was so tender, and so unnecessary. If Luke were just trying to get through this, wouldn't he dive right in, get it over with? But he didn't—he was taking his time, stroking Oliver slowly and smiling up at him.

"Holy shit," Oliver breathed. "Holy shit."

"Is this—is this okay?" Luke asked.

"Yes," Oliver gasped. "Very, very okay."

Luke gave him a shy smile. "You'll—you'll tell me if you want—if you want me to—"

"Anything," Oliver said. "Whatever you need."

Whatever Oliver needed to do to keep this going, he was willing to do. If Luke wanted him to hop on one foot and moo like a cow, he'd do it if it meant that Luke would keep touching him. And then—oh God—and then Luke licked his lips and placed them around the head of Oliver's cock, his tongue licking the underside as he slid the tip into his mouth.

Okay. Oliver was... definitely dead now. He'd died, and this was heaven, and he wasn't quite sure what he'd done to merit ending up here, but this was most certainly too good to be happening in real life.

"Oh God," Oliver whispered as Luke took more of Oliver's cock into his mouth. "Oh God, oh God."

Luke's mouth was hot and wet and tight, and this was way better than Oliver had ever imagined. He got it now, why people talked about blow jobs like they were the second fucking coming of Christ. This was... well, *divine*.

That was just how it felt as Luke began to slowly suck Oliver in and out, moving his hand in rhythm with his mouth. That didn't even take into account how everything multiplied when Oliver let himself look down and see Luke Wolitzky, the hottest guy in school, who Oliver had had a crush on since seventh grade, with Oliver's cock in his mouth. It was too good, too much.

Oliver ripped his gaze away. He didn't think he could last very long if he kept watching Luke. It was obscene, Luke's beautiful lips sliding up and down his shaft, Luke's eyelashes fluttering against his cheeks as he closed his eyes. Oliver couldn't take it. He let his head fall back on the bed and threw his arm over his face.

But then Luke took all of Oliver down in one go, and Oliver practically convulsed.

"Fuck, Luke," he whined.

Luke pulled off and then did it again, and Oliver's free hand fisted the comforter on top of his bed as he tried not to come on the spot.

"Fuck."

"Is that... is that good?" Luke asked, and Oliver, despite his better judgment, moved his arm and looked at Luke, just in time to watch him do it again.

His whole body shook.

"Fuck," he whimpered. "Fuck, yes. It's—it's so good."

Luke did it a fourth time, and this time, it pushed Oliver

right up to the edge. God, he didn't want to come so quickly, didn't want this to end so soon, but Luke was too enthusiastic, the way he was looking at Oliver as he sank his mouth down around him almost too much, and Oliver knew he couldn't last.

"God, Luke," he warned as Luke pulled off. "I'm gonna—I'm gonna come. I don't think I can—I'm gonna—"

He meant it as a warning, and he expected Luke to pull away, to let Oliver finish himself off. But Luke didn't do that. Instead, he took all of Oliver down again and fuck, it was too much, too good, and Oliver came, right into Luke's mouth.

Luke didn't move at all, didn't flinch, just looked up at him with those big blue eyes, which only made Oliver come harder. When Oliver finally finished, when his body gave one last shudder, Luke pulled off and swallowed—visibly— and Oliver thought he could have come again, just from seeing that.

"Oh my God," Oliver whispered. "Oh my God."

His head flopped back down on the bed. His entire body seemed to have turned to jelly. When Luke moved back up the bed and lay down on his back next to Oliver, Oliver flipped over and curled his body against Luke's without even thinking, without wondering whether he was being too clingy. He just wanted to be close to Luke.

"Hey," Luke said after a minute—or maybe an hour, Oliver couldn't tell—of them just lying there, arms around each other.

"Hey," Oliver replied.

"You okay?"

"Okay?" Oliver laughed—giggled, really, but he didn't even care. "I'm... I'm fucking great."

Luke laughed too. "Good."

"Did you really doubt it?"

"I don't know," Luke said. "You're so quiet."

Oliver pressed up onto his elbow. "I'm quiet because I'm not entirely sure my brain still works. But I'm... I'm definitely good."

"Good," Luke said again, and he pulled Oliver closer.

This time, though, Oliver couldn't get comfy with his head on Luke's shoulder. Because now he wondered what Luke was thinking. About everything—about what they'd just done, about Oliver, about their whole... thing. And suddenly Oliver became all too aware that he was still half-naked and Luke was totally dressed.

He didn't feel embarrassed. No, he felt guilty. Because it hit him, just then, that he hadn't offered to return the favor.

He had to admit, he'd been a little relieved when Luke had taken charge of things when Luke had said that *he* wanted to blow *Oliver*. Because in addition to it making Oliver feel like Luke actually did want him, it meant that Oliver didn't have to pretend he had a clue what he was doing. But now he realized he was being selfish.

And so, after shifting uncomfortably a few more times on Luke's chest, Oliver pushed himself back up, smiled at Luke, and then kissed his neck. They'd both been careful not to give each other any hickeys since that day—not that Oliver was the main offender in that area—but his lips weren't on Luke's neck very long anyway.

He moved quickly to Luke's collarbone, and then unbuttoned the final button on Luke's polo so he could kiss his chest. But when Oliver started to move lower, Luke's hands stopped him.

"Oliver." Luke's voice was quiet. "What are you doing?"

"I'm—I was going to—" Oliver stammered. "I mean, I thought—do you not *want* me to?"

"It's not that I don't want it," Luke said. He reached out and stroked Oliver's cheek with his fingertips. "It's just—I don't want you to feel like you have to, you know?"

Oliver flushed. How the hell had Luke read his mind? It wasn't that he didn't want to—um, *hello*, six years of fantasies—but he had to admit that those fantasies hadn't been at the top of his mind just now. A sense of indebtedness had been.

"You know you don't *owe* me anything, right?" Luke asked.

"I know that." Oliver tried to make his voice firm. "I do. I just... I want to show you, you know? Show you that I like you. That I—fuck." He winced, shutting his eyes. "That I care. Or whatever."

He only opened his eyes when he heard Luke laugh, a light, silvery sound.

"Oliver, I know that," Luke said. "Incredible as it seems... I don't really have any choice to accept that someone as amazing as you would like someone as ordinary as me." He stroked Oliver's cheek again. "I like you too, you know."

"But then why don't you ever talk to me?" Oliver burst out.

Fuck. That was *not* what he'd meant to say. Not at all. He *knew* why Luke didn't talk to him, he knew it and he accepted it, and it was fine. It wasn't like he—

"Shit."

Luke's voice cut through the tremors in Oliver's brain, and when Oliver looked at him, Luke was wincing.

"No, I'm sorry," Oliver said hurriedly. "I didn't mean that. I get it, you know? I totally get it, I'm not saying you have to—"

"I was trying to take my cues from you," Luke said quietly. "You weren't talking to me at school. Not after the first time I came over, not even after the day I kissed you. And I just..." he was silent for a second. "I thought you were trying to make it easier on me. And I was grateful for that." Another pause. "But I didn't think about it—from your point of view."

"Luke, it's fine," Oliver insisted. "I'm not saying you have to like, give me your pin or whatever the hell that even means. I'm not asking you to take me to prom or whatever. Just forget I said anything at all. It's not even important and I—"

"Come to the winter formal with me."

"What?"

Oliver could *not* have heard that correctly.

"Come to the winter formal with me," Luke repeated, slowly, as though Oliver might have wax in his ears.

"You're kidding, right?"

"Not at all." Luke shook his head. "I mean it. You saw those flyers. You saw the fucking tinsel. Let's go to that dance together."

"Luke, I don't go to school dances," Oliver said. "I've never been to one in my life."

That was a stupid excuse. And it wasn't that he didn't want to go, exactly. He'd always thought dances sounded stupid, but the idea of going with Luke...

"Great. There's a first time for everything," Luke said stoutly. "Let's fucking do it."

"But what about—"

"What?"

Oliver bit his lip. He didn't think Luke had really thought this through. And yet—and yet, he really, really wanted to say yes. If Luke was serious about this. God, Oliver wanted him to be serious.

"What about what your friends will think?"

Luke was quiet for a moment, but when he spoke, his voice was fierce.

"What friends?" He shook his head. "Those guys are assholes. You told me so yourself, remember?"

"Yeah but—"

"And remember what you said? That you could be my friend?" Luke took Oliver's hand, then fixed Oliver with a solemn look. "Fuck everybody else. Will you come to the winter formal with me? As a friend, or as a date, or as a—" Luke paused, and Oliver's heart leaped.

Say boyfriend. Say boyfriend. Say boyfriend.

"As whatever will make you say yes," Luke finished. "Whatever makes you say yes, Oliver, that's what I want."

It wasn't what Oliver wanted.

Not exactly.

But what was wrong with him, being disappointed that Luke hadn't said a word that had never been on the table in the first place, a word Oliver had never said he wanted?

What does boyfriend even mean, really? Isn't what you already have enough?

Why did he need more? He had Luke, right here, literally in bed with him, and Luke was asking him to the fucking winter formal.

Don't ruin this. Please don't ruin this.

"Yes," Oliver said finally, smiling so big that his mouth hurt. "Yes, okay, let's go to the stupid dance together."

Luke brought Oliver's hand to his lips and kissed it, and it was so ridiculous, so cute, that Oliver couldn't help laughing. Luke was here. Luke wanted him.

This was enough.

19

LUKE

*W*ithin five minutes of waking up on Friday morning, I felt like puking—and the feeling stayed with me the whole day. For once, I didn't mind the fact that my juicer just sat on the counter, mocking me, because I was too nervous to swallow anything anyway.

I ended up getting to work even earlier than usual, not so much because I was trying to look impressive as I just ran out of things to do at home that morning. On my way to the office, I got a text from Oliver.

OLIVER: <3

And for the next two minutes, at least, things felt a little better.

I popped my head into Harvey's office when I got into the building—not really expecting him to be there. I did a double-take when I saw him sitting behind his desk. It was only 7:15 in the morning. Since when did Harvey show up before 10?

"Oh," I said, trying not to sound surprised. "Um, morning. How was your flight back?"

"Luke," Harvey said, barely looking up from his computer. "Good, glad you're here. We have a phone call at 9 with an investor."

So we're just... not answering my question? Okay.

"Um... okay. Sounds great." I nodded. "Anything else you wanted to talk about or...?"

I left it hanging, but Harvey didn't respond, just glanced back at his computer.

Guess that's a no, then. It had been too much to hope, really, that he'd want to give me the promotion this early in the day. Suppressing a sigh, I walked down the hall to my office and tried to convince myself that today was nothing special.

The phone call went fine. MacFarlane came in late, in the middle of it, and Harvey just let it slide, but I told myself to let it go. Starting on Monday, I'd be MacFarlane's superior. I wouldn't have to do his work anymore or, frankly, put up with any of his bullshit.

Okay—that was maybe a *little* too optimistic. I'd still have to put up with some bullshit. But at least I wouldn't be stuck doing his job.

Around noon, my phone buzzed again.

OLIVER: Are you president of the world yet?

I laughed. Trust Oliver to find a way to make me laugh in the middle of the most nerve-wracking day of my life.

LUKE: Ugh, no. They said my application got lost in the mail? So rude

LUKE: And as for the VP job—no news yet

OLIVER: I'd say I'm crossing my fingers, but you've got this in the bag. So instead I'll just say that I can't wait to see you tonight

OLIVER: I've never been fucked by a vice president before

OLIVER: Should be a novel experience

LUKE: You're incorrigible

LUKE: See you soon

I tried to focus for the rest of the day. For once, I was actually grateful there was a ton of work to do. At 4 p.m., I started watching the clock. Harvey'd said the dinner was at 7, so any minute now, he should be calling me into his office. Surely he'd want to give me time to go over the offer and get the paperwork squared away before we left, right?

By 4:30, I was beginning to get nervous, no matter how much I told myself not to be. By 5:00, I was so keyed up I was practically levitating. And by 5:30, I was panicking.

Harvey was going to tell me soon, wasn't he? He had to. We'd have to leave soon for the dinner.

At 5:35, my phone rang.

"Luke," Harvey barked. "Get down here. I need to talk to you about something."

Not the warmest greeting, but that was par for the course with Harvey. And it didn't matter. This was finally happening. The reason I'd put in all these hours, the reason I'd worked so hard. Sure, it might not be the most exciting job in the world. And yeah, maybe it wasn't my *passion*. But still —this meant something. I'd made it. This was something to be proud of.

I felt like I was walking to Harvey's office in slow motion. At the other end of the hall, I saw his door open. MacFarlane stepped out, carrying his coat. His eyes widened when he saw me, and he looked, for a second, like he might say something. But then he just shook his head and walked out towards the lobby.

What was that about? I was at a loss until a crazy thought popped into my mind. Harvey hadn't—there was no way he'd *fired* MacFarlane, was there? He might be worse than useless, but he was also part of Harvey's family. I knew it wasn't very likely, but maybe it was like, a sign that Harvey wanted things to change after he gave me the promotion.

Caught up in that daydream, I was actually smiling by the time I reached Harvey's office.

"Hey, Harvey," I said, trying not to sound like I'd just been fantasizing about MacFarlane's unemployment. "You wanted to—"

I stopped. I wasn't sure what I'd expected to see, exactly, but it definitely wasn't Harvey standing up and putting his coat on, which was exactly what he was doing.

"What are you—"

"Oh, Luke," Harvey said, as though he were surprised I was there, like he hadn't just called me down a minute ago. "Listen, I need you to get the quarterly prospectus ready for tonight. I want to be able to share it with our clients, and I don't have time to do it myself. Can you get that together and then meet us at the restaurant?"

"I—what?" I blinked, confused. "You—that's all you—I mean..." I trailed off. I knew I sounded like an idiot, but I couldn't help it. Was that really all Harvey had called me in for? "Um, yeah. I guess I can—I can do that."

"Good," Harvey said. "Good. I'll see you there, then."

"Was—was there anything else you wanted to talk to me about?"

Harvey cocked his head to the side like he didn't understand the question. "No, I don't think so. You did good work on the Peterson reports, so those are all squared away. Just this."

"Oh. Okay."

"Excellent," Harvey said, buttoning his coat and grabbing his briefcase. "I know you'll impress our investors tonight with everything you do—and everything you've done—for the company.

"Thanks?" I said, wishing it didn't sound quite so much like a question.

Maybe he was going to tell me *at* dinner? Do it in front of our investors and make a splash or something? It was the only thing I could come up with that made any sense at all —and even so, it wasn't a *lot* of sense.

"Okay, then," Harvey said. "I'm meeting Gordon Devereaux for drinks before dinner, so I'll see you at 7."

"Right," I said, following Harvey out into the hall. "See you then."

I stood and watched him walk out into the lobby, and after he'd disappeared, just stood around staring at nothing. God, I felt dumb. And disappointed, somehow, even though nothing bad had happened. So I had to prepare a prospectus for tonight? That was fine—I could do that in my sleep.

Maybe Harvey just wanted to keep me on my toes a while longer?

Well, good, then—it'd give me one last chance to show him how right he was in making this decision. I'd make this the best damn prospectus Harvey'd ever seen. I nodded to myself and walked back to my office. This was nothing I couldn't handle.

And it wasn't. In fact, I was so full of nervous energy that I got it done in record time. It was 6:45, and I actually had time to walk to the restaurant instead of hailing a last minute cab. Which worked for me, actually. If Harvey wanted to announce the promotion in front of clients, I wanted a chance to burn off some of that energy so I could be calmer at dinner.

I ended up getting to the restaurant early enough that I thought I might be able to find Oliver in person and give him a heads-up that I might need to stay at the dinner more than 15 minutes. I took a deep breath and then headed inside, scanning for Oliver in the bar area.

The place was full with people laughing, talking, and drinking, but not so crowded that I shouldn't have been able to find Oliver. But I couldn't see him. Maybe he just wasn't there yet? I pulled out my phone and shot him a quick text.

LUKE: Hey, so Harvey STILL hasn't talked to me about the

promotion and I think he might want to do it AT the dinner? I'll keep you posted but if you don't wanna stay, I can meet you back at your hotel. Sorry.

God, I wished Oliver were here. Even if I had to wait through an interminable dinner, just seeing Oliver's face for thirty seconds would have made me feel better. He always made me feel better, I realized then—no matter what.

Maybe I could still get out of this early if I just faked food poisoning right after Harvey made the announcement? I sighed, giving the bar one last, hopeful look before walking over to the hostess's station.

"Right this way, sir," she said. "A number of your party are already here."

A number? I followed the hostess as she threaded her way through the restaurant and around a large column. I'd expected Harvey and Gordon Devereaux to be here, but she made it sound like there were more. I was still early, though. Aside from MacFarlane, who the hell else would be here already? I stopped short as we turned the corner.

Harvey was at the table, with Gordon and MacFarlane, like I'd expected. But they weren't alone. There was a fourth person sitting with them.

It was Oliver.

There was no way to hide the shock on my face. How could I? I'd thought he wasn't even in the building yet, and now here he was, sitting next to my boss. My jaw dropped about a thousand feet, and I could tell everyone was staring at me, and there wasn't anything I could do about it.

What the hell was Oliver doing there?

"Luke, you made it," Harvey said—again, as though he was almost surprised to see me. "You know Gordon, of course."

I smiled and nodded, stuck out my hand and greeted him on autopilot. It was hard to pull my eyes from Oliver's face. What the fuck was happening? I could tell, as I looked at him, that he was uncomfortable. But that still didn't explain what he was doing here.

"And I don't know if you'd have met Oliver Luna," Harvey continued. "He's been shaking things up over in Silicon Valley for the past five years."

"Uh, right," I said, still trying to process what was happening. "We've uh—"

"We've met, actually," Oliver said. His smile was friendly, as though this were all a pleasant surprise. It gave no indication that there was anything deeper between us. "We went to high school together. Good to see you again, Luke."

"Yeah." I blinked. "Uh, yeah, you too. I didn't, um, I didn't know—"

"I'm in New York for some family business," Oliver began, but Harvey interrupted him.

"I saw Oliver at the bar," Harvey said, "and I collared him."

Oliver laughed nervously and gave me a look that seemed to offer an apology and beg for help at the same time.

"He said he was waiting for someone," Harvey went on, "but we got to talking about investment opportunities, and I got him to agree to join us for a drink."

Oliver laughed again, that same tight, nervous sound. "Harvey's a real bulldog. I didn't even know who I was talking to at first," his eyes cut over to me, "but he wouldn't let me go."

"Well, you said you were interested in investing across a spectrum of asset classes," Harvey said. "And there's no one who does event-driven, value investing better than Mortimer Bancroft. In fact, while we're waiting for the others to join us, Luke, why don't you show Oliver the prospectus. You want another drink, Oliver?" Harvey asked.

"No, really, I'm okay," Oliver said.

"Oh, don't be so straightlaced," Harvey said. "We're all friends here."

He ordered a scotch and soda for himself, an IPA for Oliver even though he insisted he didn't want one, and then gestured for me to get something for myself as I sat down awkwardly next to MacFarlane.

"I didn't realize you were interested in Mortimer Bancroft's approach to investing," I said as I passed Oliver the prospectus, tilting my head to the side and trying to convey, *"What the fuck is happening?"* without words.

"I didn't either,' Oliver said, returning the look. "To be honest, I was just waiting for a friend, but Harvey here introduced himself and—"

"And I don't take no for an answer," Harvey said, with a smile that seemed pleasant as long as you didn't notice the predatory gleam in his eye. "And that's exactly the approach we use in our investing, as well. Aggressive, and unwilling to settle for anything less than the best."

"Honestly, I'm surprised you recognized me," Oliver said—I was pretty sure for my benefit.

"What, and not know the movers and shakers in the tech industry?" Harvey scoffed. "The IPOs on your companies were some of the most impressive in tech history. And even after you sold your stake in them, they've continue to soar. You know, with our support, we'd be able to extend your reach exponentially. Whatever it is you want to do—another venture of your own, or providing investment capital to other startups, we can help.

"I'm not really sure I—"

"Of course, we'd rely on your expertise there," Harvey continued. "But with our experience and your insider knowledge, we'd be able to move very aggressively in that arena. That's actually something MacFarlane's been working on for the past year."

I turned to stare at MacFarlane in confusion. He'd been working on *what*? Since when? Since when had he been working on *anything*?

But sure enough, MacFarlane took the lead from Harvey and began talking about Mortimer Bancroft's plans to expand into the tech sector while I watched, baffled, and Oliver watched, deeply uncomfortable, and Harvey beamed like a proud father.

I racked my brains, trying to figure out a way to end the dinner, or at least get me and Oliver out of it. But as more and more of our clients showed up, I realized it was hope-less. If I pulled the food poisoning thing, Oliver would still be stuck.

But I couldn't do that anyway—I needed to wait for Harvey to announce the promotion. Though that did seem to have taken a backseat in Harvey's mind, given the way he spent the next thirty minutes plying Oliver with drinks and trying to sell him on Mortimer Bancroft.

Jesus Christ, this was awkward. The only silver lining was that at least no one knew about me and Oliver—so it was mostly only awkward for us. It might even be kind of funny, eventually, once the night was over. But right now, I just wanted to sink into the floor. Poor Oliver, I'd never meant to suck him into my work insanity.

I tried to give Oliver an out after a few minutes when I remembered he'd said he was meeting someone.

"Did you say you needed to leave?" I asked him abruptly. "I thought you mentioned needing to meet a friend."

Oliver just smiled and waved my concern away. "No, I told my friend I needed to reschedule. So I'm in no rush."

Goddammit. Oliver was trying to be supportive. Somehow that just made me feel worse.

"Glad to hear it," MacFarlane chimed in. "While we have you here, let me tell you more about..."

I tuned it out. This was excruciating. It was one thing for Oliver to tell me I should quit my job. It was another thing for him to see what my job was like first hand. How smarmy and sleazy it all felt. How everything reeked of greed and ostentation, and underneath all that, desperation.

There's no way he'll respect you or your job after tonight.

Just when I was beginning to think Harvey had completely forgotten about the promotion, and I'd started to wonder if I should excuse myself to the restroom and pull the fire alarm, Harvey asked for everyone's attention.

"Enough shop talk for now," Harvey said, laughing lightly and looking incredibly pleased with himself. "As you all know, I've built Mortimer Bancroft from the bottom up. As a smaller hedge fund, we have to be quick, efficient, and ruthless to get our share and beat the market—but we work round the clock to do that—and to provide our most important clients with the top-notch service they deserve."

He smiled around the table at everyone gathered there. I was pretty sure he meant the smile to look gracious, but it just came off looking smug.

"And that's why," Harvey continued, "we've invited our favorite clients here to celebrate with us—well, and soon-to-be favorite clients," he added, giving Oliver a gross smile. "We're glad you've put your trust in us, and we'll work tirelessly to continue to earn it, day in, day out."

"Hear, hear," Gordon Devereaux said, but Harvey continued talking.

"On this occasion, I also want to talk about Mortimer Bancroft's future. We've been building and growing and continuing to look for ways to serve you better. As we look to expand into new areas, that's going to mean new challenges and responsibilities—and new leadership at the company."

Oh, fuck. This was it.

"With that in mind, I'm pleased to announce that we'll be adding a managing vice president role to Mortimer Bancroft. And I'm sure you'll join me in congratulating MacFarlane Carithers Boyd as he steps into that role."

For the second time that night, my jaw dropped.

Only no one noticed this time, because everyone was too

busy congratulating MacFarlane and clapping. Everyone except Oliver, that was.

Oliver looked at me from across the table, his eyes wide in disbelief. I felt my face flush as I tried to pull myself together. God, what must he think of me? I forced myself to smile and clap along with everyone else while MacFarlane mouthed platitudes.

Was this really happening? How was that possible? Harvey had been saying for months that the promotion was mine.

"Just a little more, Luke. Keep it up, Luke." Even when he'd been an asshole, I'd assumed he was just motivating me to try harder.

And instead, it was just... this.

Why the fuck had I done anything at all?

The conversation moved on, but I was barely aware of what anyone was saying. I must have been participating—minimally, at least—but I had no idea what was coming out of my mouth.

Harvey had promoted MacFarlane. MacFarlane! That fucking idiot. Who never did his job, and when he did, did it badly.

I'd always assumed Harvey had kept him on because he needed to—but promoting him? That went beyond any kind of sense. Harvey knew just as well as I did how incompetent MacFarlane was.

And this whole time, I'd been doing all of MacFarlane's work. Harvey knew that—he'd fucking assigned it to me half the time. How could he do this?

I felt like such a fool. I'd been used—and worse, I'd practically begged for it. Asked Harvey to treat me like this, thinking it would be worth it in the end.

He'd completely played me. More than played me, he'd led me on. I rewound the past six months in my mind, every conversation we'd had since the managing VP job had been on the table. It wasn't just, *"Keep up the good work and I could see you in this role."* Harvey had told me the promotion was meant for me.

But he'd never put anything in writing, and every sentence had been couched in plausible deniability. The promotion was *"mine to lose."* He'd *"really like to be able"* to give it to me. He thought I *"had what it took."*

And I'd fallen for it.

There was nothing I could go back and point to, to say that Harvey had lied. And even if I tried—it wasn't like I had any power over him. If I wanted to keep my job, if I wanted to keep working with Harvey or anyone who knew him, anyone he could damage my reputation with...

Harvey had me exactly where he wanted me. And as I glanced across the table, his eyes met mine, and he cocked an eyebrow as if to say, *'And what are you going to do about it?'*

I drew my eyes away quickly—and my gaze landed on Oliver instead. His face was unreadable. No longer shocked. He was just... watching me.

God, he must think I was so stupid. I'd told him so many times, promised him, that all this work, all the shit I was dealing with, was worth it—for this, for this promotion that was supposed to be mine.

I looked away, my face heating up again. It hadn't been worth it. I'd just let them lead me on. I'd gone to work for assholes and gotten played, and why had I ever expected better? I wasn't passionate enough to do something I really wanted. I'd chosen the safe route, chosen something I knew didn't make me happy.

I'd gone into an industry full of dicks and—surprise, surprise—I'd gotten fucked.

"You'll have to excuse me, but I'm afraid something's come up. I need to be going."

Oliver's voice cut through the din conversation like a knife, and my head snapped up. He glanced at his phone and made a regretful face to Harvey. Oliver was leaving? Now?

"Oh, come on," Harvey said. "The night's young. Stay. Celebrate with us."

"I can't," Oliver said curtly. "It turns out I'm meeting someone after all. It was nice to meet you all. Good to see you, Luke."

His eyes cut to me and held mine for a second. What was he trying to tell me? I couldn't leave now. Not after this. Not when it would be clear to Harvey and MacFarlane, if not the rest of our investors, how upset I was. I couldn't let them know they'd rattled me. Couldn't show weakness. I might be devastated, but I'd be damned if I let them see.

"You too," I said, staring at Oliver in confusion.

Maybe he was just leaving because he couldn't stand to be around me anymore. Maybe he'd finally seen how pathetic I truly was. It made sense. And it was bound to have happened sooner or later.

I watched Oliver's back retreat through the restaurant, that sinking realization settling into my bones. As his tall, slim figure cut through the crowd, it felt like I was watching him walk away forever. It was hard to breathe. I followed him with my eyes as he stepped out of the way of a server and then, turning a corner, he was gone.

It was like I'd been punched in the stomach. Oliver was gone. Why did that feel so final? And how the hell was I supposed to handle that, on top of a night like this?

And then, all of a sudden, I really did feel sick to my stomach. Shit. I couldn't be this weak. But I could feel bile rising in my throat, and I knew I needed to get out.

"I'm sorry," I said, standing so quickly I almost knocked my chair over. "I'm sorry, I just—I think—I'm going to be—"

I grabbed my briefcase and ran. I didn't even stop to get my coat from the coat check—I had to get outside immediately. I pushed through the tightly packed bar area and burst out into the chill of the night air. There wasn't really any greenery outside the restaurant, but 50 yards down the sidewalk, there was a tiny tree, fenced off from dogs. I stumbled to it, hunched over, and retched.

Nothing came out, but that didn't stop my body from heaving over and over again. The perks of not being able to eat all day, I supposed. I was still standing there, my hands on my knees, waiting for my body to stop shaking when I felt a hand on my shoulder.

"Hey," Oliver's voice said softly behind me. "Let me help."

My body shuddered one last time as I straightened up. Oliver's eyes were luminous in the dark—they looked like they could drink me in. Honestly, at that moment, I wanted them to. I wanted to disappear.

"You okay?" Oliver said.

I shrugged. "I... I don't know."

"Good point," Oliver said. "That was a stupid question. Can I try again? You don't look okay. Can I give you a hug?"

I glanced towards the restaurant involuntarily. Everyone was inside—and even if someone came looking for me, we were far enough away from the front of the restaurant that they probably wouldn't see. I looked back at Oliver. He must have read the hesitation in my eyes.

"It's okay," he said. "You don't have to."

"I just—" I closed my eyes for a moment. "I'm sorry, Oliver. I'm so sorry. I'm such a mess."

"Hey, you have nothing to apologize for."

"Don't I?" I looked at him in desperation. "I fucking told you, told everyone I knew, that I was getting this promotion. That everything was going to be worth it. You stayed here tonight because you thought I was going to—"

"I stayed here because your boss dragged me over, and then once you got here, I didn't want to leave until you did. It had nothing to do with the promotion."

"Then why did you—" I stopped. I sounded pathetic.

"What?"

"Why did you leave just now?" I asked, and something inside me broke.

"Because I was mad," Oliver said. "Because I was so pissed at Harvey I didn't think I could sit there any longer and watch him treat you like that. And since I didn't think you'd want me to punch him, I just thought—oh, Luke, did you think I left because I was mad at you? No, God, no, I would never —oh, Luke—"

I launched myself at him. I needed him in my arms right then, more than I'd ever needed anything. Fuck who saw. Fuck the whole world. I needed Oliver.

"I thought you were—oh God," I gasped. I was shaking again. "I thought you were embarrassed of me. That you must have thought—must have seen—how fucking stupid I've been."

"Oh, Luke, no," Oliver said, squeezing me tight. He tucked his face into my neck, and I breathed in the scent of him and felt a little more stable. "Never," he whispered. "I'd never think that about you."

"I'm sorry I made you leave though, regardless. I'm sorry about this whole night. You didn't even get to eat dinner. I'm sorry."

"Don't be," Oliver said with a laugh. "Honestly, it's probably for the best. I've never punched anyone in my life, so staying in there would have gotten really embarrassing for *me* real fast."

"It's okay." I laughed a little bit raggedly. "I'll teach you. And I'm sure you'll have plenty of other chances to practice on him in the future."

I felt Oliver's body stiffen, and then he was pulling away

from me. He tilted his head to the side and gave me a confused look.

"Okay, much as I'd like to punch that guy, when would I see him again?"

I blinked. Now I was confused.

"I mean, I'm not saying you need to tag along to any work dinners again anytime soon. But you're probably gonna have to talk to him again at some point if we keep—I mean, I know I haven't come out yet at work, but I'd want to, and I'd want him to know that we—"

"Wait but—" Oliver's look had gone from one of mild confusion to one of who-the-fuck-is-this-alien-I'm-talking to. "You're not going to keep working for them, are you?"

"I—"

"Because call me crazy, but I wouldn't think you'd really want to stay at a place like that. And now, you don't have to feel bad about quitting. Hell, you could quit and move to California with me! You can do whatever you want now."

"What?"

"I mean, not really." Oliver laughed nervously. "I was kidding. Sort of. I was just trying to say that you can literally do whatever you want now, and you don't have to feel guilty, you don't have to feel like you owe them anything. You can quit with a clean conscience and figure out what you *actually* want to do instead of just what other people tell you you should want."

"That's not—that's not what I'm doing. I don't just do what other people tell me I should want, Oliver."

"Okay, sorry. Bad choice of words, I just meant—"

"I can't just quit." I felt something gross taking shape inside me, something hot and metallic arming itself in my stomach. "I can't just—that's not how it works. And I don't just do what people tell me to. Honestly, if anyone's telling me what I should want, it's you."

"Luke, that's not what I—"

"I'm not quitting," I said stubbornly. "I can't. Not now."

"Why not? Your job is shitty, you don't even like it, and they treat you horribly. And now that you know you're not getting the promotion—"

"I can't quit."

"Why not?"

"Because that's not how it *works*," I said. "I need a fucking job, Oliver. I have bills to pay, student loans, rent. I'm sorry I don't live in a world where money grows on trees like you do, but some of us have to work."

"I work," Oliver spit out. "And I'm not going to apologize for liking what I do. For having found a world where, for once, I finally fit in. Where I'm not some weird guy people are afraid to be around."

He closed his eyes and drew a deep breath before speaking again.

"Luke, I'm sorry. I don't want to fight. I just don't get why you don't see how much of the world is open to you. If you need to take time off, you have options. You could move in with your mom—that would take care of rent, at least."

"I'm 26 years old. I'm not living with my mom. I'm an adult."

"Well, you're also incredibly privileged if you think it's that bad," Oliver said, sounding annoyed. "Do you have any idea how many 26-year-olds still live with their families in this country? In the world? Luke, you have *so much* going for you, and on top of that, you're fucking amazing. No one's going to judge you if you need to take some time and—"

"I'm not moving in with my mom."

"Fine then," Oliver said. "Don't. Keep your apartment. I have money as you seem so desperate to remind me. Let me pay your rent, your student loans. Hell, move in with me—we can get an apartment together. There are *options,* Luke. You just can't see them because you're so terrified of what it means if you admit that this isn't the right path for you— because you're terrified of making a mistake."

"I'm not fucking terrified," I shot back. "I'm just—"

I stopped, biting off my words. I wasn't thinking clearly, and I knew it, but I was also fucking pissed at Oliver. How did he not see how insane everything he was saying was?

"Jesus Christ," I whispered. "I can't—I can't think about all of this now."

"But Luke, you can't just—"

"No." I shook my head. "No. This is crazy. Move in together? Oliver, you've been back for what, a month? You're just gonna get an apartment here, like that? Or did you really want me to come back to California with you? Because I can tell you right now, both of those things are insane."

Oliver flinched, and something twisted in my heart. How the hell had we gotten here?

"I just—I can't do this right now," I said softly. "It's too much, too fast. We need—we need to take a step back. I need time to think."

"Oh." Oliver's eyes were glued to the ground.

"I know you were just trying to help, Oliver. I know that. I know you want me to be—" I choked on my own words, my heart breaking "—want me to be this wonderful person. But have you ever considered that maybe I'm just... not?"

Oliver finally lifted his gaze to meet mine, and I could see the pain in his eyes—pain that I knew I had put there.

But if I'd put it there, it was only because this whole time, I'd let him believe—I'd tried to get myself to believe—that I was someone I wasn't. Someone brave. Someone principled and passionate. Someone bigger and better than I was.

Maybe it was time for us to both stop lying.

I shook my head. "I just—I need—"

I wasn't even sure what I was trying to say, but it didn't matter. Before I could finish the sentence, Oliver turned and walked away.

20

LUKE

7 YEARS AGO

"*Y*ou look so handsome, sweetie."

Luke jumped when he heard his mom's voice behind him. He hadn't even heard her come upstairs, much less come up to stand behind him as he scrutinized himself in the bathroom mirror.

To be fair, though, he probably would have missed a bomb going off in the next room, he was so preoccupied. He was supposed to leave for the dance in just a few minutes, and he was so nervous he could barely think.

"Thanks," Luke said, blushing a bit. "Though I think you're kind of contractually obligated to think that."

"It's still true though." She put a hand on his shoulder and squeezed it for a second. "You know that I'm proud of you, right? No matter what?"

"Um. Yeah. I guess?" Luke looked at her in the mirror, confused. What had brought that on? "Thanks."

"And you're sure you don't want a ride?" she asked for at least the eightieth time that day.

"Yeah, I'm sure."

He and Oliver had agreed to meet *at* the dance. Neither one of them had been quite brave enough to have the other one pick him up in front of their parents.

Well, Oliver might have been. But Luke definitely wasn't, and Oliver had let it go.

You're not good enough for him.

The thought had been running through Luke's mind all day —all week, really, ever since he'd asked Oliver to go to the dance with him.

You're not good enough for him. You don't deserve him. You're going to ruin everything.

The thoughts beat like a drum as Luke kissed his mom goodbye, stepped out of the house, and walked towards Astor Hills. He tried to ignore them. Tried to counteract them by telling himself he could do this, he could do this, he could do this. But his stomach roiled like a snake pit and the thoughts, no matter how hard he tried to suppress them, kept coming back.

Luke had asked Oliver to go to the dance on impulse. Oliver had seemed so unhappy about Luke not talking to him at school, and Luke had hated that—and hated knowing he was the one hurting him.

It wasn't fair, Luke knew, to ask Oliver to be with him outside of school, but not even talk to Oliver on campus. And Luke had wanted, so badly, to live in a world where he was better than that. Being around Oliver always made Luke feel braver. Made him willing to dream of impossible things.

The problem, though, was that when Luke wasn't around Oliver, he got distinctly less brave. And as Luke had walked home from Oliver's house that night, still giddy from what they'd done, coming down from the drug that was Oliver's presence, he'd realized he'd made a mistake.

Like it or not, Luke and Oliver lived in the real world. This wasn't a fantasy, this was high school—and it wasn't even the end of high school yet where nothing mattered anymore, it was November. Could Luke really go through the rest of high school with everyone knowing he was gay?

Around Oliver, sure, everything felt possible. But that wasn't realistic. Luke dreaded the thought of what people would say if they knew. He wasn't brave enough to come out, he knew.

Luke had thought about playing the whole thing off—but he couldn't do that to Oliver, ask him to pretend it was a joke. It would hurt Oliver's feelings, for one thing, plus Luke could already hear the point Oliver would make about how homophobic a joke like that would be, how harmful. He wouldn't be wrong.

Besides—this was Oliver they were talking about. No one would believe it was a joke, even for a second. If Luke showed up to the dance with Oliver as his date, everyone would assume that they were together for real. And they'd be right. Luke wasn't sure he could handle that.

And yet, every step he took carried him closer to Astor Hills, closer to a life he wasn't ready for.

Luke's phone buzzed in his jacket pocket, and he pulled it out, his stomach twisting in knots as he read.

OLIVER: *Hey, just got here!*

OLIVER: *I'm just inside the doors*

OLIVER: *See you soon!*

Fuck.

Somehow, those texts clinched it for Luke. He'd fucked up. Oliver was excited—so excited—and Luke was going to hurt him.

He should have said something to Oliver the same night that he'd asked him to the dance. Explained that he really did like Oliver—maybe more than liked him—but that he was scared.

But Luke hadn't wanted Oliver to think less of him. To realize that Luke wasn't as brave as he was. Because if Oliver knew that—if he knew how much of a coward Luke really was—there was no way he'd even want to talk to him.

And as the days had passed and the dance had gotten closer, Oliver had gotten more and more excited about it. He'd blushed and made fun of himself for caring about something as dumb as a school dance, but Luke could tell that Oliver was looking forward to it, and he couldn't bring himself to tell Oliver then. He hadn't wanted to hurt Oliver's feelings.

But now, only a block away from the school, Luke understood something he should have understood from the beginning, should have realized before he'd ever kissed

Oliver all those weeks ago. Luke was going to hurt Oliver. No matter what.

Luke could see the school building now, and he walked towards it with dread in his stomach. Everyone was going to be looking at them. Watching them. Judging them.

Luke could already hear the whispers all around them. And he knew, he *knew*, that Oliver would pretend not to notice, pretend not to care. And he'd want Luke to do the same.

Oliver was going to want to dance together, to hold hands, to have the school dance experience that he'd never had before, and Luke was going to ruin it for him because he wasn't strong enough to do any of that. He wasn't strong enough to be the guy Oliver wanted him to be.

Luke tried to slow his steps, but there was only so much distance between him and the school now. He'd be at the gym doors in just a minute or two, no matter how slowly he walked. Luke could see a line of cars pulling up outside the gym, kids getting out in evening wear and fancy dresses. The lights spilling out of the open doors were warm and welcoming, but Luke had never felt colder, or more distant

Oliver was waiting just on the other side of the doors.

Waiting for Luke, with an expectant smile on his face. The thought of going in there, meeting him, taking his hand... Luke made it halfway across the parking lot before he froze. He was hidden behind the line of cars in the dark. All around him, he could hear the babble of voices, students laughing and talking, having fun. All Luke wanted was to disappear.

If Luke didn't go inside, if he bailed on Oliver now, he would hurt him. He wouldn't just ruin the night, he'd ruin everything between them. There'd be no fixing it. If he didn't go inside, he'd show Oliver what Oliver should have known from the beginning—that Luke didn't deserve him.

But if Luke did go inside, he'd do the exact same thing. Everyone would stare at him—at them—and Luke couldn't take that. He couldn't. And he'd still ruin everything with Oliver by freaking out, by freezing up, by showing Oliver just how much he cared what everyone else thought of him.

Either way, Luke was going to hurt him. Either way, he was going to let him down.

Luke closed his eyes in pain and slowly, slowly, turned and walked away.

He couldn't even make it off the school grounds before he started crying, tears falling onto his cheeks in the dark. Every step he took away from the gym was a step away from Oliver—and away from what he and Oliver had had.

God, you're already thinking in the past tense.

It was a sad thought. Luke knew he was fucking everything up between them. But there was nothing else he could do. He wasn't strong enough. It had to end—it was always going to, Luke realized now. He wasn't the guy Oliver wanted. He wasn't the guy Oliver needed. He was just... himself.

Luke thought of Oliver's texts, sitting on his phone. Pictured Oliver waiting for a response, waiting for Luke to walk through the door. Waiting for Luke to be the person Oliver thought he was.

He couldn't even bring himself to text Oliver back. He was too ashamed. And what could he possibly say?

I'm sorry. I'm an asshole. I was right all along—you never should have liked me, this never made sense. I'm sorry for hurting you. For making you think I was better than I am. I'm so, so sorry for everything.

It was better this way. Oliver deserved better than Luke. So let Oliver hate him. Let Oliver loathe him, for how much of a coward he was. Luke deserved it. And maybe, just maybe, that would help Oliver get over Luke faster. Maybe, if Oliver felt so much anger, it would hurt less. Luke hated the thought of Oliver in pain.

He felt sick. Sweat was cooling on his body now, leaving him cold and clammy. His chest felt tight, and he dreaded the thought of walking home, of coming up with some explanation for why he was home early. He dreaded spending the rest of the night curled up in his empty bedroom, his empty house, his empty life.

Luke felt like he might vomit. Which only made it weirder when he heard the sound of someone actually vomiting coming from the bushes five feet in front of him.

Luke stopped, more out of habit than actual curiosity. Everything felt a little numb right now, a little pointless. It was probably someone from the dance who'd gotten wasted before they arrived.

Luke really wasn't in the mood to talk to anyone, but a general sense of decency compelled him to wait and make sure whoever it was was okay. And how pathetic was that, that he could be decent to a stranger throwing up in the bushes, but couldn't muster up the courage to be decent to the boy he—

"Kyle?" Luke said as the person behind the bushes straightened up unsteadily. "Is that you?"

"Luke?" Kyle sounded disoriented. "What are you—what are you doing here?"

What was Luke doing there? Just ruining things. Just destroying a relationship that had barely even gotten off the ground. Just ending the most important thing in his life, Luke realized. And he couldn't tell anyone about it.

"Are you okay," Luke said instead, ignoring Kyle's question entirely.

Luke took a step closer, concerned, in spite of himself. He and Kyle still hadn't spoken since that day in the hall. Kyle still hadn't apologized, though Luke knew he'd never really explained what Kyle needed to apologize for. Still, he couldn't help feeling a little worried. Kyle didn't *look* okay.

"I'm fffine," Kyle said, his words coming out soft and slushy. "Jussht need to—"

He doubled over and started barfing into the boxwood hedge again. Luke sighed and found himself walking around, putting a hand on Kyle's shoulder.

"Jesus," Luke said, glancing down at the puddle on the ground. "How much did you have to drink?"

"Not—not muchh," Kyle slurred. "Just some beerssh at Andy'ssh. But then hissh brother made—" he paused to retch "—jello shotssh."

"Oh God."

Andy's older brother was that group's usual alcohol hookup, since he still lived at home with his parents. And in

Luke's experience, he put so much alcohol into his jello shots that they barely even solidified and tasted like paint thinner.

"Did you eat anything tonight?" Luke asked.

Kyle moaned as he straightened up.

"No," he said sadly. His voice sounded a little clearer now. "Pizza didn't come before it was time to come here."

Luke nodded slowly. "Everyone else is inside?"

"Yeah." Kyle looked unhappy. "I got kicked out."

Luke sighed. Kyle needed to go home and sleep it off, but he could use some water first—and if he'd been kicked out of the dance, that meant the closest water fountains were unavailable.

"Alright," Luke said, reaching out to steady Kyle again as he swayed. "Come on. We can walk to the diner and get you some water and something to eat."

Kyle frowned again. "Why are you being so nice to me?"

Luke shrugged helplessly. "Because I don't want you to die of alcohol poisoning?"

"Yeah, but—" Kyle started to shake his head, then reached out to grab Luke when the movement made him wobbly. "But—but you don't like me anymore."

"Kyle, it's not that I don't—"

Luke stopped. How could he explain it? He'd known Kyle his whole life. And yeah, Kyle was kind of a dick. He always had been. But he'd also always been Luke's friend.

"I'm sorry," Kyle said, into the silence. "I know I'm an asshole."

Luke gave him a long look. Kyle was an asshole—but then again, who was Luke to judge?

You're no better than him. If anything, you're worse. Kyle's never pretended to be anything other than what he is. You're the one who's a liar.

"Forget about it," Luke said finally. "Come on. Let's go."

It wasn't what he wanted to be doing—helping his drunk friend sober up while his heart broke inside his chest. But then again, there was nothing that would qualify as something Luke wanted to do right then, except crawling into a hole and dying.

You don't even deserve that. You feel shitty because you're a shitty person. You don't deserve to feel better about that.

And so Luke headed into town with Kyle, away from the school, away from Oliver—away from the person he'd thought, for a moment, he might have been.

Luke wasn't a good person. He wasn't smart, or kind, or brave, like Oliver. At best, he was mediocre. At worst—and right now, he was definitely at his worst—he was an asshole. It was time to just accept that.

Time to stop pretending.

21

OLIVER

7 YEARS AGO

*O*liver paced around the living room in his suit—one he'd bought at a thrift store because he'd never actually needed to wear one before this and his dad had refused to spend money on something Oliver might only use once. It felt weird. Oliver had never worn a tie before, either. He felt hot, and jittery, and found himself fixating on the tie. Was it making it harder to breathe?

Oliver reached the wall, turned, and walked back to the other side of the living room to inspect himself in the mirror, pulling at the tie uncomfortably.

"Leave it," his dad said from his reclining chair where he was watching the game. "You'll only mess it up."

"It's too tight," Oliver complained.

"It's not too tight," his dad said. "That's what ties are supposed to feel like."

"You're sure about that?" Oliver gave his dad a skeptical look. "I haven't seen you wear a tie in years."

"I've worn one a lot more recently than you have," his dad said grumpily. He sighed and waved Oliver over with his beer. "Get over here, let me do it."

Despite the fact that his dad hadn't wanted to spend money on the suit, he'd been insistent that Oliver pick something out that looked "normal," which apparently meant a suit that made Oliver feel like he was a pallbearer. Still, though, he was grateful for his dad's help, so he walked over and let his dad fix his tie.

Oliver had had no idea how to tie a tie, or how cufflinks worked, or whether he'd even needed a jacket at all. His dad had had to help him with all of this. Oliver flushed, remembering how he'd almost choked when his dad had asked if he needed to buy a corsage.

"What?" he'd said, panicking. "Why would I need to—"

"For her to wear, Oliver," his dad had said patiently. "That's the thing you do—or at least, it was in my day. You bring her a corsage, she'll have a boutonniere to pin onto your jacket." He'd frowned. "She didn't talk to you about this, this girl you're going with? Usually they want corsages—though if she wanted a boutonniere, I suppose we could get her one of those too."

Oliver had blushed. His dad had been shocked when Oliver had approached him about needing a suit, about going to the dance at all, and his jaw had hit the floor when Oliver had said he was going *with* someone.

Someone. Oliver had been careful not to specify who, never to use a gender. He didn't like lying to his dad, but he was pretty sure his dad wouldn't be thrilled to hear Oliver was going to the dance with a guy. His dad had just assumed it was a *"she."* And Oliver hadn't wanted to mess things up by explaining.

It was the closest he'd felt to his dad in—well, Oliver didn't know how long. And his dad had actually been happy enough not to have to get a corsage. *"Damned expensive wastes of time,"* had been his actual words.

At the time, Oliver had been sure they weren't getting each other boutonnieres. Luke had never mentioned anything about that. But now that it was almost time for Oliver to leave, he felt a flash of panic. Maybe he was wrong, and Luke had just assumed that Oliver would know he needed to get Luke something. What if Luke showed up at the school with something for Oliver to wear, and Oliver didn't have anything for him?

There's nothing you can do about it now. And if he got you something, he can just wear it instead of you—that way it'll be more fair.

"There, that better?" Oliver's dad asked gruffly, pulling Oliver back to the present.

It was. It was looser now, Oliver could tell, but evidently it still passed muster with his dad.

"Yeah," Oliver said, wishing his throat didn't feel quite so much like sandpaper.

"Good," his dad said, sitting down again. "Now *keep your hands off it.*"

"Okay, okay."

Oliver resumed pacing.

"You're sure you're supposed to meet this girl there?" his dad asked a few minutes later.

Oliver had changed direction at that point and had begun pacing up and down the living room, from the front door to the kitchen.

"Yeah," Oliver said, remembering the conversation with Luke.

He wished they weren't meeting there—he wished Luke could have come here or vice versa, that they had just told their parents they were meeting their *other dates* at the dance but walking over together. Oliver tried not to think about having to walk in alone.

But Luke had suggested meeting at the school, and Oliver hadn't wanted to disagree. He still couldn't believe Luke had asked him to the dance in the first place. And after all, what did Oliver know about dances anyway? Maybe this way was better.

"And you don't want a ride?" his dad asked.

"Yeah, no, I'm good," Oliver said quickly. If he couldn't go *with* Luke, he'd go alone. Somehow, his dad driving him would only make him feel worse. Besides, what if he wanted to meet Oliver's date or something? Oliver cringed at the thought. "Thanks, though."

Oliver glanced at the clock for the millionth time as he turned and completed his current circuit to the kitchen and back. 9:00 p.m. on the dot. The dance started at 8:30, technically, but Luke had insisted that no one would show up that early. They were supposed to meet at the school at 9:15, which meant that Oliver needed to start walking. Now.

His stomach flipped over. It was finally time. It was finally happening.

"I should go."

It was going to be fine. It was going to be better than fine—it was going to be amazing. Oliver was going to the dance with Luke, and he could put up with a million nervous, solo walks in exchange for getting to be Luke's date. For Luke letting everybody know that they were, well, together.

His stomach was full of butterflies. Luke liked him and wanted to be with him. And beyond that, Luke wanted other people to *know* he was with Oliver. That was what tonight meant.

And Oliver knew it was stupid, knew that school dances were dumb. But some tiny, ridiculous part of him couldn't help but feel giddy at the thought of slow dancing with Luke tonight.

Oliver walked to the front closet to get his coat, and when he turned around, his dad was getting up from the couch and walking over to him.

"What?" Oliver asked, confused.

"Just making sure you've got everything. Phone?"

"Yep." Oliver patted his pocket to double-check.

"Money, if you need to take a cab home?"

His dad had insisted he take it, in case he needed a ride, and had made him promise not to get in a car with anyone who'd been drinking. Oliver knew he wouldn't need it, but it had been easier just to take it. He could always stick it back in his dad's wallet later tonight.

His dad gave Oliver a long look and then, out of nowhere, reached up to straighten Oliver's hair. Oliver jumped in surprise, and his dad's face grew heated in embarrassment, which only made Oliver's cheeks turn pink in response.

Fixing his hair was something his mom used to try to do. She'd never been happy with the fact that Oliver liked it long, or that he didn't spend any time brushing it. Oliver couldn't remember a single time his dad had cared about what he looked like.

But he was trying now, Oliver realized. Trying to be the kind of dad he thought he should be. The least Oliver could do was let him. So he tipped his head down—he'd been taller than his dad since eighth grade—and let him fuss with his hair.

"You never take a brush to this, do you?" his dad said, more to himself than Oliver. He pulled his hand away, then straightened Oliver's tie a final time and nodded. "You look good, kid. You look good."

"Uh, thanks?"

His dad cleared his throat. "Now, I know you're a good kid, but I also know that sometimes there's drinking at these things. And you know that if you or your date—"

"Dad, we're not—"

"No, no, let me finish. If anyone, anyone at all, tries to get you to do something that you don't want to do, you can always say no. Or you can blame me and say I'll beat your ass if you put a foot out of line. I'm not saying—"

"God, Dad, that's really not—"

But Oliver's dad bulldozed onwards.

"I know you've been hanging out with a different crowd these days. You and this Luke kid. He seems alright. And if you like him, I'll give him the benefit of the doubt. I'm not trying to tell you what you can and can't do—I know these years are when kids your age start experimenting. But if *anyone* tries to pressure you into anything, you can always call me to pick you up. No questions asked. Got it?"

"Yeah, Dad, I got it," Oliver said, his face on fire.

"Good." His dad gave him a final look. "I'm proud of you, Oliver. And I love you. I know I don't say it much, but I do. No matter what. You got that?"

"Yeah. Um. I love you too, Dad."

Oliver escaped into the chilly night with relief.

It was so bizarre. His dad was paying so much attention to him, and it was all so off-base. He seemed to think Oliver was going to a kegger instead of a heavily chaperoned school dance.

The upside, though, was that now Oliver had to hurry if he wanted to meet Luke on time. That was good. That meant he was focused on not being late instead of freaking out about everything else on the walk. The porch lights on the houses he passed made tiny pools of gold in the dark as he made his way to the school.

Astor Hills wasn't far, and since Oliver was racing the clock, he made it there in twelve minutes instead of his usual fifteen. Threading his way through a parking lot packed with cars, Oliver compared what he was wearing to what he saw. Did his suit look normal? It was hard to tell, since everyone had coats on, but all the guys Oliver saw did at least seem to be wearing dark pants and nice shoes. So was Oliver, so that was good.

He approached the double doors to the gym on the heels of a throng of underclassmen and walked inside. Everything was strangely bright in the vestibule that he entered. A long hallway stretched out to the right towards the rest of the school. Two folding tables had been set up across it, decked out in snowflakes and tinsel and white tablecloths. They were selling tickets there—Oliver could see both Ms. Bowman and Grace Tighe through the crowd. There was a coat rack behind them, and as Oliver watched, pairs of students approached the tables, bought their tickets, and handed over their coats.

All the girls, Oliver noted with dismay, were wearing corsages on their wrists. And all the boys had boutonnieres attached to their lapels. Fuck.

Another set of doors in front of the tables led into the gym itself. Music was blasting from the speakers inside—something that sounded Top 40-ish, though Oliver didn't listen to popular music enough to be sure. The lights were dimmer in the gym, but it was packed with moving bodies and strobe lights and a disco ball, and Oliver started to feel a little nauseous as he looked inside.

Everything's fine. You're just nervous. You'll feel better when Luke gets here.

Speaking of which—it was now 9:15 on the dot. Oliver's heart was pounding as he found a patch of wall and leaned against it, looking back out towards the parking lot. He felt awkward and exposed and kept looking at his phone. 9:16 now. Only a minute late. But still.

He fired off a series of pointless texts to Luke, just to give himself something to do. Groups of students kept entering the vestibule, filling it up and then emptying it out as they progressed into the gym itself. Oliver felt conspicuous standing against the wall. He was the only person waiting like this. God, where was Luke?

Oliver glanced at his phone again. 9:20. No Luke, and no text responses either.

It's fine. It's fine. He probably just got held up. It's cold, and he's walking, and he's not looking at his phone. He'll be here soon.

Oliver could see the ticket table out of the corner of his eye, and he had the sinking suspicion that everyone over there was watching him, wondering what he was doing. He was used to people staring at him, whispering. But that didn't mean he liked it.

Somehow, tonight was even worse than usual. Maybe because instead of snide remarks and peals of laughter, all he heard was silence—that, and the weight of their eyes. The curiosity and confusion. They weren't making fun of him, not with Ms. Bowman standing right there, but they were still staring, and somehow that made Oliver feel even more like a misfit.

He tried to put his head down and ignore them, but the vestibule really wasn't that big, and there wasn't all that much else to look at. Oliver glanced at his phone again, as though he could will Luke into existence, or at least will a response to his texts. Nothing. And it was 9:25 now.

"Oliver, honey, everything okay?"

He looked up with a start and saw Ms. Bowman at his elbow. She was smiling, but her eyes were filled with concern.

"What? Oh, yeah." He shook his head quickly. "I'm fine. Just... waiting."

"Okay," Ms. Bowman said, clearly unsatisfied. "Do you want to buy a ticket while you wait? Or two?"

She added the *"or two"* ever so casually, but Oliver was sure she'd just said that to be kind, not because she actually believed he'd want to buy two. She probably thought he was here on his own and just too scared to go inside. Because surely Oliver Luna wouldn't have a date. Even the teachers knew that.

"Um, I'll—I'll wait. It should just be a little—" Oliver shook his head. "I'll wait."

His heart was beating even faster now, and he could hear his voice slipping back into that lisp he'd always had, the one he'd never quite gotten rid of. It still came back when he was nervous, and goddammit, he was nervous now.

Ms. Bowman smiled, nodded, and walked back behind the table, but now Oliver wanted to die. Everyone was staring at him, he was sure of it. He couldn't bring himself to look over, though, because he knew he'd see one of two things in their eyes—contempt, or pity. He didn't know which would be worse.

And now it was 9:30, and Luke was fifteen minutes late. That wasn't accidental late. That wasn't the kind of late that you didn't text someone to warn them about, right? There was no way Luke hadn't seen his texts, Oliver realized, because if

Luke knew he was going to be this late, wouldn't he have pulled his own phone out to give Oliver a heads-up?

And that was when it started to hit Oliver. That darkness lurking at the edge of his mind for the past two months? That fear he'd been pushing away? That bone-deep certainty that this was all too good to be true? It was real. His fears were right. And Luke wasn't coming.

Luke wasn't coming, and he'd probably never planned on coming, and Oliver was a complete and utter fool.

He tried to fight it. Tried to fight one last-ditch campaign against that wave of despair and hurt. Maybe Luke had gotten held up with his mom. Maybe he'd forgotten his phone at home. Maybe he'd been hit by a car and was on the way to the hospital right now.

But each excuse Oliver came up with felt flimsier than the last, and he couldn't stop the pain from flooding into him. It filled every part of his body, and as Oliver stood there, just trying to stay upright, his vision started to go dark around the edges.

Luke wasn't coming. Because he didn't care. Because he didn't like Oliver. Because he never had.

If Luke had cared at all about Oliver, he wouldn't do this to him.

Oliver tore at his tie again. He couldn't breathe—his inhales and exhales sounded like the gasps of a dying man, which was, Oliver realized, exactly what he felt like.

Surprise, surprise, you're being melodramatic again. Surprise, surprise, you set yourself up to get hurt.

You got your hopes up when you knew you shouldn't, and now you're shocked when you get exactly what you knew was coming all along? Could you be any more pathetic?

Oliver was dimly aware of voices babbling next to him, and he realized with a start that he wasn't alone in the vestibule anymore with the ticket sellers. He looked up, trying to focus on the world around him—a world that wasn't collapsing and suffocating him in its rubble.

"Come on, Andy," a girl's voice was saying. "Can't we go later?"

"I wanna go now," a male voice replied, a little slurrily.

When his eyes finally focused, Oliver realized he was staring at Andy, Luke's friend. Ex-friend—he started to correct himself before realizing that maybe he was wrong. Why should Oliver believe they weren't still friends? Why should Oliver believe anything Luke had ever said?

Dana Silverman, a girl in their class, was hanging off of Andy's arm, trying to pull him back into the gym as Andy stubbornly tried to make it to the door. He looked very drunk.

"If we go now, he's just going to be puking still," Dana said. "It's just gonna be gross. Can we please *not*?"

"He's done puking," Andy insisted. "He's going to the diner with Luke. I wanna go."

Oliver's heart stopped.

"Ugh, Andy, please. No." Dana took a step closer and smiled winsomely up at Andy. She was, Oliver noted absently, very pretty, in her sparkly purple dress, her black hair done up in curls. "Come on, do you really wanna go hang out with Kyle and Luke, instead of me?"

She pressed herself up against Andy's body, tilted his chin down to her, and kissed him deeply.

Kyle and Luke.

Oliver tried to process what he'd heard. Luke wasn't in the hospital. He wasn't running late. And he hadn't forgotten his cell phone somewhere. He just... wasn't coming. Because he was with Kyle—the guy he was *"never really friends with in the first place."*

Oliver could feel tears pressing up at the backs of his eyes, and his next inhale was as much a sob as it was a breath.

"Ahem."

Ms. Bowman cleared her throat, and Dana and Andy sprang apart.

"In or out," Ms. Bowman said to the pair of them. "But regardless, you know the rules about that kind of behavior on school property."

"Yes, Ms. Bowman," Dana said demurely. She took Andy's hand. "Come on, let's go back inside."

"Jesus, I don't fucking wanna go back inside," Andy said, angry now. "You can fucking go if you want, but I'm done with this bullshit."

"Andy, what are you—" Dana began, but Andy cut her off.

"I said go!" Andy yelled.

Dana took a step back while Ms. Bowman walked around the tables again and approached Andy firmly.

"This is all bullshit," Andy ranted. "And I'm fucking done with it."

Oliver had no idea what had set Andy off, but he was clearly pissed about something. Andy glared over at the ticket sellers, at Ms. Bowman, who was still walking towards him, and at Dana.

And then—oh God, why had Oliver waited around for this? —Andy looked over at Oliver. And instead of looking angry, Andy's face shifted into a malicious grin.

"Luna!?" Andy barked. "What are you doing here?"

"I'm not—" Oliver stopped.

Not because he didn't want to dignify the question with a response, but because if he said another word, he could tell he was going to break into sobs. He should have walked away the second Andy and Dana had come in. He should have left ages ago, in fact, instead of standing here like a pathetic idiot, waiting on someone who was never going to come.

"Don't tell me you were going to the dance with someone," Andy said incredulously. "Please don't seriously try to tell me that. Who would go with you?"

The words cut straight into Oliver's chest.

He wasn't supposed to care about assholes like Andy. Normally, he didn't. Or at least, he could pretend.

But not tonight. Not when Luke hadn't even bothered to text Oliver to tell him he wasn't coming, hadn't had the courtesy to admit that he'd been lying this whole time.

"I don't pretend when I'm with you."

Out of nowhere, Oliver remembered what Luke had whispered to him in the library that night. Oliver had believed him, but Luke had lied. That's all this had ever been for Luke—just one more lie in a life full of them.

"Do you have a boyfriend or something?" Andy continued, as though Oliver had answered, as though he could have kept up this one-sided conversation with Oliver all night. He snickered. "Or were you just going to hang around and hope that one of us took pity on you?"

Oliver knew he should say something, do something, but he couldn't move, and every word Andy said was like a stab wound. This couldn't be happening. He couldn't handle this, not all of this, not all at once.

"Because I've gotta be honest, Luna, it's never gonna happen. No one here wants you. Not even if you offered to blow the whole team. So why don't you just—"

"Andrew!" Ms. Bowman said sharply. "I will *not* allow that kind of language, this kind of bullying to happen on school grounds. You're coming with me now, and we're going to—"

Oliver didn't stay to hear the rest. He bolted.

Luke wasn't coming. Luke had never been coming, had never wanted anything more than to fuck with Oliver's head and take what he wanted. Oliver was just the fool who'd trusted him. Who'd let himself get hurt. Who'd asked for it.

Tears streaked down Oliver's cheeks as he ran out into the night.

I wasn't sure how I got home.

I didn't even realize I'd gone *home* home until I heard the loudspeaker announce the Garden City station. I hadn't even realized I was on a train. Numbly, I got off and stepped out into the train station parking lot.

Somehow, it felt even colder than it had in Manhattan. Not just the night, but the town. The world. Me.

Everything felt cold.

I walked home in a daze, not really thinking of anything. Just listening to Luke's words on repeat in my head. *I can't do this. I can't do this. I can't do this.*

I knew I'd been a coward to run away, but I'd heard those words coming off of Luke's lips, and I knew what was coming next. I knew I couldn't bear to hear it.

Maybe you're wrong. Maybe he was just freaking out. Maybe he'll calm down. Text you. Say he's sorry, he didn't mean it.

Or maybe he wouldn't. Because maybe he did mean it. And maybe I'd pushed too hard, too fast, like I always did.

I slipped into my dad's house as quietly as I could. He wasn't expecting me home, and I didn't want to wake him up. With any luck, I'd be up and out so early that he'd never know I'd been here at all.

I took off my jacket and walked up to my room, sitting down on my old twin bed, my phone in my hands. I stared at it, willing Luke to text, to call, to do something. But, of course, he didn't.

This was Luke we were talking about. I knew what Luke was like, and I knew I'd scared him away. I knew better than to push him like I had. But I'd done it anyway. Because this was me we were talking about, too.

God, all I wanted to do was text and say I was sorry, to beg for forgiveness. Except Luke had asked for time, hadn't he? If I texted him now, I'd only make things worse. I knew what came next, after *"I can't do this."* And if Luke had somehow, miraculously, *not* made up his mind already, me pushing him now could be the thing that tipped him over the edge.

I don't remember falling asleep. I don't remember what woke me up, either. I just know that when I surfaced next, I was curled up on top of my *Star Wars* comforter, my shoes still on, my phone gripped tightly in my hands. It was 2:13 a.m. I tossed and turned, willing myself to go back to sleep, desperate not to be conscious right now, but that worked about as well as willing Luke to call me had.

Finally, I gave up, got out of bed, and walked downstairs. Maybe I could go for a walk or something to clear my mind. But when I got to the bottom of the stairs, I saw the stove light on in the kitchen, and when I walked over, I found my dad sitting in the shadows at the kitchen table drinking, wonder of wonders, a cup of coffee instead of a beer.

"Dad?" I rubbed my eyes, confused. "What are you doing up? I thought you were—when I got home, your door was closed and the lights were off. You have to sleep—it's important. You need your rest."

"I was asleep. But then I woke up."

"Oh shit, it wasn't me, was it?" I winced. "I tried to be quiet."

"Nah, it wasn't you." My dad chuckled. "Didn't even know you were home till I came down and saw your jacket on the floor."

He pointed out to the living room, and I flushed. Typical me, I'd just dropped my jacket in a heap by the front door.

"Anyway," my dad went on, "I figure, if my body doesn't want to be asleep right now, why force it? Besides, I might say the same for you—you shouldn't be up either."

"Fair enough," I said with a sigh.

My dad pulled a chair out from the table and motioned for me to sit down. At a loss for anything else to do, I sat and started fiddling with the salt and pepper shakers.

"Couldn't sleep?" my dad asked.

"Yeah." I opened my mouth to say more, then stopped. I didn't even know where to begin.

"Anything on your mind?"

I shrugged. What could I say? My dad wouldn't be happy to hear I'd been hanging out with Luke again. He'd never forgiven Luke from the first time around, when I'd run home crying from the dance and, in between hiccups and sobs, told my dad everything. And I didn't want to stress him out, not when things were already complicated with his health stuff. It was easier just to keep things simple.

My dad reached out and squeezed my shoulder. "It's gonna be okay, kid."

"Thanks, Dad."

We sat there in silence, not doing anything, just listening to the clock ticking on the wall. Somehow, though, I felt a little bit better, just sitting there in the dark. Maybe it was because for once, my dad and I weren't arguing. I didn't feel all the way better, not by a long shot. But a bit of my agitation faded away.

"I got those prescriptions filled," my dad said after a while. "And I scheduled that appointment, about the surgery. I go in next week to talk with the doctors."

"What?" I blinked and looked at my dad in surprise. "But I thought you didn't want to—"

"Well, I thought so too. But then I thought about what you would say if you were here. And I thought about you coming all the way back home, just to help me out, and how I've been acting. And I figured..." he shrugged. "Can't hurt to talk to them, at least."

"Dad, that's—" my voice broke.

"I love you, kid." My dad's voice was gruff. "I want to be here for you."

"I love you too, Dad." I paused. "Thank you. That, uh—that means a lot."

"Well, you hounded me into it," my dad said with a smile. "Should probably be me thanking you. If I didn't have you in my life—didn't have someone who cares as much as you do..." He shook his head and then gave me a pointed look. "I hope Luke knows how lucky he is."

"What?"

I stared at my dad. I must have misheard. He couldn't possibly be saying what I thought he—

My dad snorted. "I'm old, Oliver, not dead. And I remember what it looks like when you're trying to hide something from me. Granted, it's your right to keep things to yourself if you want. But still—"

"You're not mad?" I asked, baffled.

"Mad? Why would I be mad?" My dad looked at me like that was the most ridiculous thing he'd ever heard.

"Because I'm—because I lied about it. Because you don't like Luke. Because I was—"

"No, kid, none of that. You're an adult. You can make your own decisions, and you know what's best for you." He gave me a long look. "I don't want to see you get hurt again. And I can't say I like the guy. But if you think he's worth it, well, I'll support you."

"Oh."

"So." My dad gave me an expectant look. "Everything okay there? Or is that the reason you couldn't sleep?"

"Jesus, since when did you become psychic?" I grumbled, a little annoyed at how transparent I apparently was. "You never seemed to care about this stuff before."

"I always cared, Oliver. I wasn't always great at showing it. But I always—well, I can try to get better. If you want me to stick around and live longer, this is the price you gotta pay. I'm gonna start badgering you.

"That's, um..." I laughed. "Encouraging and threatening at the same time. God, I can't believe you've known about Luke this whole time."

"Kid, you spent the first week you were home never leaving the house or my side. Then Luke comes by one day and suddenly you're spending all your time in the city, staying over 'with friends.' You said it yourself, you weren't a social butterfly in high school. Doesn't take a genius to figure it out."

I flushed. "Still. This is humiliating."

"So what happened?" my dad asked. "And don't try to tell me nothing happened, because nothing isn't the reason you come home without any warning, sneak into the house, and then wake up in the middle of the night saying you can't sleep. Were you with Luke tonight?"

"Yeah," I said. I felt so tired all of a sudden, exhaustion creeping over me at the thought of having to explain all of this to my dad. "Yeah. I was."

"And?"

"And... I don't know. I did just what I did last time. I ruined it."

"What? I don't believe that," my dad scoffed. "You couldn't ruin anything. That kid looked head over heels for you when I saw him."

"Yeah, well, thanks, but I did." I sighed. "I pushed too hard. And he—I mean, he had every right to tell me that. I wanted —what I was saying—" I shook my head and looked at my dad helplessly. "I thought he wanted the same thing I did. And I just—I fucking brought it on myself."

You fell in love with him. Or maybe you'd never really stopped loving him. And you pushed too hard.

"Oh, Oliver. My dad reached over and pulled me into a one-armed hug, ruffling my hair. It was a bit awkward, and it kind of felt like getting hugged by a robot, but still, it was nice. "You just have a big heart, is all. You feel things so strongly."

"I know. That's the problem. I feel things *too* strongly, and I move too fast, and I set myself up to get hurt."

"No, no, that's not what I'm saying at all," my dad disagreed. "Yeah, you feel a lot. But that's not a bad thing. Hell, I think we could all stand to learn something from you. You don't want to end up like me, right? Old and alone."

"Dad, you're not—"

"My point is, don't you go thinking there's something wrong with you. There's nothing wrong with you. And if Luke can't see that—well, then he's not the one for you."

"I know." I put my face in my hands, propping my elbows up on the table. "I know that, rationally. I know that's what I should tell myself. But I just—" I looked at my dad from between my fingers. "How do I stop it from hurting now?"

"Can you talk to him?" my dad asked quietly.

"I don't know. I want to, but I don't wanna push him away. He hasn't officially—like, I don't even know where things stand right now. We kinda had a fight, and he said he needed time, and I just—I don't know what to do."

"Well," my dad said, running his thumb along the rim of his coffee mug. "That's fair. You can give him some time. But it's also fair for you to need to talk to him, to hear him tell you what he wants. Maybe give him a day, let him get in touch?"

"But what if he never does?" I asked plaintively. "He never— he never did back—back in senior year, I mean. He never even spoke to me once, after that night. What if he just... stops talking to me again now?"

"Well, if he tries to do that, you got one of two options. Either you get in touch with him, and you make him talk to you. Or you tell me, and I'll give Bill a call and we find someone to break his kneecaps."

He said it so straightforwardly that I laughed in spite of myself.

"Of course, I'd recommend the former," my dad continued. "I'm not sure I trust Bill not to crack under police pressure, and I don't know if they'd still let me get my heart surgery from prison."

"You're impossible." I sighed. "I don't know what to do. We were supposed to go to this brunch thing tomorrow, but if Luke asked for space..."

"You should go," my dad said decisively. "Hell, that's better. Then you'll actually have to talk to each other in person instead of through your damn phones like everyone your age does."

"But I can't—"

"Don't even think of backing out of it." My dad fixed me with a hard stare. "You let that boy break your heart and run away once already. He doesn't get to do it again. You be brave. You go and make him talk to you."

"But I'm *not* brave, Dad."

"Like hell you're not. I've never met anyone braver than you. Who's the kid who stood up to all those bullies in school, who refused to change himself for them? Who's the kid who moved across the country to pursue his dreams? Who's the kid who puts everything on the line when he believes in something?" My dad shook his head. "I may not know where you came from, but I'm always proud you're my kid."

"Thanks, Dad."

"You're welcome." He nodded stoutly. "Talk to Luke—if he's smart, he'll see what he's got in you. And if he's dumb—well, I don't want an idiot dating my son anyway."

I just stared at my dad and started laughing again. Somewhere along the line, my beer-drinking, football-watching, chain-smoking father had become *Dear Abby*, and I loved him for it. Things weren't always easy between us, but my dad was doing his best—and he'd always, always, accepted me for who I was.

"I think I needed to hear that," I said when I finally got my laughter under control. "Thanks."

"Yeah, well. I needed you to talk some sense into me. I'm just returning the favor."

I slept better after that conversation. I still didn't know what to do about Luke. I was still terrified that no matter what I did, things were going to end badly. But I was at least able to turn my brain off for long enough to pass out.

I didn't bother to set an alarm, so it was the smell of coffee that woke me up the next morning. It was only 10 a.m. I wasn't sure when the last time was that I'd woken up this early of my own accord. With Luke, sure, but that had been because his alarms went off at six, and I'd spend the next 15 minutes trying my best to keep him in bed with me, curling around him and—

No. Fuck. I wasn't going to think about that.

I wandered downstairs and found my dad in the kitchen, eating an apple, of all things.

"Okay," I said weakly. "I was willing to let it slide last night because I was tired and sad. But seriously, who are you and what have you done with my father?"

"What do you mean?"

"An apple?" I arched an eyebrow. "Really? You expect me to believe that my father would eat a piece of fruit of his own volition? Nice try."

"What?" my dad said, looking injured. "So sue me, I care about my health."

"Since when?" I snorted.

"Well, since, you know... oh, what do you know about it

anyway?" My dad handed me a mug and gestured to the coffee maker. "People can change."

"Right." I filled my mug up and sat on the edge of the counter, just enjoying the taste of the coffee and trying not to think about anything.

"You're up early," my dad said after a moment.

"10 a.m.?"

"Well, early for you."

I shrugged. "Yeah. Just not my night for sleeping, I guess."

My dad gave me an astute look. "You know, if you left now, you could probably get into the city in time for that, uh, whatever it was. Brunch."

He said the word *"brunch"* like it was French and he wasn't quite sure what it meant.

I barked a laugh. "Yeah. Maybe. But I'm not going to."

"Really?" My dad blinked. "Huh."

"Huh, what?"

"Nothing. Just... never woulda pegged you for someone who'd give up so easily."

"Dad, it's—"

"But it's your call, of course. Maybe I was wrong."

"Oh, come on, it's—"

"I mean, I thought I was talking to the guy who'd built two companies from the ground up. Who'd defied everyone's expectations. Who was an example to everyone he met—especially to his father—but I guess I—"

"Okay, okay, I get it," I groaned.

"Do you?"

"Yes," I said, exasperated. "I do. You're disappointed in me or whatever. But you're forgetting something important."

"And what's that?"

"Luke. All those things you're proud of me for doing—all that stuff you think shows I'm so brave or whatever? That was stuff I knew I could do—stuff I knew I could make happen with hard work. But I can't control Luke, Dad. Me *'wanting it bad enough'* isn't enough to make this work. He needs to want it, too. And he doesn't."

"How do you know that?" my dad asked.

"Because I know *him*, Dad. I know what he's like."

"People can change, Oliver. Hell, look at me." He pointed to the apple in his hand.

"It's not the same thing," I said stubbornly. Which wasn't necessarily true, but I could tell I was losing the argument and it was making me irrational. "And since when do you defend Luke?"

"I'm not defending the guy. I'm defending you. I think you deserve an answer from him, whatever happens. And I want you to get that."

"So what, I'm just supposed to show up at a brunch with all of his friends and force him to talk to me? In front of everyone?"

"Damn right," my dad said, taking another bite of his apple. "Don't you let him off the hook."

"Um, yeah, except that puts me *on* the hook for being totally humiliated in front of a bunch of strangers."

"So pull him off to the side," my dad said. "Oliver, I know you. And I can tell when you're arguing because you believe your point, and when you're just arguing to argue."

His look left no doubt as to what he believed I was doing now.

I sighed. "Ugh, this is going to be so awkward."

"And what, you're gonna let that stop you?"

My dad's eyes grabbed hold of mine and wouldn't let go. I stared back, determined not to give in, but my dad didn't blink, and slowly, I felt my anger fade to frustration, and my frustration, eventually, fade to fear.

"What if he says he doesn't want to be with me?" I whispered.

My dad's eyes didn't waver. "Then you hurt. You hurt for a while, I bet, because you've got a big heart. But you'll get through it. And you'll know that you're brave enough to do even the things that scare you the most. And that it was worth it."

Was I brave enough? I didn't like the idea of getting hurt again. I'd tried so hard *not* to have feelings for Luke precisely because I hadn't wanted to end up in this situation.

But here I was.

What if my dad was right? Trying to keep my feelings from

getting hurt, trying to pretend I didn't *have* feelings—that wasn't brave at all. But admitting I had them, admitting they were there, and that Luke could hurt me, and that I wasn't going to let that break me—that was brave.

Seven years ago, I'd been too scared, too hurt, to tell Luke how I really felt. To ask him why. To show him how much I cared.

I didn't want to be scared anymore.

I set my coffee mug down on the counter and then looked back at my dad. He raised an eyebrow in a silent question. I nodded. I could do this.

"Can you drive me to the train station?"

23

LUKE

I spent the next twelve hours curled up in bed, crying. I'd never actually done that before. I hadn't felt this bad since—well, since seven years ago. But that night, I hadn't let myself curl up and sob like I'd wanted to, and it felt like maybe now, I was crying the tears I should have cried that night too.

It was kind of pathetic. The little voice in the back of my head had a field day with its running commentary on how dramatic I was being, how maudlin. How embarrassing. How I didn't deserve to cry like this, because I was the one who'd fucked everything up, and all I was feeling now were the consequences of my actions. It was my own damn fault.

That only made me feel worse, which, perversely, felt right. So I just let the voice berate me. It was no more than I deserved.

I lay in bed and let every bad decision I'd ever made cascade over me. Letting Harvey treat me the way he did. Letting MacFarlane take advantage of me. Being stupid enough to trust that Harvey was telling me the truth, that he wanted me to succeed. Being stupid enough to take the job in the first place, hell, to go into finance at all.

I was too boring to have a passion, too dumb to be brilliant, and too scared, too selfish, to do anything better with my life. I was too scared and selfish to ever think about more than just myself. To look beyond myself and see who I was hurting.

I'd been scared and selfish seven years ago, too, abandoning Oliver and never even having the guts to tell him why. I'd fucked up so badly, and I'd been hiding from that decision ever since. Trying to ignore its consequences—as if that were possible, as if my entire life since that night wasn't one long string of consequences.

That was the night I'd decided I'd rather hurt other people than be honest and risk getting hurt myself.

And that was still who I was. I'd been right—Oliver was going to see that eventually, and I'd hurt him again, and he would regret wanting to be with me. It had just happened so much sooner than I'd expected. I'd thought I'd get more time with him.

Oliver wanted me to be brave. To be someone I wasn't. That's all he'd ever wanted, and I kept finding ways to let him down. I hated myself for that.

I hated that I put up with how Harvey treated me, and I hated that I wasn't going to quit, that I was too scared to quit, too scared to admit I had no idea what I was doing, with anything, in my entire life.

The only thing I'd ever known for sure was that I needed Oliver.

That I *loved* Oliver.

But I wasn't good enough to keep him. I felt small and worthless. Because that's what I was, at my core. So I curled up in a ball, hugged my knees to my chest, and cried. I just wanted the hurt to go away, but it wouldn't because it wasn't supposed to—I was supposed to hurt.

I wanted Oliver. I needed Oliver. But I couldn't have Oliver because I'd pushed him away. I'd known exactly what I was doing, and I hadn't been able to stop myself.

How could Oliver not see that everything he was offering me was a terrible idea? That I didn't deserve his help, his affection, his care? I wasn't special, and if I let Oliver keep thinking I was worth his time, it would only hurt him worse when it all eventually came crashing down. How did he not see that he should have chosen someone better?

And how was I supposed to get through this night, get through the rest of my life, wanting him so badly?

I needed Oliver in my arms. I needed the scent of his skin, the light scratch of stubble on his cheek in the morning, the tangle his legs made with my own under the covers. I needed Oliver's laugh, his relentless belief in possibilities, in the future, in me. I needed his brilliance, his kindness, his Oliver-ness.

I loved him.

I grabbed a pillow and hugged it fiercely to my chest, wishing to God I didn't feel so alone.

I must have fallen asleep at some point because when I opened my eyes next, it was light out. Not just light out—the light was slanting in from the wrong angle. Even when I got back from my morning runs, the light was still low, the sun hovering on the eastern horizon, but now, it was slanting all the way in from—

I picked up my phone in confusion. 9:00 a.m. Jesus, I'd slept late. Why hadn't I set an alarm before I—

A sharp pain stabbed my chest as memories from last night swam to the surface of my mind. Fuck. So that hadn't been a dream.

I opened up my messages app, filled with a half-formed hope that maybe Oliver had texted me last night and I'd forgotten about it. That we'd talked. That somehow, I'd fixed things. But there was nothing.

And why should there be? I was the one who'd told him I needed time. I was the one who made a specialty of abandoning Oliver. Why the hell should he contact me?

What I did have waiting for me was an email from Harvey.

Luke,

I trust you're feeling better and that you've put last night's outburst behind you. You're still a valuable part of this company. I don't know what we'd do without you.

I expect we'll see you Monday. We have a meeting scheduled with Gordon at 10. I understand this may be a hard time for you, which is why I won't insist you come into the office this weekend, as I will be doing. But I do need you to have these reports ready to go on Monday morning.

—H

He'd attached a set of files to the email.

My heart sank. I wanted to be indignantly outraged that Harvey would send me an email like that right after last night. That he'd expect me to just keep working, like nothing had happened—and on the weekend no less. Except, well, I wasn't surprised.

I couldn't deal with it, though. Couldn't deal with any of it. I lay there for a while, hoping that if I just didn't move, maybe I'd fall back asleep or cease to exist, but neither of those things happened, unfortunately. So I did the only thing I could think of—I went for a run.

It was the world's shittiest run. I felt like I was just sort of dragging my body across the concrete. A sloth could have moved faster. And somehow, everything hurt. It was like all the pain in my heart had metastasized and spread little tendrils through every part of my body.

I only made it a mile before I had to sit down and—well, I don't want to say rest because I'd barely gotten started. Sit down and feel sorry for myself. It was cold, and I was underdressed, and I buried my face in my hands and shivered, regretting every decision I'd ever made.

"Luke?"

I blinked and looked up. Nick was standing in front of me—and instead of a pea coat and puppy hat, he was wearing winter running gear and looking at me, confused.

"Are you okay?" he asked, jogging up to me, breathing hard.

Apparently, Adam had been right about Nick running again. Nick gave me a concerned look.

I did my best to act like I hadn't just been wondering if I might actually be warmer if I threw myself into the Hudson, and whether being sopping wet in freezing cold February water might be a pleasant distraction from everything else going on inside my head. I plastered a smile on my face, nodded enthusiastically, and opened my mouth to tell him everything was fine.

"Yeah, I'm—"

I couldn't get the words out. They caught in my throat. Nick's look went from mild concern to definite worry, and he walked over to the bench and sat down. I turned, ready to wave him off, tell him to get back to running, that *really*, I was *fine*. But instead...

"Everything's so fucked up."

Nick gave me a sympathetic look. "I'm sorry."

"It's just—it's not—I just—" I stumbled over my words, trying to figure out how to explain, or how not to explain, how to simply form a complete sentence with this giant hole in my heart. I looked at Nick in anguish. "I ruined everything."

"With..."

"With Oliver. And everything else in my life. But mostly Oliver," I said, shaking my head. "And everything's so fucked."

Nick nodded slowly. "I'm sorry, Luke. That sounds really

awful." He gave me a sidelong glance. "Do you wanna talk about it? Totally fine if you don't."

"I don't even—I'm not sure how to—" I tried, bumbling through my brain's lexicon, trying to figure out how to string words together meaningfully.

"Yeah," Nick said. "Yeah, I know how that feels."

We sat in silence.

"He thinks I'm someone I'm not," I said finally. "He thinks I'm like, this amazing person who's capable of all this stuff and so much better than I actually am. He has all this faith in me, and I just—I don't get it. I don't deserve it. I'm not— I'm not actually a very good person. I'm not the person he thinks I am. I was only ever going to hurt him."

Nick just looked at me, nodded, and didn't say anything. After a while, I couldn't take it anymore.

"Well?" I demanded. "Aren't you going to tell me to envision my best-case scenario for this? Ask me what I want? Give me some kind of useful wisdom that I can use to fix my life and not feel like a complete failure?"

And Nick—Nick laughed at me. He *laughed* at me, at my suffering, at my no-one-else-has-ever-felt-anything-as-truly-sad-as-this-in-the-history-of-the-universe pain. How dare he? I glared at him, offended—and then realized what I was doing.

"Sorry," I said, laughing weakly. "I'm just... a mess."

"You're fine," Nick said. "I've been there, trust me. I was only laughing because God, do I recognize where you are and it *sucks*."

"So there's not, like, a magical cure for this?"

"Afraid not," Nick said, giving me a sad smile. "But I'll tell you one thing that's helped me in the past."

"Yeah?"

"You said that Oliver thinks you're someone you're not, but he's wrong, and because you're actually such a terrible person, you're doomed to hurt him, right?"

"Uh... yeah. That's pretty much it in a nutshell."

"Okay," Nick said slowly. "I'm not trying to invalidate your wallowing or whatever because believe me, I get it. Sometimes we just need to luxuriate in beating ourselves up for every bad decision we've ever made. But... have you considered the possibility that maybe *you're* the one who's wrong, and not Oliver?"

"Wait, what? What do you mean."

"Well, I'm just thinking out loud here. But I'm guessing you like Oliver a lot because this all feels pretty serious for a guy you were only just getting back in touch with a few weeks ago."

"Well, we have a history. It's not like I—" I shook my head ruefully. "But yeah, you're right. I um... like him a lot."

I love him. That was what I wanted to say, but it felt too scary to say out loud.

"So if you like him so much, you must have a pretty high opinion of him, right?"

"Yeah?"

Of course I had a high opinion of Oliver. He was fucking

amazing. That was why it hurt so much to know I was hurting him.

"So I'm just saying," Nick said gently, "that if you like Oliver and think so highly of him and all of that... couldn't you maybe do him the favor of thinking he might just be right about this? That maybe you're not so terrible? That maybe he wouldn't fall for you if you weren't worth it? What would happen if you trusted him?"

"I'd lose everything," I said—no, wailed. I looked at Nick helplessly. "I'd quit my job, I'd have to find somewhere new to live, I'd have no idea what I was doing with my life. Literally the only thing I'd have—"

I stopped short, my brain screeching to a halt. Because it hit me. If I lost all of that, the only thing I'd have left would be Oliver.

And suddenly, looking at it that way, holding my job and apartment and the identity I tried to project to the rest of the world on one side, and Oliver on the other, and asking myself what was more important, what would hurt more to lose, what I couldn't live without...

It wasn't even a contest. It was Oliver. I'd choose Oliver every time.

I turned to Nick, my eyes wide.

"I need to... fuck, I need to fix this."

Nick smiled. "Yeah?"

"Yeah." I nodded, my brain tripping over itself trying to figure out what to do next. I pushed myself up off the bench.

"I need to go—I need to—shit, there's so much I have to do. Thank you—thank you so much."

"I'm not sure I really did anything. But you're welcome."

"Have fun at your party!" I called as I started jogging north.

"What party?" Nick asked, and I remembered belatedly that it was supposed to be a surprise.

Well, I could apologize to Adam and Ben later. For now, I had work to do.

I knew I had to find Oliver, to apologize, to beg for forgiveness. But I needed to show him I was serious, first. I needed proof.

Fifteen minutes later, I stepped into the elevator at work, and it whisked me up to the Mortimer Bancroft offices. I took a deep breath as I stepped into the lobby, then walked to Harvey's office. The door was closed, and I could hear voices coming from the other side of it.

I knocked once.

"Come in." Harvey used the same imperious, entitled tone he always had—how had I not realized how obnoxious that was until last night?

I opened the door and stared in surprise for a moment. MacFarlane was in Harvey's office too, lounging in one of the chairs on the other side of Harvey's desk. I wasn't sure I'd ever seen MacFarlane in the office over the weekend—but honestly, seeing him there now just made me even more confident I was doing the right thing.

"Luke," Harvey said. "I assume you got my email. Do you have those reports ready?"

"No." I shook my head. "And I'm not going to."

"No?" Harvey blinked. "Luke, I understand you may be upset about how things have worked out, but you're still an employee of this company, and—"

"Actually," I smiled. "I'm not."

"What do you mean?" Harvey demanded.

My smile broadened. "I'm not an employee of this company anymore. I quit."

"You what?" MacFarlane exclaimed. Harvey didn't say anything—he just watched me with an inscrutable expression, but MacFarlane leaned forward and tapped his finger on Harvey's desk as if to make a point. "You can't just quit, you have to—"

"I can," I said. "And I am. Quitting. Right now." I cocked my head to the side. "My boyfriend helped me realize that the way you two were treating me was ridiculous, and that I deserve better."

"Your boyfriend?" Harvey said, his eyes widening.

"Yeah." I grinned. "You met him last night. Oliver Luna? We're together."

Now it was MacFarlane who stared at me, dumbfounded. I guess he'd really never expected me to out myself to Harvey. I should have done it years ago.

Harvey's eyes narrowed. "You might have said something."

"I could have," I agreed. "But I don't think it would have made a difference. You've used me from day one. This company only works because of all the work I do. And if you hadn't realized that after two years and decided to treat me appropriately, I really didn't see how knowing that I was dating someone whose money you wanted a piece of was going to help. And frankly, it's none of your business."

"You can't just quit, though," MacFarlane interjected. "Luke, you have responsibilities—"

"Most of which should have been yours." I cocked my head at him. "Enjoy being vice president, MacFarlane. I think you'll find it a real eye-opening experience, now that I'm not around to do all your work for you."

"Come on, Luke," Harvey said. "I'm sure we can work something out."

"You know? I really don't think we can. I'm done. And this isn't a two-weeks-notice thing. It's a now thing."

"You're going to have a tough time finding another job in our industry if this is how you leave things, Luke." Harvey's voice was deathly quiet.

"Maybe." I shrugged. "But I'm not so sure I want another job in this industry. And honestly, I'm not sure Mortimer Bancroft is going to be around in another six months anyway." I turned to walk out the door and smiled over my shoulder. "But all the same—best of luck."

I was shaking by the time the elevator reached the ground floor again. Shaking with joy. I couldn't believe I'd actually done that. I'd expected it to feel awful. Instead, it had just felt... freeing.

I was free—and I'd never have realized how happy it would make me, how badly I needed this, if it hadn't been for

Oliver. I hadn't realized how badly I needed *Oliver* in my life. There was so much I needed to tell him.

But when I got to his hotel, the same concierge as before told me that he hadn't seen Mr. Luna all day, and was I absolutely sure that Mr. Luna wanted to see me, given my track record of coming to find him only to get stood up. He did let me call Oliver's room again, but there was no answer.

I pulled out my phone and stared at Oliver's number. He hadn't contacted me yet today, though that was hardly surprising, given how horrible I'd been last night. I could just call him, and ask where he was. But that was assuming he would tell me—that was assuming he'd even pick up the phone.

What I had to say had to be done in person. But where would Oliver be if he wasn't here? He wouldn't have flown back to California or anything, right? Probably not, given how things stood with his dad's health. But he—

Oh.

His dad. I hadn't thought about that. I wasn't sure Oliver would have gone back to his dad's after last night, but if he wasn't at the hotel, it was the next best place to check. Even if it did mean having to talk to Oliver's dad again. He already hated me, and if Oliver had told him anything about last night... Yikes.

But I had to find Oliver, and I wasn't going to let anything stop me.

An hour later, I got out of a taxi in front of Oliver's house, hit with the sudden memory of the last time I was here, standing on this exact sidewalk at dusk. Oliver had kissed me that night, and I'd been so scared, so unsure, of what to do next.

I was still scared—but there was one thing I was dead certain about. Whatever happened next, I needed Oliver by my side. I gulped, walked up the steps to his front porch, and rang the bell.

Please be home. Please be home. Please answer the door and don't slam it in my face like you have every right to. Please let me explain how sorry I am, how wrong I was, how badly I want to make this up to you. Please be—

The door opened, and Oliver's dad stared at me.

"Oh," he said, his voice gruff. "It's you."

I could do this.

"Hi, Mr. Luna," I said, pushing my hands into my pockets nervously. "I uh—I'm sorry to bother you. I'm sure you uh, have things you'd rather be doing than talking to me. I was just wondering, is there any chance that Oliver is home? I just—he's not at his hotel back in the city, and I really wanted—needed—I mean, what I'm trying to say is I need to see him. Oliver. If he's here."

Well, that had gone smoothly.

Oliver's dad regarded me silently for a moment before finally speaking. "He's not."

Oh.

"I'm sorry," I said again. "I know, um, I know you don't like me. Hate me, probably. You have every reason to, and that's fair. But I—I need to see Oliver because I have to tell him—I have to tell him I'm sorry. I have to tell him I was wrong and tell him—tell him—tell him that I love him."

It all came out in a rush, and I could feel my cheeks turning scarlet. Oh God, that was *not* what I'd meant to say. Oliver's dad was probably going to laugh in my face and tell me—

"He went into the city," Mr. Luna said. The look he gave me was maybe one percent softer than before, but his voice was surprisingly gentle. "Said you had some brunch thing."

"He *went* to that?"

It had never occurred to me that Oliver might still go—hell, *I* hadn't planned on still going.

"Well, he didn't want to," Mr. Luna continued. "But he went anyway. To talk to you." He gave me a hard look. "Because he didn't think you were going to have the cojones to talk to him yourself."

"That's not—that's…" I flushed. "That's fair. I deserved that. But I have to find him."

"Go find him, then," Mr. Luna said, folding his arms across his chest. "I'm not stopping you."

"I—um, okay, then." I couldn't tell if Mr. Luna was mad at me or not, but it didn't really matter. Nothing mattered, except talking to Oliver himself. "Uh, thanks."

"Don't thank me—thank Oliver, if he decides to hear you out," Mr. Luna said.

I was halfway down the walk when he called out again.

"Oh, and Luke?"

I turned around. "Yeah?"

"Don't you dare hurt him."

"I won't."

Because that was the only other thing I was sure of. I'd do whatever it took to make sure I never hurt Oliver again. I just needed to find him, first.

24

OLIVER

I stared at the restaurant from across the street.

It was 12:05, which meant I was a little late. I had no idea if Luke was in there yet or not. Part of me wanted to stay outside longer and keep *"waiting"* for him like I had been for the past five minutes. But let's be real, I wasn't waiting so much as I was delaying.

It wasn't a big deal. Or at least, it shouldn't have been. Luke had invited me to come. And granted, that had been before last night. But still. Micah was going to be there. His friends had told me to come. It wasn't like I was crashing.

I just had to go in there and tell Luke I wanted to talk to him. Tell him how I felt, but also tell him I needed an answer. That he couldn't just leave me hanging.

And that, I realized, was exactly why it was so hard to go into the restaurant, its red and gold decorations sparkling in the windows, its vestibule packed with people. I was convinced that somehow, I'd go in there and discover that was exactly what Luke was going to do.

Walk away, and leave me with no explanation.

But even if that was what was going to happen, standing out here wasn't going to help anything. It was time to go inside. Time to be brave.

The restaurant was packed. I opened the door onto a crush of people and scanned all the heads I could see for Luke's. I couldn't see him, but maybe that was because they'd already sat down? I pushed forward towards the host's stand, but before I made it more than two feet, someone snagged my arm.

"Oliver?"

I turned in surprise to see Micah grinning at me.

"Hey!" He pulled me into a hug. "I'm so glad you came."

"Hey," I said, reminding myself to smile. Just because I felt weird was no reason to spread it to anyone else. "Good to see you. How are you?"

"Oh God, exhausted," Micah said.

I tried to listen to his story—something about babysitting again and being up half the night with Bea as she puked everywhere—but I kept searching the crowd for Luke. Where was he?

"Anyway," Micah finished, "I got like, three hours of sleep, total, and then I get here, and our table isn't even ready yet, which is a travesty, so I think we can all agree my life is pretty much the hardest in human history, ever."

He paused and laughed. "You're not listening to me at all, are you?"

"I—what? No, of course, I am. I'm just..." I trailed off, flushing. "Sorry."

"Don't worry about it," Micah said. "I realize it's actually a pretty boring story."

"I'm just um—" I swallowed. "I was actually looking for Luke? Do you know where he is?"

"Luke?" Micah blinked. "I thought he was coming with you."

"Oh. Uh. He's—yeah, we didn't—I mean, we came... separately," I stammered. *Real smooth, Oliver.* "I was just hoping to uh—I kind of need to talk to him."

Micah frowned. "Is everything okay?"

"Yeah, no, I'm fine." A blatant lie. "It's just—it's not—it's kind of..."

God, I had no idea how to explain it without explaining everything.

"Is everything okay with you and Luke, is what I meant," Micah said. "You seem kinda... well, not great, if I'm being honest."

"We just—it's hard to—" I shook my head. This wasn't working. "We had a fight. Kind of. I guess. And I just—I really need to talk to him. But if he's not here—"

"Ohhh," Micah said, his eyes softening in comprehension. "I'm sorry. I bet we can find him, though." And before I could say anything else, he looked over and shouted, "Hey, Gray, Tyler, we need you."

Just what I wanted—more people who knew about my quite possibly about to end relationship. I knew Micah was just trying to be helpful, and I loved him dearly, but his version of helping could be a little... well, *"enthusiastic"* would be the nice way to describe it, but *"unrelentingly pushy"* were the words that came to mind right now.

"Gray, Tyler, this is Oliver," Micah said as a tall, muscular brunette and a shorter, blonder guy who looked kind of familiar joined our conversation.

"Oh, shit," the blond guy said. *"You're* Oliver. God, I've been so curious about you for so long because Luke hasn't said *anything,* and you know it's gotta be good if he's so tight-lipped about it. Oh, I'm Tyler, by the way."

He stuck out his hand, and I shook it, my brain still slightly dazed.

"Hi," I said weakly. "I uh—it's good to—I'm just, I was really only—"

"Oliver, huh?" the other guy said—he must have been Gray. "Damn. Well, it's nice to meet the guy who's finally gotten Luke to settle down and put—"

"It's really not that big a—" I tried to say, because this was getting out of hand, but Micah interrupted both Gray and me.

"Oliver's actually looking for Luke right now. We were wondering if you knew anything about where he might be."

"Us?" Tyler scoffed. "Luke doesn't tell us anything. That would involve, you know, opening up about stuff. Admitting he has feelings, etcetera, etcetera." He looked at me. "You're sure he's not just late? Did you text him?"

"He's—I didn't—it's kind of complicated," I said, fully aware of how dumb that sounded.

Micah snorted. "They had a fight."

"Micah," I said, aggrieved.

"What? How are they supposed to help if they don't know?" Micah protested. "There's nothing embarrassing about having a fight."

"Who's having a fight?"

All of us turned to see Luke's other friends, Adam and Ben show up. They must have just gotten there because they were pulling off hats and scarves as they made their way to us through the crowd.

"No one," Tyler said quickly, seeming to sense that I didn't want to talk about it. But it was too late.

"Luke and Oliver," Micah said unrepentantly, and I couldn't decide if I wanted to punch him or sink into the floor. "And now Luke's not here, and we're trying to figure out where he is."

"Oh, shit." Ben winced and gave me a sympathetic look. "I'm sorry, man."

"Yeah," Adam said. "Is there anything we can do?"

Five sets of eyes turned and focused on me and yeah, sinking into the floor was the winner. That was definitely what I wanted to do.

"Um, no, that's really... thanks. I mean, I appreciate it," I said, stumbling all over my words. "I didn't mean for—it's really not a big deal, I just thought—I can go. I *should* go. I don't want to ruin brunch for everyone and—"

"Holy shit, what's everyone doing here?"

Yet another person joined our group, but at least this new guy, with dark hair and confused eyes, took everyone's attention off of me for a second.

"Oh," Adam said ruefully. "Um. Surprise?"

I guessed that made the new guy Nick.

"What?" Nick laughed and shook his head. "I thought this was just supposed to be..."

"Yeah, we lied," Ben said, grinning. "It's a surprise party. But we uh, we got a little distracted by Oliver, and you're not supposed to get here for another fifteen minutes."

"Yeah, way to ruin your own surprise party," Adam said with a laugh. "Definitely blaming you for this and not us at all."

Nick rolled his eyes. "Terribly sorry about that. Next time I'll —wait. Did you say *Oliver*?"

He turned and looked at me, and I decided sinking into the floor was no longer enough. I wouldn't be satisfied until I was actually sinking down to the earth's core, as that was the only place where my cheeks being bright red and completely on fire wouldn't seem so out of context.

"Oh, shit, yeah," Adam said. "You guys haven't met yet. Oliver, this is Nick. Nick, this is Oliver. Luke's uh—"

"Did he find you?" Nick asked, his eyes wide.

"What?"

"Luke," Nick said, stepping forward and looking at me very intensely. "Did he find you? I talked to him this morning when he was running and he said he had to go—well, he didn't exactly say *"find you,"* but that was definitely the subtext."

"He what?"

My stomach had dropped into my shoes. No, beyond my shoes. My stomach was currently residing in the earth's core where the rest of me should have been.

"Yeah." Nick nodded quickly. "He said he had to go fix things and literally ran off to go, well, find you, I assumed." Nick paused. "He also told me to have a good party, which makes a lot more sense, now."

"Oh sweet," Adam grinned. "Then we can blame Luke for ruining the surprise. Excellent. I love it when things aren't my fault."

"He didn't—" I shook my head, not able to process what Nick was saying. "I haven't heard—he hasn't—I haven't heard from him. I don't know where he is. I thought he was here, but no one's seen him, and I don't even—"

"Oliver?"

I swear to God, I almost had a heart attack right then and there, and I know I'd told my dad not to joke about stuff like that, but I'm honestly not sure I was joking, because finally, *finally*, the voice I heard behind me belonged to the one person I'd been waiting to hear from, and I'm pretty sure my heart skipped at least five beats.

I turned, slowly, and tried to remember how to breathe again, Luke was pushing through the throng, his cheeks red from exertion or cold, I wasn't sure, and he looked—well, he looked gorgeous, just like he always did. I stood there, numb, as he got through the last bunch of people separating the two of us, just staring at those impossibly blue eyes of his as they locked onto mine.

"Luke." My voice caught in my throat.

I took a step towards him, then another. Oh God, I just wanted to touch him, to kiss him, to tell him whatever he needed to hear to get him to stay.

But no. I needed to be brave. I needed to tell him what *I* needed to hear, which was an honest answer about what he wanted. About if things were really done between us. Whatever he said, I could handle it. I just needed him to tell me— I couldn't let him walk away from me again without an explanation.

Dimly, I heard Micah say, *"Well if it isn't the man of the hour,"* and Nick grumble, *"Hey, I thought that was me,"* but it was like they were talking in another room, another universe, like everything else had been blacked out and muted except for Luke, standing right in front of me.

"Luke," I tried again, a little stronger this time. "I need to—"

"I love you," Luke said. And everything in my brain flew out the window.

"You—you what?"

"I love you," Luke repeated. He twisted his hat nervously in his hands. "I know that's insane, I know it's barely been a month, and I know I've fucked everything up and you probably want nothing to do with me anymore but I just, I had to tell you, even if you never want to see me again. I love you."

"You love me?" I blinked, still convinced I wasn't hearing him right. "You *love* me?"

It came out all high-pitched. Really attractive.

"Yeah. Yeah, I do."

"But you—you said you needed—you said it was too much, that I was moving too—"

"I was scared," Luke said, shaking his head. "Oliver, I was so scared. I still am. I'm fucking terrified. Because if you've changed your mind and you don't want me, or if you change your mind three months from now when I still haven't found a new job and don't know what to do with my life and you've realized you've made a mistake—that would kill me. But I—I can't let that control me. I have to trust you."

"Luke, I would never—"

"I've been such an idiot," Luke said. "I was so afraid of letting you down that it seemed easier to push you away. But I realized that the only thing I really can't live without... is you. Nothing else matters." Luke took another step towards me. "So I quit. This morning. I walked right into Harvey's office—he was actually there on a Saturday, for once—and I quit. Effective immediately."

"But Luke, that's your job."

"Not anymore," Luke said, laughing helplessly. "You were right. It was never going to make me happy. And I was only clinging onto it out of fear. But I can't worry about that. About making everyone else happy. The only thing I care about is you."

"I just want *you* to be happy, Luke," I said. "I just want you to be yourself. And not be scared that that's not enough."

Luke shoved his hat in his pocket and took my hand. "I told you this seven years ago, and it's still true. You're the only person I feel like I don't have to pretend with. I know you have no reason to forgive me. Not for abandoning you seven years ago and never explaining, not for pushing you away last night. For being so afraid of what everyone else would think that I let myself hurt you. But if there's any way I can convince you to give me a second—well, a third—chance, I promise you, I won't waste it."

"Luke, I—"

"I will show you how much you mean to me. Every day. I will never let you forget how important you are to me. The most important person in my life."

"*Luke*, I—"

"I mean it, Oliver. Whatever it takes. Hell, I already talked to your dad and told him what I told you—I love you. And if I can do that and live to tell the tale, I can do anything."

"You talked to my *dad*?"

Luke laughed. "Yeah. I tried to find you after talking to Harvey. I went to your hotel—they definitely think I'm stalking you, by the way—but you weren't there, so I thought maybe you'd gone to your dad's, but he told me you were here, and I just—Oliver, I just need you to know that—"

"I love you."

"—I will do whatever it takes to—wait." Luke stopped and tilted his head to the side. "You *love* me?"

"That's what I've been trying to tell you. Only you wouldn't stop talking."

"I thought I—"

"I love you," I said, trying to control the urge to giggle hysterically. "I love you. I'm not sure I ever really stopped. I know that sounds gross and creepy, and maybe *I'm* the stalker, but I think I fell in love with you when I was eighteen, and I don't think I've ever stopped."

"Me too," Luke whispered. "Me too."

"Jesus, just kiss already, we get it," Micah's voice cut in from somewhere behind us.

"Oh my God," I said, leaning forward and burying my face in Luke's neck. I'd completely forgotten they were all there. Watching and listening to us.

Luke's arms went around me, and I felt his lips on my cheek before he whispered, "Sorry my friends are the worst."

"Don't be," I snorted. "Micah's the really obnoxious one, and he's more my friend than yours."

"Whaddya think," Luke said, laughing all warm and rumbly in my ear, like the tail end of a summer thunderstorm. "Should we appease them? Kiss a little?"

I knew my cheeks were on fire, but for once, I didn't actually care. "I think we could manage that."

So we did.

***

"So on a scale of one to ten, how mortified are you right now?" I asked Luke with an arch look as we stepped out into the cold.

His friends had basically shoved us out the door and insisted we go home, Micah suggesting that we probably wanted some *alone time*, which would have been fine if he hadn't also been miming a blow job while he said it, and even Nick saying that it sounded like maybe Luke and I had some things to talk about privately. So with promises to meet up with them later, we'd left the restaurant and headed back to Luke's apartment.

Luke laughed. "Honestly? Probably about a seven." He tugged my hand to bring me close and pressed a quick kiss to my lips. "But I think that's a good thing."

"Yeah?"

"Yeah." Luke laughed wryly. "I've spent my whole life trying to avoid being embarrassed—I think maybe I need to just inundate myself in embarrassing situations now to make up for it. Realize it's actually not that bad. In fact," he said, raising my hand to his lips and kissing my knuckles. "I think I could get used to it."

I chuckled. "'*Not that bad*' and '*could get used to it,*' huh? The most romantic things anyone's ever said to me."

"Shush. You know I wasn't talking about you." Luke grinned at me as we crossed the street and began our walk back to his apartment. "Besides, I'll say plenty more than that when we get home. And I'll do more than just talk."

"You'd better. The past 24 hours are a memory I'd like to

forget, and I feel like the best way to paper over them is copious amounts of sex."

"Your wish," Luke said, with a sparkle in his eye, "is my command."

I smiled happily into my scarf. I still couldn't believe it. Not just how Luke felt about me, but that he'd come to find me, to tell me. Hell, he'd even told my dad. And while I would have supported him if he'd needed more time at his job, I was unreasonably happy that he'd decided he didn't. I didn't care what Luke did next—as long as it made him happy.

We walked in silence for a while, but it was a warm, giddy kind of silence. The kind that made it feel like the sun was shining just for us, the kind that gave the old piles of snow on the sidewalks a sparkle and sheen. The kind that made the whole world shimmer.

"You know," I said as we turned up Luke's block. "I think I was actually telling the truth."

"About what?"

"I think that actually may be the most romantic thing anyone's ever said to me. That they could get used to me."

"Oliver, I was just—"

"Because it means someone wants me around long enough for that to happen," I continued. "That they *want* to get used to me."

"Oliver—"

"And I just—I know you were joking, but I just want you to know that it—"

"Oliver."

I stopped, finally, and looked at Luke as we came to a stop outside his building. He was smiling in what looked like exasperation.

"Yeah?"

"I'm already used to you," Luke said, pulling me close. "I've been used to you since the day you walked back into my life, and I don't know what I'd do if you went anywhere. Please don't, okay? And I was joking about being embarrassed—I am in no way embarrassed by you."

He kissed me again, sweet and slow, and warm, so warm against the cool of the afternoon air. When he pulled away, he smiled.

"Got it?"

"Got it." I smiled back.

Going up to Luke's apartment was strange. I'd been there so many times in the past month. It felt more familiar to me than anywhere else in Manhattan—more than anywhere else in the state of New York, really, other than my dad's house. And yet, the last time I'd been here, everything had felt so different.

As soon as we got into the apartment, Luke pressed me up against the door. I guess he hadn't been kidding about wanting to get home. *Home.*

Wherever Luke was, I realized—that was home. And it always had been.

There was no other way to explain the past seven years, other than one long attempt to forget—and the final acknowledgment that I couldn't—where, and who, home was for me. Luke had been home from the moment he'd kissed me in my bedroom all those years ago.

We left a trail of clothes on our way to the bedroom, and Luke, for once, left them where they were. I'm not entirely sure how we even made it to the bed—it was all a blur of lips and tongues and fingers in hair and twisting buttons as we tore everything off each other.

"Like Hansel and Gretel," Luke said when I pointed out the very *Oliverian* mess. "So we can retrace our steps."

"I'd really rather not though," I said as we crashed onto the bed, naked. I let Luke roll me onto my back, and I wrapped my legs around him. "I'd much rather stay here."

"Yeah?" Luke said, stroking my cheek with the back of his fingers.

Something in his voice made me look more closely. Luke's eyes, that beautiful marine blue, had a hint of a question in them. And something that looked a little like fear. Luke was asking me something. Something he was still afraid I might say no to.

"Always," I said to Luke's unspoken question.

I pulled Luke down for a kiss, and Luke let himself be pulled. I realized for the first time, then, that it was usually Luke who led, Luke who was the one in control. And suddenly that made sense, too. That was probably less scary for him than waiting for me to take the lead—and risking the possibility that I wouldn't take it. The possibility that I wouldn't want him.

Impossible as it seemed, Luke, my perfect, beautiful, kind,

smart, funny, *did-I-mention-perfect* Luke, thought that he was nothing special and worried that I wouldn't want him. Worried that there was something in him that would drive me away once I saw it. And before I knew what I was doing, I was pushing up and over, taking the lead and talking as I did.

"There is nothing," I said, "*nothing* you could do that would make me want to leave. You got that?" I kissed Luke's Adam's apple, then slowly trailed kisses up to his ear where I whispered, "Because you're *you*. And it's you that I want. There's nothing you're hiding from me, nothing you're going to spring on me. I've seen all of you—and I want it. I want you."

"Even if I have no idea what I'm doing with my life and it turns out I don't *have* any passions and this is as interesting as I get?"

Luke laughed, but I could tell the question wasn't really a joke.

"You could be unemployed for the rest of your life, and I'd stay," I said firmly. "You could collect and trade rare Allen wrenches on the internet, and I'd stay. Hell, you could do nothing but watch sports with my dad and drink beer, and I'd stay."

"God, you really shouldn't, though," Luke laughed. "Not for that last one. *I* wouldn't even stay for that."

"Well I would. So there."

"You won't have to," Luke said seriously. "Because that's not gonna happen. I'm gonna—I'm gonna figure something out."

"Luke?"

"Yeah?"

"That's fine—as long as that's what you want to do, and not something you think you should do because it's respectable, or it looks good, or it makes someone else happy, okay?

"Even if I don't know what that is yet? Even if it's just Allen wrenches? Or miniature trains? Or spoons or something?"

"Even if it's just spoons," I said. "I promise, baby."

"Baby?" Luke's eyebrows shot up.

"Sorry." I grimaced. "It just slipped out."

"No," Luke said. "No. Don't be sorry at all." He laughed. "The number of times I've had to keep myself from saying that. I just didn't wanna overstep."

"Please." I pressed my lips to Luke's. "Step as far as you want. Step all over me."

Luke burst out laughing. "Somehow I don't think that's quite what you meant. Unless—"

I snorted, feeling myself flush. "Well, lucky for you, I'm not going anywhere, so you've got plenty of time to figure out what I meant."

"I like the sound of that," Luke said, wrapping his arms around me and pulling me down into a hug. "I like the sound of that a lot."

I kissed my way down Luke's chest and onto his stomach, loving the feel of his cock, hot and hard, pressing up beneath me. Luke groaned as my chest brushed over his shaft, and I smiled and stroked my fingers along it lightly.

"Fuck," Luke moaned.

"Someone's sensitive today," I said with a grin.

"Yeah, well," Luke grimaced, "remember that idea I had where I was too busy and too stressed last week to have sex, and I just needed to focus on work?"

"Yeah?"

"Let's never do that again."

"Agreed." I bent down and licked a long stripe up the underside of his cock. "I'm so glad we've settled on spoons as a new hobby for you. I think it'll give you a much better work-life balance."

Luke laughed and moaned at the same as I swirled my tongue around the tip of his cock.

"Fuck," he gasped. "That's what I should have told Harvey. That I was stepping down to spend more time with my family—by which I mean my boyfriend and my spoons."

"Gotta spend time with them," I snorted. "Those tiny teaspoons will grow up into tablespoons before you can blink."

"Good point," Luke said. "You really have to appreciate these days while you have the—"

But he never finished his sentence because I swallowed down around his cock right then and must have distracted him. Whoops. It was probably rude of me, but I found myself remarkably unremorseful.

It was way too much fun, sucking Luke off, touching, teasing, licking, never establishing a rhythm. But all too soon, Luke's hand gripped my shoulder and pulled me back up.

"Babe, you're gonna make me come if you keep that up. It's been a while, remember?"

"Babe?" I arched an eyebrow.

"What's wrong with 'babe'? I thought we decided that was okay?"

"We decided 'baby' was okay," I laughed. "'*Babe*' though... it just sounds so... *hetero*."

"Says the guy who's actually slept with women," Luke said with a grin. "Do forgive me, baby. My apologies."

"That's right. I demand the full two syllables and nothing less."

"Far be it from me to deprive you of your due. But seriously." Luke gave me a pleading look. "I'm not gonna last if you keep that up, and I'd really like to—"

"Ugh, are you going to demand to give me sexual satisfaction again?" I tried my damndest to suppress a grin.

"I know, it's a real hardship. I don't know how you put up with me."

"Sometimes I wonder."

Luke reached between us and stroked my cock—which was, for the record, almost painfully hard and leaking precum, so it's not like I really had a leg to stand on.

"You were saying," he said, grinning as I moaned.

"Well, I guess it wouldn't be the *worst* thing in the world," I said, not even able to pretend I wasn't whimpering as he swiped a finger across my slit and then licked it. "Hold that thought."

I reached over to Luke's nightstand to grab the lube and condoms, and then paused as an idea occurred to me. I came back to Luke, pressed the bottle of lube into his hands, and bit my lip.

"Second thoughts?" Luke asked, his breath hitched.

"No," I said quickly. "God, no, not at all. It's just... I was thinking. If we're doing this—I mean, if you just want this to be like, just us, and not date anyone else—"

"Which I do." Luke squeezed my hand. "I thought that was obvious. I love you. No one else. Just you." He gave me a confused look. "What's wrong?"

I flushed. "Nothing's wrong. It's just—ugh this is embarrassing, I've just never asked anyone this before, so I don't know how big of a deal it is, and maybe it's not a big deal to you at all but um, I've been tested recently—I do it whenever I get a physical, and I haven't been with anyone else but you since then, and I don't have any—"

"Oh." Comprehension dawned in Luke's eyes, and he smiled. "Oh."

"I mean, it's totally fine if you don't want to—" I said, blushing.

"I do." Luke brought my hand to his lips again and kissed it. And it was such a Luke gesture—so sweet and so tender, and no one else had ever done that to me before, but Luke did it all the time, and it just made me feel *safe*—that I basically melted into a puddle right there on the bed.

"Don't be embarrassed," Luke said. "It is a big deal. Actually, I've never had sex without a condom either. Never been with anyone long enough for that to come up." He smiled up at me, and it was almost shy, which was so sweet it was like stabbing a candy cane through my heart. "I got tested three months ago. And I don't have anything either."

"So do you want to—"

Luke smiled, it spread across his face like sunshine. "Yeah. If you do—I'd—I'd like that."

"Me too," I said, and somehow we were both bright red and laughing, and I collapsed down onto Luke's chest. "God. We're such nerds."

"We really are," Luke said, kissing my neck and stroking my back. "Good thing I've always liked them."

"Good thing," I said, grinding down onto him.

I loved the feeling of Luke's body under me, his cock rubbing against mine, our skin slick with sweat. Luke's hand slid between us and began to stroke us together as I uncapped the bottle of lube and squeezed some onto my fingers. I found my entrance and bit my lip to stifle a moan as I pressed a finger inside.

"Fuck," Luke breathed. "That's never gonna stop being the fucking hottest thing I've ever seen."

"You can't even see anything," I gasped, pushing my finger in further, then sliding it out and back in again.

"I can see your face," Luke said. "That's all I need."

I rutted forward into Luke's hand as I added more fingers, slowly loosening myself up and preparing for Luke's cock.

"Please," I begged when I knew I could take it.

"You ready?"

I nodded, speechless, and started to roll off of Luke, but Luke stopped me.

"I wanna see you on top."

I flushed again.

"What?"

"It's just—" I shook my head. "I was just thinking about that night, after the reunion. How embarrassing that was."

"It wasn't embarrassing. It was just—we just didn't know each other yet. Or, well, we were pretending to be different people. We don't have to do that anymore."

"But what if that position is cursed or jinxed or something," I asked, only fifty percent joking.

"Then we'll just have to unjinx it," Luke said. He stroked my cheek. "I promise it's not jinxed, Oliver. If you want, we can do something else, though."

"It's not that I don't want to. I'm just—" I squeezed my eyes shut. How could I explain the cocktail of emotions I was feeling? The desire I had for Luke, and the strangeness of knowing it was reciprocated. I was afraid it would overpower me. "What if I freak out again or something?"

"Then I've got you," Luke said. "I've got you."

Trust him. You're asking him to trust you. Trust that he's right here, with you, all in. Trust that this is real.

"Okay." I nodded slowly. "Yeah. Okay."

"You sure?" Luke winced. "Shit, have I already asked that today?"

Sweet Luke. Always asking if I was sure. Luke, who cared about me, who loved me, as improbable as that seemed. He *loved* me.

"Yeah." I smiled, letting the warmth of that idea warm me to my core. Luke loved me. "Yeah, I'm sure."

I climbed back on top of Luke and slicked his cock with lube, then lined myself up above him.

"Take your time," Luke said as I leaned back on his cock, feeling it press against my hole.

I nodded, and then, my hand braced against Luke's chest, I sank down, his cock pressing into me. God, it felt good— and like it had been too long. Only a week, and in a life where I'd gone two years between getting laid, that hardly counted. But it felt like something missing was finally sliding back into place.

Luke's blue eyes were wide and wild, and he mouthed something that was too soft to hear. *"So beautiful,"* was what it looked like.

"Fuck," I groaned, adjusting to the stretch. "Oh fuck, you feel good."

"You're so perfect," Luke whispered.

I began to move, slowly, just luxuriating in the feel of having Luke inside me again, of being filled. I rotated my hips, just barely moving up and down on his cock, and was rewarded not only with how good it felt, but with the moans of pleasure I was bringing out of Luke.

Luke brought his hand to my cock and began to stroke me as I thrust back onto him. We were so in sync, I wasn't entirely sure where his body stopped and mine began. It didn't matter. We were together. But Luke wasn't the only one who'd gone without for a week, and I wasn't sure how long I'd last, either.

"Fuck me," I murmured as I collapsed down onto Luke's chest, and Luke was only too happy to oblige.

He shifted his legs, bracing against the bed, and hipped up into me. I moaned into his neck. Fuck, I was coming undone. My heart felt like it was trying to beat its way out of my chest, crushed between me and Luke. My breath came out in gasps, and all I could manage to do was whisper Luke's name, over and over and over.

"Are you okay?" Luke murmured.

"Yeah," I gasped. "I'm just—you feel—it's just—you're so—"

"I know," Luke breathed, stroking my back. "I feel it too."

And somehow, that reassurance that I hadn't even known I'd needed was like the last piece of the puzzle. I wasn't alone, Luke was right here with me, and he felt the same as I did.

"Oh, Luke," I groaned. "I'm gonna come."

"Come for me," Luke whispered, and as I did, he released inside of me. It felt right.

Luke stroked my back as I melted down onto him again, seeming to sense that I wanted to stay connected, stay just like this. He kissed every part of me he could reach, his fingertips leaving trails of goosebumps on my skin.

"I love you," I tried to say, but my face was smushed into Luke's neck and it came out more like, *'Awbugoo.'*

"What was that?" Luke laughed lightly.

I tried again. "I love you."

Luke smiled. "I love you too."

When he finally pulled out and went to the bathroom for a washcloth and water glasses, I was practically in a stupor of post-orgasm happiness. I knew there was so much more to talk about, to figure out about our future. But for the moment, everything was perfect, just like this.

I couldn't stop staring at Luke as he filled the water glasses in the bathroom. Luke grinned back at me, and maybe it was that that distracted him because as he walked back and set the water glasses down, I heard a bump and saw him wince.

"Dammit," he said, hopping on one leg as he got back into bed. "What if all I want to do with my life is just get a new bed? I've always hated this one."

"Then I support you," I said, letting him pull me close. I studied Luke's face as he looked around the room, his expression unreadable.

"You know," he said after a minute, "I've never even really liked this apartment all that much."

"Really?" I asked drowsily.

"Yeah. I only ever lived here because it was close to work. Who lives in Midtown?" Luke shuddered, and I laughed.

"What would you say," Luke continued after a moment, "if

we—and I mean, only if you wanted, obviously, but what if we—what if we looked for a place... together?

"Really?"

"Really," Luke said. "I mean, I can completely understand if you're like, not eager to sign a lease with someone you just started dating a month ago—"

"But have known for thirteen years—"

"Who might not have a job really soon—"

"When I have more money than I know what to do with—"

"But I have some savings—"

"Again, the money—"

"And I promise, I really am gonna look for—"

"Luke," I cut in, "Not to be an ass about it, but the money thing *really* doesn't matter. Do you wanna just be my personal accountant? I could literally afford to pay you a salary just to do that, and if you actually were investing my money, you'd probably pay for yourself. God knows all I've ever done is let it sit in a savings account."

"You've *what*?" Luke looked at me, horrified. "Oliver, you should be doing so much more with—do you really not have anything invested in—I can't believe no one's ever sat down with you and—"

"See." I laughed. "There we go, that's one possibility right there. You can fix my financial habits. But just... trust me. The money thing really doesn't matter."

Luke laughed. "Not to sound ungrateful, but I'm not sure I really want another job in finance actually? I was kind of thinking—maybe this is dumb—but I was kind of thinking about teaching? Or something with kids, maybe?"

"I don't think that sounds dumb at all. I think that sounds wonderful."

"But don't worry," Luke said hurriedly. "I'm still happy to talk to you about the joys of market-indexed mutual funds. And I'll do it for free."

"Oh yeah?"

"Well... on second thought, I might need some kind of compensation. But it wouldn't have to be cash," Luke snickered.

"Well, if I'm really interviewing you," I grinned, "then I think it's only fair that I ask you about your relevant skills and experience. Before I take you on."

"Oh, I'd be more than happy to give you a taste of my skills. And even happier for you to take me on." Luke kissed his way down onto my neck.

"You sure you don't want to take a little break?" I said, gasping as Luke's tongue flicked across one of my nipples.

"Oliver, I've got weeks—no, *months*—of stress to burn off here. I don't need any kind of break."

"Well, in that case," I said with a laugh, "maybe you can tell me a little more about the duties you carried out in your previous position?"

"My previous position, huh? I can do more than just tell you. I can show you..."

25

LUKE

"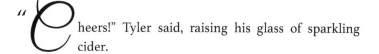heers!" Tyler said, raising his glass of sparkling cider.

"Cheers!"

Oliver, Gray, Adam and Ben, and Nick all raised their glasses too. My mom and Oliver's dad were deep in conversation in the corner of my mom's back porch, but they each made a halfhearted nod in the direction of raising their glasses before going right back to whatever discussion they were having. Undoubtedly about Nassau County property taxes or something equally fascinating.

"No, no," I said, shaking my head. "We can't cheers until Micah gets here."

"But Micah was supposed to get here ages ago," Oliver whined. "Who knows when he's gonna show up, at this rate? I just wanna celebrate your accomplishments and make you deeply uncomfortable. Is that too much to ask?"

"Yeah, Luke, come on. We just wanna tell you how great you

are. Why should that make you want to die or walk across hot coals to get away from us?" Tyler said, grinning.

"I hate you all," I grumbled.

"Excellent," Tyler retorted. "And now that that's been settled, can we please get back to the matter at hand?"

"Yes, definitely," Oliver said. "Ooh, and I wanna say something after you say your thing," he told Tyler. "So don't let me forget."

"I'm actually going to die." I shook my head. "Right here and now. Are you really this heartless?" I gave Oliver my best puppy dog eyes.

"Utterly and completely," he said, smiling broadly. And then, as if that weren't enough, he leaned in and kissed me on the nose.

"I'm never telling anybody anything from now on," I groaned.

It really wasn't that big a deal. All I'd done was get into an alternative-route teacher certification program. I hadn't even completed it yet. It was only May, and I had three months of intensive training and summer school ahead of me. But Oliver had insisted on having a party, and I hadn't been able to talk him out of it.

"You can't let them see it bothers you," Adam leaned over and said with a laugh. "Take it from one attention hater to another. Letting them know you're uncomfortable only encourages them."

"It's true," Ben agreed. "It's way more fun torturing someone with compliments when you know just how much they hate being told how sexy, and talented, and perfect they are."

He kissed Adam on the cheek, and Adam rolled his eyes.

"See?" he mouthed silently at me.

"Annnnyway," Tyler said. "As I was saying, let's all raise a glass of our alcoholic or non-alcoholic beverage of choice in honor of Luke, who is not only the strongest, most loving, caring, helpful big brother in the entire world, he's also the most patient person to ever go through a legal battle with. Luke, you put up with so much whining from me, and I know you're going to say that it wasn't that bad and you wanted to help, but seriously—I wouldn't have made it through the last year without you. Also, Dad would still have a lot more of my money."

He snorted. "But you helped me get through it, and you know what I thought when I found out we won the suit? *'Luke told me everything was going to be okay. And he was right.'* So, to you, Luke, for always being there for me, for being incredibly giving, and," Tyler grinned up at Gray, "for lending me your high school uniform on the day I auditioned and met this guy. That was pretty solid, too."

"To Luke," Gray said, and everyone raised their glasses again, and only like, 25% of me died.

God, I'd been so happy when Tyler had won the suit. I'd known he would—our dad really hadn't covered his tracks all that well and had just relied on Tyler never bothering to look—but it had been so rough on Tyler, and I knew he needed the win. But everything else—I mean, it was nice to get thanked, I supposed, but that was just what you were supposed to do, wasn't it? As a brother, and like, a decent human being?

"Okay, my turn," Oliver said. He smiled at me and took my hand. "Luke, I will keep this short because I know you hate this, but I just wanted to say, I'm super proud of you for taking this leap, for giving yourself the chance to figure out what you want and then going for it. *Of course*, you being you, the thing you want to do is in service of others, but what matters most to me is that you're doing it because you want to. I'm so proud of you, and I love you, and now I'll stop talking because I can see you trying not to cringe at every word that comes out of my mouth."

Oliver pulled me into a one-armed hug as everyone raised their glasses again, and I leaned up against him, just enjoying the warmth of him at my side.

"Speeeeech," Ben demanded, cupping his hands around his mouth. "Make a speech, Luke."

"Oh my God," I groaned, though it was hard to be too mad when I had my arm around Oliver. I glanced around the porch at everyone and saw Adam grinning as if to say, *"I told you so."*

I closed my eyes for a moment and took a deep breath.

"Okay, so for the record, you're all terrible people," I began.

"True," Nick nodded. "Very true, continue."

"*But*, I suppose, I'm glad that you're *my* terrible people. And I love you all, and this is very nice, and please everyone stop looking at me now."

"So eloquent," Oliver grinned.

Thankfully, the conversation moved on after that.

It ended up being a really nice afternoon, though no one knew where Micah was, which was a little strange. But Tyler and Oliver got into a deep discussion about a documentary they'd both seen on electric sewing machines, and Gray and Ben found all of my old sports equipment in the garage and insisted on setting up the badminton net and yelling *"shuttlecock"* at the top of their lungs, and I think even Oliver's dad had a good time—the last time I checked on him, at least, he and Nick had been passionately agreeing with each other about how terrible Connecticut was.

"See," Oliver said, coming to stand next to me as the sun began to set that evening. "I told you this wouldn't be so bad."

"And you were right, as usual." I snuck my arm around his waist. "Thanks for organizing this. Have I told you lately how much I love you?"

"Only twice this morning while I was brushing my teeth and once at the grocery store while we were getting salsa." He grinned impishly. "But if you wanna tell me again, I suppose I won't *complain*."

"Good. Because I love you. A lot." I knocked my bottle against his.

"Yeah?"

"Yeah. Even more than this smoothie. And that's saying something."

I'd had some champagne earlier, but I'd picked up a super-green smoothie at the store along with our salsa, and I hadn't been able to resist the temptation to break into it.

"Oh, shit!" Oliver said. "That reminds me. I got you a present, and I just got the email that the package was dropped off with the doorman."

"You what? You didn't have to—"

"I know, I know," he said, waving away my objections. "But I wanted to. Besides, it's kind of a present for me too because it means you might finally stop complaining about your chlorophyll intake levels. You, my friend, are the proud owner of a brand new juicer."

"Oh my God." I shook my head. Oliver had refused to let me buy a new juicer for way too long, insisting he could fix my old one. "You're ridiculous."

"Please, I'm not ridiculous, I'm just finally admitting defeat. Besides, it's practical. Now you don't get to whine about me wanting to eat takeout all the time because you can still drink all the kale you can handle."

"Well you shot yourself in the foot because now you're going to have to drink kale too." I beamed innocently in the face of Oliver's sudden misgiving and, for good measure, returned the nose kiss from earlier. "You're very welcome."

"Ugh, no." Oliver shook his head. "I take it back, this thing's going straight back to the store. I'm sure I can return it for a panini maker, ooh, or a deep fryer."

"If you even so much as think of bringing a deep fryer into our apartment..."

"What?" Oliver smiled broadly. "What would you do."

"I'd..." I barked a laugh. "I'd probably learn to love deep-fried food."

"Aww, Luke, you'd do that for me?"

"Anything for you." I leaned in and kissed him for real this time.

Oliver made a face. "Eww, gross, you taste like green stuff."

"I know," I said sweetly. "Get used to it."

"And this is how you treat me," Oliver said, in mock outrage. "After everything I've done for you."

"Hey, I tried to warn you," I said with a laugh. "I told you I wasn't very nice, but *somebody* thought he knew better and said there was nothing I could do that would make him leave. You've got no one to blame but yourself."

"Oh God, you're right."

"And don't even bother hoping I'll return *you* to the store," I said, pulling him into my arms. "You're stuck with me now."

"Yeah?" Oliver's arms snaked around my neck. "You mean it?"

"Yeah." I smiled, pressing my forehead to his. "You're a keeper."

THANKS FOR READING!

Check out some of my other books no the next page! But before you do... want to know what's next for Luke and Oliver?

After Midnight

Free Bonus Chapter

You can read *After Midnight*, a free, explicit bonus epilogue for *Oliver Ever After*, just by joining my mailing list. *After Midnight* is an explicit follow-up, taking place after the end of *Oliver Ever After*. Sweet and sexy, it's the perfect happy ending for Luke and Oliver! You know you want that, right?

Oh, and also, you'll be notified of my new releases and when I have more free stuff, you'll be the first to know.

Sign up at: http://eepurl.com/diQHrb
www.spencerspears.com

ALSO BY SPENCER SPEARS

Have you read the first two books in the *8 Million Hearts* series?
Check them out below!

Adam's Song

Gray for You

Stay tuned for the next *8 Million Hearts* book. In the meantime,
check out my *Maple Springs* series!

Billion Dollar Bet

Beneath Orion

Sugar Season

Strawberry Moon

Adam's Song

They say it's a bad idea to fall for your best friend. But since when do I say no to bad ideas?

Adam: It's not like I wanted to fall in love with Ben. When we first met in college, I thought he'd be like every other hot jock who'd made my life hell in high school. It's not my fault he turned out to be sweet, funny, and insanely talented. We moved to New York after college to break into the music business and of course Ben got signed by a major label— they'd be stupid not to want him. But even though he's a famous popstar now, he still wants to be friends with a nobody like me. Honestly, if he didn't want me falling for him, he should have been less goddamn perfect.

Well, except for the part where he's straight. Did I forget to mention that?

In my defense, responsible decision-making has never been my strong suit. Case in point—collapsing on stage, guitar in hand, after discovering my then-boyfriend, now-ex was cheating on me, and downing a bottle of bourbon in response. But I'm cleaning up my act—no more hiding in the closet and no more bad life choices. But that also means no more waiting around for the day Ben magically decides he likes di...sgustingly sappy guys with secret crushes on him (aka me).

So why did Ben have to pick now to make me question everything I thought I knew about us?

Ben: It's not like I planned this. I was on tour when Adam collapsed back in New York and he wouldn't even let me come home early to visit him. But that's Adam for you—brilliant, breathtaking, and pathologically afraid of vulnerability. All I wanted was to be there for him—and him coming out didn't change that in the slightest. Yeah, I couldn't help seeing him a little differently. And no, I couldn't quite explain why I was suddenly noticing the curve of his back, the freckles on his cheeks, or wondering what his lips tasted like. But whatever weird awakening I was having, Adam needed support, not more confusion.

And then I kissed him. Whoops.

And I know it's fast. I know it's unexpected. I know my label would be livid if they found out I was dating a guy. But I also know—deeply and inexplicably—that this could be something real. I just have to convince Adam of the same thing. Beautiful, broken Adam who looks at the world through 14 layers of irony. Adam, who'd rather get an appendectomy than admit that he needs someone. Adam, who still doesn't know all of my secrets.

So do I convince him to risk everything—on me?

Adam's Song is **Book 1** in the **8 Million Hearts** series. *While each book can be read on its own, they've even more fun to read together. Adam's Song is a 120,000 word m/m romance full of snark, sweetness, and a healthy serving of steam. Friends-to-lovers and hurt/comfort themes. No cheating, no cliffhangers, and a guaranteed HEA.*

Gray For You

Who auditions for gay porn without realizing it? Me, apparently...

Gray: I'm not the kind of guy you take home to meet your mother. I'm an ex-adult film star with a GED and a giant co...llection of movie credits I can't talk about in polite company. I might be good at helping other guys get their happy endings, but I've more or less given up on finding one of my own.

Until Tyler Lang walks into my life.

That's right, my co-star for my final film is Tyler Lang-- America's heartthrob, until he disappeared from the radar last year. Tyler's got a reputation for being a bad boy, a partier, and apparently straight, but the sweet, vulnerable- looking kid who shows up at auditions is completely different. And now that I'm getting to know him, I can't help wondering what it is that's made his eyes so sad--and wishing there were some way I could make it better.

I'm not supposed to get a happy ending. So why the hell won't my heart listen?

Tyler: I know what you've heard about me. Another spoiled child-actor, all grown up and out of control. I wish I could tell you you're wrong, but the truth is, I'm a little bit of a mess. Okay, so maybe I'm a *giant* mess. And now, after getting arrested with an ez-bake oven's worth of drugs I don't even remember buying, I'm washed-up at the grand old age of 21.

After a year of rehab and community service, all I want is to work again. So when my agent sends me a new script, maybe I don't read the fine print as carefully as I should. Which is how I end up auditioning for an adult film. A high-brow, literary adult film. But still. There's no way I can go through with this. After all, I'm so deep in the closet I'm not sure I'll ever find my way out. And I *wouldn't* do this movie-- except for one thing: Gray Evans.

Strong, kind, and honest, Gray makes me feel seen in a way I've never been before--and makes me want to be better. And somehow, around Gray, everything seems possible. Like maybe there's a world where I'm not a total screw-up. Maybe there's a world where I can come out, and not tank my career. And maybe, just maybe, there's a world where Gray, who's smart and brave and so together, could want someone like me.

Gray For You is Book 2 in the 8 Million Hearts series. While each book can be read on its own, they're even more fun to read together. Gray For You is a 150,000 word m/m romance full of snark, sweetness, and a healthy serving of steam. Movie star romance and hurt/comfort themes. No cheating, no cliffhangers, and a guaranteed HEA.

Billion Dollar Bet
What would you bet for a chance at true love?

Hopeless romantic Kian Bellevue can't help falling for the
wrong guys. Maybe it's because he lost his parents so young,
maybe it's just his caring nature, but he can't stop diving in
when he should be heading for the hills. And just when he
decides to swear off guys for the summer, he meets drop-
dead gorgeous Jack Thorsen, who might just be the man of
his dreams.

It's not fair, because Kian doesn't even have time for guys
right now. His hometown of Maple Springs, Minnesota is
considering selling miles of pristine wilderness to a Wall
Street billionaire who wants to open a resort and play at
being a hotelier. But Kian's spent his whole life fighting
against big businesses and he's ready to go toe-to-toe with
the mystery mogul - until he realizes that the billionaire is
Jack himself.

Billionaire Jack Thorsen is married to his work and likes it that way. Growing up in foster care taught him to look out for himself and since the day he left for college, he's never stopped striving. Despite his best friend's urging, he's not looking for a guy. Even after he meets sweet and sexy Kian Bellevue, he's still determined to keep his guard up. People can't hurt you if you never let them close.

But it's not like Jack doesn't have a heart. When he finds out that Maple Springs, the home he left behind, is on the brink of bankruptcy, he proposes to buy their unused public lands and create an eco-resort. It's an obvious win-win - who could oppose it? That is, who, other than Kian, the guy he can't get out of his head.

Jack needs Kian on his side if he wants the town to vote in favor of his resort and he's not afraid to play dirty. His proposition: Kian spends the summer with him. If Jack convinces Kian to support him, Kian will get the town on Jack's side. But if he fails, Jack will withdraw the proposal completely. It's a crazy bet, but Kian would be crazy to turn it down - right?

There's only one problem. Jack - tall, handsome, and emotionally unavailable - is exactly Kian's type. And Kian is surprisingly good at breaking down the barriers Jack spent years putting up. With their hearts on the line as well as a hotel, will both men risk it all for a chance at love?

Billion Dollar Bet is Book 1 in the Maple Springs series. While each book focuses on different characters and can be read on its own, they're even more fun to read together.

Billion Dollar Bet is a 55,000 word m/m romance novel with sizzling summer heat. No cheating, no cliffhangers, and a guaranteed HEA.

Beneath Orion
What happens when two stars collide?

The first lesson Colin Gardner ever learned was not to trust. The second was that love hurts. Growing up in an abusive family, he turned to the night sky for comfort and buried himself in science. It wasn't easy being the only gay guy in school and Colin made peace with the fact that he'd never fall in love. He won't risk that pain. Especially not for a guy who's never dated men before. No matter how much he's tempted.

Charlie Keller doesn't date. How could he risk his kid growing attached to someone when it might not last? The divorced dad's life revolves around his daughter, his dog, and his job as Maple Springs' resident handy-man. But when Charlie helps Colin out in a pinch, his world changes forever. Charlie can't ignore his attraction to Colin, but he can't act on it either - can he?

As winter deepens, Charlie and Colin are drawn into each other's orbit. But when Charlie's ex-wife threatens to move his daughter across the country, he realizes his worst fears might come true. And when Colin's past comes calling, it raises demons he's not sure he's strong enough to fight. Will Colin and Charlie's love flame out, or can they find a way to make a new constellation - just for the two them?

Beneath Orion is Book 2 in the Maple Springs series. While each book focuses on different characters and can be read on its own, they're even more fun to read together.

Beneath Orion is a 55,000 word steamy, contemporary, gay-for-you M/M romance. No cliffhangers, no cheating, and a guaranteed HEA.

A MAPLE SPRINGS NOVEL

SPENCER SPEARS

<u>Sugar Season</u>

They say it's better to have loved and lost. They have no idea what they're talking about...

Police officer Graham Andersen already had his happy ending. A whirlwind romance, a young marriage, more happiness than he knew what to do with. And then it was over, almost as soon as it began.

After his husband Joey died, Graham knew he'd never find that kind of love again. But what he'd had with Joey was more than some people ever got in life. He'd had his chance at happiness. He couldn't ask for more.

When chef Ryan Gallagher is swindled out of his savings right before he can open his restaurant, it almost seems right. One more failure for his long list, one more way he'll never measure up to his older brother. Joey might be gone, but he still finds a way to overshadow Ryan.

With no money and no prospects, Ryan has no choice but to move home to the family that rejected him and his sexuality.

But when he goes out to the local bar one winter night, he never dreams the hot guy he's hitting on used to be his brother's husband.

Both men insist that they're not interested. And yet neither can resist the desire they feel. But relationships require love. Love requires risk. And both Graham and Ryan know this life offers no guarantees. After a long winter in both their hearts, are they finally ready for spring?

Sugar Season is Book 3 in the Maple Springs series. While each book focuses on different characters and can be read on its own, they've even more fun to read together.

Sugar Season is a 75,000 word steamy, contemporary, second chance m/m romance. No cheating, no cliffhangers, and a guaranteed HEA.

<u>Strawberry Moon</u>
Trevor: It was supposed to be a one-night stand.

Josh isn't even my type. I mean, physically, sure, with those hopeful green eyes and hips that fit perfectly in my hands, he's insanely sexy. But the guy talks too much, tries too hard, flirts way too shamelessly. From the moment I met Josh, I knew he'd drive me crazy.

I didn't think it mattered for one night. I suck at relationships, so I stopped trying long ago. I didn't expect to ever see Josh again. And I definitely didn't expect him to turn out to be sweeter, kinder, and genuinely a better person than a guy like me deserves. I should know better than to want someone like him.

It was supposed to be a one-night stand. So why the hell can't I let him go?

Josh: It freaking figures.

The night I finally have some meaningless fun--and,

incidentally, the hottest hook-up of my life--I manage to pick the one guy in the bar who I'm gonna have to see for the rest of the summer. How was I supposed to know that Trevor had a competing claim on my grandma's cabin? Or that he's the only person who can help me get it ready to sell by the end of the season?

It would be so much easier if I could hate him. Trevor's got that whole tall, dark, and mysterious thing down - emphasis on mysterious. He's aloof to the point of arrogance and deals with emotions about as well as a tree-trunk. He swears he's no good for me, but the more time I spend with him, the more I know he's wrong.

It freaking figures. So what the hell am I supposed to do now?

Strawberry Moon is Book 4 in the Maple Springs series. While each book focuses on different characters and can be read on its own, they've even more fun to read together.

Strawberry Moon is an 85,000 word m/m romance with enemies-to-lovers, out-for-you, and hurt/comfort themes. No cheating, no cliffhangers, and a guaranteed HEA.

Check out the rest of my catalog at:
www.spencerspears.com

Made in the USA
Middletown, DE
08 February 2022